THE TOWPATH

JESUS MONCADA was born in 1941 in Mequinensa, the town
on which this story is based. He has published two volumes of
short stories. This is his first novel; it has won six literary prizes
in Spain.

Jesús Moncada

THE TOWPATH

*Translated from the Catalan
by Judith Willis*

HARVILL
An Imprint of HarperCollinsPublishers

First published in Catalan in 1988
with the title *Camí de sirga*
by Edicions de la Magrana, Barcelona

First published in Great Britain in 1994
by Harvill
an imprint of HarperCollins*Publishers*
77–85 Fulham Palace Road,
Hammersmith, London W6 8JB

This edition has been translated with the
financial assistance of the Spanish Dirección General
del Libro y Bibliotecas, Ministerio de Cultura.

1 3 5 7 9 8 6 4 2

© Jesús Moncada 1988
English translation © HarperCollinsPublishers 1994

A CIP catalogue record for this book
is available from the British Library.

ISBN 0 00 271284 9 hardback
0 00 273005 7 paperback

Photoset in Linotron Garamond 3 by
Rowland Phototypesetting Ltd, Bury St Edmunds, Suffolk

Printed and bound in Great Britain by Clays Ltd, St Ives PLC

Although the fabric of this novel is woven from events taken from the last century in the life of the ancient town of Mequinensa, particularly those which sealed its fate from 1957 onwards, the author wishes to make it clear that it has not been his intention to write a history of these events, at least not in the usual sense of the word. He also wishes to state that the characters in the book are fictional beings and that any similarity to real people, living or dead, is purely coincidental.

PART ONE

Days at the Eden

I

Columns and supporting walls suddenly gave way; as the house came toppling down, Horseshoe Hill reverberated with the thunderous roar of rafters and beams creaking, stairways, ceilings, coves and partitions collapsing, glass shattering and bricks and tiles smashing. And then a cloud of dust, the first of many which were to accompany the long agony that lay ahead, rose up above the town and slowly dispersed in the bright spring morning air.

Years later, when the tragedy that began that day in 1970 had become a dim memory, time shrouded in cobwebs of mist, an anonymous chronicle collated a number of moving personal accounts of the event. The first in chronological order – though not the most poignant – related how the clock on the belfry had stopped the previous evening against a louring backdrop of purple and sickly yellow storm-clouds streaked with black. For the chronicler this was a clear omen of what was to pass on the morrow, a sign that the past was gone for good. Another lurid account which described the night that followed this uncertain dusk was full of suspense: it spoke of the eerie silence in the empty streets, a silence that was mirrored indoors as the townspeople prayed that dawn should not break. The most vivid of all these recollections, however, was of the sinister bang on Horseshoe Hill at eleven o'clock the next morning; according to the chronicle, the townsfolk were profoundly shaken by the onset of the disaster.

These accounts were certainly all very impressive. But this wasn't the only factor they had in common; there was something else, something of maybe no significance, and yet it helps explain what happened that ill-starred day. They were also all, without exception, completely false.

To start with, Honorat del Rom, one of the town's two pharmacists, who outlived the events long enough to be around still when the chronicle appeared, pointed out in an ironic footnote to the document that the town clock, mounted on the church tower, hadn't broken on 11 April 1970. It was a dilapidated relic, as old as the hills, and often went wrong; there was nothing unusual in seeing its hands stationary on all four faces. But that day it was working and – should anyone wish to split hairs – its only fault was that it was seven or eight minutes ahead of the official time. According to the chemist, this quite invalidated the theory that the clock had supposedly predicted what was to happen the following day, and meant that any other speculations on the matter could be ignored.

And the storminess of the evening didn't fit the facts either. Nobody denied that it would have been a very suitable setting for the prelude to the drama had it occurred as the chronicle claimed. Unfortunately, it was a dreary twilight, not even on a par with the kind that the town normally enjoyed, let alone the more spectacular ones that the chemist didn't get around to mentioning. It had been feebly borne up the Ebro valley by a southwesterly sea-breeze, its red light had imparted a lukewarm glow to the quays, where the town's old boats were gradually rotting away, and it had then slipped off upstream and darkened as it reached the west, the same as any other evening, amidst purple gleams of little account.

The night was almost as run-of-the-mill as the dusk: a common or garden black. Except for the darkness, which is always vaguely disquieting, there was nothing to warrant talk of any unusual tension – over and above the unremitting tension that the town had put up with for so long now that it had become part of the fabric of its everyday life. It was just another night for the local populace: from the Justice of the Peace who, sick and tired of his lady wife's faded charms, was getting down to business under the courtroom table with a cousin of the council secretary's, thrusting slowly, deeply and powerfully into her as she melted in deep-throated agonies of pleasure and crumpled the municipal Register of Deaths beneath her hips, to the nightwatchman who was up and down the streets like a baker's sieve. The only exception, of course, was Pasqual de Serafí. Laid out on his double bed, surrounded by the enervating drone of his family's laments, he was coming to terms with the death that had sneaked up on him as he read the sports pages at the barber's that afternoon. The town had its own time-honoured ways of coping with the presence of death, so there was nothing untoward to disturb the passing hours; and when dawn

4

drifted up the Ebro and its rays of light caught the patent-leather cap, the steel baton and the gold buttons on the uniform of the nightwatchman as he walked home down Witches Street, the whole town was peacefully asleep.

Dawn's rosy glow crept across the sailing barges moored at the silent wharves, climbed up the riverside wall and slowly spread over the rough-textured houses that huddled on the slopes of the mountain beneath the castle. Daylight could barely penetrate the tangle of streets and alleyways. The town had lived alongside the lignite mines for nearly a century now and the coal dust had stuck to it like a shadowy skin; the same patina seemed to cling to the buildings – where whitewash didn't last a minute – the people and even the rivers, which were continuously crisscrossed by black boats and whose beds were darkened by coal from capsized vessels. Eventually, however, as happened every morning, the first red gleams faded and the light of day dispelled the darkness, revealing the ancient, decrepit, much loved and frequently reviled outline which emerged, ochre and black, from the night.

An intense yet provisional life took hold of the streets. Now, contrary to what accounts in the chronicle were later to maintain so melodramatically, hardly anybody noticed when eleven o'clock came and went. The town didn't hold its breath; hearts didn't miss a beat; the noise didn't echo through streets and squares like a death knell, or boom down the Ebro valley, along the banks of the Segre or over the silent wharves and lifeless mines presaging disaster. It was a brief thud in a town so accustomed to hearing drills from the mines that nobody gave it a second thought.

Other rumours circulated but oddly enough, seeing that they were just as false as the first ones, they were not recorded by the anonymous chronicler. Even so, they too formed part of the dense web which many townspeople used to stifle the rumblings of their guilty consciences. Deep down, this was the secret justification for the chronicle, and what led to its being accepted as true by most of the people who lived through these events.

Because after numerous years' talking about it non-stop, brooding about it and suffering in advance (strange phenomena appeared in old Caterina's tarot cards, stirrings from the underworld), the fact is that other than the chemist, Honorat del Rom, who was at that moment painfully rooted to the spot at the corner of Fish-Hook Alley and Horseshoe Hill, no one else realized what had happened. The town's fate was already sealed, so nothing would have changed had the reverse been true, but years later, when the sinister nightmare had become a dusty memory, a mere speck of ash, some residents began to invent apocryphal stories in order to look good in the eyes of history.

But not everything was in the chronicles or so easy to dismiss. For instance, was there any truth in the rumour circulated in cafés and on street-corners that Llorenç de Veriu got wind of the occurrence? Some people said that he came back to the town to take a last look at the house on Horseshoe Hill, which he had built with his own hands in 1936, when he and Carme Castell were to be married. Most preferred to think that even if news of it did reach Llorenç, it still didn't bring him back to life, as he lay, a handful of inert, anonymous dust, in the distant soil of the wasteland of Teruel, where nearly thirty years earlier, during the Civil War, he had been mown down by a Fascist machine-gun.

The townsfolk deceived themselves when they persisted in seeing 12 April 1970 as a key date in their collective drama; similarly, they were wrong to feel guilty about not witnessing the event at first hand. Knocking down No. 20, Horseshoe Hill, which was the start of the whole town being demolished – and bureaucratic chance singled out that house as it could have done any one of those already empty – was merely the opening scene in the final act of a long nightmare. By the time the bulldozers tugged at the steel cables attached to the columns and the building came down amid clouds of dust, the destruction of the town had been going on for more than thirteen years.

II

During the night, the town was briefly shaken by a harsh north wind, although someone was to insinuate later that this was no northerly but a strange blast that issued from a place where no wind had ever blown from before. A gust whistled down Horseshoe Hill, dispersing the dust from the ruins of Llorenç de Veriu's house, swirled round Saints Square and flung open the unfastened balcony windows at the Torres i Camps mansion. Once inside, it howled through rooms and corridors; curtains were ruffled, the pendulum of the huge study clock was knocked off balance and the crystal drops of the dining-room candelabra were set tinkling before it died down and finally petered out in the Hall of the Martyred Virgins.

Many years had passed since the picture which gave its name to the room had disappeared from the wall where it was hung on arrival at the house; more even than the sixty-seven that had padded out Senyora Carlota de Torres' redoubtable contours. It had been brought back from Italy by her mother's brother, a much-travelled man who was secretly branded as a mason, an atheist and a godless roué, and who, they feared, would cap it all by leaving nothing in his will when he finally popped off. The painting depicted a group of buxom pink females unashamedly displaying their charms through the sheerest of gauze veils, a pure textile illusion. So suggestive were these ladies that the picture would not have had pride of place in the drawing-room were it not for his parents' indulgence, his sister's fear of upsetting her bachelor brother – since, for all her misgivings, she still had hopes of inheriting from him – and the assent of the local rector, a frequent visitor to the house. The priest, a pot-bellied, thrifty and beatific gentleman, studied the picture with an attention to detail that was maybe a trifle excessive, bringing sarcastic remarks from Camilla, one of the maids, in the privacy of the kitchen. After many long-drawn-out mid-afternoon cups of hot chocolate with langues de chat, he finally gave his verdict: while there might not be sufficient grounds for agreeing with the profligate uncle when he claimed with a leer that the painting depicted young

Christian maidens in a Roman amphitheatre, about to be devoured by the lions, neither could he see any reasons for disagreeing. If nothing else, this ambiguous pronouncement helped to allay the worthy doubts of the worthy family.

A series of factors brought the picture's presence in the hall to an end: the "unfortunate event" as they euphemistically termed the untimely disappearance of the dissolute uncle, who died in Paris, France, in mysterious circumstances which the family went to great pains to hush up; the discovery that apart from his cat Lucretia, who was adopted by his landlady at the hotel on the Left Bank of the Seine where his death occurred, he had left nothing but debts; the promotion of the gluttonous priest to a canonry at Lleida cathedral and the subsequent appointment of a new, tough rector, an inquisitorial and intimidating skeleton of a man, who, on his first day, roundly condemned the orgy of flesh portrayed in the painting; the scruples of the deceased's sister, which coincided rather suspiciously with her disappointment over the inheritance; and the additional expenses caused by his dying abroad and his body having to be transported back to the family vault in the town cemetery. And so the picture was relegated to the attic of the immense mansion, the most imposing building in the town's large Plaça d'Armes, and only visited by an emotional Senyor Octavi who, spied on by Camilla, climbed up there on clandestine pilgrimages to contemplate the fresh beauty of the nymphs his greatly missed son had passed off as Christian virgins.

Despite this change in circumstances, the hall was always known by the apocryphal name of the painting, *The Martyred Virgins*, although the gust of wind that blew in there that April night in 1970 was doubtless unaware of its history and entered purely by chance.

The hall was in a sorry state the next day. The first batch of the dust which would become an obsession with the town after the demolition of Llorenç de Veriu's house, had coated it in a ghostly white film. Even the massive portrait of Senyor Jaume lay invisible beneath the dirt. His daughter's furious voice echoed round the house the moment the disaster was discovered. The three maids – Carmela, Sofia and Teresa, who had taken over from Camilla, Adelaida and Veronica, and who, apart from their mistress, were

8

by now the sole inhabitants of the house – were summoned from the ante-room and came at the double to clear up the mess. They dusted walls, mouldings, lights, curtains and furniture, swept floors and then took down the painting and began carefully wiping the canvas with damp cloths, under the stern gaze of their mistress.

This exhumation, so to speak, in the course of which Senyor Jaume de Torres once more saw the light of day, had a profound effect upon his daughter's immense humanity; as his likeness gradually emerged – first the tip of his nose, then his left ear-lobe – she recalled the painting of the portrait sixty years earlier, when she had been a little girl and such an awkward, lanky and scrawny thing that no one could ever have foreseen the weight she would put on in later life, which was to earn her locally the nickname Stout Carlota.

The painting of the picture had been a fascinating process; she had been so enthralled by it all that she could still remember every detail. One day, old Joan, the carpenter from Oar Square, turned up at the house carrying a frame with a canvas stretched and nailed on it, covered in a fine matte white. The three workmen from Torres i Camps Ltd, Manufacturers of Liquorice Extract, who came with the carpenter, felt slightly uncomfortable in the presence of the ladies, cowed by the luxury all around them. They left an easel in the hall with a box of paints and a folding chair. Later on, the keen anticipation aroused among the ladies of the house (Grandfather was up in the attic, gazing ecstatically at the pseudo-martyrs) reached its climax when Senyor Torres came home from the factory earlier than usual in the company of Aleix de Segarra.

After endless protestations ("No, Adelina, I'm not important enough; don't insist, you know I'm a simple sort of fellow . . ."), Senyor Torres went through the motions of giving in to his wife, although privately he told himself that he fully deserved to accede to her request. Who was it after all who, even before marrying the Camps girl, had sorted out the muddle the family had got into over inheritances? Who was it who had put the factory on its feet again, flushing out undesirable elements who were lining their own pockets and taking advantage of the ineptitude of his father-in-law and the negligence of his brother-in-law – that no-good reprobate who would have done better to die before squandering his part of the

9

family fortune? Who was it who had disentangled all the legal paperwork and got back several family properties which had been all but lost? As well as confirming beyond any shadow of a doubt their right to own the lignite mines after a fiendishly tricky dispute over a will? Which household in the town could now compare with the union of the two families, the Torres and the Camps, to which he had brought not merely his wit and energy but his own far from contemptible patrimony? And naturally, all this had not been achieved without some effort and sacrifice – and here must be included the nights with his wife, not the least painful part thereof. Senyor Torres did not take pleasure in his wife, she had never been to his liking. Being a connoisseur of full, well-rounded beauty, he was totally uninspired by that skinny bag of bones. Her three pregnancies (Jordi, Robert and Carlota) had caused her to wither up, in contrast to what he had hoped (without too much conviction, to be honest) on seeing other ladies endowed by motherhood with a certain ripeness. It was, then, a sense of duty, similar to that of controlling the production of liquorice extract or coal, or overseeing the contributions of share-croppers and tenant farmers, but without the enthusiasm with which he performed the latter tasks, which induced Senyor Torres to quench the fires of his wife's passion with praiseworthy selflessness. Luckily, her rather inert nature, coupled with lengthy sessions in the confessional, which reinforced her qualms of conscience, meant that these fires were seldom aroused and, when they were, they were far from volcanic. Senyora Adelina's lack of passion so disappointed Camilla that she gave up her spying sessions at the keyhole of the bedroom door exactly one week after their return from honeymoon. She lost no time, though, in uncovering where it was that the master sought compensation for these lacklustre, penitential nights. As it helped to keep him cheerful, and the atmosphere in the house was consequently calm and relaxed, she gave no more thought to the matter.

That afternoon, Senyor Torres was even more pleased with himself than usual. Humble, modest, self-sacrificing, he had decided to give way to his family's entreaties – "purely so you won't pester me any more" – and add his portrait to the collection of his wife's relatives who hung on the walls of the exceptionally long corridor; they were exhibited there until they disappeared in order of seniority and oblivion into any one of the many out-of-the-way rooms where surly gentlemen, languorous infants and tightly corseted ladies lined up in a grisly procession of ghosts, almost invisible as the pigments darkened. The only exception to this forced march into the darkness beyond was Nicanora de Camps, Carlota's great-great-aunt, who was reputed to have been the mistress of the entire corps of officers of a cavalry brigade on the death of its general, her husband – a slow-witted disciplinarian with a carroty moustache, who died a hero's death in Africa. The distinguished lady returned to the family seat at the end of her life and was a source of wonder to the towns-folk. One of the blacksmiths from Bakers Hill spread the rumour that she regularly sharpened her late husband's sabre to cut off chickens' heads, and the maid who attended her as she lay dying revealed that during her final delirium she ordered cavalry charges against the Moors of the Rif. Her portrait was impregnated with her own strong personality and gave off such a daunting sense of bad temper that no one ever dared to move it from its original spot on the most visible part of the ante-room wall, from where it should theoretically have been displaced by her nephew who died on the banks of the Seine.

From that first afternoon when Aleix de Segarra, the artist, weighed up the best place to position his model in order to catch most light from the balcony, little Carlota followed every single brush-stroke in the evolution of the work. She was fascinated by the paints and the way he mixed them on his palette; she loved the smell of the turpentine and the amber colour of the linseed oil, but most of all she was intrigued by Aleix, who was so different from the people in her family circle and whom her father seemed to treat with a hesitant mixture of shocked respect and affectionate condescension.

Aleix, in common with the Torres i Camps clan, belonged to one of the town's old aristocratic families, but to the majority group who were in decline because of their members' spinelessness and inertia. Lacking their ancestors' predatory instincts – which in some cases had been revitalized and continued with the force and unscrupulousness of former days – the rest had degenerated into habitués of gentlemen's clubs, bitter hags or sanctimonious old biddies. In order to survive without working, they ended up selling

11

off their birthright at a loss, and letting themselves be slowly fleeced. Some went to live in the city, squandered all they had and came home empty-handed to rot inside the walls of their decrepit mansions where the coat of arms over the doorway opened onto nothing more grandiose than chambers and halls festooned with dusty grey cobwebs. The local mattress-maker was an accurate barometer of the gentlefolk's distress. When they had no paintings, furniture, antique carvings or weapons left to sell off to the dealers – a greedy gang of thieves always ready to pounce – the proud gentry would get rid of the wool from their mattresses. They surreptitiously sold it off via the mattress-maker to the brides-to-be who were preparing their trousseaux and wished to enjoy the comfort and status conferred by owning a woollen mattress rather than the millet-leaf palliasses which most of the townspeople slept on, but who didn't have enough money to buy one new. And in this way, many impoverished and broken aristocratic bodies sank inexorably towards the bare bed springs – either in easy stages or in one fell swoop – a descent which provoked not only aches and pains but also wisecracks from the lower orders. Particularly outspoken on this subject was Arquimedes Quintana, the finest sailor on the Ebro, who held court at the Quayside Café. The captain frequently pointed out that once the wool from the mattresses had been washed in the river (since high-class bedbugs were just as fierce as their proletarian brothers, and the grime that poured out was one and the same), it often returned to the very people from whom it had originally been stolen.

The Segarras hadn't reached the wool stage yet. They were half way between the Torres i Camps and ruin, but on the way down. Of their former wealth they still retained some farms, the one-time nunnery on Ferryboat Lane and the family home on River Street where Aleix, who had been orphaned at the age of fifteen, lived with his paternal uncle, Ignasi, and the latter's wife, Malena, surrounded by the collections the family had built up over the years. Nineteenth-century French paintings and archaeological finds from the various cultures who had inhabited the town down the centuries rubbed shoulders with the Romantic landscapes of his late Uncle Damià, the mechanical inventions of Grandfather Hermes, some of Aleix's Cubist experiments and the mythological sculptures of Aunt Severina, also now departed, whose automata were stored up in the attic.

After living in Barcelona for a few years and making the odd brief visit to Paris, Aleix had settled back in the town when still young. He worked hard but preferred to keep his own oeuvre, which didn't include commissioned portraits such as that of Senyor Jaume de Torres, hidden away. Apart from his Aunt Malena nobody else saw it and he was to destroy most of it himself during the cataclysm which would turn everything upside down many years later. That afternoon in 1914, however, when he was preparing to embark on the portrait of Senyor Jaume de Torres under the watchful gaze of little Carlota, the events which were to make an indelible mark on Aleix de Segarra's life and death were still lying dormant in the seed-bed of the future.

In complete contrast to what one might have expected of Senyor Jaume de Torres' apotheosis, the painting of the portrait was interrupted by certain incidents which left their mark on it. The first occurred in the course of the second sitting, when the picture was nothing more than a sketch in very dilute sienna, lightly smudged with grisaille. The model sat by the balcony overlooking the square and bequeathed his image to pictorial posterity from a wickerwork armchair whilst delivering an endless and tedious speech in which the Torres i Camps family – he, of course, being its head and particularly its brain – obviously had the starring role. Had Aleix seen the new sailing barge under construction in the Ebro shipyard? Once it was finished, the firm's fleet would number half a dozen vessels, one more than that of the young widow Salleres, and the deadlock in the river power of the two families would be broken: this deadlock was as provoking as it was unfair – and indeed almost downright offensive as far as the Torres i Camps side was concerned. Had Aleix noticed the warehouses which would one day encircle the huge central courtyard of the liquorice-extract factory where carriages from the entire region unloaded tons and tons of liquorice-root? Had Aleix heard at the Quayside Café – seeing he rarely went to the Casino de la Roda, the gentry's meeting-place, where he was regarded as a lost cause, practically a renegade – that the Torres family (here his mother-in-law frowned since he had failed to mention the Camps side of the family, forcing her son-in-law to hastily rectify his error) was about to buy the farm at the Plana dels Voltors?

As Senyor Jaume expected, Aleix said nothing but concentrated instead on his subject's flabby red features, bulbous nose and slightly arrogant black moustache. The artist was merely an audience with no right to speak. It was his job to get on with the painting – an activity closely associated in Senyor Jaume's mind with a Bohemian life of irresponsibility and debauchery – and to listen to the great exploits of the household.

In contrast to the first day, when he had been unstoppable, the second sitting didn't give Senyor Jaume the chance to get very far with his triumphal monologue. He was just about to launch into another tedious list of his remarkable achievements as Aleix painted a hint of a shadow beneath his heavy jowls when a commotion broke out on the main staircase. The three maids – Camilla, Adelaida and Veronica – came rushing to the ante-room from the kitchen; Carlota's mother and grandmother were both horrified and stopped their crocheting, Aleix's brush came to a halt on his subject's double chin and Senyor Jaume de Torres wriggled round in his wicker armchair while his little daughter looked enquiringly towards the door and her grandfather, peacefully reclining open-mouthed on a corner of the sofa, continued his afternoon nap.

"How dreadful!" they heard Camilla exclaim.

"May God have mercy on his soul!" interjected Veronica.

"What a disaster, what a disaster!" repeated Adelaida in her strident voice.

Standing at the door in front of the three horror-stricken maids was Ramon Graells, Senyor Jaume's right-hand man, and in the corridor a group of sailors and miners had congregated, not daring to come in.

Of what happened next, the part that stuck longest in Carlota's mind was the expression on her father's face. He turned pale and his skin became almost transparent; one could sense his lips trembling beneath his moustache. His eyes were open wide in an unbelieving stare – only seconds earlier they had been gazing on things in a haughty, aloof manner and now they were fixed in terror on his right-hand man.

14

Apologetic and deferential as though he himself were to blame, Ramon Graells described what had happened. Strange words pervaded the room, names of things on the river unfamiliar to Carlota. Only the word "death", a black gleam that flickered between the words of the narrator, was linked in her mind to funerals and mourning and the still-inexplicable disappearance of certain members of the family, whose portraits changed places along the corridor.

The event related by Graells to the consternation of the ladies and their maids and the deep dismay of Senyor Jaume, causing the artist to turn pale, was to be padded out over the years as it went the round of local society, but the nub of it always remained a mystery. Once things were back to normal, once funeral masses and condolences were over and done with, pending a burial that would never take place since there were no remains to be buried, one single undeniable fact stood out from the whole tangled web of conflicting versions, hypotheses and speculations that surrounded the truth of the affair: just before midday on 12 June 1914, the *Rapid*, a sailing barge belonging to the firm of Torres i Camps, laden with a cargo of flour, had capsized in the Ebro, in the Lliberola Gorge. Two of the crew managed to survive by swimming away and the third, who was no more buoyant than the stones of the riverbed, hung on to the gangplank that floated his way as the ship went down, and was washed ashore, dazed and half-demented with fear, a few kilometres downstream, almost within sight of the town. Nothing was ever discovered of its captain, Josep Ibars, the vessel itself or Gatell, the ship's dog. Sailors and fishermen tirelessly searched the waters, the whole riverbank was alerted from the town to the sea, but on this occasion the Ebro refused to give up its prey; no other remains of the shipwreck were ever found. This gave rise to the legend secretly told one day to Senyoreta Torres by Veronica in a corner of the kitchen where the young girl would conceal herself to spy on the goings-on, regardless of her mother's orders. Carlota learnt that the captain, like all dead people denied the repose of the grave, had become a soul in torment. This was no fairy-tale; on the contrary, it came on good authority. Didn't Pere del Pla – who never told lies – swear that he had come across the missing ship in the middle of the Canota Valley? Neither Pere del Pla nor his crew could ever forget the blood-curdling spectacle of the ghostly *Rapid*, enveloped in a haze, her oars still moving though there were no sailors to pull on them. The image of the captain haunted them even more; Josep Ibars in person with his beret tipped slightly over his left ear, silently guiding the ship. And if it was not the spirit of Gatell the dog, then what was that sinister beast which one night ran into the house of the sailor's widow and scampered out again in the direction of the wharf, carrying in its mouth the spectacles of the departed captain, who must be in need of them in the afterlife?

Sometimes, particularly in winter or on foggy evenings, added Veronica, just as darkness was falling, the *Rapid* would tie up at the town pier, and the deceased captain, in an effort to drive the chill of death from his body – so it was said – would take a turn round the cafés and taverns, polishing off any drinks he came across on the counter or the marble-topped tables. The customers watched their glasses being raised and emptied unaided, as though the alcohol were simply evaporating. At any rate this was what kept happening to Robert de Tàpies, who was forced by the ghost's unquenchable thirst to order one glass of rum after another to make up for Ibars' depredations. The story captured Carlota's imagination and she enquired whether the tormented captain had ever drunk the coffee or liqueur of her father, Senyor Jaume de Torres. The maid stopped plucking the chicken she had decapitated a short while earlier with one of the sabres that had belonged to the late general's wife (when there was poultry for the chop she always smuggled it in from the panoply in the hall, despite Senyora Adelina's prohibition) and cast a shocked glance at Carlota through the snowy flurry of chicken feathers that floated in the peaceful atmosphere of the kitchen. Begging her pardon, but had the young miss gone mad? How could she ever think, she snapped at her crossly, that a humble workman, even a captain of Ibars' standing, would, even once he had passed on, dare set foot in the Casino de la Roda, the gentlemen's café?

The picture and Carlota de Torres had grown old together, although she was not conscious of the gradual darkening of the painting's oils, pigments and varnishes. She didn't notice the faint yellowing that had turned his shirt front from cobalt-blue to green, that had tinged his once-white shirt with amber and had dulled the originally luminous sky that hung above the view of the town which served as a backdrop to the figure. She was blind to these changes which ran parallel to the mysterious biochemical processes in her own body, which had turned her from a little girl bewitched by the artist into an old woman raging at the dirt that invaded the Hall of the Martyred Virgins. The hours that the portrait spent covered in dust were sufficient, however, to break the habit of seeing it every day, the reason why these changes had passed unnoticed. And so, while it was being cleaned, when one of the maids – we can't be sure if it was Sofia, Carmela or Teresa, who had taken over from Camilla, Adelaida and Veronica – dusted off a fragment whose yellowed tones had lost the brilliance that had been engraved on young Carlota's memory, the search for its former freshness rolled back time once more.

She walked down the picture's streets, the streets of memory; she recalled the warm, dry light of those summer days when it was being painted; she inspected everything as though she owned it, going from one façade to another, through the still air of a town ignorant of its future ups and downs. She reached the fumes emitted by the liquorice-extract factory, the red brick edifice built on to the old stone fortress that formed the town wall on that side; from there, following the blue-grey reflection of the smoke from the chimney in the River Ebro, she made her way towards the boat moored at the Widows' Wharf.

The barge floating on the river in the picture was the *Carlota*. Her father had hurried to get it finished so that it could take the place of the *Rapid*, lost in the Lliberola disaster. The boatbuilders worked flat-out in the yard, an enchanting, mysterious world wreathed in smoke and smelling of wood and pitch, where she was taken to see the ship. The first time, it made her think of the rib-cage of a huge, terrifying beast, but on successive visits she saw how it took shape, how it was fitted out and how Aleix de Segarra painted her name in carmine on its prow . . .

The launch of the ship was one of her most vivid memories. The ceremony was entrancing, magnificent. The old inquisitorial drybones had died of a heart attack while scourging himself at the end of a fast, and his replacement, the new rector (who belonged to the same school of thought as the Lleida canon) had resumed the afternoon visits to the Hall of the Martyred Virgins. It was he who donned his ceremonial cope and, surrounded by choirboys, went down to the wharf to bless the boat. With the help of her father, she had then smashed a bottle of champagne over the prow, where her name stood out in red characters on a white triangle. After a long-winded speech by Senyor Jaume, family and guests went on board to the excitement of the crowds who had gathered on the quayside to witness the ceremony. Her first recollection of the old river devil Arquimedes Quintana dated from that journey down the Ebro. The captain, an ungainly yet robust giant of a man standing at the helm, stared at the cluster of gentlefolk and treated his passengers with a supercilious attentiveness that unsettled them. It was also the first time that she saw Robert Ibars, the son of the captain of the *Rapid*, which had gone down in the Lliberola disaster. The lad, a strapping youth of fourteen, was standing alongside Arquimedes; her parents went over to talk to him and the skipper. Carlota remembered the slightly nervous and apprehensive look on her mother's face as she ran her white hand through the orphan's rebellious black hair, and the surly stare with which he responded to her caress.

Sofia ran a duster over the collar of Senyor Jaume, motionless in his precarious painted eternity, and then rubbed it over his shirt front. The mistress fidgeted anxiously in her armchair. From under the film of dust there emerged a scrap of waistcoat whose colour matched his suit and some links of his silver watch-chain . . . Then, from the recesses of time, like an unstoppable gust of wind, the whole scene rushed back, the second of the incidents that took place during the painting of the picture. Her father was pleased with the launch of the *Carlota* and had almost forgotten the loss of the *Rapid*; now that these distractions were out of the way, he had decided to go ahead with the portrait. It was one of the final sittings. Looking smugger than ever, he was telling Aleix about his important plans for the future of Torres i Camps Ltd. Her mother had just ordered Camilla to bring in the afternoon snack, Granny was crocheting and Grandpa was dozing as usual in his corner of the settee. The artist was examining his work, nearly finished by now, and adding the final touches. He had accentuated the light on the leaves of the rubber plant to the right of his subject and was preparing to highlight the shine on his watchchain: he dabbed a spot of yellow paint on to the tip of his brush and gently brought it towards the canvas . . .

The spot of yellow paint was to be associated for ever more in Carlota's mind with the shattering of the glass of the balcony windows and the terrifying crack of a shotgun.

III

While Carmela was carefully wiping Senyor Jaume's right sleeve in his portrait in the Hall of the Martyred Virgins, Estanislau Corbera, in thoughtful vein at the Quayside Café, was remarking, "If he'd stayed in good health, today would have been old Arquimedes Quintana's one hundred and thirtieth birthday."

Having passed on this information, the café owner – whose round, ruddy-cheeked, beady-eyed face Honorat del Rom often likened to a puppet's, the way it poked out of his white shirt-collar behind the stage setting of the counter – leant against the cash register with a gesture of profound, viscous, all-embracing lethargy. His head nodded a couple of times and, had the church bells not suddenly rung out, shaking all the panes of glass in the café, the tip of his nose would have hit the number seven key on the till. And the chimes also unsettled the customers waiting for Pasqual de Serafí's funeral to begin. The death-knell forced them to remember the deceased and to say a few words about him. But on the face of it at least, poor Pasqual – may he rest in peace – had led a very uneventful life: like most men of his generation, he went to work in the mines when he was still young, married, had children, fought in the war (in the Republican Zone) and after the defeat, went back to digging up coal until the day he retired, three years and six days before his heart gave out as he read the football scores while waiting his turn at the barber's. Nothing out of the ordinary was known of him, except for his passion for chess. With the best of intentions, those present recalled his by no means inspired performances at local competitions and the odd provincial tournament, and the incident which took place during the first year after the war when a Monarchist schoolteacher wanted to clap him into gaol for being a Red. The accusation caused quite a stir but was dropped because Serafí was a good worker at Senyor Jaume de Torres' mine and was needed there. It all came about because one day, when Pere made an unforgivable blunder and was stupid enough to lose a game that was already in the bag, he angrily threw the white king into the fire at the Sportsmans Café. There wasn't really very much to reminisce about and the subject was rapidly concluded; although they did make a gallant effort to stretch it out, even making specific reference to the doubtful virtue of mothers who brought treacherous good-for-nothings such as the aforesaid schoolmaster into this vale of tears. They mused for a short while on the fragility of human life; in passing, they reflected on the deceased's good fortune, since not only had his death been quick and painless, but he had been lucky enough to be spared the heartache of seeing the calamitous destruction of the town. Then, once they had warded off the danger that might have befallen them had they failed to appease the mysterious force Pasqual de Serafí could already have become, the talk turned inevitably to last weekend's football – full of unexpected twists, with cast-iron predictions shattered and the league table turned upside-down.

"One hundred and thirty years old," murmured the café owner as his customers got involved in heated arguments over brilliant passes, daring tackles and the referee's unbelievable stupidity. No one paid any attention to Estanislau's odd mania for recalling the birthdays of dead people. His customers were never taken aback if, just as he was about to pour them a measure of spirits or a cup of coffee, he said in a solemn, mournful voice, "If he'd stayed in good health, today would be poor Napoleon Bonaparte's one hundred and ninety-ninth birthday," to which he immediately added, "We are nothing," steeped in resignation and usually accompanied by a spasmodic blinking of his right eye. And so, regardless of his customers' indifference – with the exception of Honorat del Rom, the chemist from Bakers Square, who used to play along with him (he once caught him out by three days over Garibaldi's birthday) – the landlord would commemorate the days when famous names of the past were born or died, along with those townspeople who had made the journey to the cemetery; he kept a careful mental list of them and had just added the unfortunate Pere de Serafí to its tail end.

"If he'd stayed in good health, today would be Arquimedes Quintana's one hundred and thirtieth birthday."

These words were now addressed to Robert Ibars, better known as Nelson, and stopped the retired sailor in his tracks; they set off in his memory the transformation of the café which the recollection of old Arquimedes so often evoked. As usual, General O'Donnell's infantry regiments appeared in impeccable formations at the tables normally occupied by the card-players; the field artillery took up position on the white marble counter between the cash register and the coffee machine, a couple of inches away from Estanislau's nose; General Prim's Catalan volunteers marched in through the large French windows that overlooked the Ebro, while beneath the light over the billiard table, now transformed into the relentless African sun, a mob of Moorish cavalry troops took shape, a dazzling hotch-potch of turbans and tunics in the golden dust . . .

Battle commenced beneath Nelson's nostalgia-soaked eyes: cannons roared, guns cracked, bullets whistled, sabres, bayonets and daggers flashed. Headlong gallops, terrifying charges, fights to the death, cries of victory and groans of agony were heard one after the other among the chairs, tables and cast-iron columns of the Quayside Café. A furious Moor who had come from Heaven knows where, possibly from the tall shelves where the cobwebby bottles of spirits stood, his djellabah stained in fresh-spilt blood, ran over the counter towards Nelson. The old sailor saw him draw close with a fearsome scowl on his face and raising his scimitar . . . Somebody opened the café door; the glaring sunlight landed on the Moroccan, who crumbled and was scattered like dust. The acrid smell of burnt gunpowder was the aroma of coffee once more, the cannon-balls were reduced to footballs from the Sunday league, and the light over the billiard table resigned itself to playing its usual role again after illuminating for a short while the battlefield of Tetouan in Morocco in 1860.

Robert Ibars, known to everyone, including his wife, as Nelson, blinked as he unwrapped the sugar and dropped it into the coffee Estanislau had just served him. The victims of the massacre of Tetouan had been nothing but piles of anonymous bones buried in godforsaken graves in the African earth for over one hundred years. And nearly forty years had passed since the death of old Arquimedes Quintana. But on that day, his birthday as the café proprietor had reminded them, the ghost of the old chap, which was always hovering above him in a kindly, protective way, solidified into a real presence, alive and kicking, crossing the borders of time. He felt that these recollections were being dredged up from the depths of the past by the dead man's memory, not his own.

The former bargeman's intuition was shared by others in the town who were thenceforth affected by similar sensations; although he never put it into words, he suspected that his recollections were so extraordinarily intense because of the jolt that had been given to the town's collective memory by the destruction of Llorenç de Veriu's house on Horseshoe Hill – which people were only just starting to notice. Maybe the streets, squares, houses and the two rivers were releasing their memories in despair, hoping that someone would gather them up before the demolition and their inevitable dispersal. Whatever the reason, people's powers of recall had never been as sharp as now. His first memories of the old fellow, who could almost have been his great-grandfather, came from far back, when he, Robert, was just a young lad and would go down to the quayside to wait for his father's barge to come in. He nearly always bumped into old Arquimedes. The sailor would make a fuss of him, he would give him seashells and conches or take him on board his barge. He was the most respected captain in the whole hundred miles of the river between the town and Tortosa, and Robert would listen open-mouthed, particularly when he recounted his part in the battle of Tetouan. He always loved this story. He still seemed to hear him clearing his throat and see him tugging his right ear before launching into his version of the battle.

He described how they had set off in 1860 and, not being one to reveal details of his love-life, merely hinted at the last night spent with his fiancée, the first of the four official wives he was to have during the course of his long life. The years never dulled the impact leaving the town had had on him. He remembered it all: the crowds of people on the quayside who had gathered to see the troops off, the tears, the farewells, Senyor Camps' words vibrating with patriotic fervour. The worthy gentleman reassured the soldiers that they wouldn't be lonely: his brother-in-law the renowned cavalry general, the husband of Senyora Nicanora de Camps, would look after them in the hostile, godless lands of Africa. Next he saw the parched, luminous, ochre-coloured town which was not to be blackened by coal for several years, even though prospecting had just begun in the area. The town merged with the horizon as the boat sailed down the Ebro after crossing the confluence with the Segre alongside the last houses. And an instant later, a brief, awe-struck glimpse of the port of Barcelona, followed by the blazing sun of Morocco. At this point, the narrator's powers of recall were so strong that it was said that the Moorish fez and the musket inlaid with mother-of-pearl that had been kept on the shelves since the days of Estanislau's grandfather were found near the billiard table one winter's night when old Arquimedes had yet again been regaling his fellow drinkers with the tale. Whenever the ghost of Josep Ibars, Nelson's father, tossed back half a dozen glasses of Robert de Tàpies' rum, the latter would remark with great conviction – marred only by the indistinctness of his speech – that the crack on one of the café's marble table-tops had been made by General Prim in person. Conjured up even more vividly than usual by old Arquimedes' words, the soldier from Reus galloped in through the French windows overlooking Church Square and rode through the café like a centaur. Before making his exit through the riverside door, the General, covered in blood and dust, lashed out with his sabre at Silveri Tona, whom he had undoubtedly taken for a Berber, being swarthy-skinned and looking for all the world like a real Moor. Silveri miraculously dodged the swipe, but the blade cracked the marble table-top and because of this incident it was christened the General's Table.

After the Catalan volunteers' attack, the tale became even more animated and the enraptured audience was fed detailed information on charges and countercharges, manoeuvres and stratagems, moments of faint-heartedness or bravery, all leading up to the high spot of the action.

"Don't ask me how, but there he was, right on top of me. I saw the gleam of his dagger and instinct led me to parry his thrust with my rifle; I didn't manage it too well because then I felt a blow to my cheek. That was a blow and a half, by Christ! It all happened in a flash. He lunged at me a second time, trying to finish me off. I fired at him at close range, the shot sent him flying up in the air and then he fell to earth like a stone, dead as a doornail. All around me there were shouts, bangs, horses galloping. Something warm was trickling down my neck and I realized in horror that my thigh and left sleeve were soaked in blood. I touched my face; the bastard had cut my ear off. My first thought was, 'Arquimedes, there's no hope for it, the Moor's done for you.' I was scared rigid, I threw down my rifle and ran off like a madman. And where do you think I was making for, lads? The quack? Don't make me laugh! For him to polish me off good and proper? If that's what you're thinking, you're pretty wide of the mark . . . I'll tell you where: I was making for the town, the Segre, the Ebro, the boats, Carme . . . I even felt like seeing Senyor Camps and the other old buggers at the Casino de la Roda . . . I still can't understand how I got out of there alive. Suddenly I felt a crack on my skull. Everything started spinning round like a top, I felt sick and night fell in the middle of the day.

"When I came round, the orderlies were carrying me on a stretcher. The cannons had stopped firing and I could just hear guns going off in the distance. The wound wasn't bleeding any more, but it felt as if the drums of the whole regiment were banging inside my head. 'You've been lucky, mate,' said one of the fellows transporting me, who turned out to be from Tortosa. 'You've only had your left ear shaved off; you won't die of that. They did a better job on our friend here though. Look!' And then I realized I wasn't alone on the stretcher; sitting on my legs there was a severed head staring at me with its glassy eyes wide open. God's ballocks, it was horrible! It fair scared the shit out of me. The poor sod's cap was still fastened by the chin-strap and his teeth were clenched round the cigar he'd been smoking when his head was blown off. In spite of the dust and the blood-stains, his face looked familiar to me. I was feeling pretty ropy but as I listened to the stretcher-bearers telling me that they'd found no signs of a body, I finally placed the head in my memory. I remembered him standing in the doorway of our church – still attached to the rest of his body of course – the day he'd got married to Nicanora de Camps. Well stone the crows, I said to myself, if it isn't a small world. And then I fainted again. Who'd have thought it – it turned out that that day we'd covered ourselves in what they call glory for some odd reason. And, believe it or not, yours truly was as near as dammit a hero. A filthy blood-bath, that's what it was. But I have to admit I've always felt sorry for that ear of mine buried in Africa. Poor thing! What can it be

25

doing there all on its own? I sometimes hear strange sounds and gabbling voices and I can't help wondering if they're noises from Morocco that are coming to me via my old friend who I left behind on the battlefield. And Heaven help me, I feel pretty bad about the Moor too: I didn't really want to have to finish him off. Though I'm glad I'm the one who's here to tell the tale. But he, poor chap, was at least defending his own patch; we were sent there to defend the pockets of folk like the Camps, the Salleres, the Romagueras and the Torres."

Nelson also knew that once the General's widow came home – with great shows of grief as she disembarked at the Town Square Quay, numerous speeches, flags unfurled and patriotic tears, courtesy of family and friends – to stay there for ever more, she often summoned Arquimedes to go and tell her about the battle where her husband perished so gloriously. The veteran skipper of the Camps' barges, and subsequently of those of the firm of Torres i Camps, had no choice but to go along to the room where the picture of the Martyred Virgins had yet to be hung, and retell the tale. But he always left out the scene of the severed head and particularly what happened next, which he had been told about in confidence by the fellow from Tortosa. Despite the peremptory orders they had received, it had been impossible to locate the general's body and so the stretcher-bearers filled the coffin with the hero's head (complete with cigar) and the remains of a beheaded tribesman who they secretly clothed in the acclaimed warrior's dress uniform.

Half a century later, when the widow was in her grave and there had been no hint of protest from the Great Beyond – a state of calm which the Quayside Café's regulars put down to her having found the tribesman's body to her liking, for it was sturdy and better-armed than that of the hero of Tetouan – the phantom of war in Africa stalked the town once more. To show their support of Barcelona, shaken by the events of the Tragic Week,* the townspeople stopped the departure of three recruits who had been sent to Morocco to defend Spanish interests in the mines of the Rif. Robert Ibars,

* The Tragic Week: the name popularly given to an anti-clerical, anti-military uprising in July 1909 brought about by the call-up of 40,000 troops, mainly from Barcelona, to fight an undeclared colonial war in Morocco. (Translator's Note)

the future Nelson, was only ten years old and his recollection of the events was a jumble of crowded meetings in the Plaça d'Armes, arguments, riots and also the fear in the town when it was learnt that a boat full of Civil Guards was sailing up the Ebro. The town had no permanent police force at the time and the paramilitaries only came in exceptional circumstances. The women, terrified by the army's brutality in Barcelona, feared for their menfolk's safety and persuaded them to stay indoors. Then they went down to the quayside and waited for the boat to arrive; an ominous sail had just been sighted, swelling in the southwesterly breeze that was blowing that summer afternoon in 1909. When it tied up, the women began to applaud the contingent, hoping to mollify them and avert a disaster. Disconcerted by this welcome, the guards came ashore and made for the Town Hall amid a chorus of cheers. The next day, however, after a brutal night of arrests, interrogations and beatings, two barges set sail from the Town Square Wharf, laden with prisoners. Among the principal suspects was Arquimedes Quintana who, along with Robert's father, was one of the ringleaders of the disturbance. The detainees were about to be brought to trial when the international condemnation triggered by the fierce repression in Barcelona and the execution of Ferrer i Guàrdia, the fall of the government and the constant pressure exerted by the townspeople on the verge of revolt secured their return. Led by the veteran of Tetouan, they marched ashore in silence at the Widows' Wharf.

One hundred and thirty years . . . In the rest of the town and the time zone to which it belonged it was half past ten; in the Quayside Café it was already quarter to eleven. Some strange unexplained quirk of the café's founder, respected by his son, meant that the establishment's clock was always kept fifteen minutes fast. A lorry drove down the road that ran by the riverside wall above the wharves jammed with barges in various stages of decomposition. The café and the square were filling up with people waiting for Pasqual de Serafí's funeral. Nelson had been joined by Eduard Forques – by family tradition a builder of river boats and by irrepressible vocation a tenor saxophonist – Horaci Campells, the municipal nightwatchman, and Manolet who ran the cake-shop on Fish-Hook Alley. They sipped their coffee and talked about what had been an obsession with the townsfolk for the past thirteen years since the agonizing prelude to the disaster had commenced, a prelude that had come to an end the day before, with the demolition of the house on Horseshoe Hill.

Nelson said nothing. His thoughts of old Arquimedes, which had been set off by Estanislau, were transporting him back to one summer morning many years earlier. A crimson glow set the river on fire and highlighted the black outlines of the ships on the quayside where the sailors were preparing to get under way. The bargemen's silhouettes were splashes of red and blue bustling round among the oars and the rigging. The rasp of the pulleys and the noise of the boat-hooks as they cut through the black water mingled with the captains' orders and the cries of the sailors. He was both excited and confused: he was a bewildered teenager, feeling out of place in all this activity. The *Carlota*, the brand-new ship of the Torres i Camps fleet, was preparing to set off on her maiden voyage one week after her triumphal launch. And he, Robert Ibars, formed part of the crew. He could still recall the celebrations, his own feelings of wonderment at the crowds of smartly-dressed gentlemen and ladies with enormous hats – "crows and parrots" as old Arquimedes called them – and Senyoreta Carlota who had glanced at him with a mixture of curiosity and insolence. And the next day, Arquimedes, the veteran of Tetouan, had turned up at his house to tell his mother that he was taking her son off sailing with him for the firm of Torres i Camps. The captain had raised the issue with Senyor Jaume, who no doubt agreed to employ one of the dead man's sons in order to salve his conscience, since he had done nothing for the widow of his employee who died at Lliberola.

"Climb on board lad," old Arquimedes told him that morning. The other crew-members, who were busy fitting the oars, grunted a few welcoming words. When they set sail, he purposely didn't look at the quayside; he knew that his mother, dressed in her widow's weeds as though the blackness inside her heart were not enough, was watching him anxiously, one shadow more among the many, since darkness still enveloped the riverside alleyways.

They left the waters of the town, which he knew like the back of his hand, and his delight grew as old Arquimedes showed him the river, which was a new world to him. Whenever he had gone down to the wharf he had been overcome with a desire to embark on a journey on one of the boats. But his father had never wanted to encourage him to take up such a hard life and never allowed him on board, contrary to the opinion of Arquimedes Quintana, who had always suspected that the lad was a born sailor. That morning, the old man had been describing their route as they went: over there was Riba-roja, and on that side, Ascó, the castle they had sighted later on was Miravet . . . The veteran of Africa was right: he had a feel for the river coursing in his blood, which had been handed down to him from generations of sailors, and even if the sight of all the villages strewn along the bank came as a surprise, nothing was foreign to him in the fresh water that guarded his father's lost bones in its muddy depths.

It was a peaceful trip. On the way back, the men had to tow the boat as far as Miravet, travelling on foot alongside the river. They spent the night there, although the captain didn't sleep on board – provoking malicious comments among the crew – and from there on a strong, steady southwesterly carried them home. The only disturbing event occurred at the rocks of Cova Plana where they sighted a boat laden with coal sailing downstream.

"It's the *Sant Lluís*!" exclaimed Jaume Tàpies. "Damn the fool who gave it a licence to sail!"

"The bottom of the river's where it belongs."

"What a bunch of cowards! You should be ashamed of yourselves," muttered the old man.

As the boats passed within inches of each other, the crew of the *Carlota* were careful not to look at the other barge; Arquimedes was the only one to hail them. The captain of the *Sant Lluís* was so haunted by the idea of death that he had had a coffin built and always took it with him in his cabin along with a bundle containing his shroud. When he lost a crew-member he was hard pressed to find a replacement and everybody tried to avoid the sinister barge which carried the grim reaper on board.

They were still unsettled by this ominous encounter when they reached the town. As they very carefully began to unload the splendid frame they had picked up at Tortosa for a large picture Aleix de Segarra was painting, a group of sailors came over to the gangplank where the old fellow was supervising the operation and gave him the news that had set the whole town agog. A crown prince had been shot dead in a distant place called Sarajevo and at home somebody – it wasn't known who – had just taken a shot at Senyor Jaume de Torres.

IV

As the bells rang out for the funeral of Pasqual de Serafí, an expert driller and a mediocre chess-player, Senyora Carlota de Torres recalled the crack of the shotgun and the state of utter confusion it had led to on that far-off day which had been reawakened in her memory by the cleaning of the portrait. Veronica had let out a scream far more terrifying than the shot itself as the tray of hot chocolate slipped from her hands; Senyor Jaume had fallen from his armchair clutching his blood-stained face; a bottle of turpentine had crashed on to the tiled floor where the liquid ran into the blood and cocoa; and in his fright Aleix de Segarra had flung his palette in the air, which proceeded to land on Grandma's bosom. Indifferent to the world's ups and downs, Grandpa carried on snoozing peacefully at one end of the sofa.

Once Camilla had managed to allay the initial fears and calm everyone down, Aleix discovered that for all the blood spattered around the room, Senyor Jaume's wound was just a nick on his cheek and looked much worse than it actually was, caused as it was by a shard of glass that hit him when the bullet shattered the balcony window and that the crimson on grandmother's blouse came from the painter's palette, not from an injury. The projectile had lodged itself in part of the moulded ceiling after piercing Senyor Jaume's portrait. It had been fired with breathtaking accuracy and had made a hole right in the middle of his forehead.

News of the event spread like wildfire and the entire Casino de la Roda showed up to express their solidarity with Senyor Jaume, who received them looking pale and nervous and unable to hide the persistent tremor in his hands. To meet his friends he sat among the ladies, who were over-excited and spiced up their accounts with wild gestures and the occasional fainting-fit; Camilla's reassuring presence was then required with the bottle of smelling-salts or *Aigua del Carme* elixir. In tones which ranged from the bombast of the last Baron de Sàssola to the laconicism of Romaguera, an important local landowner, the visitors expressed their sense of outrage at the attack. There was no doubt about who was to blame: it was clearly the work of the Anarchists, that bunch of murderous lunatics whose aim was the destruction of society. They had obviously singled out the town to strike at one of its most illustrious residents . . . Senyora Salleres' mines administrator – who by night obediently doused the widow's fires of passion – set off a roll-call of bloody events by recalling the recent murder of a Barcelona industrialist, an unsuitable thought which caused the victim to quake even more violently. Don Praxedes de Torrents, a pious and saintly cuckold, continued in the same vein with a few less than heartfelt words (he was a Liberal after all) about the minister Canalejas, who had been assassinated in Madrid a couple of years earlier. The Chevalier de Monegre – a jaundiced skull wedged between a moth-eaten hat and an oil-stained shirt-front – expatiated on the attack on King Alfonso the Thirteenth – "on his wedding day no less!"; and when the Baron managed to get a word in again, he added a historical footnote to this chapter of disasters by harking back to the bombs at the Liceu Opera House in Barcelona, a notorious *fin-de-siècle* bloodbath. He later repeated these same remarks almost word for word, with a few variations which came to him while he dined on one solitary pickled sardine served up on his last Limoges porcelain dish, to a semideserted Casino de la Roda. Barely half a dozen gentlemen had decided to brave the gloomy streets where they all fancied they could see the malicious gleam in the Anarchist's eyes.

The next day, a carriage arrived in the town with two Civil Guards and an official from the regional court, a plump, sanguine individual with a pronounced tic in his right eye which made him look as though he were inciting people to commit unspeakable crimes. The official took evidence from the witnesses, made a lengthy examination of the damage to the moulding in the hall and removed the projectile with the assistance of a carpenter. Once he had studied the holes made in the balcony window and the picture, and praised the portrait for being such an excellent likeness of its subject, he wrote in his report that the bullet had been fired from outside, from a spot difficult to pinpoint exactly, but probably from somewhere among the acacias lining the side of the square next to the Ebro. Two days after this brilliant deduction and endless sterile investigations which bored him beyond belief, the official, still displaying a constant invitation to naughtiness in his eyelid, upped and left and went back to the city with the Civil Guards. Senyor Jaume de Torres didn't dare venture outdoors and was careful to go nowhere near the windows or balconies, fearing a fatal bullet-wound. In the meantime, a heavy silence descended on the town. In the secrecy of the kitchen, Camilla dug up the old spine-chilling tale of the bar-room braggart, Pere dels Sants, who saw the shadows in Washtub Alley turn into daggers. Carlota, yet again flouting her mother's orders not to gossip with the maids, heard how the selfsame official had failed to get anything out of the alleyway's residents, who must undoubtedly have heard the fight at midnight and seen Pere fall, struck down by the eight daggers which time would later multiply, as it would also multiply the number of dogs who came to lick the blood off the pavement. The victim's betrothed was silent too, although she must have known the names of the killers; and so were those who could have pointed out the spot on the quayside where the daggers were flung into the nocturnal waters of the Ebro. The town kept quiet then as it did now. It was defending itself against outsiders armed with weapons more terrible than daggers or guns: officials who came brandishing papers. They scrawled unintelligible words on them and then people were hauled off to gaol or had their homes, lands and boats seized. And anyway, asked Camilla, seeing the young lady both intrigued and scared by this blood-curdling tale, what business was it of the city people what went on in the town?

As Senyora Carlota recalled, life suddenly got back to normal a few days later. Her father stood openly at the French windows once more, he lost his fear of going out and recovered his former devil-may-care attitude. Only his mother-in-law's implacable stare could wipe the smug, triumphant smile off his face.

Carlota never knew what had happened. Camilla could have given her some idea. But when, in adult life, Carlota sought to unravel the mystery behind the story of the Anarchist, her father wouldn't give her a straight answer; her grandmother and mother were dead by then and many years had passed since Camilla had left the family's employ. The maid was the only one to learn of the meeting between her grandmother and Graells, the administrator, and of a secret conversation between mother-in-law and son-in-law while the rest of the family slept. It was a stormy interview: his mother-in-law treated him as a fool, a coward and a scoundrel. How had he been so careless, and how, for pity's sake, had he let things go so far? Had he taken leave of his senses? What about the scandal? She had had to discover the truth for herself. What did he think he'd gain from burying his head in the sand? Didn't he see that the shot was a warning? The attacker had hit the portrait on purpose instead of blowing out the brains of the original. If he'd wanted to finish him off, he'd be dead and buried by now . . . She would sort it all out, not for his sake but to save her daughter from shame and suffering. Poor Adelina mustn't find out what a degenerate – and a useless one at that – she was married to. After a protracted stream of abuse which Senyor Jaume occasionally tried to interrupt with feeble protestations, cut short by his mother-in-law, a lady as formidable as the late general's wife, she slipped out of the house accompanied by Graells. When she came home at daybreak, the first groups of miners were making their way to work, lighting the still-dark streets with their carbide lamps, and the sailors were getting ready to cast off from the wharf. She talked briefly with her son-in-law – no shouting this time – who had waited in his office for her to get back, and then silence descended on the house.

Nobody ever mentioned any of this to Carlota. And neither did she ever hear of a christening in the old town of Gràcia in Barcelona a few months after the attempt on her father's life. It was 13 December 1914, and the city was keenly following events in the war that had broken out in Europe as a result of the assassination in Sarajevo. The Russians were in the process of recapturing Belgrade that day, but Joaquim Castells couldn't care less. The owner of the brand-new Cafè del Sol felt a glow of pride as he looked tenderly at his daughter, a former factory worker at Torres i Camps Ltd, Manufacturers of Liquorice Extract, cradling a baby in her arms, a lovely little girl who in the course of time was to grow more and more like Carlota de Torres; so much so that in years to come, no one from the town who happened to be in Barcelona would fail to go and see the double of the high and mighty lady from the mansion on the Plaça d'Armes serving coffee in Gràcia. Since leaving the town unannounced with his family six months earlier as a consequence of a visit from Senyora Camps at dead of night, Joaquim Castells had changed beyond all recognition. Nobody would ever guess that just a few months back, the café proprietor was working in the lignite mines on the banks of the Ebro or that he had the reputation of being the sharpest shot in the area.

Fifty-six years after that christening of which she knew nothing, Senyora Carlota de Torres let out a sigh. The priest, surrounded by choirboys, was walking towards Pasqual de Serafí's house, and the droning of his Latin chants floated up from the square. But Carlota was oblivious to it all; she was in another time. She was looking at the unfinished portrait pushed into a corner of her father's study. The period of mourning for her grandfather, who had gone straight from dozing on the settee to dining with Saint Peter, meant that it had to be put off yet again. Eventually, in the autumn of 1915, with the bullet-hole carefully patched up and repainted by Aleix de Segarra, and a black armband added to one of the subject's sleeves in memory of Grandpa, the painting, gleaming with varnish and housed in the magnificent frame which Arquimedes Quintana had brought from Tortosa, was hung on the salon wall, occupying the spot where once upon a time the spurious Christian martyrs had shamelessly flaunted their provocative flesh-tints.

The guests were unanimous in their praises, which were heartfelt and flattering. One of Senyor Torres' cousins put it in a nutshell when she said, "If only it could speak!" This was easily and amply rectified by the model: Senyor Jaume sat at the head of the table surrounded by his wife, his mother-in-law and his three children, and gabbled away non-stop. The host was placed directly beneath his painted likeness, and wellbeing and optimism radiated from him, as evidenced not only by his loquacity but also by the splendour of the occasion, his daughter's fourteenth birthday party, where no expense had been spared. The rector's hasty blessing had poured Latin words over the magnificently decked table bearing victuals of undeniable rotundity, accompanied by the crisp wines of the Terra Alta which set the crystal decanters and goblets afire with a vigorous red blush. Except for the first part of the meal, during which the guests attacked their food in silence and with a zeal that was fodder to Camilla's sarcasm in the seclusion of the kitchen, the conversation centred on the main topic of the day: the war that had been raging in Europe since the assassination at Sarajevo. The large-scale blood-shed in the fields of France and the steppes of far-off Russia, the skirmishes on the eastern front, Joffre's unsuccessful attacks in Vosges, the opening of an Italian front in the Trentino and the problems of the Middle East were the key points covered in the guests' chatter, even though most of them had a rather fanciful idea of where the places in question were located.

Despite the underlying rift at the party between Allied supporters and Germanophiles, which surfaced in heavy-handed remarks that had nothing to do with the celebration, neither side in the town actually wanted the conflict to end. Was there no way, secretly wondered scheming voices at the Casino de la Roda, of making it last forever? Senyora de Torres offered up prayers, masses, rosaries and novenas to saints both male and female, imploring them to extend the fighting indefinitely: why should these not be heeded? After all, didn't the rector say that the Germans were a bunch of Protestant heretics? And what about the French? Not only had they beheaded their king but they had carried out a massacre in the town in 1808 after a horrendous siege which, albeit at best a doubtful honour, figured among Napoleon's victories on the Arc de Triomphe in the Place de l'Etoile, Paris, France. And there was nothing to be said for perfidious Albion, as Baron de Sàssola called it in the preamble to his bitter tirades on Gibraltar and other such grievances. To tell the truth, there was no need to make a song and dance about it if for once they were on the receiving end. Particularly if the ructions benefited the town in such a surprising and spectacular fashion . . . For when, dear Lord, exclaimed Senyora Camps, had such a thing been seen before? Trade had bucked up during the Spanish-American war, but it was nothing compared to now. The moment the carnage began, Barcelona put in orders for endless supplies of coal: tons and tons of it, whole mountains of lignite to provide the steam to fuel an industry that had been given an enor-mous boost by the war. Such unprecedented demand shook up the coalfield and forced it to get moving. The pits still working began to mine coal flat out. Those that had closed down after the short-lived prosperity of the war in the Caribbean, came back into production; new ones were opened. The fleet of sailing barges was inadequate and new vessels had to be built to ferry the mineral down the Ebro as far as the railway stations. The yards had fresh life injected into them and were swarming with boatbuilders. Men were needed in the mines, on the river, everywhere. A flood of people came looking for work; the town was bursting at the seams. Trade, previously sluggish, took a turn for the better. Shops sprang up on the main street, the Carrer Major, which ran from the old Moorish market square – the nucleus of the medieval town – to the new part, which had spilt over the inner walls and necessitated the raising of an outer wall in the eighteenth century. The latest fashions from Barcelona went on display in bright shop windows beneath signs made by Aleix de Segarra who, besides painting names on barges and portraits of industrialists, enjoyed letting his imagination run riot on the nameplates he was commissioned to design for the shopkeepers.

In the Hall of the Martyred Virgins, the wine's red glow passed from the crystal decanters and goblets to the cheeks of the guests; the table contained all shades of gastronomic satisfaction on the faces of the local worthies, whose features twitched with the movements indispensable to chewing and swallowing. In the case of the Baron these were slow and laboured since he was missing several teeth – which, after bitter experience, his dentist refused to replace until he was paid a stack of outstanding bills; and in the case of the mayor's wife, they were very obvious due to the black wart on her chin: this excrescence translated the slightest movement of her jaws into a rolling and pitching that drove Senyor Jaume de Torres to distraction.

While they satisfied their hunger, chronic in some cases, the dignitaries conversed with mounting enthusiasm. By the dessert course, the hubbub in the room was deafening. But the gaiety was nearly brought to an end by an extremely baroque toast proposed by the Baron de Sàssola to young Carlota. He made heavy hints about her future and the family pact which everyone suspected had been made to marry her off to Hipòlit de Móra, a shy, confused youth wallowing at that moment in the delights of a bowl of cream. When another guest, Senyora Salleres' mines administrator (the widow absented herself from such tedious get-togethers on the grounds of her mourning) raised his glass to coal, may it continue to bring them prosperity for ever more, the voice of Sadurní Romaguera, made shrill and strident by his contained fury, cut through the hum of conversation like an icy blast of wind. The gentlemen were too scared to say anything while the landowner delivered his speech. What price was the town paying for this dubious prosperity? What would become of the land if people carried on leaving it to go and work in the mines or on the river, lured there by the prospect of a fortnightly wage packet? Land was the basis of society. Romaguera had such contempt for coal that he wouldn't allow any prospecting for deposits of lignite on his property, much to the impotent fury of his eldest son. Anything other than land led to debauchery, the overturn of the natural order, confusion and chaos.

He was getting carried away. His wife didn't know where to look; she was conscious that nearly everyone was watching her – particularly the ladies – and enjoying her humiliation at the hands of her husband whose outbursts were, after all, notorious. Malena de Segarra, Aleix's aunt, was the only one to take pity on the wretched woman; grown weary of the speech, she tried to cut it short with a deliberately frivolous remark which would distract her fellow-guests. But her mention of the new dress shop on the Carrer Major fell flat. The landowner shot her a furious glance and proceeded to inveigh against the intolerable expectations of the workers who were growing more insolent and demanding by the day; he went on to attack the decline in the town's moral standards since the outbreak of war in Europe and the new prosperity in the mines. Here most of the guests struck hypocritical poses. The overfed rector, his understanding clouded by copious libations, began shaking his head disapprovingly with clerical restraint and the ladies prepared to look shocked at what, in reality, they knew full well.

Did anyone doubt that the devil, Satan himself, was the master of the town's night-life? Who else could be responsible for that ante-chamber of Hell, that den of iniquity called the Eden, which had opened up directly opposite the rectory? A hotbed of sin, vice and perdition (Romaguera was quoting the words the priest uttered in righteous indignation every Sunday in his sermon at high mass), the Eden was a weed that must be uprooted without further ado. Taking this as a reference to himself, the mayor, Senyor Gelabert de Móra, Hipòlit's father, who was seated between the schoolmaster and Doctor Beltran, one of the town's two young doctors, attested between a spoonful of cream and a swig of ratafia to the strict legality of the establishments which had proliferated over the past few months. If the Eden complied with the law, what could the authorities do about it (other than secretly pocket a rake-off from the gambling profits, a detail the mayor failed to mention)? If Pere de Tobes gambled away his house at cards; if Joaquim de Tamariu spent three nights in a row in the dressing-room of an Italian chorus-girl, Simonetta Tamburini, and all hell was let loose when his wife came to drag him off home amidst clouds of face-powder and broken bottles of eau de Cologne, fisticuffs and hair-pulling; if Eustaqui Salvador ran off in a fit of unbridled passion with the waitress Filomena London (the *nom de guerre* of Casilda Valls, a lass from Tarragona); if a tipsy shipwright climbed on stage in the middle of a performance and bit one of the chorus-girls (His Worship the mayor didn't specify where); if the variety shows ended the way they did (His Worship the mayor preferred not to enter into the sordid details in the presence of the ladies); if all this and more took place without disturbing public order, what was the Town Hall meant to do about it?

It would be some time before Carlota de Torres learnt that Senyoreta Estefania d'Albera, a few years her senior and the primm-est of the angelic-looking young ladies invited to dinner, could have added a wealth of extra information to the mayor's necessarily sanitized version. But that young lady, who was now engrossed in daintily eating her bowl of cream with a silver teaspoon, did not consider it appropriate to inform the assembly of the Eden's latest record in amorous resistance. The title had been held until then by a sailor from Ascó but had been won off him two nights earlier by Cebrià de Sansa, a bargeman by profession, when he had one of the chorus girls eight times running in the presence of a reliable jury, whereas the sailor from Ascó had retired in the sixth round of his bout with Signorina Tamburini. And neither did she feel it was the right moment to divulge the name of the winner of the beautiful bosom competition held last week among the waitresses and chorus-girls; nor to let slip the nicknames by which each of the people in the Hall of the Martyred Virgins that night was known at the cabaret. Why should she reveal that every Saturday night old Arquimedes got up on to the billiard table, raged against the King, denigrated the bourgeoisie and as a finishing touch proclaimed the Republic, while Aleix de Segarra – a musician as well as a painter – played the revolutionary Hymn of Riego on the piano, lustily accompanied by a chorus of sailors and miners?

Senyoreta d'Albera could have added all this and more to the words of the town's chief authority. But she didn't, maybe because she didn't want to embarrass the clerk of the court whom she had blackmailed the information out of. The wayward girl, complained the official, using a novelettish adjective, was always threatening him that if he didn't tell her about the nights at the Eden, she would never again dress up in her nun's habit to perform fellatio on him, an activity in which she excelled, bringing him to the point of ecstasy during which, as the whole town knew, he would bellow out whole articles of the penal code as he writhed in pleasure.

Romaguera was meanwhile replying to the mayor. He stuck to his guns and warned of other perils that the plague of money would cause, railed against the miners, predicted trouble even at the liquor-ice-extract factory which had until then been a model of harmony. Who would stop the workers later on if their demands weren't nipped in the bud? The riffraff must be made to realize that they should be grateful for their wages: the weeds, he repeated sourly and menacingly, with the pompous support of the Baron, must be uprooted . . .

Among the many things made public by Camilla, the words pronounced by Romaguera that night were to be engraved forever on the town's memory. Besides arousing the maid's secret indignation, since she herself was a member of that riffraff whom the landowner had attacked, the speaker's contempt, so fibrous and dry when the other guests were sunk in postprandial somnolence, had angered Senyor Jaume's mother-in-law. The good lady was just about to forget her duties as hostess and explode with anger when the sound of loud music in the square set the crystalware on the tables chinking, roused the guests out of their leaden drowsiness and sent them over to the balcony to listen to the concert of the Riverside Harmony Band which Senyor Jaume had hired in honour of Carlota.

On 13 April 1970, many years after that birthday when the maids – Carmela, Sofia and Teresa, successors to Camilla, Adelaida and

Veronica – were cleaning Senyor Jaume's portrait, the present surfaced and blotted out Senyora Carlota's memories. No longer was the band, drenched in the autumn mists, playing the paso doble they had chosen to get the concert going, thereby resolving in Solomonic fashion the struggle between the helicon player, a supporter of the Germans, who wanted a Strauss waltz, and the tuba player, an Allied supporter, who insisted stubbornly on a Verdi march. Instead, the Latin incantations from Pasqual de Serafí's funeral wafted in through the windows of the Hall of the Martyred Virgins.

V

The rector was sweating profusely beneath his heavy ceremonial cope, which felt more uncomfortable than ever in the warmth of the spring morning. Puffing and panting, he climbed up the flight of steps leading to the church door as the bearers of Pasqual de Serafí's coffin came to rest at the bottom; while the square filled up, he seized the opportunity to draw breath before offering up the prayers for the dead. The regulars from the Quayside Café had just joined the crowd, led by Estanislau, who began to philosophize at length about the human condition, about how our lives are but a brief dream and about the uncertainty of fate; then he suddenly went off at a tangent and started rambling about the unexpected and extortionate rise in the price of coffee. His monologue culminated in a sigh of resignation which he let out a mere inch from old Nelson's right ear, just as the rector struck up his chants.

The skipper didn't notice; and neither did he hear the priest's Latin words or the muttered conversation between Nicolau de Monegre, Honorat del Rom, Eduard Forques, Horaci Campells and Manolet de Ribes. The flood of memories released by the café-owner's allusion to Arquimedes Quintana's birthday refused to subside; on the contrary, it swelled unstoppably in his mind. Every word, every sensation brought back shreds of recollections; the fragments fitted together like pieces of a jigsaw depicting old images of the veteran of the African campaign. After the prayers for the dead, the funeral procession turned into the Carrer Major and as Nelson's group passed near the corner of the alleyway leading to the Widows' Wharf, something startled him: the former stables of the firm of Torres i Camps stood beneath the arcade, and rising above the rhythmical, muffled sound of the procession, he seemed to hear the braying of Trèvol the mule . . .

The brays of the mule really had sounded in the alleyway one misty morning in 1916, when a deck-hand from the sailing barge *Carlota* had led Trèvol by the halter from the warmth of his stable out into the wintry cold and down to the Widows' Wharf. Despite the frost and the early hour, the landing-stages were unusually busy; the arrival of the animal – small, but strong and lively – aroused comment among the people there, most of whom were sailors, workmen and miners. At the foot of the *Carlota*'s gangplank, Senyor Jaume de Torres, escorted by his right-hand man, was talking to Arquimedes Quintana, who was wearing his cap as he always did, tipped over the ear he had lost at the battle of Tetouan. One of the skipper's cheeks bore a large black scratch and as he spoke, he occasionally grimaced in pain. An odd sort of mimicry meant that others of those dotted round the wharf pulled similar faces: Jordi Ventura, Senyora Salleres' captain, as he waved his right hand, Tomàs de Xerta, one of the Torres i Camps men, whenever he closed his livid, puffed-up left eye, Pere Cistella, as he moved his numb knee, Jaume Glera, when he opened his abnormally swollen lips . . . Now, such a wide range of injuries and the number of people affected – far more than just those on the quayside – might lead one to suspect a common origin. However, the chronicles of that period (anonymous as usual) shed no light on the matter. Intrigued by the affair, the town bailiff launched an investigation, contrary to the wishes of the clerk of the court, but abandoned it almost immediately because of a strange swelling on his cheek and a pain, undoubtedly rheumatic, which he got after a chance meeting in the darkness of Witches' Alley with some of those allegedly involved. That same night, Senyoreta Estefania d'Albera, who lay on the official's bed when her mother thought she was at the novena for Saint Casilda, and egged him on, the wayward girl, with glimpses of her red garter beneath her nun's habit, learnt from him of the total lack of evidence to back up the rumours of a skirmish at the Eden, caused by the plan to change the system of sailing up the river.

When the southwesterlies didn't blow and the barges couldn't come upstream under sail, the crew-members were given the onerous task of towing the boats. Now they were talking of replacing men with animals. Senyor Jaume de Torres was behind this plan, which sought to reduce the cost of transporting lignite, but it had created a great deal of suspicion, which had apparently come to a head in the alleged battle of the Eden. The civil servant however, denied that the fight had ever taken place. But just supposing, he said,

43

trying to side-step the issue, that it really had, there was no proof that anyone had said that the system of using animals to tow the boats, which had been adopted many years back in the plain around the Ebro estuary, would work upriver, where the towpath was often steep, difficult and in certain stretches non-existent. And there was no reason to think, said the clerk as he continued his report to Senyoreta d'Albera – that little minx who by now was revealing an inch or so of her thigh, above her garter – that the alleged conversation had turned sour with certain insinuations proffered by Jordi Ventura, Senyora Salleres' captain, no doubt inspired by his long-standing jealousy of Arquimedes Quintana. Despite his age, the veteran of Africa was to undertake a trial run in the *Carlota*, the flagship of the Torres i Camps fleet. And it was quite far-fetched to imply that Baltasar Teula had punched Jordi Ventura against the wall for loudly casting aspersions on the virtue of his mother, said the clerk. Of course – by now his voice had sunk to a scarcely audible murmur as Senyoreta d'Albera's artful performance continued with her slipping out of her panties – had that happened there might well have been a meteoric exchange of insults at the Eden:

"Good-for-nothing!"

"Son of a bitch!"

"Bastard!"

And then the disaster: the hysterical squeals of waitresses and chorus girls would have swelled the general pandemonium and the Eden would have turned into a battlefield. In years to come, the chroniclers could have revelled in describing the débâcle: in reporting the punch Arquimedes Quintana received from a sailor from the Feliça Lignite Mines, to which the veteran of the African wars responded with a hook to the jaw that knocked him out cold; in expressing their horror at the rain of blows Tomàs de Xerta landed on Jordi Ventura who had just thumped him in fury; in showing sympathy for Aleix de Segarra who hadn't harmed a fly, but whose face came crashing down on to the keyboard of his piano thanks to a sailor from Ascó who hit him on the back of his neck for no reason at all; in describing the entry of the municipal night-watchman, Claudi Campells (the father of Horaci who would take over from him in later years) who, having hidden his spiked stick behind the bar so that no one could say he had an unfair advantage,

44

joined the fray and with a kick to the backside sent a towman from Miravet rolling across the floor and stopped him from strangling the café-owner. In similar fashion, the chroniclers could have recorded the screams of the chorus girls as they were dragged under the billiard table in a whirl of petticoats by some of Salleres' crewmen who were taking advantage of the situation, or the war-cry of Joan Canyes, the libertarian shoemaker, the second before a blow from the left fist of a miner from the Carbonífera pit made him lose sight of the world: "Death to the bourgeoisie! Long live Bakunin!"

But in any case, stammered the clerk of the court – who by now was reduced to a slavering wreck by the sight of the jet-black curls on Estefania's eager and welcoming sex as she lay open-legged on the silk-fringed flowered bedspread – it was all lies, mischief-making and evil nonsense. The assortment of injuries borne by most of those who had gone down to the quayside that morning to see Arquimedes leave on board the *Carlota* was sheer coincidence and there was no reason to think otherwise.

As Pasqual de Serafí's funeral procession jerked, squeezed and corkscrewed its way along the narrow streets and twisting alleys of the medieval town, old Nelson recalled his resentment as he watched the *Carlota* pull slowly away from the Widows' Wharf with a cargo of twenty tons of lignite. His foot was bandaged up after an accident during the loading of some barrels and he had had to stay behind just when he would have been most useful on board. A year's sailing with Arquimedes had made him a bargee through and through, and in spite of his youth, which meant that he still wasn't allowed into the wild goings-on at the Eden, he was already being spoken of as captain material, the successor to the old man who, his severed ear at its most alert, was setting off on a difficult journey that morning. There was low dense fog and the black outline of the boat vanished immediately to the rhythmical sound of the oars.

Two days later, it was learnt from ascending crews that Arquimedes Quintana had reached Tortosa; on the return trip he was going to test whether beasts of burden could take over the job of towing the boat.

Then, all at once, the weather changed and the worries and doubts began. A chilly December became more like April: the mists cleared, a warm breeze blew through the valley and the heavens opened. The downpours caused the Segre and the Ebro to swell alarmingly high; no barges could set sail. On the fourth day, the rain suddenly stopped; on the fifth, the Ebro, a furious torrent of blood-red waters, began to quieten; and on the sixth, the first boats held up by the storm arrived back home, but not the *Carlota*. Senyor Jaume de Torres was apprehensive: the wreck of the *Rapid* was still fresh in his mind, and, fearing disaster, he didn't go to the mine or the factory; he spent most of his time on the balcony of the Hall of the Martyred Virgins, staring at the confluence of the two rivers. At the quayside everybody scanned the waters hoping to glimpse the silhouette of the *Carlota*, but the widow of Pere Botes – an evil bastard in the habit of throwing a large bucket into the water, tied with a rope to the rear of the barge to increase the boat's resistance and exhaust the towmen – swore on the Bible in the Town Square to a group of terrified women that the ship had gone down with all hands lost. The toothless, greasy old hag laid special emphasis on the passing of Arquimedes Quintana: the eels would devour him in punishment for his audacity at seeking to change things which had remained unaltered since God ordained them thus. Speculation was rife in the town's cafés and social gatherings. To the secret satisfaction of Romaguera, the gentlemen at the Casino de la Roda assumed that the *Carlota* was lost. In the Eden, where carpenters and builders were hastily repairing the damage caused by a fight that had never taken place, no one was in the mood to resume hostilities. Aleix, his neck still sore from a blow he had never received, added his anxiety to the dismay of the singers, waitresses and chorus girls with whom he would climb up on to the roof and peer at the river. Or else he would visit the pharmacist, whom future historians would refer to as Honorat del Cafè – because of his weakness for coffee – to distinguish him from his son and heir Honorat del Rom – the rum-drinker – who was yet to be born. The chemist would position himself on the roof of his house and study the Ebro with a marvellous brass telescope that had been in his family since the war against the French, when his great-grandfather had shot dead an arrogant Napoleonic horseman. In the course of one of the battles during the siege of the town, the officer galloped in through the Segre Gate and got as far as the Plaça d'Armes after running through two of the townspeople with his sword. Once there, he was quickly dispatched by a bullet from the chemist, who claimed as his booty the magnificent long-distance telescope that he found in his saddle-bag. Miraculously, the instrument was not discovered, a fact which saved the pharmacist from execution, when Suchet's troops captured the town and ransacked the house. Since then, its lens had observed stars and planets, Cabrera's soldiers during the Carlist wars, naked females and distant sails, but its reconnaissance was fruitless that winter of 1916: there was no sign of the *Carlota*. Not until the afternoon of the seventh day, when distress had been replaced by a conviction that some disaster had befallen her, did the boat appear in the spyglass's field of vision, sailing up the troubled waters.

"Here they come," exclaimed Honorat del Cafè from the roof. His cry echoed from street to street; the whole town rushed down to the quayside and climbed aboard the boats tied up at the water's edge to welcome the *Carlota*. The chemist had come down from his look-out post on the roof to the Widows' Wharf and was now describing everything in full detail.

"I can see Trèvol the mule together with a deck-hand who I guess must be that ugly brute Pere d'Atura; the animal is walking up the riverbank along the towpath, hauling the *Carlota*. They've done it! And I can see the old pirate Arquimedes too, standing by the stern, taking the helm. I'd almost swear his ear's grown back . . . Hold on! What the devil's that? What the devil . . ."

The crowd couldn't yet see what the chemist could distinguish perfectly and they were agog with curiosity after his last words. But instead of clarifying his statement, he just carried on emitting cries of disbelief, which got louder and louder as the ship drew near.

"What is it, Honorat?" Senyor Jaume de Torres enquired anxiously as he reached the landing-stage.

"Saints preserve us!" was all the other could say, still looking at the *Carlota* through his spyglass.

"For pity's sake, Honorat, what the hell is going on?"

"Well, bugger me . . ."

"For Christ's sake, Honorat!" Senyor Jaume exploded in exasperation, clutching his arm.

"If you touch me it wobbles and I can't see a thing!"

"Give the confounded thing to me."

The shouts of the crowd interrupted the tussle between Senyor Jaume and the chemist. The *Carlota* had sailed straight into the town and old Arquimedes' voice could be heard ordering the sailor on the bank to let go of the towrope joining the mule to the boat; freed from the task of pulling the boat, the mule continued upstream, making for the ferry-boat crossing opposite the liquorice factory. No optical instrument was needed now to see what was causing the chemist to gasp: at first it was just a red smudge on the rice straw that protected the *Carlota*'s cargo of earthenware; but as the sailing barge drew closer, the mass of colour acquired details. A cheer rang out on the docks. But it was impossible to say how much of this was due to the successful voyage of old Arquimedes and his crew and how much to the spectacle of the lovely Françoise Herzog – a magnificent vision of scarlet feathers and blonde hair – the bright new star of the nights at the Eden, whom the townsfolk were to know for ever more as Madamfranswah.

Amid the frenzy of the first performances by the Eden's new artiste, the patrons gradually learnt what had happened on the journey. They discovered that after an unremarkable voyage, old Arquimedes had reached Tortosa and, once the coal had been off-loaded, he had had a wash and gone to the barber's for a shave. He had put on his smartest suit and made for one of the town's hotels with the four crew members, who had also spruced themselves up. In bar-rooms heavy with the reek of cigar smoke and the smell of rum the rear towman described all the ins and outs of their meeting with Madame, who had been expecting them. Everything had been pre-arranged between her, the owner of the Eden and Arquimedes Quintana, the only ones apart from Aleix de Segarra to be in on the secret. The audience felt the same tingle of excitement as had the crew of the *Carlota* the first time they saw the beauty gazing at them with a blend of humour and surprise, and a touch of fear in her eyes. The rear towman also gave a full description of how they had carried the artiste's baggage to the boat: the front towman and the deck-hand, bent beneath the weight of an enormous zinc bath-tub, were followed by himself and a porter from the hotel with two trunks, while Madame brought up the rear on the arm of Arquimedes Quintana. In the opinion of the rear towman she seemed very taken with the fierce-looking giant, who laughed loudly and waved with gentle irony at the locals who stood gawping at the motley crowd.

It was a tougher job to get the front towman to talk. According to the shipwright from l'Arenal, who knew his weak point and wanted to loosen his tongue with drink, the crafty old fox didn't say a word until the eighth jigger of rum, but once he got going, there was no stopping him. Trèvol the mule? Good old Trèvol, God bless him! A marvellous beast; you'd think he'd been towing boats all his life. Scared of the river? What good-for-nothing nincompoop was spreading slander like that? Whoever it was, he'd got it all wrong. They'd had their work cut out? Of course! What merit would there have been in it otherwise? And anyway, once they'd taken on earthenware at Benissanet, it got harder for the mule. It wasn't the same towing an empty barge as one laden with pitchers, pots, basins and mugs . . . All things considered, it had gone pretty well, apart from the odd dressing-down old Arquimedes gave the rear towman for showing off in front of the lady who'd come all the way from France. They would have been back in two days. But Arquimedes Quintana had suddenly stopped in mid-sentence while talking to the boatman on the riverbank and stood absolutely still, like a statue . . .

The towman's account was interrupted by the usual controversy over Arquimedes' mysterious ability to sense the river's hidden dangers. For some people it was a gift he had inherited from generations of ancestors and had been in his blood since before he was born. For others – a minority, encouraged by Aleix de Segarra who sometimes affectionately poked fun at them – Arquimedes Quintana's knack came from his injury at the battle of Tetouan: the Moor's dagger had opened up a secret channel in his ear which enabled him to hear the voice of the river. During the course of this debate, the towman was knocking back rum as if it were water and when he was allowed to go on with his tale, his speech was slurred as he recounted how the old man had anxiously urged Trèvol on as fast as possible in order to take refuge in a branch of the stream near an uninhabited farmstead on the bank. The air soon grew heavy, the sky darkened, a torrential downpour began to pepper the surface of the Ebro and the river was veined with streaks of earth. As he described the beginning of the storm and the flood, his mind was fuddled with rum. From this point on, the account of their days in the farm waiting for the weather to improve and the waters to subside turned into a meaningless splutter which the rest could make neither head nor tail of. So nobody could confirm the truth of the rumours of a love affair with Arquimedes Quintana during the flood that were circulated the moment that Madamfranswah set foot in the town.

The success of this voyage meant that all the mines in the area immediately went over to the use of beasts of burden for towing. They each built their own stables on the alleyways leading to the wharves, the crews were reorganized and the former towmen, now replaced by mules, were recruited as deck-hands on the new barges coming out of the shipyards and swelling the river-traffic.

This wasn't the only innovation in a navigation system older than the river itself. A few months after the journey of the *Carlota*, it was learnt that Senyora Salleres was having a marvellous vessel built: its tonnage would be superior to that of the biggest sailing barge, it would sail faster than the wind and could tow pontoons and colliers. This item of news provoked secret feelings of anger in the Hall of the Martyred Virgins and immense anticipation everywhere else from the Casino de la Roda to the lowliest tavern. No one knew the details. Senyor Jaume de Torres set spies to report on his competitor's activities, he attempted to bribe those working on the project and tried to pump Aleix de Segarra about it, seeing that he was involved on the artistic side, but he failed to learn anything.

The circle who met every Thursday at the boatbuilders' workshop in Ferryboat Street abandoned the intense debate they had been indulging in for months on the subject of perpetual motion and took up speculating on the characteristics of the mystery vessel which was to revolutionize river transport. However, Pere Metges displayed scepticism and indifference when he raised serious doubts as to whether anything genuinely innovative could be designed without consulting him first.

"He should stick to what he knows best," said the inventor referring to the widow's administrator who appeared to be the architect of the scheme. He, Pere Metges, had designed every possible artefact to do with the river, from an automatic fishing-rod and an amphibian barge equipped with articulated legs, to an underwater excavator which only needed a few slight adjustments before it was brought in to mine the seams of lignite that lay beneath the beds of the Segre and the Ebro. The boatbuilder, who had seen the plans, privately said that it was lucky for Pere Metges that these inventions had never been put into practice.

Excitement at Senyora Salleres' boat even eclipsed the great German offensive of late March 1918 which got as far as threatening Paris. According to Honorat del Rom's interpretation of events many years later – arbitrarily repudiated by the official history of the conflict – the German High Command was inspired to take this action by the ceaseless prayers of Senyora Adelina de Camps. This lady went with Carlota every afternoon to kneel on her own private prie-dieu before the altar her great-grandparents had given the parish church and which she had generously endowed with new statues, candelabra and paintings since the beginning of the war as a pious entreaty for the killing to continue.

After many weeks of mystery and conjecture, the launch of the ship was finally scheduled for the last Sunday in May. On the appointed day, vast crowds flocked to the quayside: balconies, windows and roofs with a view of the river were thronged with people. Sunshades blossomed over the groups of women and painted the spring morning red, blue and pink. The corseted ladies declared themselves entranced by the event and chatted away nineteen to the dozen, wondering what this extraordinary ship would look like and taking advantage of the occasion to voice their shocked disapproval of the widow's amours. The conversation took another tack at eleven on the dot when the good-humoured group from the Eden arrived in the square. Silveri Tona, the guitarist, dressed in navy blue and wearing a straw boater, Aleix de Segarra in a wide-brimmed hat and black smock with a bright red kerchief round his neck, and Arquimedes Quintana in his Sunday-best cap, his good waistcoat and new espadrilles, still smelling sweet from his recent soaking in Madamfranswah's tub, surrounded the Madame, who was attired in a pink dress with matching sunshade. Behind them came the waitresses, chorus girls, gamblers and regulars en masse. The ladies reacted with studied indifference to the presence of this odd bunch while their husbands peeked sidelong at them, their mouths watering at the mere thought of the beautiful Parisienne. However hard it was for them to swallow the fact that such a delightful lady should have a counterpane the colours of the French flag, not even the Germanophiles could remain impervious to her charms. Grandmother Camps' reproving glance at the singer's décolletage – her glance here encountered that of her son-in-law – coincided with the arrival of Senyora Salleres in the company of the civic authorities, sweating in their black suits and stovepipe hats and half-strangled by their high collars. They were followed by the deafening sounds of the River Harmony Band playing a march full-blast, energetically conducted by Forques the boatbuilder.

A rocket took off from the widow's mine, one kilometre upstream from the town, exploded over the intense green of the irrigated lands on the right bank of the Ebro and smudged the deep blue sky with a tiny fleeting cloud. The crowd standing in the square, on the balconies and the docks suddenly fell silent. A distant humming had started up, a compact noise wherein could be distinguished, as it grew closer, a series of successive bangs like a string of firecrackers. The booming grew louder until a unanimous cry went up from the throng as the vessel rounded a bend and hove in sight in the middle of the Ebro. While the *Polyphemus* – for this was its name – cut through the calm green waters and approached the Town Square Wharf, leaving behind a wake of foam, the wide-eyed spectators spotted all its intricate details. A sudden ripple on the river's surface reflected the bright gay colours that Aleix had painted on the hull of the huge barge, which was equipped with paddles like a steamer. At the prow, an awe-inspiring figurehead, carved by a sculptor from Lleida, depicted the mythological giant whose name the boat bore; his single eye; stuck in his forehead, seemed to be staring suspiciously at the crowd on the wharf. The letters on the sides of the prow were painted in scarlet and stood out amid wreaths held aloft by flaxen-haired mermaids with full breasts, modelled on those of Olga Sagristà, a vivacious singer from the Eden and the secret sweetheart of Senyora Salleres' assistant. The gunwale bore another floral wreath and the sort of mudguard that covered the paddles was an encyclopedia of stylized aquatic plants, among which there darted an angler's heaven – carp, barbel, chub and shad pursued by sinuous silver eels.

"Three cheers for progress!" cried the widow's administrator in a less stentorian voice than he would have wished for such an occasion. The former office-boy, who had been promoted to administrator on account of his mattress skills, was still feeling weak from the night before: undoubtedly stimulated by the historic event that was to occur the following day, she had squeezed him so dry that his subsequent incognito visit to the cabaret singer's dressing-room had turned out to be despairingly platonic.

"Three cheers for progress!" the clerk of the court chimed in generously.

"Hear hear!" chorused the local worthies, but they could not drown the alarming counter-chant that had sprung up among the groups of artisans, boatmen and miners:

"Three cheers for progress and the old floozie!" bellowed a shipwright.

"And the dead man's horns!" burst out a Torres i Camps skipper.

"That pipsqueak is referring to the posthumous cuckolding of the deceased," added Claudi Campells the nightwatchman, librettist of the shows at the Eden and a prize pedant in questions of language.

"Three cheers for progress!" the gentry repeated discordantly.

"Three cheers for Socialism!"

"Three cheers for the eels!"

"And the frogs!"

"Stuff the Germans!"

"Quiet, you bastards!"

"Riffraff!"

"Pansies!"

"*Vive la France!*" contributed Madamfranswah, waving her sunshade enthusiastically and arousing the anger of the pro-Germans; they were not conversant with foreign languages but a malicious know-all translated the songstress's words for them.

The band, urged on by the priest, struck up a brisk march. The municipal corporation walked over to the platform that had been raised on the landing-stage, from where the mayor was to read a stirring speech, an ardent hymn to the new age ushered in by the launch of the *Polyphemus* and the rosy future that lay ahead for their

53

town and its two ancient rivers. But the speech was never delivered; the mayor cleared his throat, flung his arms wide open in a grandiose gesture, and was about to begin when disaster struck.

VI

The demolition of Llorenç de Veriu's house was first noticed by the townsfolk en masse on the morning of 13 April 1970, on their way past during Pasqual de Serafí's funeral. Other demolitions were to follow, but the impact they had was largely offset by their sporadic nature at first, their patchy distribution round the town, and the fact that the flattened houses were empty because their owners – distant, nebulous heirs, mere names on the land register – had left the area. People had more pressing matters on their minds and paid only scant attention to the phenomenon, in spite of subsequent statements to the contrary in the chronicles, and the odd exception such as Honorat del Rom. And so it was that late that autumn, thanks to an unknown heir who had never even set foot there, the Eden was unceremoniously razed to the ground.

No one had been inside the café-concert since 1919, and it was so huge that three attempts were needed to bring it down. It occupied almost the whole block between Rectory Street and Widows' Wharf; but a barber's shop had opened in what had once been the entrance-hall, and a mining company had turned the courtyard that backed on to the river into stables, thereby effectively sealing it off from the outside world. So the immense mausoleum, whose only visitors were the cats that prowled through the jungle the garden had become over the years, remained inviolate at the heart of the town until the demolition gang burst in fifty years later through the back-room of the barber's.

The first to fall was the café. Beams and tiles crashed to the ground, wrecking the spiders' dusty realm, an aerial graveyard which held the swaying remains of the victims who had fallen into their deadly clutches – flies, bees, butterflies – and shattering the Valencian ceramic counter. Until the dust settled, the pale light of that November morning could not penetrate the rubble, which still contained the bottle of rum that Ramir d'Anglesola, the Eden's founder, had knocked back as he gazed despairingly round the empty

55

building before shutting it up for good on a day that nearly no one remembered.

The collapse of the theatre, which led off the café, through a large velvet-curtained door, was more dramatic. The first time the machines pulled, nothing much happened because of a miscalculation over exactly where the steel cables should be attached; the ceiling just rocked slightly and there was a sudden, loud flutter as some bats were disturbed. It wasn't until the third attempt, after a chorus of blasphemies from the workmen, slightly unnerved by the bats, that they managed to bring it down. The moulding round the stage, a Baroque fantasy in coloured plaster which framed the performances of Madamfranswah – "the great *vedette* from the play-houses of Paris, France" as she was always announced by Ramir d'Anglesola – fell on to the backdrops. They had been used for the first time on her opening night when the tremendous racket and the roar that went up to greet her had drowned out the piano-playing of a happy, smiling Aleix, clad in formal dress to mark the occasion.

Once the Eden had been demolished and the last remaining echoes of Madame's saucy melodies still trapped in its walls were set free to float up into the grey morning air along with the chords of Aleix's piano, the great Silveri Tona's guitar and the provocative twittering of the chorus girls, one of the workmen uttered a curse and pointed in terror to where the dressing-rooms had stood. There was a moment's panic, then a member of the gang who was more intrepid than the rest cautiously went over to where his mate was pointing and established that the head poking out from the rubble wasn't human but in fact a carving. It had an outlandish appearance and was somewhat scary because of the way its solitary eye stared out from the middle of its forehead, not to mention its injuries – some of them old and others sustained during the demolition – so they left the bizarre object to rot among the ruins. And thus it was that the luckless figurehead of the *Polyphemus* finally saw its ambitions dashed; for when the Eden was in full swing it was hoped that it would become the pride of the river, and this hope had been cherished ever since, even after the accident on the day when Senyora Salleres' great ship was launched. It had been fitted with an aircraft engine to turn its paddles and this engine exploded with a terrible bang, blowing the ship to smithereens in front of the Town Square Wharf. Miraculously, other than a few people whose clothes were ripped or who were jostled as the panicking crowd fled and tripped over, flinging hats, caps and sunshades in the air, the only casualty was a member of the crew who broke his leg. After this calamity, the figurehead was salvaged by Aleix during the clean-up and stayed put in Madamfranswah's dressing-room, waiting for another motor vessel to be built. This at any rate was what the beautiful Senyora Salleres had stated resolutely as she marched off, leaving her administrator stretched out in a dead faint beneath the band's tuba, between a startled little girl and the judge's moth-eaten top hat.

The artist deposited the poor giant in a corner and from here it witnessed Madame's nights of love under and over the tricolour she used as a coverlet. The sight of her bed and her bath-time ritual brought a tremble to its olive-wood frame; Arquimedes Quintana and Aleix de Segarra, both regular onlookers as the songstress soaped herself down every day in the tub that the veteran of the African war had carried upstream on board the *Carlota*, told how the ripe fullness of her superb body caused Poseidon's son to blink his avid, awestruck eye. However, the figurehead's wait proved fruitless: the glorious future that the mayor was predicting for the town and the river only seconds before the blast of the explosion lifted him in the air and set him down on top of the Justice of the Peace, was not to be. Within a few months, Germany had been defeated and in November the armistice was signed at Compiègne; demand for coal from the town's mines, once so brisk, suddenly plummeted. The landing-stages soon filled up with piles of lignite that industry had no use for; with no cargo to transport, the barges stayed in dock. Disaster struck.

The first to leave were the gamblers. Nobody went near the green baize tables any more and the gambling fraternity who had descended on the town in its heyday soon upped sticks. Nelson could still remember seeing those peaky faces, sallow in the oil-lamp's glare, as the crowd of reprobates left town on the small number of boats that had started up again, reviving the mediocre trade of pre-war days. The next to depart were the migrant workers who had flocked there from far and wide to work in the mines. Cafés and businesses began to fold. During the long afternoons at the Casino de la Roda as he listlessly played chess or cards, the rector would recite long rosaries of complaints about the fall in donations and alms and the slump in Masses and sales of candles. Even – and at this point the rector would always heave a plaintive sigh, seeking to arouse the interest of the other members – even Adelina de Camps, such a saintly lady and so generous once upon a time, had forsaken her charitable ways and now, since the end of the war, hardly ever came near the church, may the Lord forgive her! These sly hints had no effect on the local dignitaries, most of whom were as broke now after the brief prosperous interlude of conflict in Europe as they had been before. The priest's finances never amounted to more than the pittance he received from his long-time faithful parishioners and from other less orthodox spirits such as that old devil Arquimedes Quintana. Every year the rector had the same misgivings, which he dismissed every year with the same thought as he pocketed the sailor's money: who was he, a mere minister of the Church to turn down a donation, even when it came from a godless Republican to pay for a Mass – which he never said anyway – for the eternal rest of the Moor whom the captain had dispatched at the battle of Tetouan?

November 1970 saw heavy fogs and freezing rain; these conspired to fade the colours on the giant stranded among the remains of the dressing-rooms. Mud covered his wooden head and Polyphemus, whose brief life lasted just one far-distant morning on a calm, luminous Ebro, shut his eye for good, taking with it the image of the last days at the Eden in 1919.

His tender blue pupil had seen the number of clients go rapidly downhill. After this decline, his wooden slumbers were only disturbed by Madame's baths. No longer was there the hustle and bustle of the variety shows, the tinkling of Aleix de Segarra's piano or the shouts and brawls between rival gangs of sailors and miners. Crews from foreign parts were rarely seen. Once the professional gamblers left, the mammoth sessions that lasted for days on end dwindled to dull, lifeless games. Gone too were the secret visits to the dressing-rooms paid by gentlemen who went there to treat themselves to what they criticized so fiercely. The vast bald pate of Senyor Eugeni Salses – La Margarida Coal Merchants Ltd – no longer lay embedded between the quivering thighs of Candelària Llançà, a petite girl from up-country who drove men wild. Romuald Rodera – Rodera & Co., Suppliers of Lignite – no longer came knocking at the door every Wednesday (other than Ash Wednesday) his eyes crazed with sin, to leave later, wracked with guilt, his cheeks covered in lipstick and face-powder and Signorina Tamburini's sickly-sweet perfume clinging to his moustache, to go and wake up the rector and beg absolution. The chemist from Rampart Square would still pop by; Victòria Planes used to insist he purify himself first in the bath-tub and carefully sponge off the smell of medicine that always clung to his skin. By now the unexpected visits of the man in the mask who would ask for two or even three girls were few and far between; once when a silver medal engraved with his initials turned up in Candelària's sheets, Arquimedes Quintana had returned it to the mayor's office with exasperating gravity.

The figurehead also witnessed the outcome of the meeting between Senyor Jaume de Torres and Madamfranswah. The factory-owner was besotted with the singer but had no way of making her his. Since the business with the shotgun, his mother-in-law had spied on him with the aid of a network of accomplices in an effort to forestall any future indiscretions with the ladies which would upset her daughter – who was in the dark about the truth of the other matter and had swallowed the story of the ruthless Anarchist hook, line and sinker – and entail another financial blood-letting. For Senyora Camps this was just as painful as the humiliation entailed in going to plead with the father of the little tart in an effort to avoid scandal (how unconvincing she had looked, for all her tears, in the role of the seduced young maiden!). Senyor Jaume de Torres was forced to limit himself to the occasional night at a brothel the few times he visited the city, the only alternative to his insipid marriage bed, where the most daring of their vices, as Veronica testified, was when the Senyora, behaving with what was for her extreme depravity, would consent, after a great deal of fuss and with the exciting and sinful sensation of sinking to the depths of those strumpets at the Eden, to letting her husband tickle her navel with the tip of his curled waxed moustache.

An opportune sprain of his ankle on an inspection tour of the mine prevented Senyor Jaume from joining a family trip to Barcelona to attend the wedding of his wife's cousin; here was the chance he had been waiting for. As he stood on the balcony of the Hall of the Martyred Virgins waving his hat in farewell to his family who were leaving on the *Carlota* to catch the train at Faió station, he was like a cat on hot bricks. Scarcely had they embarked when Senyor Jaume sent Graells to the Eden while he reflected on the best way to get rid of the maids for the night. To his amazement, the reply did not come back via his messenger; it was Camilla who informed him of Madame's acceptance, who took charge of dismissing the other servants and prepared the dinner. The singer was stony broke and had hopes of raising enough cash in the course of the evening to return to France.

The party ended prematurely. Having been witness to a longer bath and a more painstaking *toilette* than usual, the figurehead suddenly saw the dressing-room door fly open less than an hour after the *vedette* had left; Madamfranswah came in, threw herself face down on the bed and sobbed bitterly onto the white fringe of the counterpane decorated with the national colours of France. She was inconsolable and refused to answer the concerned enquiries of the waitresses and the guitarist. They had come running when they saw her sweep through the building like a madwoman but could get nothing out of her. The arrival of Camilla, just when the white strip of the bedspread had become soaked in tears and Madame had moved on to the blue strip, didn't shed much light on things. All the maid knew was that while her master – whose limp rather tarnished his image as a Don Juan – was accompanying the lady to the bedroom after dinner, she had let out a shrill scream, freed herself from his arm and fled from the house like one possessed. The repetition of a name amid her tears was connected in Camilla's mind to the exact spot where she cried out. The maid had an inkling of the truth but it was Madamfranswah herself who confirmed that her intuition was right: she was the lady from Paris, France whose arms had cradled the dying older brother of Senyora Adelina de Camps, the beloved libertine whom the artiste, unaware that fate had brought her to the home town of her erstwhile lover, had just recognized among the family portraits displayed along the corridor.

*   *   *

The melancholy goodbyes of late autumn 1919 returned to the figurehead's eye before he was buried for good in the ruins of the Eden. His blue pupil flickered as Silveri Tona, the guitarist, once again recited his valedictory poem to his friends – Arquimedes Quintana, Aleix de Segarra, Ramir d'Anglesola, Claudi Campells and other shadows since departed – who had met for a poignant farewell meal. It saw Madame as she walked out of her dressing-room for ever, leaving a scarlet feather from her best dress lying on the unmade bed. The rest – Madame's departure from the Widows' Wharf in the company of Camilla, who was leaving with the guitarist, by whom she was expecting a child, and the adieux of Arquimedes Quintana and the painter once they had loaded the singer's enormous bath on to a barge – didn't belong in the memory of the poor figurehead left forsaken in the dressing-room, but in the memory of an autumnal Ebro where the first seagulls were starting to fly upstream.

PART TWO

Thirteen Saints Island

I

A year after the house on Horseshoe Hill was knocked down, the demolitions had become a familiar sight. Long periods of stagnation were followed by frenzied bursts of renewed activity, like outbreaks of a waning epidemic suddenly returning to its former virulence. And then the streets would ring once more with the sinister noise of the bulldozers, while people put on a show of false normality among the ruins; clouds of acrid dust engulfed everything for a few days until the wind blew it away or one of the rare showers that soften that harsh land turned it into a muddy shroud.

Each demolition was preceded by the trauma of clearing the chosen house in order to hand it over naked to the machines. This brought many unsuspected objects to light; folk were amazed to discover things they had been living alongside for donkey's years and were so used to seeing that they no longer noticed. However, such was the endless string of rarities that, although these finds initially aroused curiosity and conjecture – often simply because of the little scrap of the town's life they contained – eventually they left even the most inquisitive spirits cold.

When the Vidal family dragged the Death-dealer screeching and scraping from the cellar there was a general lack of interest. The cannon, which would have been a source of wonder in different circumstances, was a relic from the Napoleonic Wars and had been abandoned in an olive-grove after the siege and capture of the town by Suchet's troops. In 1814, it was found by the Vidals' great-great-grandfather, a barber, surgeon and polygamist, who was an expert in leeches, cupping-glasses, distillations of essences, mysterious aphrodisiacs, linseed poultices and snake-fat plasters. Being a handy sort of fellow, he restored the damaged gun carriage and left the weapon as good as new. During the Carlist Wars, he brought the cannon out of the back-room of his shop, where it normally resided, and placed it on the battery at the Widows' Wharf, so as to contribute to the defence of the town, a bastion of Liberalism in the struggle against the forces of General Cabrera active on the other bank of the Ebro.

One pitch-black night, the sandal-maker who was on guard at the battery thought he heard the splashing of oars and, somewhat impetuously, raised the alarm.

"The Carlists!" he cried out, shouldering his blunderbuss.

The warning was passed down the quayside to the Segre fort and the town walls. The sentinels followed the sandal-maker's example and started firing at random. The townsfolk leapt out of their beds, dressed as fast as they could, seized their weapons, set off for the defences, where the attack was apparently centred, and began bombarding the shadows. The cannon thundered seven times, fired by the surgeon and his three wives – one legal one and two obtained by droit du seigneur – whom the gallant artilleryman addressed before the fray, exhorting them to set aside their amorous rivalries and concentrate on the battle which would go down in History, a word which, according to the chronicles, he always pronounced with a capital H. In a chance lull in the firing, the townsfolk realized that there was no sound from the riverbank.

"Victory!" exclaimed the sandal-maker as he held his blunderbuss aloft after a few seconds of expectant tension. "Victory!"

"A magnificent trouncing, there's not a single one of them left alive," decided the barber, resting proudly on the cannon, surrounded by his wives, all three of them with their faces streaked by the smoke from the gunpowder, as the victory cry echoed along the bulwarks.

At daybreak, a bleary-eyed sun awoke the townsfolk from their slumbers; after the fever of the victorious battle, fear of another attack had made them stay inside the fortifications. Stiff from the cold night air, they stretched lazily and peered out through the loopholes; what they saw left them speechless. Where were the dozens of Carlist bodies, the remains of the enemy boats they had expected to see floating near the wharf? The dawn light, muted by a purplish mist, illuminated a calm Ebro with no sign of the foe. Their disappointment was tempered by the words of the barber, enthusiastically seconded by the sandal-maker, to the effect that the defenders' shots had been so accurate and deadly that they had caught the enemy in the middle of the river and all evidence of the skirmish had been swept away in the current. Without doubt, the macabre flood of Carlist corpses was at that very moment sowing terror and dismay in the villages downstream. On hearing the surgeon's words, several of the heroes recollected the screams of agony or the sinister noise of the bullets whizzing out of the darkness, which had gone unnoticed the night before. Things started to fall into place: the landlord of the Old Boar Inn, for example, had a scratch on his cheek which was now attributed with a clear conscience to a blow from the sabre of a Carlist who had managed to scale the bulwark. The enemy, who was an officer (a boatbuilder, who had been next to the publican during the attack and could therefore recall him perfectly, stated this for a fact) stood for over a week on top of the parapet with his sabre held high, poised to slay Alexandre Molina, the founder of the dynasty of innkeepers. And there he remained until the apothecary – the great-grandfather of Honorat del Café and consequently great-great-grandfather of Honorat del Rom – albeit a sceptic, felt a twinge of superstitious pity for the Carlist, who had been left in such an uncomfortable posture by the reconstructed battle. So he decided to jog a few memories and remind them that the doctor had resolved the affair by firing his pistol at the enemy officer. Once the merciful bullet pierced his skull, the image of the Carlist toppled from the rampart and was released from his awkward position; he was borne away in the Ebro with his red beret floating by his side. Meanwhile, at the Town Square Café, the forerunner of the Casino de la Roda, the doctor, who had in reality crouched quaking behind a parapet, swelled with pride at the apothecary's explanation. Full of gratitude, he himself embroidered the exploit and made a mental note to reject the malicious allegations contained in certain anonymous letters where some busybody had maintained that the chemist, an irreproachable gentleman when all was said and done, was carrying on with his wife.

The Death-dealer, the hero of that fierce struggle, stood on the gun-emplacement until the end of the war, covered in a piece of sacking used to harvest olives. Then it was taken back to the shop where the barber would often polish it in an intimate ceremony, continued by his descendants. He extended the privilege of attending this ceremony not only to his children by his legal wife but also to the offspring of his concubines, who had shown them-selves selfless artillerywomen on that glorious night. And so the cannon, which was wheeled out of the back-room of the barber's in the summer of 1971 and left on the pavement to be carted away the following morning along with the rest of the Vidal family belongings, was gleaming and well-greased.

Maybe it was a bid to regain the attention that its past merited rather than an act of vandalism, as some suggested, that set off the gun, which had been loaded since the time of the Carlist wars. In the black of that cicada-studded July night, the flash must have been terrifying, although no witnesses were ever found to testify to it, not even false ones. The bang did awaken the whole town how-ever, and, except for those who jumped out of bed to hide under-neath, fearing that the rocket which the Americans had launched into space the previous day must have fallen to earth and crashed in the middle of the Plaça d'Armes, everyone else went outdoors to find out what had made the noise. Other than the nightwatchmen and Senyora Carlota de Torres, who couldn't sleep because of the heat and was standing naked at the second-floor window of her house, hoping for a breath of air, nobody else was in time to hear the sinister whistling of the projectile. The bullet described a parab-ola above the roofs and landed in the back yard of the Civil Guard barracks, slap on top of the coops belonging to the post commander, where it wreaked havoc among the chickens.

The presence of the formidable coffin full of onions, most of them sprouting, in front of No. 6, Holy Innocents Square, aroused even less interest than the Death-dealer. The slaughter of the paramilitary poultry (under cover of night and with total disregard for rank) had, after all, created quite a stir and inspired a fruitless search for terror-ists, instigated by the commandant's wife. The only reaction to the coffin was an occasional shudder, nervous glances from pedestrians who nearly tripped over the macabre receptacle and a couple of mis-guided souls who asked who the dead man was and when the funeral was being held; the very opposite, in fact, of what happened many years earlier when it was a talking-point for some time, so difficult was it to forget the events of the first Tuesday in September 1920.

Atanasi Costa was a real sight, nearly seven foot tall and of enormous girth, rather surprising in someone from a family of fairly weedy specimens, whose stunted growth invariably meant that the army denied them the honour of defending their homeland. But people were used to him, they hardly noticed the lad or his remarkable feats. The fact that when he chose, Atanasi would unaided raise the mast on Nelson's barge (where he worked as a deck-hand), that he would single-handedly carry a barrel of soft soap up the gangplank or box the ears of a petty officer who ran a whorehouse in Tortosa if he felt like having his run of the girls for free, formed part of the natural order of things. However, the sight of him carrying a coffin so immense that it could only have been built to house the outsize death of its bearer was a different kettle of fish and the townsfolk found it disconcerting. But then, after the initial shock – a travelling salesman from Reus fainted when he chanced on the ghoulish scene and had to be brought round with a nip of brandy – people began to follow Atanasi. By the end of Carrer Major he had gathered quite a crowd of people with nothing better to do and housewives clutching their bags and shopping-baskets. News of what was happening spread fast: by the time the giant got to the carpenter's, the workshop was packed with an inquisitive throng, contrary to the wishes of Serafí de Llosa, the carpenter.

In the Quayside Café – one of the few to have survived the 1919 slump in the coalfield, and now home to the regulars from the Eden, which had been closed for over a year – a thorough analysis was made of developments once Atanasi reached the carpenter's. The giant's demands and the carpenter's reply were assessed. The latter, an irascible, fair-haired man whose secret ambition was to be a bullfighter, had declared himself delighted that Atanasi had recovered (a kindness the people at the carpenter's had applauded as did those at the Quayside Café) when he had been thought dead from a strange illness which, at least according to the certificate signed by Doctor Beltran, had led to his demise. However, he had continued after a pause and a little cough, he himself was in no way to blame and, try as he might, he could not understand why the coffin was being returned. Hadn't he done a good job? Was it the wrong size? Was there something wrong with it? No, there wasn't, was there? He had done his part, he had delivered it and been paid; the rest, in other words the unpredictable quirks of fate, which apparently included the unexpected resurrection of a bargeman, was outside the control of a humble craftsman. Surely no one could allege ill-will. This might have been true if it were a coffin for a normal-size body, neither tall nor short, thin nor fat, although it would have been the very devil to sell it to somebody else. Like it or not, it was a second-hand casket – "second-death," chipped in Honorat del Cafè – even if Atanasi's mortal remains never actually lay there because of his recovery while being wrapped in his shroud. But who would want such a monstrous coffin, one that no Christian thereabouts could fill? The only person it could just about fit was Arquimedes Quintana. But now he was over his bad patch – the slump, the closure of the Eden and Madamfranswah's departure – he was as fit as a flea and looked as though he would last for years . . . Both the audience at the carpenter's and the customers at the Quayside Café found these words reasonable and they also praised the ex-deceased's reaction. He weighed up what had been said and just when many people feared, or hoped, that he would tear the other to pieces, he nodded, lifted up the coffin and started off home. The crowd followed him again. Before he opened his door, Atanasi – known from that day on as Atanasi Resurrecció – feeling rather bewildered and grateful for their company, stretched out his hand to the first one in the group. The sight of the coffin and the gesture repeated at funerals since time immemorial made the people step automatically into line. The procession was silent until, somewhere round the seventh handshake, a benighted soul stammered out the traditional words of condolence; everyone unthinkingly adopted a look of remorse and the women burst into uncontrollable tears . . .

The coffin ended up in the attic and the family gradually lost their initial awe of it. After a little time, they left clothes in it; later on they used the lid to make a shelf until the casket's macabre nature was forgotten and it became just another household object. In 1971, fifteen years after the second and final death of Atanasi Resurrecció in France, where he had been living in exile since the Civil War of 1936, when his grandchildren carried the box full of onions out on to the street as they were emptying the building, nobody remembered its history.

*   *   *

Apart from a few odds and ends, the large mirror was the only thing left of the former splendour of the Baron de Sàssola's mansion-house. This was the final stage in the decline that began with the second Baron and ended when the last member of the family to bear the title died in the workhouse at Aitona in 1920 – the pathetic old moth-eaten buffer whom Senyora Carlota de Torres remembered from her childhood parties in the Hall of the Martyred Virgins. Properties and estates had been gobbled up by creditors and now, a year after the beginning of the town's destruction, the last owner of the mansion, no relation to the old family, was stripping it prior to demolition. Fate had decreed, though, that the mirror, a collector's item coveted by the antique-dealers, would not leave the town.

Senyora Carlota de Torres was given detailed information about the accident by Carmela: how the cable broke with a whip-like crack as the removal men lowered the mirror over the balcony; how their mates in the street who were holding the rope cursed as they overbalanced and fell; how the workmen on the balcony cried out; how the family shield on the façade had been chipped by a corner of the looking-glass as it broke, and how it finally shattered. But one thing she was not told: in the brief instant it took to fall, a host of images crowded on to the mirror's dusty surface, struggling to escape from that glass fog. Jordi Ventura, a retired skipper on Senyora Salleres' boats, was standing daydreaming in the square and was the only person to witness at first hand the mirror's crash on to the pavement; from that day forth he began to have terrible nightmares. He tried numerous potions which did him no good, but was eventually cured by a witch from Lleida who transferred the dreams from the mind of the sufferer to that of the hunting dog who belonged to the tailor in Chub Square. Scarcely had the crone finished casting her spells than the dog started to grunt, to execute bizarre leaps, to roll its eyes and bare its teeth. It tore pieces out of trousers and waistcoats, attacked the tailor's dummy and ripped the skirt of the tailor's wife before darting off like greased lightning down Saint Francis Alley and hurling itself into the Ebro. Its demented brain carried away the scenes that the mirror had contained for nearly two centuries until set free by the accident. But it was not the image of the nights of passion enjoyed by the

71

founder of the family, the flamboyant Baron de Sàssola who made his fortune in the Americas, was ennobled by His Majesty King Charles the Fourth, King of all the Spains, and retired to his native town with his young wife, a girl from a Barcelona family, as aristocratic as it was impoverished – it was not this that sent the dog mad. And neither was his insanity caused by the endless evening rosaries led by the rector, or the sinful siestas which Senyoreta Nicanora de Camps – the future widow of the heroic general at the battle of Tetouan – took many, many years later in the company of one of the aristocrat's descendants. The root of the dog's madness lay in the agony and death of the first Baron de Sàssola which had been engraved on the misty recesses of the glass more than one hundred years earlier.

"The agony of an exemplary Christian," the rector had quavered, seeking to conceal the Baron's despair. For the aristocrat's suffering had not been eased by the absolution he received after his appalling confession, nor by the consecrated oil. The dying man stared openeyed at the Baroque mirror that hung in the room. Unseen by the priest, who learnt of their presence from the Baron, figures were invading the room. Reeking of pestilence – a combination of the bitter smell of feverish sweat, the stink of excrement and putrefaction – these were the terrified slaves who had been cast mercilessly into the Atlantic when an epidemic broke out among the negroes crammed into the hold of the brigantine. They wished to be present at the death of the former slaver, who had grown rich on the slave trade and not from growing tobacco and sugar-cane as he had always claimed. Images of men, women and sacrificed children had lain buried in the trader's soul for forty years; his weakened state had now caused them to be released and they were returning through the mirror. The grey light reflected inside the room by a wintry Ebro became the fog of the Atlantic; the sound of pistols came from the looking-glass and the thud of the sailors' machetes slaying a group of recalcitrant slaves on deck. The Baron's fevered pupils reflected once again the desperate features of the Mandingo clutching on to the boatswain's neck as he tipped him over the side and threw him into the ocean.

The images of this massacre were imprisoned in the mirror on the death of the first Baron de Sàssola and set free again by the mishap when the house was being cleared; but they disappeared for good with the poor hunting dog drowned in the Ebro.

The old Ford was discovered in the stables at Nasi's house. It had been left there by its owners, who had made no attempt at all to clear the building. The children were delighted with the old banger and used all their patience and ingenuity to drag it out, festooned with cobwebs and throwing up clouds of dust, on to the streets amid a chorus of barking dogs. That evening, someone in the Quayside Café remarked that it must have been the first car to be seen in the town, but this assumption was wrong. The first one was definitely not the rusty fossil from Nasi's stable but a Model-T Ford that exploded its way down Carrer Major in early 1920. Its driver, a mining engineer from the city, took it three times round the Plaça d'Armes, well aware of the admiration it was causing, then drew to a halt at the door of the Torres mansion, where they wined and dined him to keep him sweet during his inspection trips to the coalfield. The fellow always used to come by sailing barge and his presence tended to pass unnoticed by everyone other than the miners. The old foremen would listen attentively to his expert advice (long-winded and full of technical jargon, on how to tunnel galleries, locate seams, blast rocks, lay rails and shore up roofs), which they had not the least intention of following; and the engineer, satisfied at having passed on a shred of his knowledge to these poor ignorant souls would go back to daydreaming in his city office. But on this occasion, the engineer's arrival by car caused quite a stir.

As he got out of the automobile, the stentorian voice of Senyora Feliça de Roderes rang out from the west side of the square, where she maintained permanent sentry duty from her favourite balcony. The engineer still had one foot on the running-board of his Ford and was taken aback by the darkly-clad figure who leant over the railing and proclaimed that the presence of the wheeled monster was an unmistakable sign that the end of the world was nigh. The young city gent – as he himself confessed to Senyor Jaume over dinner – could not avoid a shiver running down his spine. However, her words had little effect on the locals since they were so accustomed to her dire warnings, trotted out unaltered during eclipses, storms, carnivals or floods and resurrected in later years with the invention of the cinema and the telephone, that they weren't really bothered by yet another divine curse or planetary cataclysm. They had even given Senyora Feliça de Roderes' customary platform the nickname of the "Balcony of the Apocalypse". And so the bystanders went on examining one of the machines which most of them had only seen in illustrated magazines, while Senyor Jaume de Torres, embarrassed at the woman's outburst, hurried down to the square to rescue his guest amid a welter of jumbled excuses.

A few months later, the riparian sibyl let fly again and loudly predicted calamity when a paternal uncle of Carlota de Torres became the first person in the town to buy a car. She may not have been right about the end of the world, but Feliça was spot-on about the car: during one of its jaunts round the town when its driver was showing it off, its brakes snapped at the end of Saint Francis Alley. Nelson and his crew were busily unloading sacks of rice at the Town Square Wharf and all of them – most notably the giant Atanasi, who had died and come back to life two weeks earlier – helped fish the driver and his fiancée out of the Ebro, stunned and half drowned after the plunge which had put an end to their dizzy descent of the hill.

Although they kept their mistress informed of events in the town, neither Sofia or Teresa felt that the discovery of the car was worth mentioning. They hardly noticed the heap of old iron that the children brought out on to the street. And even if they had told her, she probably wouldn't have associated the cobwebby relic with the splendid vehicle, her father's gift on the occasion of the wedding of his daughter to Hipòlit de Móra. She had sat by her mother on the back seat in her wedding dress and driven the hundred metres from the Torres mansion to the church steps.

Francesc, the youngest son of Sadurní Romaguera, might possibly have remembered the Ford confined to Nasi's garage since the Civil War, but by the time he appeared in the town, on the day after its discovery, the car had vanished. That same night, somebody, most likely one of the rag-and-bone men who were lurking around during the demolitions, had spirited it away.

II

It was the ladies' custom to sit beneath the portrait of Senyor Jaume de Torres – whose bullet hole from 1914 had been reopened by the energetic scrubbing it had received the previous year after the invasion of dust from Llorenç de Veriu's house – and distil the venom of the town's gossip, or else gleefully hatch endless intricate and malicious plots as they dipped their biscuits in their cups of hot chocolate.

There was an atmosphere of tension the day after the old Ford came to light. The daily get-together dragged on rather tediously until almost the final sip from the thimbleful of extra-dry anisette which the hostess always served with fresh lemonade after the thick, cloying chocolate, so often marred by the sinister grittiness of dust from the demolitions – an insidious forewarning of death and the grave.

They had been pretending all along. They feigned interest in irrelevant matters and made trite remarks about how awful things were in the town because they didn't dare broach the subject that all of them wanted to discuss, except for Carlota de Torres. She knew nothing of it and listened to their prattle with mounting annoyance. They insincerely declared themselves relieved that Arcadi de Sàssola, the nephew of the last Baron, was back home. Surly and foul-mouthed, the slaver's descendant lived a solitary life at the Corner Café where he worked as a waiter and only came out once a year. When his big day came, Arcadi would conscientiously dress himself up in the fashion of his youth, saunter down to the coach stop, causing quite a stir with his suit from the 1920's, an impeccable straw boater and an ivory-handled cane, a relic of his family's former wealth; he climbed aboard the coach to Lleida and on arrival at the city vanished. When his year's savings ran out – and they never lasted more than seven or eight days – Arcadi would come back to the bus station, dirty and unshaven by now, with bags under his eyes, ravaged by his debaucheries, unsteady on his feet and without a penny to his name. He lay down on a seat in the coach, with his straw hat over his face, and slept like a baby until the bus reached the town and made a detour, thanks to a long-standing pact with the driver, who deposited his passenger at the door of the Corner Café. Once there, the customers would welcome the return of the prodigal waiter with good-natured ribbing; amid their laughter the proprietor resolutely sent him off to the wash-house and walked behind him shouting insults, "You filthy pig, you degenerate, you disgusting fornicator, go and scrub yourself clean with bleach; you stink of loose women!" He wouldn't let him touch a thing until he was as fresh as a daisy. This year Arcadi's disappearance had lasted longer than usual and they had been starting to get worried at the café, when he had finally turned up, the previous day, after an absence of twelve days, looking more of a wreck than ever.

The guests in the Hall of the Martyred Virgins rapidly concluded this story; they wasted no time in questioning the truth of the convoluted tale of corrupt police, romantic whores and sinister thugs that Arcadi had used to explain his delay. The ladies also made a brief reference to the accident with the Baron's mirror and the clearing of certain pretentious houses which, in the event, had turned out to be little more than repositories of junk. Where were the supposed riches of the Plana, Vallcorna or Veriu families? When it came to it, what had emerged from the mysterious attic hideaway of Ceferí de Valls, that eccentric who was rumoured to be the illegitimate son of a bishop, and who Senyoreta Estefania d'Albera, the oldest of the ladies present, could scarcely remember? No jewels, no pots of gold coins in secret hiding places; just documents, parchments and crates of old books thrown away to the incomprehensible despair of Honorat del Rom, who spent days scrabbling through the filth at the rubbish dump to rescue them. This was not the first time, as Nàsia Palau pointed out with a shudder of disgust, that the chemist had indulged in such crackpot behaviour. It ran in his family. At the beginning of the demolition, when the Campells house was cleared, he was running round like a maniac in search of the customers of a certain shopkeeper who wrapped his vegetables in paper cones made of old yellowing plates covered in scrawls. They had surfaced in a trunk from the house and the greengrocer was using them as wrapping paper. Honorat looked deranged, Nàsia remembered perfectly hearing him mutter, "How stupid can you get! Using Goya etchings to wrap up beans!"

They changed subject but the tale of the rector's housekeeper didn't manage to spice up the assembly, even though Carlota de Torres, whose maids had kept her well informed, went into great detail about how the poor woman, flustered by people knocking at the door in the middle of the night for the father to attend a dying man, went to open the door dressed in the priest's cassock. What with the darkness, her sleepiness and haste, she had mistaken it for her dressing-gown.

The decision to raise the matter was taken by Estefania d'Albera, a decrepit, evil-tongued old spinster who in the privacy of her own bedroom would still slip into her sexy nun's habit and let herself be swept away in a tide of nostalgia, remembering her promiscuous past with the clerk of the court who had died of typhoid in 1922.

"They say that . . ."

"What?" exclaimed pampered, cross-eyed Nàsia Palau.

"What?" tinkled soft, plump Teresa Solanes.

"What?" blurted out pale, insipid Isadora Rubió.

"Seeing that you're interested," continued Senyoreta Estefania, knocking back her anisette and casting a sidelong glance at Carlota de Torres, "they say that Francesc Romaguera arrived in town last night."

"Oh!" said Isadora Rubió in surprise.

"Oh!" said Teresa Solanes in amazement.

"Oh!" said Nàsia Palau in astonishment.

"You spiteful bitch!" thought Carmela; and she put a jug of lemonade down on the table as she stared at the former mistress of the clerk of the court. "Damn and blast you!"

Senyora Carlota de Torres didn't open her mouth and although Estefania d'Albera understood from her hostess's stony silence that she had drawn blood, she didn't dare pursue the matter and chose to go off on another tack. However, her sudden interest in the nocturnal affairs of Horaci, the town's nightwatchman, didn't really catch the imagination of Isadora, Teresa or Nàsia. Disappointed at Estefania's refusal to go on with the subject of Romaguera, they began yawning and, under the pretext of vague things they had to do very urgently, scurried away.

Alone now, and even more annoyed by their hypocritical thank-yous on the way out, Carlota stood next to the table for a short while, her head hung low, then she picked up the jug and smashed it against the drawing-room wall. After insulting Carmela, Sofia and Teresa as they cleared up the pieces of glass and the slices of lemon that shone like golden coins scattered on the floor, she went round the whole house, muttering, banging doors and terrifying the ancestors in the pictures that hung in rooms and corridors – except for the general's wife. When she had calmed down, she went back to the hall and slumped into an armchair.

"Wind the thread, unwind the thread. Then start all over again . . ." mumbled old Carmela, turning on the tap of the gas cylinder in the kitchen. She had to admit that gas was quicker and cleaner than coal, but she still couldn't get used to it. She missed the old coal-fired ranges which had disappeared shortly after the beginning of the town's agony, to be replaced – saints preserve us! – by these clean, white stoves that made her think of those awful machines at the hospital.

"Wind or unwind, the thread's always the same," concluded Sofia, listening to her words.

"There are some things in life you can never blot out."

"Never."

"They're like the Ebro and the Segre," added Teresa. "The water never stops running."

"Listen to Miss Know-it-all," taunted Sofia. "Where did you learn that? In bed with Senyor Jaume?"

"For God's sake keep your voice down."

"Don't fret yourself, dear! The dead are hard of hearing . . ."

"But the living aren't."

"If you mean the mistress, you needn't worry about her. Do you think she doesn't know her father used to chase you on the side?"

"I know somebody who couldn't wait to be caught but didn't even get a look-in . . ."

"You cow!"

"That's enough of that!" interrupted Carmela. She knew how these squabbles ended: in a catalogue of grievances where truth, insinuation and blatant lies tarnished everything. There was no need to stir things up, to unearth old stories; the new ones were bad enough. What point could there be in raking over the love-life of Senyor Jaume – "may he rest in peace" the maid was careful to add –? He had always been ready to chase any woman, so long as she wasn't his wife, who was such a skinny shadow of a woman that you could scarcely believe that she had given birth to three great big children, two boys and a girl. Many years had passed since Senyor Jaume pinched Camilla's well-built thighs before she ran off with the guitarist from the Eden; and then she, Carmela, had taken over from her as housekeeper in 1919. A long time, too, since Senyor Jaume, an old man by now and a widower but still hot-blooded, would corner Teresa in the darkness of the corridor. That time was gone for good; best not hark back to it.

Now that she had nipped the maids' quarrel in the bud, Carmela's thoughts returned to her mistress. Why had Romaguera had to reappear? The destruction of the town had dredged him up from the depths of the past, as it had laid bare the contours of the buildings waiting to be demolished. Maybe it would have been better for the houses to sink without trace along with their contents, to make a clean sweep and start again without all that old lumber impregnated with other years and other lives. Without the Romagueras, ghosts of time past. But objects weren't to blame. She knew this full well. As she sat in the middle of the vast kitchen enveloped in a dim light that gleamed pallidly on china, aluminium, silver and copper, the old maidservant grasped the folly of this idea; there was no purpose in battling against time, the immutable enemy, since its seeds lay buried deep inside objects and once in a while they brought forth shoots of anger. It had been pointless to see the Torres' retired administrator, Ramon Graells, the night before, and get him to send somebody to tow away the old Ford that the children had dug out of Nasi's garage. The Graells lad, the living image of his father and as smarmy as they come, had told her that the car was now a burnt-out heap of metal lying in a ravine in Vall Seca. Pleased with his own efficiency, he had failed to notice her shiver when she heard where he had set fire to the old jalopy. The flames had engulfed the car, but it wasn't the rusted bodywork and dirty, cobweb-strewn upholstery that contained the mark of a few hours of dubious happiness and the impatient imprint of death. It had been useless to set fire to the Ford, almost as useless as trying to prevent the mistress from hearing that Sadurní Romaguera's youngest son was in town: there would always be an Estefania, a Nàsia, an Isadora or some other merciless hag waiting to reopen old wounds.

The thread that Carmela was alluding to was tied to one morning in 1925. Inside the gloomy hall, in the viscous blackness that rose from the quayside full of rotting ships, Senyora Carlota de Torres seemed to see once more the sun that had dazzled her at the railway station at Faió, when she and Hipòlit de Móra had alighted from the Barcelona train on return from their honeymoon. One of her sailing barges was supposed to meet them in this village, which lay downstream from the town; they brought coal here from the Torres mines, the most important of the few that had survived the 1919 slump and that were still working at virtually full capacity. But there were no sailors there to welcome them, to collect their luggage or take them to the boat.

"I suppose you sent the telegram," she said in annoyance on seeing the empty platform.

"Yes, of course I did. Maybe the stationmaster knows something or has a message for us."

He was nowhere to be seen. After waving the train off with his red flag he had vanished into thin air.

"It's all very odd. Look . . ."

Past the heaps of lignite en route for the factories of Barcelona and through the shimmering heat, pierced by the repetitive sound of the cicadas, they could see two barges tied up at the wharves; but no crew on board or shovelling the shiny black mineral, now grey beneath the whitish film of the heat haze.

Thoroughly perplexed, Hipòlit began hypothesizing. The telegram had been held up, there had been a last-minute hitch in the barges' journey, or maybe a boat had run aground – quite probable with the low level of the Ebro in summer, which led to danger in backwaters and shallow stretches where it was not unusual for boats skippered by second-rate captains to get stuck. This string of conjectures solved nothing and only intensified his wife's exasperation to the point where she nearly exploded. She felt offended and humiliated. Who would ever have thought that Carlota de Torres i Camps

– she never used her husband's surname – would have to wait amid a pile of suitcases, abandoned at the very railway station where they loaded *her* lignite, alongside a river plied by *her* vessels and *her* sailors and which she felt belonged to her as of right? Where were the Torres i Camps workers from Faió? Spurred on by her anger, she began to pace furiously up and down the platform from one end to the other. She opened her sunshade, then shut it. She looked down the path, muttered something and opened her sunshade again; while Hipòlit, puffing and panting, moved the suitcases out of the glare of the sun, put them in the shade of the porch and said he would telegraph the town.

Night robbed the geraniums on the balcony of their colour and stained the corners of the room black; stars were now floating on the calm Ebro. But Senyora Carlota de Torres didn't get out of her armchair to put on the light. She heard the muffled noises of a town witnessing its own death throes, sometimes in anguish and sometimes delirious with a strange excitement. On any other occasion, this would have rekindled her deepening anger, which one day would lead her to the brink of disaster. However, that evening a different anxiety was gnawing away at her: Francesc Romaguera must be walking down those scarred streets, consumed with an ancient hatred which left no room for forgetfulness, pretending to know nobody, avoiding people as he had done the few times he had been back to the town since the end of the Civil War in 1939. And yet again he wouldn't knock at the Torres' door. In spite of this, the mention of his name was enough – as wily old Estefania d'Albera knew – to fetch her a secret blow with the same force as on that day in 1925 at the railway station at Faió.

When she saw the Ford jolting over the ruts and coming round a bend in the road, Carlota de Torres felt relieved that this ridiculous situation was coming to an end, and she prepared to fire off her heavy guns at the family. The car stopped at the station, but the person who got out wasn't her father or his inseparable sidekick Ramon Graells; it was the tall, stocky figure of Francesc, Sadurní Romaguera's youngest son. He and Carlota had been childhood friends although they had scarcely seen one another since they had both been packed off to school, she to a convent boarding-school in Lleida, and he to Madrid, where he stayed with his aunt and uncle and studied to be a lawyer. The boy only visited the town in August, when Carlota was on holiday with her family in some spa or other. Francesc had changed so much that she found it hard to connect his appearance now with the image she had of him nearly ten years back. They greeted one another and Carlota's anger melted immediately. Francesc quickly loaded the baggage on to the roof-rack and couldn't help smiling when he saw Carlota occupy the front passenger seat, relegating Hipòlit to the back seat next to two suitcases which didn't fit on top. They swept out of the station. Francesc suddenly became serious and began to explain the reasons for the lack of activity on the river and the family's absence at the station. As they went up the Ebro along the stony road that ran parallel to the towpath trodden for so many years by the feet of men and, since Arquimedes Quintana's famous voyage, by the hooves of animals, Carlota learnt of events, first in surprise and then in fury: a strike had brought the coalfield to a standstill. Yes, they had received the telegram from Barcelona saying that they were arriving, and had intended going to meet them at Faió, but at the last minute it had been thought better for Senyor Jaume and Graells not to risk travelling. It was advisable for them to lie low. Francesc's father, who had been the town's mayor since General Primo de Rivera's coup d'état in 1923, had recommended this at least until the arrival of the troops they had requested from the city to enforce law and order. And this was why Francesc, who had been on holiday in the town since Carlota had left on her honeymoon, had gone to rescue the damsel in distress (now it was his turn to forget the poor fellow on the back seat, half squashed by the suitcases each time the vehicle jolted).

A strike? The Torres miners out on strike? Carlota couldn't take it in, although Francesc's words left no room for doubt: miners, carriers, drillers, blacksmiths, stablemen had taken a stand, they were refusing to work if they weren't given a pay rise and better working conditions. The sailors had joined in too. The barges weren't sailing; whether empty or laden with lignite, they were in dock awaiting the outcome of the negotiations between owners and workers, but the talks were getting nowhere. And what about the factory, she enquired, how had the workers there reacted? Francesc, growing more serious by the minute as he outlined developments there, replied that the factory-workers had fallen in with the rest; Carlota felt as though she were hearing his father's voice. At meetings in the Hall of the Martyred Virgins and get-togethers in the gentlemen's club, Romaguera senior became furious whenever reports came in of workers' unrest anywhere, and would demand that a firm, unrelenting stand be taken to deal with situations that could lead to disasters such as that in Russia where the proletarian masses – "Godless wretches fit only for the gallows!" – had overthrown the Tsar and imposed Communism. The coalfield had been a model of peace and quiet in the wake of the 1918 crisis and the departure of the foreign workers, but discontent had been simmering for some time now, and this could not be allowed to go on. The trouble-makers must be rooted out on the spot. Socialists, Bolsheviks, Anarchists, Republicans: throw the lot of them into a sack with a big stone and heave them into the Ebro. These views drew feeble protests from Senyor Jaume, who was horrified at Sadurní Romaguera's increasingly ruthless pronouncements and feared that violence would erupt. Francesc was in agreement with his father, which pleased Carlota. She had never had any say in the conflicts at the mines or the factory and anyway her notion of them was very basic, rooted dangerously and exclusively in class pride; but she found her father's behaviour weak, almost cowardly, and could not help despising him a little when she heard him argue with Sadurní Romaguera about the workers.

Carlota de Torres i Camps felt overwhelmed by Francesc. His presence, his words stirred her in a strange, unfamiliar way. She felt a persistent tingling down her spine, which was soaking wet from perspiration and sticking to the leather seat; her heart was pounding while Hipòlit, whose only contribution to the marriage – beyond two mines, land and shares which in Carlota's eyes justified the union, arranged many years back between the Torres and the Móra families – would be the spermatozoa required for three pregnancies, was wrestling with the suitcases to stop them from squashing him.

They met the first group of miners by the loading-bay of the Amat mine and were forced to slow down. They were blocking the road, and the windscreen framed a mass of sombre faces, which moved aside as the car crawled past, almost at walking pace. Francesc Romaguera had turned pale; Carlota pretended not to notice the eyes staring at her through the windows, which made her almost unbearably nervous. She had never felt these people so close to her before. She had always looked on them as strange, remote beings. She would point them out, almost like zoological freaks, to her friends from the city, former classmates from the convent boarding-school in Lleida whom she often invited to the town. Along with a look round the factory, a visit to one of the family's mines was always scheduled for such trips. Often escorted by her father, arrogant, talkative and gallant with the young ladies, or else under the overweening protection of the solicitous Graells, she enjoyed scaring her friends. She would take them to the entrance of the main gallery where they were overawed by the sight of truckloads of lignite being towed by animals glistening with sweat and dust. She made them go inside the mysterious world of the smithy with its showers of fiery sparks. She led them to the stables and down to the docks to see coal being loaded on to the sailing barges. At dusk they would step out on to the balcony and watch the miners, black as embers, walk home by the light of their carbide lamps. A filter had always existed between her and that world; reality belonged on the other side. Now, all of a sudden, the miners had stopped being anonymous silhouettes and had become living, threatening beings, with the audacity to hold up Carlota de Torres' car. The crowd of workers eventually thinned out and the car picked up speed. The scene was repeated before they reached the ferry station, and as they motored through the olive-groves a couple of stones ricocheted off the Ford's bonnet. The crossing was the final straw. The ferryman didn't even acknowledge them; some peasants moved over to the other side of the platform, pointedly drawing well away from the car, fearful that the strikers might retaliate, so Francesc Romaguera informed Carlota, if they showed the travellers any kindness.

It was an odd sort of return, quite different from how Carlota had imagined the end of her honeymoon in Paris. The town was unrecognizable; the bitter, previously hidden, face of a happy world. Handing out the presents they had brought back from Paris helped to cheer things up over dinner. Afterwards, as she gazed through the windows at the groups of miners on their way to a meeting, another image, that of Francesc Romaguera, occupied her thoughts with an unsuspected, unfamiliar and disquieting force. Her body, which Hipòlit had failed to excite with his clumsiness, was now aroused. Her obsession gave her no rest. Two days later, she found an excuse to summon Francesc to the house. She called Carmela, the girl they had taken on when Camilla ran off with the guitarist from the Eden. The girl was a little older than herself and had gained the trust of her employers through her loyalty and obedience. She had been the close companion of Grandmother Camps until her death just over a year since, when she had immediately become Carlota's confidante. She listened to her mistress's instructions, nodded and left the house to go and ask Francesc Romaguera if the revolver that they had just found in the glove-box was his.

"Wind the thread, unwind it . . ." mumbled old Carmela, alone in the kitchen.

Her mistress sat in the hall at the other end of the house, but she could follow the thread of her memory and join her own recollections on to it, in the same way that the Segre joined on to the Ebro; she recalled the darkness of that distant night which had enveloped her the moment she stepped out of the Torres mansion to go and ask Francesc Romaguera about the gun which Senyor Hipòlit had found while checking the Ford and which he had been too scared even to remove. As she turned into Bakers Hill, she collided with a crowd of miners. They had been holding a meeting at the Bridge Mine and were now on their way to the Town Hall. Frightened by the black mass that looked like an excrescence of the night itself, she flattened herself against the wall. The men didn't notice her. She recognized a few, including Terrer; from what she had heard of the conversations between Senyor Jaume and other members of the bourgeoisie while eavesdropping at the door of his office, the mine-owners held him to be the instigator of the workers' demands, the organizer of the strike fund and the chief ringleader of the stoppage in the coalfield. He had come to the town two years previously and although little was known of him, beyond the mysterious revolutionary past he was reputed to have had, he became a leader. He lived at the Eel Inn, where every day after work he

85

gave free lessons in reading and writing to anyone who was interested. This had transformed it into a meeting place where the workers drew up their first proper set of demands. Inevitably, the outsider was the target of the middle class's hatred, the *bête noire* of the powers that be at the Casino de la Roda. Carmela had only seen him occasionally; she recognized him by his Barcelona accent when he addressed a few words to old Arquimedes Quintana who was walking alongside him, unmistakable on account of his huge bulk. She thought she glimpsed her brother too – she was always arguing with him and telling him to steer clear of trouble, so that he could get a better paid job in the mines or at the Torres factory. The rest were a sea of indiscernible faces lit here and there by a miner's lamp.

"The Civil Guards!"

The troops, who had arrived that afternoon in barges requisitioned at Faió, came out of a side-street and charged at the strikers. Fists flew and there were cries of pain. The maid was petrified and darted off to the bakery on Bakers Hill where she crouched against the bundles of rosemary piled next to the door.

"Son of a bitch!"

"Come on!"

"Bastards!"

"Make for Sun Alley!"

Carmela heard a groan nearby; a miner appeared in the circle of light cast by the lamp at the bakery door. He stumbled forward, clutching his head. A Civil Guard seized hold of him but the enormous figure of Atanasi Resurrecció barred his way and landed the policeman such a mighty punch that he ended up sprawled against the bakery door.

Shots rang out. Carmela felt someone take hold of her arm.

"What the hell are you doing here?" old Arquimedes asked her as Llorenç de Veriu dragged away his wounded comrade. "Do you want to get yourself killed? Clear off."

The bunch of miners managed to turn down Sun Alley, pursued by the Civil Guards. There were people moaning on the ground. Carmela ran off in the direction of the Romagueras' house, staying close to the wall. When she passed by the Old Boar Inn, she saw that Englishman whose name she never remembered leaning over the balcony; he was looking anxiously towards the wharves where the clamour of the strikers was at its loudest.

Clouds obscured the moon and intensified the darkness. But neither Senyora Carlota de Torres in the hall or old Carmela in the kitchen noticed it. The thread of memory was drawing mistress and maid to that day, forty years past, when, in the wake of the collapse of the miners' strike after two months of struggle, the body of Arnau Terrer was found on the banks of the Ebro, his heart pierced by a juniper branch.

III

As he walked up Sun Alley, old Nelson didn't realize that he was
cutting across Carmela's memories, focused on the exact spot where,
in 1925, the Civil Guards had just charged at the rioting strikers.
Had the gust of bitter memory taken hold of him, had it made him
relive that moment, the old fellow would have instinctively moved
his head as he had done, just in time to dodge the rifle butt which
merely brushed against his left thigh. Instantly recovering his youthful energy, he would have punched the figure who had him pinned
against a wall; the Civil Guard would have fallen like a stone, and
a second later the flash of a gun would have cut through the darkness
above the shouts and scuffles of the writhing mass. He would have
felt a jolt as someone scurried off and bumped into him, and, as he
retreated towards the bakery, he would have come across Arquimedes Quintana and Llorenç de Veriu tending a wounded man.
Arquimedes was rebuking a woman: "What the hell are you doing
here? Do you want to get yourself killed? Clear off!"

If Nelson had found himself in this flurry of memories, he might
have recognized the fugitive who stole away hugging the wall as
Carmela; and he might have wondered what the sly young madam
– said by the town's gossips to be permanently lying spread-eagled
beneath Senyor Jaume de Torres – was up to in that inferno. If old
Nelson had found himself inside Carmela's head, he would have
seen himself aged twenty-five, a fully-fledged riverman, captain of
the *Neptune*, the finest barge in Senyora Salleres' fleet; his reputation
as an outstanding navigator was confirmed by the English guest at
the Old Boar Inn, who once said to him at the Quayside Café,
"Robert Ibars, you are a greater sailor than our own Admiral
Nelson!"

Mr Oliver Wilson came to the town in October 1922. He got off
the train at Faió station and journeyed up the Ebro in a sailing
barge belonging to a fellow from Ascó known as the Bishop because
of his pious ways, attested to by the large collection of medals which

88

he always wore round his neck: from a Virgin of Carmel, the patron saint of sailors, whose task it was to protect him from shipwrecks and other misadventures on the river, to a beatified Italian miracle-worker. The latter commanded the sailor's blind devotion because, in conjunction with a powerful disinfectant that burnt his skin, she had just rid him of a virulent and tenacious bug that he had acquired on the bed of sin from a Tortosa prostitute. (*"Phthirus pubis*, commonly known as crabs," Honorat del Cafè, a lifelong agnostic, had murmured mischievously as he handed him the bottle over the pharmacy counter, not realizing that the Latin name, interpreted by the sailor as a liturgical formula, enhanced the merits of the preparation). A week after the miracle, when the sailor was starting to forget his infuriating itch, Mr Wilson's arrival at the Town Square Wharf excited a great deal of curiosity. The Bishop, followed by the crew who were laden with the foreigner's luggage, escorted him to the Old Boar Inn.

Later, when he had learnt more Catalan, Mr Wilson confessed to Aleix de Segarra and old Arquimedes Quintana that the first time he had stepped inside the inn, nothing there led him to suspect the drastic change of direction, the irreversible turn of the tiller that his life was to undergo in the old house. He usually attributed this momentary lapse in his prophetic powers – which he had had since birth – to the Bishop's miraculous hardware interfering with his brain's magnetic field. The regulars at the Quayside Café, who subjected everything to the harshest scrutiny, reached the conclusion that there must be a grain of truth in the Englishman's words: in the time he had been there, Mr Wilson had sensed with remarkable foresight the flood tides of the Segre and the Ebro, an unprecedented snowstorm, the shipwreck of a skipper from Miravet, three caved-in mines, the adultery of the rope-maker's wife, the nightwatchman's gallstone and the premature confinement of the judge's wife. In any case, whether the reason for the temporary decline in his powers was the negative influence of the metal or exhaustion from his journey, there is no doubt that the stranger walked into the Old Boar Inn defenceless and unprepared.

On his travels round the world, Mr Wilson always conformed to the stereotype of the phlegmatic Englishman. All kinds of women (formidable Valkyries, fiery Italian beauties, native women in

Polynesia, lethargic dusky maidens in the Caribbean and Japanese women like porcelain) had left him cold, unmoved; but he was like putty in the hands of Agatòclia Molina, the splendid widow who owned the inn. The loyal subject of His Majesty King George the Fifth was so bowled over by the riverine beauty that, despite his exhaustion, he didn't sleep a wink. Three nights later, while Mr Wilson was doing his best to get Agatòclia out of his mind and concentrate on the task that had brought him to the town (a geological study of the Ebro basin) the landlady walked into his room without knocking.

Just then, the Bishop was going through agonies because of the Englishman. He was staying overnight in the town and had lingered in the Quayside Café on his own to round off the evening with an after-dinner glass of rum, unaware of what lay ahead. Scarcely had he sat down when the customers at the next table began chatting about a sailor from downstream, an ungrateful so-and-so. Luckily, they didn't appear to know his name, which afforded the Bishop some relief. He sat cringing at the table, not daring to get up and leave since he didn't want to attract their attention, being the only other person in the bar besides them; and thus he had to sit through the tale of the wretch who returned evil for good. For instance, said Honorat del Cafè, echoed by Aleix de Segarra and re-echoed by old Arquimedes Quintana with a wink at Estanislau between two puffs on his pipe, scarcely four days had passed since an Italian saint had delivered the scoundrel from an attack of the crabs that were giving him a sore rudder, and the rascal repaid her kindness by taking a Protestant heretic on to his barge. Yes, English, and a Protestant to boot! And not just that: to make matters even worse, he was running round, calling him Mr and Your Excellency, carrying his bags for him and getting him a room in the town . . . If the Vatican got to hear of it – and hear of it they would because Feliça Roderes, the tireless watchdog of the Balcony of the Apocalypse, must at that very moment be penning one of the vitriolic anonymous letters she sent every month to Rome – the captain would avoid neither excommunication here on earth or the everlasting crabs of hell in the afterlife. The wicked Englishman, the devil-worshipping heretic, the subject of perfidious Albion must really be laughing up his sleeve at him!

At that very moment, contrary to the suppositions of the customers at the Quayside Café, the Englishman was not laughing; he
was succumbing instead to the delights of the riverside Venus who
had just scuppered his plans for geological meditation and seemed
to have no intention whatsoever of letting him waste his energy on
metaphysical ruminations on the soul of an Ebro sailor. While he
was dressing next morning, Mr Oliver Wilson, drowsy and still
flabbergasted, looked out of his balcony at a strange procession
making its way to the quay down St Francis Alley. He recognized
the crew of the boat he had travelled on from Faió, led by the
eccentric bemedalled pirate. They were escorting a priest in his best
vestments, flanked by two altar-boys bearing lighted candles. The
Englishman, however, could never have imagined that he was the
cause of the procession. A couple of months would have to pass,
the time it took him to move from the tedious clientele of the
Casino to the Quayside Café where he became friendly with Aleix
de Segarra, Honorat del Cafè and Arquimedes Quintana, before he
learnt, amidst much mirth, of his responsibility for the Bishop's
night of penance, which had culminated in the early-morning ceremony when the rector, on receipt of a sizeable donation from the
sailor, agreed to exorcize the barge and purify it of any trace of the
Protestant heretic who had come on board at Faió.

When he was thrown out of town in the turmoil provoked by
the death of Arnau Terrer, the Englishman took with him Agatòclia
Molina, who was to become Mrs Wilson two months later in Liver-
pool. He also took a half-finished study of the coalfield and the
manuscript of a secret collection of love poems where he compared
the landlady's hips to the beauty of the geosynclines of the Palaeozoic
era and the curls of her pubic hair to the delicacy of certain fossil
ferns, along with other even more intimate reflections of a part
erotic, part geological, part palaeontological nature. The couple left
on the *Neptune*, which was sailing to Tortosa with a load of wheat.
A group of people, embittered at their defeat in the great strike,
went to see them off at the docks; when Nelson shouted to weigh
anchor, the handkerchiefs waved until the boat disappeared downstream in the still hesitant light of an early August morning. But
Nelson wasn't the one recalling this day nearly half a century past;
it was Carmela, in the Torres' kitchen. If he had been recalling it,

he would still have caught the air of gratitude and warmth surrounding the geologist's departure, the sniffs of a sentimental Estanislau Corbera, the sober demeanour of Honorat del Cafè, the sadness of Aleix de Segarra and the desolation of Arquimedes Quintana in the harbour dappled with hazy flecks of gold which would soon merge into a dazzling sun. Nelson would have seen the ends of Mr Oliver Wilson's sandy moustache betray the tremble in his lips as he stood on the sacks of corn next to Agatòclia, and wave goodbye with his hat.

But Nelson wasn't the one recalling this scene; it was the maid from the Torres house. And for Carmela, the image of the Englishman was still coloured by the same hatred she had felt when she witnessed his departure that far-off summer of 1925 from behind the curtains at the balcony window of the Hall of the Martyred Virgins.

As he rounded the corner of Sun Alley, where he had inadvertently stepped on Carmela's memories, the figure of Nelson, now skipper of a boat rotting helplessly in the town's silent wharves, was reflected in Julia Quintana's green eyes. She had been looking out for him for some time. Julia felt relieved as the old bargeman began slowly trudging up Rampart Hill. While waiting for him at the window, she had started to wonder if Robert – unlike everyone else, she couldn't bring herself to call him Nelson – had maybe not gone to the Quayside Café, in which case Estanislau Corbera wouldn't have given him the message. If she wanted to talk to him, other than when they chanced to meet in the street – and when this occurred they both preferred to keep it short – Julia would go and see the café proprietor. If she went to Nelson's house or simply sent a message, it would spark off a fit of jealousy in his wife. She had been a real beauty when young but had never come to terms with the childhood friendship between Robert and Julia – the only daughter of Arquimedes Quintana, who was longing to have a little girl but only had boys with his first two wives.

"My seed is too coarse," he would remark with a humour tinged with melancholy, "I always father boys; as strong and healthy as can be, but boys. Perhaps I should sweeten it with honey before I chase the lady."

Neither honey – if he ever did try it, because nobody was too sure if he did or not – nor any of the magic formulas secretly employed first by Carme and later by Joana, had any effect: each pregnancy meant another boy in this world. Shortly after his third marriage, when Marina Torrents, not known for her clairvoyant gifts, stopped him on the Town Square Wharf to tell him that his wife would become pregnant and would bear him a daughter, the African veteran, who was nearly sixty by then, was sceptical. The prophecy came true though. Julia was born on the same day as Carlota de Torres and a few months after Robert Ibars, in the autumn of 1900. This earned Marina Torrents the reputation of being a witch and some gold earrings from the sailor.

After the *Rapid* sank in the Lliberola Gorge and Arquimedes Quintana took care of Robert, the son of the missing captain, and began to train him up to be the best bargeman on the Ebro, the boy spent a lot of time at the old man's house. In Julia he had a friend, the only person who could smooth down the rough edges of his character and guide him tenderly and understandingly. With the lukewarm consent of her father, who eventually gave in to her although it meant losing Robert as a member of the *Carlota*'s crew, she advised him to leave the Torres' employ. It was crystal-clear that even though he had the old man's backing, the lad wouldn't get on there and would never be more than a deck-hand. Ramon Graells was the real power behind the throne; the only people to prosper in the Torres factory and mines were his protégés. Arquimedes Quintana was the one exception – untouchable since the days of the general's wife and too prestigious a captain for the right-hand man to risk defying. But he didn't have many years' sailing left in him and when he retired, Robert would pay the price for the mounting resentment harboured by Graells. He should go to work for Senyora Salleres, declared Julia; she needed new men to replace the two captains who had been dismissed along with the administrator after the disaster of the *Polyphemus*, which had made her the laughing-stock of the whole town. On the day that Robert had his interview with the widow, the maid showed the sailor into an enormous room. At the far end, a glassed-in veranda looked out over the wharf where the company's barges were moored, near the confluence of the Segre and the Ebro. The widow, dressed in a silk kimono and lounging on a sofa, didn't reply when he said good-day. She examined him at length while playing with a little monkey, an exotic gift from a merchant navy captain who occasionally visited her and who Robert could remember in a white uniform promenading with her along the riverside wall.

"Ibars' son . . ." she murmured, almost to herself, and straightaway added out loud, "You're very young, but everyone speaks highly of your skill as a sailor. Is it true that you're so good? Haven't you got anything to say? I can see the cat's got your tongue. I hope you've got a little bit left to tell that rascal Jaume de Torres that from next week you'll be sailing as a captain for the firm of Salleres. Now go."

When he reached the door of the room, the widow's voice stopped him in his tracks. "Robert!" She had finished playing with her monkey, who was now climbing up the back of a green chaise longue. "This year a Salleres barge must win the September races."

Senyor Jaume de Torres was not one to bear a grudge; he soon forgot Robert's defection to the widow. He even understood when in September, Arquimedes Quintana declined to take part in the festivities on the river. The old pirate excused himself on the grounds of his advancing years, although everyone could see it was because he didn't want to compete with his own pupil. But Carlota de Torres never forgave Nelson. If she ever bumped into him in the street or caught sight of him on the river from her balcony, she automatically recalled the humiliation of the Torres family, beaten in the sailing barge races for the first time in years at the hands of that grubby wretch who had learnt to sail on a boat that bore her name. To make matters worse, on the day of the river festival, a great banquet was being held to celebrate her engagement to Hipòlit de Móra and the young lady had had to put up with defeat, well aware of the guests' concealed mirth; despite the sympathetic expressions on their faces as befitted the occasion, they enjoyed seeing their hosts humiliated.

Robert's triumph confirmed him in his post as Senyora Salleres' captain; the redundancies during the crisis after the Great War did not affect him. His friendship with Julia continued, but when Robert started courting after his military service and she realized that his fiancée was jealous, she discreetly distanced herself from him, while maintaining a keen interest in everything the captain got up to, including his crazier exploits. In the nostalgic iconography of those years he enjoyed numerous adventures, which local tittle-tattle embellished with a string of unanswered questions. What became of the *Neptune* (the widow had a weakness for christening her boats with mythological names) when it disappeared with its crew? Was it true that Nelson's band of marauders journeyed down to the mouth of the river, dodged the Navy look-outs, sailed out to sea and engaged in smuggling? Were the folk from Miravet to be believed when they swore on the Bible that they had seen the widow take part in these daring expeditions and that the merchant captain seemed to be involved too? Didn't this tally with the story of the naval officer who was considered stark staring mad by his superiors because in a report he claimed to have spied a shipload of smugglers through his telescope, and standing at the helm, an elegant lady with a white parasol and a blue feather hat?

Julia knew Robert well: he was as capable of indulging in these escapades as he was incapable of boasting of them. She also knew something else from the Salleres maids: he was not occupying the widow's bed and, whether the tales of smuggling were true or false, the captain – whom the Englishman at the Old Boar Inn had by now christened Nelson – had not let her high regard for him go to his head. This was evident during the great strike in the coalfield. Robert joined in without a second thought, risking the widow's fury. Senyora Salleres screamed blue murder against the workers, but she was the only one to oppose the intervention of the Civil Guards, as requested by Mayor Romaguera with the backing of the rest of the bourgeoisie and the only one to care for her wounded miners during the troubles, paying for doctors and medicines.

Once she too had married, Julia didn't talk to Nelson again until the night of the demonstration, when, after the strikers had been dispersed, old Arquimedes insisted that Robert should stay at their house and wouldn't let him go back to his own through the streets swarming with Civil Guards. The presence of other miners and sailors had prevented them from talking in private without stirring up gossip. At the time of Arnau Terrer's death and the expulsion of the British geologist, Robert's first daughter fell ill. A week later, the captain suddenly turned up at the Quintana house, sat down next to Julia and left three hours later without opening his mouth. The little girl died that same night.

Julia was at the wake. She remembered Robert, looking pale and hollow-eyed, grieving with the men in the small dining-room. She associated this image with the smell of turpentine that came from the bedroom where Aleix de Segarra was painting the little girl's portrait as a favour to his friend; he had been most reluctant to accept the commission but took pity on the grief-stricken mother. Robert was like a statue and said nothing beyond the bare minimum needed to acknowledge the condolences. On the way back from the cemetery, instead of going home he went to the wharf, embarked on one of the widow's lighters, set the oars into the rowlocks and sailed off down the Ebro to the amazement of the onlookers who were horrified at this unthinkable break with tradition. He was discovered near Miravet, lying face down in a patch of dried up riverbed, unconscious and covered in mud, the palms of his hands rubbed raw and bleeding after his manic journey; his body resembled a broken puppet.

Her green eyes looked at him melancholically. From time to time they took on the lustre and ironic tenderness of when she was young, which led old Nelson to surmise that Julia was remembering something pleasant. They had said nothing to each other. Standing in the middle of the empty room they just looked at one another, feeling lost inside those four walls which even now still bore the marks made over the years by pieces of furniture and the portrait of the African veteran, painted by Aleix de Segarra over the course of some memorable sittings in the billiard room at the Eden. He looked away towards the window, and out into the July night, heavy with the heat of the sultry southwest wind. A cricket sitting on a vine in the yard was chirping.

"I wanted to say goodbye," murmured Julia. "We're leaving tomorrow . . ."

Nelson shivered. He knew all along it would come to this: Julia's children wanted to leave and make a life for themselves elsewhere. Other people had moved out already, even before the demolitions commenced, tired of worrying about the future; they hadn't waited to see the new town which the resolute locals had started building right by the old one and where the first families should soon be moving in. He had heard that they were leaving, but preferred to believe it would never happen. When Estanislau had told him that Julia wanted to see him urgently, his heart had sunk.

Naturally, or so Honorat del Rom maintained in one of the last sessions at the Quayside Café, the town hadn't died on the same day for everybody. Each one had felt it die at a different moment in its protracted agony, and Julia's farewell probably marked this point for old Nelson. The mysterious thread that linked them had never been broken. Through all the hard times she had been his real support, even saying nothing; such as the day he came ashore after his brainstorm on the death of his daughter, and saw Julia on the quayside. His emotions crystallized at that instant; he had to run off without looking at her, for he could not otherwise have held back the force that was pushing him to embrace her and feel every particle of his body and soul merging with hers. He realized that he loved her with his eyes, his skin, his member, his mind, his heart, his bones, his muscles. He was swept off his feet by this feeling, which his wife had guessed at before he had had an inkling of it himself. It lasted for ever: just a glimpse of her in the street would agitate him. And now Julia was leaving, vanishing from the ruined town with its wharves full of dead boats, and he sensed that he would never see her again.

"Take this, Robert. I thought you'd like to have them."

Old photographs, time past portrayed on yellowing paper. The first one showed old Arquimedes at the door of the Eden with Aleix de Segarra and Madamfranswah near the end of the 1914–18 war. The other had been taken at a dinner in 1928 held in honour of the African veteran, then eighty-eight years old, by his friends and the survivors of the seventeen crews he had sailed with until his retirement immediately after the great strike and in the wake of Arnau Terrer's death and the expulsion of the Englishman. His strength began to fail; his astounding vitality, which had made him unique on the Ebro, crumbled overnight. Useless for work, a widower and with no means of support, he went to live with Julia, who had recently married a union official from the Masos mine. His account of the battle of Tetouan demonstrated the progressive weakening of his brain: mistakes almost too slight to notice at first about where the regiments were positioned, or mix-ups over the names of generals became worse and worse. He recounted false charges, multiplied the number of times the Moor had attacked him with his scimitar when he cut off his ear, promoted himself to the rank of captain on the spur of the moment or imagined himself an artilleryman, and altered the troop movements. The cavalry general's severed head took on diverse and unpredictable features: now it was the head of King Alfonso the Thirteenth, now, Senyor Jaume de Torres. In April 1931, on the morning after he had muddled the soldier's head with that of his father, the old man embarked without telling anyone on a sailing barge from Ascó. He landed at Tortosa, had his photograph taken there with an old friend and started back up the Ebro. All the captains knew him and he was welcome on their boats. In Benissanet he and an old towman, who had been blind for years and wrote love ballads, reviled the king; in Xerta he went to see the brother of his first wife, who had advised him off the record not to marry his meddlesome sister, a warning the old man had always been grateful for, even though he hadn't heeded it; in Garcia he enquired after a schoolmistress he had had an understanding with between the period of mourning for his second wife and his wedding to the third one, but the schoolmistress had been dead for over twenty years and he himself had often gone in secret to lay flowers on her grave, as a sympathetic innkeeper friend of his tried to make him understand; in Flix he started to feel giddy and got lost in the streets, not realizing that they were buzzing with election fever. One of Torres' old boatbuilders came across him wandering aimlessly around the audience at a political meeting, rescued him and sent a telegram to the family.

As he looked at the yellowing photograph, without really seeing it, Nelson recalled the furious night-time journey down a moonless Ebro, never to be forgotten by the crew of the *Neptune* who had been hurriedly dragged away from the pre-election excitement in the cafés. How in God's name – ruminated Atanasi Resurrecció – had they managed not to break their bones on the rocks or hit an island and sink? Even Nelson would have been hard put to provide an explanation, as he did whenever he got up to one of his exploits on the river. They were on the point of collapse by the time they reached Flix. The invalid didn't recognize them when he first saw them. While his crew took a rest, Nelson stayed to look after him. By the time they were ready to return, the wind was blowing. They hoisted the squaresail and the topsail and made the journey under sail. Old Arquimedes lay stretched out on a palliasse in the stern; his long periods of silence during which he stared open-mouthed at the sky or at the swelling sails alternated with bouts of delirium and babbling. At the Merro Rock, he called for his second wife, at the Embrolla de Riba-roja he started humming one of Madamfranswah's music-hall songs, and then held a long conversation with General Prim and his first wife. As they drew near to Faió he tried to stand up, pointing at the sky with his right arm. Nelson and the deck-hands turned round and saw a hot-air balloon turned gold by the rays of the afternoon sun. Transported by the wind, the balloon was flying up the river channel behind the boat.

"It's Ponç!" exclaimed Atanasi Resurrecció.

The balloon, which had created great excitement among the whole neighbourhood and provoked inevitable warnings of planetary catastrophe from Feliça Roderes the first few times it flew over the town, was rapidly growing larger. The bargemen could soon discern its passengers leaning over the edge of the basket; sure enough, they were Ponç the engineer, the director of a chemicals firm in Flix, and his wife. The couple often took advantage of the sea-breeze to ascend in the balloon and fly up the Ebro. When the balloon was above the barge's mast, they heard the aviator's voice:

"Nelson, Nelson! Can you hear me, you wicked old pirate?"

"Yes I can! How's it going?"

"You look nice and peaceful. Haven't you heard?"

"Heard what?"

"We've won! The king's buggered off abroad and the Republic's just been proclaimed! Hurrah!"

"Hurrah!" the crew of the *Neptune* had all replied.

The wind soon bore the balloon away. They heard one more triumphant cry from the engineer and saw his wife's handkerchief fluttering. But Arquimedes Quintana, who had proclaimed the Republic so many times during those sorely missed nights at the Eden was totally unaware of it all. Death's invisible scythe had fallen and come between him and the world.

IV

She could clearly recall the sound of the trombone providing the backdrop to that night, in isolation from the other instruments in the band. Sometimes it was scarcely audible, a distant echo from the upper part of the town, where the narrow streets had reverted to their primal state and were gullies once more, channelling the rainwater from the Castle mountains to the Ebro. Later, she could hear it rise and fall as it threaded its way through the tortuous maze of streets in the medieval town; and once on the procession's unpredictable route she seemed to hear it fill the entire Church Square. Although Senyora Carlota de Torres believed that she was pinpointing it accurately in time and space, her memory was in reality playing tricks on her, probably because of the annual concerts for the Torres family birthdays and name days, when her father hired the band to play beneath the balcony. For on the night in question, no trombonist was playing in the band. The crisis in the mines at the end of the Great War had decimated the River Harmony Band. The helicon-player, a builder by trade, was the first musician to join the stream of townspeople moving to Barcelona in search of work, leaving entire streets uninhabited; he was followed by a tenor saxophonist, the bass drummer and two clarinettists. The trombonist was the last to go, along with the bassoonist. The latter found the city so unbearably noisy that he came back, but was reduced to selling his bassoon to pay for more urgent needs than music. The band was greatly depleted in consequence and the rehearsals at the Arenal shipyard became a sad spectacle. When inspiration took hold of the conductor at a key point in the piece and he called for the bass drum to make a thundering entrance, or asked the tenor saxophonist to play with more gusto, he had to be brought down to earth with a bump and reminded that the former had been working in the docks at Barcelona for two years and that the latter was also in the big city, employed at a brewery. The band was not substantially affected when the worst of the crisis was over and things returned to the sluggish normality of pre-1914, or when employment received a short-lived boost from the construction of a bridge over the Ebro, school buildings and a wall around the docks (all of these projects acquired through the good offices of a lady from the town, resident in Madrid, who had influence among the ministers of Primo de Rivera's dictatorship). Two aspiring musicians appeared, a violinist and a drummer, and for a short while, the engineer in charge of building the bridge contributed the dulcet tones of his flute. But the trombonist was never replaced and so there wasn't one among the musicians hastily assembled on the night of 14 April 1931 to celebrate the proclamation of the Republic.

The detail of the trombone was therefore a rogue memory that had crept into the flood of Senyora Carlota de Torres' reminiscences, set off by Francesc Romaguera's presence in the town during that summer of 1971; during long, sleepless hours she had been transported from their meeting at the railway station at Faió through the days of the great strike of 1925, to that night of widespread jubilation when an old bloodstained spectre was to stalk the town's streets once more.

Scarcely had Ponç's balloon flown over the wharves and drifted off beyond the bridge into the blaze of the setting sun, when the River Harmony Band started parading around the town to the strains of the Marseillaise, being already informed of the news before the balloonists sailed over and announced it from the skies. However, an hour later the instruments suddenly fell silent and when they struck up again after some time, the revolutionary melody had been replaced by a funeral march played on the Widows' Wharf. One of the maids, Veronica – who took good care to avoid divulging that she had profited from the running of an errand to join in the Republican merrymaking – gave a detailed description of what had happened to the Torres i Camps family who had gathered in the hall, concerned at this turn of events. Julia Quintana had received a telegram from Nelson in Faió, telling her that her father had died and informing her that the *Neptune* would be arriving with his remains. Seeing Senyor Jaume's shock at the death of the old sailor who used to work for the firm, Carlota's indifference and the horror of the rest of the family, Veronica, still quite moved herself, carried on describing the lamplit arrival of the barge at the quayside where the crowd was celebrating the departure of the king and the proclamation of the Republic. She mentioned that the deceased's children were there, a son by his first wife and two by his second, and didn't overlook a single one of the whole entourage of brothers-in-law, sisters-in-law, nephews, nieces, grandsons and granddaughters the sailor had acquired in the course of his matrimonial career. The Torres family were also apprised of the braying of the mule, who must have guessed that his stable was near as the *Neptune* drew close to the wharf; and of the composure of Arquimedes Quintana's daughter, who neither screamed nor showed any other signs of grief as the corpse was carried ashore, wrapped in a blanket. (At this point, the maid's voice took on a reproachful tone, indicating her disapproval of too much silence.) Finally, Veronica related how people had spontaneously formed a cortege, how the funeral march had replaced the Marseillaise to escort the body back home, and how the festivities had resumed once the shadow of death had been dispelled. Having submitted her report, the maid went to the kitchen, where she and Adelaida puzzled long and hard over the reasons for the departure of Old Whiskers, as the king was known locally, and wondered why on earth his place had been taken by a queen with the outlandish name of Republica.

She was haunted by the false memory of the trombone. The music had permeated that entire night, whose fuzzy edges seemed to overlap in a confused jumble, shot through with anxiety at the fall of the monarchy. Her father was upset and stayed in his study till late. They didn't hear him go to bed until after midnight. She was at her balcony, looking down at the revels, when Carmela's discreet tap came at the door. The Plaça d'Armes was full of people acclaiming the Republic and a whole string of names she had never even heard of. The cheers drowned out the music from the River Harmony Band, whose members were so exhausted that the tuba-player swore he would never get involved in politics again if republican celebrations were always to entail such hard work.

Carlota de Torres feared it would be bad news. Her maid's wait at the back door of the garage had almost certainly proved fruitless.

She was wrong: standing in the lamplight, behind a terrified-looking Carmela, still shaken by the uproar in the streets, was Francesc Romaguera.

It was nearly daybreak by the time the servant led Francesc back through the maze of passages at the rear of the house. The cry rang out at once, almost directly beneath the balcony of her bedroom. The first time, assuming that she had been mistaken in all the noise from the mob, she stayed on the dishevelled bed, still tingling with excitement, breathing in his smell which had sunk into her every pore. She missed the weight of his body on hers, the rough feel of Francesc's face on her belly, the strength of his hips which she had held imprisoned in her thighs as he penetrated her, his eager panting, which grew ever more rhythmical until he climaxed with a hoarse moan. She felt him tense like a bow and at the root of his cries she seemed to sense the despair of annihilation. Then she felt herself being carried away by his orgasm. Slowly recovering from her vertigo, she always reached for his spent body, lying awkwardly next to hers. She stroked him with clumsy tenderness but her lover fled hastily from her bed and all that was left of him was his smell which clung to the rumpled sheets. Carlota had preferred not to delve too deeply into Francesc Romaguera's feelings since their meeting at the railway station at Faió six years earlier, during the great strike. At that time they had met frequently, aided by Carlota's unconditional complicity and Hipòlit's involuntary collusion – he was often away on mining business. They made love for the first time inside the Ford, in the garage where she had taken Francesc under the pretext of the revolver. This was also the first time that an unrestrained, vulnerable Carlota de Torres had been swept away in a frenzied orgasm, something she had never previously experienced and which would only happen in the arms of Francesc. When he went back to Madrid, Carlota watched his boat leave from behind her balcony curtains and then she flew straight into one of her tantrums that shook the walls, unnerved everyone and forced Senyor Jaume out of the house – to go to the mine, to the club, to hell – so as not to hear her. She assumed that Francesc did not love her and that things would never change. Their relationship would consist of meetings during his occasional visits to the town. Their nocturnal encounters and embraces, always too brief to slake her desire, left her wanting more; she would seek out his smell on the sweat-drenched sheets and on her skin which she rubbed hard with her hands impregnated in Francesc's seed.

The cry she had chosen not to hear the first time rang out again, this time clear and unequivocal, with no interference from the band, whose members, starting with the tuba-player, had peeled off from the parade until no music was left by the time a hesitant dawn began to tremble on the waters of the Ebro. She couldn't blot it out: the ghost, which had supposedly been laid, was coming back to life in the streets, cracking through the crust of time. She shifted uneasily. The town that lived and breathed out there, around the house, the world that Carlota de Torres had never attempted to know or to understand, not even during the great strike, had the nerve to live for itself, to keep its own memories and to shout them out loud in the streets as a threat. What were the Civil Guards doing inside their barracks? Why didn't they come out and disperse the mob with bullets and blows as they had in 1925? The Republic! Francesc was right: all it needed was half a dozen cannon shots to put the rabble back in their place. And then a proper clean-up, starting with the band of traitors who not only turned their backs on their own class, but supported the workers. There were quite a few of that sort in the town. Not just Aleix de Segarra who, to be honest, was a naïve simpleton who wouldn't harm a fly . . . But the Civil Guards didn't intervene, even though they no longer had to be sent for from the city; since the great strike there had been a permanent, well-equipped post in the town. Their arrival took place on the same day that the nuns from Ferryboat Alley left their convent to seek a more hospitable abode than this town of unbelievers. Carlota de Torres remembered it all in great detail: the black and white line of nuns had just gone on board a barge laden high with their possessions, topped by an old harmonium and the crucifix from the chapel, when the Bishop's boat, filled to the brim with members of the force, appeared at the confluence of the Segre and the Ebro. The vessels passed within inches of each other in front of the Widows' Wharf. Horrified at the deadly sin the town had committed in allowing the nuns to leave – an opinion shared one hundred per cent by Feliça Roderes on the Balcony of the Apocalypse, but dismissed by the great and the good, who had refused to dip into their pockets to solve the problems of the religious order – the Bishop brought his boat in as close as possible in order to acquaint the Mother Superior of his distress. When he saw the sisters, the commander made his men stand to attention on top of the sacks of rice that the barge was transporting from the Ebro delta, and present arms. Standing as stiff as ramrods, they all obeyed his order, except for one plump fellow who was thrown off balance by the movement of the barge and fell on to the rail, provoking ironic glances from the women who were doing their washing in the river and from the sailors busy on the quayside. From that time on, the force became part of the town; the sergeant-major was immediately made to feel at home in the Casino de la Roda where his uniformed, mustachioed and bumptious presence served as a guarantee of law and order for his fellow members, increasingly jittery at the miners' ever more organized and excessive demands. But where were they now, wondered Carlota de Torres on the night of 14 April 1931. Why didn't they come out and quell the republican riots? Why didn't they silence the last groups, whose fearful cries portended the spilling of blood?

"Remember Arnau Terrer!"

Things looked different in 1971. Most of the places where that cry had been uttered on that night in April 1931 were now unrecognizable. Without the landmarks of that period, the rush of memories got lost among the ruins. Only one house remained standing in Creel Square, where the shout commemorating Arnau Terrer first exploded. On the route the cry had taken to the Plaça d'Armes, the mind's eye was disorientated by the scars of dead houses. The bones of Llorenç de Veriu, the first to utter the name of Arnau Terrer, had lain buried in a wasteland in Teruel for more than thirty years and his house had been the first to fall at the outset of the destruction. Carlota de Torres felt as if the cry, echoing solely in her mind, was climbing up on to the balcony of her bedroom and bringing the silence to life. She relived the same anger which had seized her on 14 April 1931, when voices no longer belonging to the previously good-natured procession had forced her to realize that the death of the miners' leader was not forgotten; it was still fresh in people's minds, six years after the day in 1925 when Arnau's corpse had been discovered on the banks of the Ebro. Senyora Salleres' prediction was coming true; she had been the only one among the gentry to condemn the death unreservedly and to guess what it might lead to.

"Remember Arnau Terrer!"

The night that the Republic was proclaimed, Carmela heard it too, near the back door of the garage, just as she was going to open up and let Romaguera out. She didn't unfasten the bolt. She waited for the group to move away and their voices to be drowned out by the songs of another bunch on Bakers Hill. Francesc appeared unmoved, but Carmela noted his tension: he was clearly affected, even though he had been absent from the town when it all happened and had not lived through the unrest that followed the death of the miners' leader.

The body was discovered by the riverside path, at the foot of a crag near the Ebro. It was lying in a juniper tree, its heart pierced by a branch. No sooner had the fisherman who found the corpse arrived in town to report the discovery than someone put forward the theory that the death had been an accident. But this immediately posed the question: what had led Arnau Terrer to go there, a good three hours away from the town, along a path used only by the few peasants who had plots of land in the area? The last people to see him alive were the friends who had walked him home the previous night as far as the corner of Saint Francis Alley and the Plaça d'Armes. He had carried on alone to the Eel Inn. But the innkeeper confirmed that Arnau had not reached home by the time that he threw out the last of his customers, nearly an hour later. And his bed had not been slept in, as he found out when he checked his room on learning of the tragedy; neither had he been with the girl he was courting. What had happened between the corner of Saint Francis Alley and the inn? Even supposing that Arnau had gone of his own will to the place where he met his death, could anyone really believe the cock-and-bull story of an accidental fall from the cliff edge on to the juniper and the branch transfixing his heart? Suspicions of a crime became a certainty that afternoon when Mr Oliver Wilson returned from one of his customary field trips and was informed of events. Surrounded by a turbulent crowd who had gathered in front of the tavern, the Englishman stated that early that morning while gathering mineral samples at the foot of the cliffs in the Ebro valley, he had seen someone hurrying back to the town along the riverside path. From the details he gave – a flat cap and a slight limp in his left leg – this person could be none other than the mayor's henchman, the town bailiff. The thug turned up that evening at the Old Boar Inn in the company of two Civil Guards and provoked the impotent rage of the people there by summarily ordering Mr Wilson out of town. The geologist was always well-mannered and correct (to the extent that on Nelson's wedding-day when he had had too much rum to drink at the reception and couldn't stand, and Atanasi Resurrecció had had to carry him back to the inn on his shoulders, he had gone to the trouble of raising his hat to everyone he met); but on this occasion he blew his top. Bellowing incomprehensible words, he lunged at the official, and the two Civil Guards were hard put to restrain him. While the geologist and Agatòclia were packing their bags, the troops mounted guard at the door of the inn and wouldn't let a single soul in. The examining judge's buggy and the van with the body waited on the outskirts of the town until the small hours before they drove through on their way to the city. The following day, a few hours after Mr Wilson and Agatòclia Molina were seen off by a silent crowd standing on the quayside, the penny suddenly dropped as to why the body was found at that precise spot by the river. It was lying a few metres outside the town boundary and so the affair came within the jurisdiction of the neighbouring town, whose judge was the illustrious Senyor Damià de Penyalver and whose forensic surgeon was the equally illustrious Senyor Ricard Canota, the brother-in-law and cousin respectively of the mayor, Sadurní Romaguera. The inquest's verdict was accidental death and a deaf ear was turned to all protests, including those of the regulars at the Quayside Café. Once the initial anger had subsided, the matter appeared forgotten, but the other town, the town unknown to Carlota, or despised by her, never let it go. Proof of this was the clamour on the night that the Republic was proclaimed. And the shouts rang out again a few nights later in the cinema of the Recreational Association where, in a hall decked with tricolours, Aleix de Segarra, still feeling depressed at the death of Arquimedes

Quintana, had been asked by the republican town council to give a piano recital to welcome in the new political era.

"Remember Arnau Terrer!"

Nearly forty years later, during Senyora Carlota de Torres' recollection of events, the memory of this cry sought to come back to life. But it got lost among the mutilated streets, and before becoming audible, disintegrated above the Widows' Wharf, next to the masts of the dead ships.

V

Saying goodbye to Julia Quintana had left old Nelson feeling profoundly dejected. On his way back to the Quayside Café, the thread
of memory that he had rediscovered in the old photographs made
him relive days long gone. At times the images were crystal-clear;
at others, they swirled round and if he tried to catch hold of them,
they evaporated like wisps of smoke.

Arquimedes Quintana figured prominently: he saw his body
stretched out in the bottom of the *Neptune* while Ponç's balloon flew
over the boat in April 1931, and he sorrowfully recalled his own
indifference in the face of tragedy. He hadn't grasped the implica-
tions of it all until the moment of the burial in the graveyard. He
sometimes wondered uncomprehendingly what lay behind his own
coldness. Neither the disembarkation at the Widows' Wharf with
all those people pressing round nor Julia's silent grief on seeing her
father's body had shaken him out of his apathy. During the wake,
it was as if he wasn't there; he hardly heard a word of what was
said. He couldn't share in the enthusiasm that the new political
situation kindled among those present, to the accompaniment of
the music from the parade. The King, the Republic . . . What
were they? What did they signify? The words of Julia's husband,
full of excitement at the changes the new regime would bring about,
meant nothing to him. Grief hit him all of a sudden at the cemetery
when Jeremies the gravedigger (a black cheroot clamped in the
corner of his mouth, a nose like a red pepper and blurred eyesight
from a lifetime on the bottle) clumsily covered over the front of the
niche beneath the bright blue April sky; he felt himself sinking,
he was alone in a dark, chilly, unfathomable emptiness. He couldn't
sleep that night and when he next sailed on the *Neptune*, he sensed
that the Ebro had also become a stranger to him. The link between
him and the river had been broken, a fact which did not escape the
notice of the crew or even − so Atanasi Resurrecció maintained −
of the barge itself, which lost its pliancy for a while. At the age of
thirty-eight, Nelson felt his energy had been burned up; he felt

old. His vision of that time was of a harrowing nightmare which ended three weeks later on a lucky but also ill-fated day, the only black mark in his sailing career.

"You've got a passenger today," Simó de Figueres, the groom, told him on seeing him enter the stables. "That little cracker of a maid has just been down to pass on the message from the administrator."

He was surprised. People were constantly travelling on the river but the owners never got involved: whether they took them or not tended to be up to the captain. If the administrator, the third one the widow had installed in her bed since the *Polyphemus* fiasco, had sent a maid at daybreak, it must be a special case.

"Who is it?"

The old stableman stroked the mule's smooth warm back before slipping its headstall on; a powerful shudder ran like a wave down the animal's skin, which gave off a hot, bitter smell of straw and manure.

"Take a look for yourself. He's down on the wharf. He got here almost the same time as the girl. They should send that young lass here more often . . . What a rump she's got on her, sweet Lord!"

He went over to the window and glanced at the landing-stages. The light from a watery sun, which had barely risen above the violet-tinted horizon, was playing on the ships; alongside stood Francesc Romaguera. A few feet away from him, a manservant was watching over his luggage.

"Go on Nelson, this is your big chance to chuck him into the river," muttered the stableman behind him. "One bastard less in the world . . . Take his lackey too; those arselickers deserve all they get. They'd sell their souls for a kind look or word from their lord and master. Haven't you ever heard that creep brag about how well he's treated? They make me sick, him and his kind! Once a year, their master offers them his tobacco pouch so they can roll themselves a fag, and hey presto, they forget the squalor they live in . . . And if it comes to it, they'll even let him shag their wives and daughters."

Nelson couldn't even be bothered to get annoyed; it would only have stirred up more trouble. He didn't own the *Neptune*; Senyora Salleres did. If the administrator told him to take Francesc Romaguera on board, that was that. He would just have to grin and bear it. As he walked out of the stables, the groom, who had got quite worked up, was still ranting and raving against the gentry; the old malcontent had found an excuse to spend the whole day cursing. It wouldn't be long before he would climb into a manger and make an inflammatory speech to the animals on the miseries of this world, somewhat mitigated that morning by the delights of the maid's hindquarters.

Nelson walked down to the quay, said good-day to everyone, invited the passenger to climb on board and told Atanasi Resurrecció to carry his luggage. From his captain's perch in the stern he could see the whole ship. His men's sullen faces showed their resentment at the presence on board of the smartly-dressed young gentleman. Romaguera sat on top of the suitcases, careful not to get smudges of coal on his clothes, and lit a cigar before half-heartedly waving back at the manservant as the gangplank was taken down and the *Neptune* moved slowly away from the quayside.

The entire town hated Francesc Romaguera, but their loathing had nothing to do with the nights that the big-city shyster spent with Carlota de Torres – nights that were public knowledge thanks to Adelaida and Veronica, who furnished full and detailed information on them, including every creak of the mattress, every moan and sigh of the encounter which they spied on from the darkness of the passageway, unbeknownst to Carmela, the incorruptible and jealous guardian of the bedchamber. In matters of dalliance, the town was unreservedly on the side of good-natured philandering, and the affair between Carlota de Torres and Sadurní Romaguera's son, although worthy of gossip six years earlier, no longer had novelty on its side. And anyway, Carlota's infidelity to Hipòlit followed an ancient, well-known tradition. Honorat del Cafè, who was now seriously considering retirement, to devote his time to the family collections of pressed flowers and pharmaceutical instruments and to his passion for reading, stated that a kind of fate hovered above each and every family, which had an ineluctable influence – sometimes more obvious than others – on all its members down the generations. And so, he pointed out merely as an example, a fore-taste of the definitive study, that Senyora Salleres was a very clear case of a family of widows where the husbands lasted just long enough (give or take a year) to leave their wives pregnant, kick the bucket and make room in the marriage bed for the chief assistant. The chemist also cited the Sansa family's consuming passion for legal wrangles; they were always involved in endless lawsuits handed down lock, stock and barrel from one generation to the next, to such an extent that it was rumoured that Juli Sansa had gone to his grave because of winning an extremely involved and complex case in a matter of minutes, when he had thought it would last him a good five years. There was no denying that all the Sabogas – unquestionably good sailors – ran aground at least once in their lifetime on Horseshoe Island, an even more surprising piece of bad luck when you considered that it was a spot free from danger, where no other vessel ever came to grief. The members of the Quintana de Roca family always died on a Thursday; the Olivers' special talent was for sniffing out seams of coal and finding mandrake roots; the Castelló family's mares were always barren and fate had decreed that the men of the Móra family would inevitably marry women who were unfaithful to them. The only time that the family seemed about to break with this tradition of deceived husbands (albeit not complaisant ones, as the chemist pointed out, since the Móras couldn't condone what they didn't know, nor did it ever occur to them to doubt the virtue of their wives) was when Desideri Móra still hadn't been cuckolded by his wife six years after their marriage. The townsfolk were becoming quite impatient and didn't relax until they heard of the lady's fall from grace with a councillor from Lleida. Once fate had had its way, the good lady who, as she confessed to a friend, was incapable of understanding the mysterious impulse that had driven her into the bed of a man she didn't even like (and who, it has to be said, proved to be deadly dull), dedicated herself body and soul to Desideri, whom she was genuinely in love with, and she was never again unfaithful to him even in her thoughts. Hipòlit de Móra suffered at the hands of his family's fate but Carlota de Torres, unlike her mother-in-law, wasn't satisfied with a brief fling. After the great strike, whenever Francesc Romaguera was due to visit the town, some administrative problem would arise at the mines, or some difficulty with the pharmaceutical company in Marseilles which imported the factory's liquorice extract; or else something needed doing with the numerous investments in stocks held by the Torres i Camps and the Móra i Torres families, requiring Hipòlit to travel to Madrid or France. However, he was always happy to do so: he seized the opportunity to visit high-class bordellos where – through the law of compensation, according to Honorat del Cafè – he always requested sweet-natured, slim blondes.

The general hostility towards Romaguera, as evidenced by the murmurings of the *Neptune*'s crew when he came on board, also went back to the summer of 1925 when he behaved even more arrogantly and harshly towards the miners than his father had done. He went so far as to slap Arnau Terrer on the face for insulting him during a disturbance at the door of the Town Hall when the strikers' representatives had tried to get in and talk to the mine-owners, who were in session with the mayor. The town's memory retained the image of the young swell spouting venom against the "red hordes", under protection of the Civil Guards after the incident with the workers' leader. At the time of Arnau's death, the Romaguera lad wasn't in town; he had been back in Madrid for a week but no one, not even the staunchest conservatives at the Casino de la Roda, would absolve him of responsibility in the crime. They remembered the threats he had issued during the troubles and his part in breaking up meetings and demonstrations. There was no doubt whatsoever over who actually issued the order to kill the miner. Scarcely a year after the crime, the bailiff whom Mr Wilson had seen on the riverside walk was the victim of a strange disease which finished him off in a week and which gave rise to much speculation. When he was on the verge of death and wracked with feelings of remorse, the terrified assassin began to curse Sadurní Romaguera, crying out that it was his fault that he had Arnau Terrer's blood on his hands. The family were alarmed and hastily shooed the mourners out of the room; they tried to silence the dying man's horrific screams with a towel over his mouth, but it was no use. Everyone heard him and the town learnt the true story: Terrer had been picked up on his way home to the Eel Inn, taken outside the town boundary and shot with a revolver, then a juniper branch had been driven into the wound to make it look like an accident . . . The bailiff, swallowing down the death-rattle that couldn't escape through his gag, died two days later one wind-tossed morning. Once he had been buried – the wine-coloured dusk among the cypresses of the graveyard enveloping the few quaking souls who made up the funeral procession – it seemed as if his revelations would fade along with the image of the murderer. However, the town's silence did not signify forgetfulness. This was made clear on the night the Republic was proclaimed, when the crowds filled the streets with the name of their leader, slain on the riverside walk.

Recent events had finally removed any doubts about Francesc Romaguera. Nelson and the crew knew the young gentleman's views on the change of regime, an echo of his father's, who was also bursting with indignation since he had been replaced by a Republican mayor. Father and son stormed at the Casino de la Roda, where they had had more than a few verbal skirmishes with the youngest of the town's doctors and other club members with Republican leanings who finally decided never to return to this patrician stronghold. During this period, the club's mirrors often reflected the monocle of von Müller – "a filthy Nazi," muttered Estanislau Corbera at the Quayside Café – the German who, with the help of the Romagueras, had bought a large estate on the banks of the Ebro. He had had a powerful radio transmitter installed as well as a meteorological observatory. Lanky, sculptural Aryan youths were constantly parading through the town on their way from Germany to the farm; as sailors and fishermen recounted in amazement, they swam in the dead of winter in the freezing waters of the Ebro.

That morning, Nelson couldn't care less. The moment they weighed anchor, he withdrew into his shell of lethargy and mechanically steered the *Neptune* downstream. The sun soon brightened the deep-blue water; on the banks, the patient mules were towing trucks along the rails of the mines' loading bays and slag-heaps. The rhythm of the oars made the captain feel drowsy. His mind was whirling with dark thoughts: the ever-present memory of his dead daughter merged with the image of old Arquimedes and a sinister weariness made him want to put an end to it all. Just one shot – the idea haunted him – and he would be free of this intolerable situation.

The wisest, most fair-minded sailors could find no explanation for what happened next other than the lethargy that had been plaguing Nelson since Arquimedes Quintana's death. ("Or the inscrutable forces of destiny playing a cruel trick," added Honorat del Cafè.)

The captain himself could not understand his blunder: the noise was terrifying, as though the keel had shattered. With a sharp movement, the tiller hit Nelson's thighs, flinging him up in the air and overboard. He saw the sky spin round like a whirlpool as he tried to grab hold of the stern bitts before falling on his back into the water. He only heard half an oath from Atanasi, who always went in for long ones, and swallowed his own – a concise "God's ballocks!" inherited from the hero of Tetouan and which he was famous for all down the riverbank – along with a mouthful of water. He felt himself hit the stones on the bottom and when he managed to stand up, coughing and spluttering, he realized the tragedy that had befallen them: they had run aground on an islet. The impact had torn the rowlock mountings from the thwarts, the mule was kicking in desperation as it struggled to its feet from the black mass of coal that had shifted over to port now that the boat was listing.

Nearly forty years later, as old Nelson walked to the Quayside Café, his mind full of the memories which Julia's departure had stirred up, he relived the humiliation of the accident, which had never been entirely dispelled. Luckily the boat hadn't been holed. Even so, several tons of lignite had to be dumped in the river to refloat it. Apart from the odd bruise, the sailors were unscathed. The only casualty was the young gentleman, who had nearly knocked himself unconscious on a thole and was bleeding copiously.

His shame jolted him out of the apathy that had beset him since Arquimedes' death. Running aground and losing the cargo stuck in his conscience, despite the widow defending him – "To hell with the coal, Nelson's still the best skipper on the Ebro," – and from that day on he could never sail past Horseshoe Island without remembering the misadventure and hearing the boat grate against the riverbed. Five years later, the island would be engraved on his mind again, but this time on account of a far greater trauma than the wounded pride of the captain of an Ebro sailing barge or the loss of a few tons of Senyora Salleres' lignite.

There wasn't a breath of wind. The world, reeling from the pitiless July heat, seemed about to explode. Crows were cawing among the yellow and red rocks lining the valley. The mule trudged slowly up the right bank of the river, towing the barge. The *Neptune* was sailing upstream on a return trip from Tortosa with a heavy load of rice and pots, and had nearly reached the town. Joanet del Pla was punting with the boat-hook to make the mule's work easier when, by Horseshoe Island, he suddenly gave a shout and pointed to a spot on the overgrown islet.

Nelson didn't take much notice. He had other things on his mind; he was worried about the still-confused rumours of a military uprising in Morocco that had been circulating round the docks at Faió that morning. Yes, Africa was a long way off and the captain from Miravet who had given him the news insisted that nothing would come of it, that it would fizzle out soon enough, but they were all anxious to reach the town, where excitement at the Popular Front's election victory in February was still intense. After all the disappointments they had put up with since the proclamation of the Republic, including some as bitter and momentous as the crushing of the miners' revolt in Asturias, optimism was in the air again. Hopes were high and everyone – the Socialists at the Quayside Café, the Left-wing Republicans at the Central Café and the Communists at the Rampart, almost opposite the Anarchists' headquarters at the Eel Inn – was confident that their triumph would bear fruit. But Nelson wasn't so sure; he couldn't see how things would turn out or which of the parties the town supported was really likely to create the heaven on earth promised at all their meetings. Their speeches made him tired, their political theories made him yawn and annoyed him; he didn't understand them. Common sense told him that the only way to make head or tail of it all was to base his judgment of the political options on the characters of their respective leaders. Being lucid enough to skirt the many pitfalls of this approach, it put things on to a more comprehensible, everyday plane, divested of the claptrap spouted by those who promised him the earth. It cut the leaders down to size, turned them into real people who drank their coffee alongside him, mined coal in the pit or worked their fingers to the bone on those damned rivers, people who married, fell ill, went out dancing, people he saw battling their way through life's ups and downs, loved and maybe hated. Yet even so, things were never that clear-cut for him, at least not in the way they were for Atanasi Resurrecció. For him, Communism was the

116

undisputed answer and he was fully behind the party. Where did the truth lie if the disagreements between those who were meant to solve the world's problems were so bitter that their in-fighting made them forget the common enemy? In the long run wouldn't they just be exchanging one master for another and have to carry on slaving away the same as always, or even worse? Was it possible to change things? Atanasi told him that in Russia . . . But Russia was a long way away and God only knew how much truth there was in the propaganda. At times he wondered whether to ask Aleix de Segarra about these issues that set his head reeling but he never plucked up the courage. The former friendship between Aleix and old Arquimedes Quintana created a barrier of respect between Nelson and the artist. Aleix made him feel uncomfortable. He didn't share that sort of unease, obscurely tinged with age-old mistrust, felt by many people who were wary of Aleix de Segarra and other middle-class Republicans even though they were clearly on the side of the workers. Was disowning one's own class in order to defend the interests of those who basically sought to destroy it anything more than mischievous children being naughty? Or was it, as certain folk stated openly, a way of having a foot in both camps so that whichever way the wind blew they'd be all right? None of this seemed likely in the case of Aleix, who had been permanently ostracized by the upper classes. His wildness during his days at the Eden had been viewed with indulgence by the conservatives, but they could not forgive him for his attitude over the death of Arnau Terrer or his unqualified support first for the Republic and now for the Popular Front. And anyway, Nelson hadn't seen much of him recently . . .

The captain had no time to start ruminating on the reason for Aleix's isolation or his alleged love life – "terrible, disgraceful, diabolic," to quote Feliça Roderes, who would drop veiled hints from the Balcony of the Apocalypse and send confidential notes to the Bishop of Lleida condemning him – because Joanet del Pla's shouts drove all these thoughts from his mind.

"What's the matter?"

"I can see a body on the island, among the osiers!"

"Holy shit!" swore Atanasi Resurrecció. "Someone must have drowned."

Nelson felt a lump in his throat. Assuming Joanet was right —
and he was bound to be, as he had very keen eyesight — he would
have given anything to be a million miles from there and not have
to get involved in fishing out the body. Having to meet this require-
ment, both humanitarian and legal, made him ill. The sight of
death was always chilling but on the river it was repulsive and
horrible. He always thought back to his father who had disappeared
in the Lliberola Gorge and who must have ended up like these poor
wretches, blown up like wineskins, spattered in mud and eaten by
the eels. On such occasions, until the obsessive images faded in
time, he hated and cursed the river.

"Where is it?"

"At the tip of the island."

He halted the mule, loosened the towrope and turned the prow
towards the island. The Ebro was dazzlingly bright, sparkling like
a mirror; a sticky bluish vapour was shimmering above Horseshoe
Island. Joanet leapt ashore and made his way across the stones to
the shape he had spotted in the undergrowth. Nelson wouldn't even
look. Who could it be? Someone from the town? Or if not, where
had the waters dragged him from; where were they desperately
searching for him? By the time he made up his mind to go ashore,
laughter was coming from among the willows. Nelson wondered if
the shock had driven the poor sailor mad. He swore.

"Come here Nelson," the other fellow shouted. "You've never
seen anything like it in all your life!"

He jumped out of the barge and went over towards the osiers.
Through the soles of his sandals he could feel the heat rising from
the stones which were covered in scales of mud that crackled like
dry leaves underfoot. He saw an arm raised in the air, a hand
with three mutilated fingers. He brushed aside the branches of the
willows; a mud-encrusted body appeared and a face with one cheek
submerged in the water and the other half eaten away. The white
of an eye shone out between two smudges of black mud; its unblink-
ing pupil stared up at the cloudless sky.

"A statue!" exclaimed Atanasi Resurrecció.

"A saint!" confirmed Joanet del Pla in a relieved voice as he
sprinkled water on the figure to sluice it down. "A church saint!"

The muddy water coursed down the statue's cheeks, revealing

the polychrome: beneath its pale pink cheeks a long, curly, black beard framed bright red lips.

"Looks like a bishop," mumbled the third boatman, who had left the mule tethered on the right bank and had swum across the channel between the bank and the islet.

Nelson placed his hand over the back of the statue's neck.

"Help me . . ."

"Leave it to me . . ."

Atanasi Resurrecció dislodged the gigantic figure – its arm moving as though it were alive – and set it straight. On its chest, where the wood was painted to look like a dalmatic, there was a crack; it was peppered with holes as though the woodworm had been at it.

"Looks like gun-shot," commented Joanet del Pla.

"You're right," said Nelson, as they rested the carving on a willow-tree. The mule-driver was searching the island and called them over.

The wing, also made of wood, its whiteness spotted with mud, was sticking out from the reeds; the blond boy was gazing at them with his blue eyes from a face without a nose.

"Well bugger me! An angel!"

His left wing was missing, he had only one hand and his body was covered in sores.

"Poor little lamb!"

The second bearded figure, nearly naked and holding a skull in his right hand, turned up near the angel and close to the fourth figure, who had white whiskers and was clasping a St Andrew's cross. The female saint, blonde and with a look of rapture on her face, had not got as far as the osiers; she had come to rest in stagnant water a few feet away from the shore, next to three horned demons brandishing iron pitchforks and an altar-front full of painted figures. Higher up, at the mouth of one of the islet's channels, the headless image of a saint lay flat on its back next to a virgin clad in a blue tunic. A black prie-dieu was caught up in the roots of a poplar which had been washed up on the island by a flood many years past.

They fished the galaxy of saints from the water and assembled them on the highest point of the island among some osiers.

"They look like dead bodies, don't they Nelson?" muttered Joanet, rather intimidated by the row of statues.

"Yes, it looks as though someone had it in for them. Come on, let's get back to the boat."

A carp pierced the surface of the water: the fish's silver gleam encircled by iridescent droplets seemed to stand still at the highest point of its leap. The sound it made as it plunged into the water underlined the eerie silence hanging over the valley.

"We should be able to hear the riddling machines from the Amat mines," Nelson said to himself as they climbed on board. But everything was perfectly still. They started sailing again. There wasn't a soul on the riverside path. They suddenly realized that they hadn't passed a single boat coming down from the town and a sinister sense of foreboding gripped their hearts. Nelson pricked up his ears; he still couldn't hear the machines. When they were almost within sight of the mine's wharf a mule came galloping through the olive-groves. On the horizon to the right, columns of smoke were rising into the sky.

On the way down from Julia's house to the Quayside Café, Nelson stopped in front of the old convent. The next day, the building would be coming down, another stage in the relentless destruction of the town. He reflected for a moment on the mystery hidden behind that door, which Honorat del Rom often speculated about, and recalled the figure of Aleix de Segarra on one of the last occasions he had seen him, up in the high galleries. The image of the painter faded, the captain ambled slowly down the alley; the thread of memory pulled him back to the day in July 1936 when the boat sailed past the Amat mine. As they worriedly scanned the empty site, something hit the stern.

"Another one!" yelled Atanasi Resurrecció. "He looks like the Saint Blaise in the town church!"

Nelson felt it graze the boat to starboard, then the bearded wooden figure floated away down the Ebro in the foam of the *Neptune*'s wake.

VI

The vibrations that heralded the collapse of the convent spread panic among the rats. Squealing in terror, the creatures scampered through the empty rooms looking for a way out through a hole or down a drainpipe. One of them ran across the foyer where the cables were still pulled tight after the bulldozers' first onslaught. It tried to run up a wall; its razor-sharp claws dug into the lady's shoe, then it climbed up her dress, above the neckline where the fiery red of her clothes ended and the smooth pink of her naked flesh began, to her pearl necklace. A stronger tremor shook the wall; the rat fell to the ground, tearing off some pearls and part of the coloured plume on her hat. But the lady kept on smiling regardless, the mischievous glint in her eyes didn't fade. The pianist alongside her was set in motion by another judder, more vigorous and prolonged than the first ones. His fingers seemed to be flying over the keys, pounding out the musical accompaniment to the dances of the chorus girls in the background. And meanwhile, on the wall opposite, an inaudible cheer came from a crowd of miners, sailors, farmhands and workmen. Another brutal crash, followed by sinister squeals from the rats, wiped the smile off the face of the lady in the feathered hat. A flake of paint came loose and disfigured her lips, laying bare the powdery white plaster on the wall where Aleix de Segarra's vast murals, steeped in ironic nostalgia, immortalized the heyday of the Eden.

This was the first mural he had painted when the departure of the nuns in 1925 allowed him to get his hands back on the convent building which had been ceded to the order of nuns by a licentious great-great-grandfather of his as penance for his sins. Although there was no mention of it in the family archives, which in any case Aleix never delved into, having little interest in the dusty sheaves of documents piled high on the top shelves in the library, it was common knowledge that Senyor Domènec de Segarra had seduced and deflowered a nun when the order, at that period thriving and prosperous, occupied a tumbledown house on Fish-Hook Street. His conquest, which evil tongues at the time put down to a trap laid by the Mother Superior rather than to the seductive powers of Segarra, who was quite old and in pretty poor shape by then, came as a disappointment to the old lecher. Once she had been stripped of her incitingly mysterious habits beneath which the libertine's desire had imagined charms enough to drive any man wild, the nun turned out to have a scrawny behind and sagging breasts and to be dull as ditchwater. And to make matters worse, she instilled the fear of eternal damnation into him. Manipulated by the chaplain at the bidding of the Mother Superior, the sinner's qualms and his desire for forgiveness led to the building being made over to the order – merely on a temporary basis, thanks to the timely intervention of some relatives who managed to put a stop to what would otherwise have been an irreversible donation. Things might have followed a different course had someone been able to tell him then what was revealed in a séance held in the Quayside Café in 1930. Aleix de Segarra's ancestor would have learnt that Estanislau Corbera's grandmother had been reincarnated as an Italian mare and had just won the Palio in Siena, an item of news which made the café proprietor's breast swell with legitimate family pride. And there were other surprising facts about various of the town's inhabitants (Honorat del Cafè had been a camp follower with Napoleon's army during the Egyptian campaign, Senyora Salleres, a Roman senator, and the tobacconist, Garibaldi). He would have seen that it was not his fate to burn in hell but to be reincarnated as a boatswain on a Dutch vessel carrying copra round the South Seas. But none of this happened, the poor chap didn't lose his fear and the building was made over to the nuns. The Segarra family didn't get it back till forty years later, when the nuns left town on the same day that the first permanent detachment of Civil Guards arrived aboard the Bishop's vessel. This coincidence was never seen as mere chance and it gave rise to a most entertaining conversation at the boatbuilder's workshop, where those present painstakingly analysed the full symbolic value of replacing habits with uniforms, crucifixes with guns and wimples with tricorns.

The day after the convent was made over to him, Aleix went round burning sulphur in the rooms, scrubbing floors, doors and windows with bleach and scattering bunches of thyme and rosemary. Once the scent had taken hold, he began painting on the walls, putting down his memories of the long-gone days of the Eden, thereby initiating a process which would last for years, until the moment when the artist was borne away in the black gust of wind that swept through the town.

The last remaining rat had found an escape route. Its hairless tail was just slipping into a crack in the kitchen pipes when another jolt hit the staircase that led from the hall to the first floor, and set the carnival painted on the surrounding walls jigging up and down. It was as if the toothless masks, the horned devils, the shameless witches with artificial flowers stuck in their behinds or the outlandish big-nosed figures with floured hair were trying to get down from the walls and start leaping round the stairs in time to the music of cowbells and saucepans. This wasn't the sugary ersatz carnival of the Casino de la Roda or the Hall of the Martyred Virgins, all ambiguous Harlequins and fairground miladies in masks. It was the traditional town carnival, the ancestral force that drove Honorat del Cafè out into the streets secretly disguised as a billy-goat, butting people with his horns, that made the fish lady from the Porxos so restless that she put on her grandfather's uniform from the Cuban war and covered her face to go and meet the cardinal – Estanislau Corbera's unsuspected disguise – and make love with him in the cabin of a barge without ever breaking the veil of anonymity; the same force that kept a terrifying black figure standing motionless for hours and hours in front of the Romagueras' house.

That tragic figure, whom everyone took to be Arnau Terrer's former sweetheart, was painted on the left-hand side of the staircase, next to two masks which concealed the artist and Malena, his aunt, who had been a widow for just over a year. They had been through the tiresome obligations on the first anniversary of his death and the macabre repetition of the Requiem Mass – the catafalque at the foot of the altar, mournful prayers and the smell of tapers – along with the inevitable formal visits with the hypocritical string of condolences. Malena had easily let herself be convinced by her nephew, only a couple of years younger than herself, to blow away the greyness of her married life under the secrecy of the mask. Why should she remain like that always, insinuated Aleix, consuming herself in memory of Uncle Ignasi, a man chosen for her by her family? Why should she stay shut up indoors for ever more and never get any pleasure from life? Why not go out into the streets and be swept along in the anonymous carnival madness that enabled the town to throw restraint to the wind and set loose a few ghosts?

In the silence of her sick-room in 1971, old Malena heard Aleix's voice as it had sounded that afternoon in 1926, relaxed and suggestive. The maids had gone to join in the fun, dressed up in clothes she had let them choose from the trunks in the attic, where they shared the dust and spiders' webs with Grandpa Hermes' mechanical inventions and Aunt Severina's unfinished sculptures and automata. Malena and her nephew were alone in the house, hearing the noise of the crowds outdoors, and she guessed that she would finally be caught in the invisible snare that she had felt growing around her for a year, as soon as her nephew (this word applied to Aleix had always secretly made her laugh) started to speak. He had never openly courted her; he was so discreet that she even doubted her own intuitions which, shortly after she had gone to live in the Segarra family home after her marriage to Ignasi just before the 1914 war, led her to guess at her husband's nephew's feelings through small, almost imperceptible details. She realized to her own horror that she felt the same way on experiencing a stab of jealousy when the Eden was still in full swing and Madamfranswah and the high jinks at the café-concert were the favourite talking-point of the ladies over their afternoon cups of hot chocolate. After Madamfranswah's departure, her jealousy resurfaced whenever Aleix climbed on board Arquimedes Quintana's boat and disappeared for days on end. Not noticing his wife's reactions, Ignasi attributed these absences to a mistress in Tortosa; he had heard some piquant remarks about her from Senyor Jaume de Torres, who was kept well informed by his boatmen of what went on between the town and the mouth of the river. When Aleix reappeared, he was treated with disconcerting coldness, the reasons for which he was unable to fathom. Ignasi's sudden death – a heart attack according to one of Dr Beltran's few correct diagnoses – intensified Aleix's shows of tenderness. Robbed of the presence of her husband, who was more of a father to her than anything else, she had felt unprotected; being alone with Aleix both scared and excited her: her widow's weeds couldn't disguise her confused feelings. She wondered whether to disappear for a while, to heed the advice of relatives who recommended a change of air to overcome the "most painful pain" – as Aunt Assumpta wrote to her from Barcelona in a letter of condolence – that the absence of the "most beloved of the beloved" was causing her. However, she eventually refused to run away to the "most peaceful peace" of Vichy which her aunt suggested would help her get over things. Being incapable of moving away from her nephew, she didn't leave the town. But at that time Aleix was hardly ever at home; she only saw him at mealtimes, if then. She lay awake every night while he was down at the Quayside Café relaxing from his day's work on the convent murals. She would hear him get in, cross the corridor on his way to the rooms on the second floor, and she would tense in anxiety and fear. When, after what she took to be him dithering outside the door of her room, the footsteps went upstairs and died away, she relaxed, but it was some while before the rapid throb of her heart, like flood water in spate, quietened. When at first she rejected Aleix's suggestion to put on a mask and take part in the carnival, it was not so much a flat refusal as a feeble attempt to stave off the terror, to justify herself to the memory of her dead husband, which had been evoked by the gloomy memorial ceremonies. But the suggestive voice of Aleix who, little by little and without daring to believe it, had eventually guessed her feelings and no longer deceived himself about his own attitude, easily overcame her half-hearted resistance.

Forty years later, Aleix's voice still lived on in Malena de Segarra's memory. It was preserved as intensely as the exhilarating sensation of excitement and release with which they suddenly threw themselves into preparing disguises that would ensure their anonymity in the hurly-burly of the streets. The paintings on the staircase held the key to those moments concealed behind two Venetian masks, the beginning of a story that would be immortalized on the walls of the first floor of the convent. The door had been sealed since then; old Malena wanted the secret to be destroyed with the building. She had sent her faithful and discreet servant, Anna, to supervise the demolition: no one must go up to the cells or set foot in the chapel.

The servant saw to it that these orders were followed to the letter. The same workmen who had had a shock with Polyphemus's head in the ruins of the Eden were put off by the high painted walls of the foyer and didn't dare climb a single tread of the staircase. They attached the steel cables to the bottom of the pillars on the ground floor, and started up the powerful machines, whose first thud had shaken the walls and sown terror among the rats.

In the cell where Sister Andrea used to flog herself to drive out the impure thoughts constantly besieging her — particularly in summer, when through her shutters she could see the half-naked bodies of the boatmen working in the Ferryboat wharf or the teenage boys swimming in the Ebro — the machines' first tug gave life to the mythological nudes that Aleix had painted on the walls, unwittingly making amends for the harsh indignities suffered there by the poor woman's body.

This was the first thing that Aleix showed her after the carnival, when he led her upstairs to the first floor of the convent. Until then she had only seen the murals in the foyer with the picture of Madamfranswah that had reawakened old jealousies. Once inside the cell and stirred by a mixture of modesty, excitement and pleasure, she recognized her own body in that of the nude goddess encircled by nymphs, bathing in a river which the landscape round about identified as the Ebro; her own body which ever since the night of the carnival had recaptured in Aleix's arms a zest and vitality that had taken her by surprise. The artist's delight in her naked form was translated into the numerous representations he made of it over the years on the convent walls. Where religious hymns and whispered prayers once echoed, the pagan feasting inspired bacchanalian songs; walls once darkened by oil paintings of martyrdoms or made cold by chilling crucifixion scenes were opened up to the light in a good-natured mythology, deeply rooted in the land. The buildings portrayed were no fabulous palaces but the farmsteads of the ancient Arab fields on the banks of the Ebro, the classical cypress trees were replaced by poplars or fig-trees, the wine that gleamed red in their cups was the rough dry juice from the grapes of Terra Alta. It didn't require much effort to see that the satyrs in the corridor were the regulars at the Quayside Café —

126

Atanasi Resurrecció playing the pan-pipes, Honorat del Cafè with a crown of vine leaves and Nelson with a goblet in his hand – and that the laughing nymphs being chased across a landscape covered in thyme and rosemary against a background of olive trees were Julia Quintana and other beauties from the town; in the ante-room to the refectory, Estanislau Corbera, looking solemn and majestic in the role of a bay centaur, presided over an uproarious orgy on the banks of the Segre, opposite a wall where another nude of Malena, a Phrygian cap on her black hair, led the people's joy at the proclamation of the Republic.

The convent was their own secret world. Aleix worked flat out. Sometimes she worried as she saw all the hard graft that went into the preliminary stages of the murals and paintings, their slow evolution; he constantly rubbed them out and began again with a tenacity which would have astounded those who saw no deeper than the Bohemian veneer of the painter's old nights of debauchery. But Aleix had to go out too. He needed to be with people, to enjoy the bustle of café life, to sail down the Ebro and make the odd trip to Barcelona. Whereas she had no life outside Aleix. External things were muted echoes of a world she isolated herself from behind the black barrier of her mourning. Naturally, there was no shortage of caustic backbiting from the members of the Casino de la Roda or the ladies who met in the Hall of the Martyred Virgins. In both places it was considered a cause for concern that aunt and nephew should live under the same roof in the Segarra house with no chaperons except the maids, "continuously exposed to the temptations of the flesh", in the priest-like terminology of Senyoreta Estefania d'Albera and "offending against the sacrosanct memory of the departed", as put with an eloquence as pompous, malodorous, flabby and pot-bellied as its purveyor, Senyor Gelabert de Móra of Ebro Lignites Limited. A healthy antidote came in the shape of a dressing down from Senyora Salleres. Infuriated by the gossip – which the administrator of the moment relayed to her in the shadowy recesses of her bedchamber – and possessing considerable family experience when it came to replacing deceased husbands, the widow railed against the entire membership of the Casino, branding them all as pansies and cuckolds and their respective wives as two-faced harlots.

She had no compunction about exposing all their guilty secrets. The townsfolk heard of the former smuggler's remarks from her maids, who repeated them in the market and the shops. They learnt that Senyor Jaume de Torres chased the maids along the corridors while his wife was at her rosary, that the wife of the worshipful Council secretary had been unfaithful with the clarinettist (and sometimes the bass drummer) of the town band and that the famous ecstasies of Senyora Sebastiana de Vidal, whose beatification Feliça Roderes had sought from Rome on three occasions, had less to do with mystical visions than a secret devotion to her bottle of anisette . . .

The gossip didn't worry Malena de Segarra one little bit. The whole town could go hang! The world inside her house and the convent was all she needed. In the good weather she spent many hours with Aleix in the high gallery that overlooked the Ebro. Hidden behind the shutters of the convent, they looked down on the quay, at the barges sailing past with their cargo of lignite and the trucks in the mine on the other side of the river trundling to and fro beneath the first arch of the bridge. They were often so overwhelmed by desire that they ended up in each other's arms on the cushions in the gallery or in the cell of the flagellant nun who died in odour of sanctity after a brutal session with the scourge. Her memories of those winters were of seagulls soaring over the grey water, the warmth of the open fire in the old refectory, the north wind rattling the windows of the empty cells, the deep sound of the conches which the river-captains used to signal the position of their vessels and avoid collisions on foggy days.

On that morning in 1971 when the bulldozers were about to demolish the convent, those ten years of happiness seemed like a brief gust of wind to old Malena: they had come to an abrupt end when the world they were living in as though it were an island was torn apart for ever.

When the impact of the bulldozers shook the building, the rats in the refectory were the only ones not to run away; they didn't budge from the walls where Malena had first seen them in January 1938. At the time, she hadn't been able to stifle a scream on entering the refectory and taking for real creatures the blotches of dirty grey with malicious little eyes and hairless tails scattered on the wall.

They were an indication of the anguish that was starting to take hold of Aleix. The military rebellion against the Republican government that began in Africa in July 1936 was no longer the short, sharp flare-up that many people had expected, but a long civil war that was consuming the entire nation. The rats appeared in a corner of the large mural he started just before the Fascist uprising, next to the sketch of a nymph who was supposed to have the form and face of the lady from the fishmongers in Moon Street. The nymph was left unfinished: the spark of life never shone in her black eyes, and her splendid body with its small firm breasts and a backside which Honorat del Cafè praised as the most provocative and pleasing, though maybe not the most perfect, along the whole riverbank, never got beyond the draft stage. Along with the rest of the composition, it disappeared under new paintings dominated by black and red, evocations of the mourning and blood that darkened the atmosphere in the town once war broke out. The death of the first inhabitant in the trenches while defending the Republic was still offset publicly by the blaze of speeches and the mummery of official ceremonies. Later on, casualties became more frequent among the flood of volunteers rushing to the front and the leaders abandoned their speechifying, useless in the face of the infinite emptiness of death.

On the convent walls, the sketches of nymphs and goddesses whose tender pink flesh tones were just coming to life against a background of ochre landscapes, disappeared beneath the body of Aleix's nephew Lluís, killed at Carrascal, surrounded by weeping women. At his side lay the two eldest boys of the late Arquimedes Quintana who had been executed in Saragossa where the military uprising had caught them. A scene painted on the right of the balcony overlooking the Ebro depicted the bodies of the *Christopher Columbus*'s crew, gunned down by enemy planes; the barge had run aground on the bank and at the helm Carbó the mule lay dying. His flanks were pierced by bullets, his bloodied mouth was open wide in despair. On the left-hand wall in a composition Aleix had painted on top of a marvellous wine-harvest scene, the livid light of a painted dawn could not dispel the darkness of night: shadows still stained the figure of Sadurní Romaguera who had been peppered with gun-shot and lay stretched out among the rosemary bushes in the ravine where they had driven him to his death in a requisitioned car, the same one in which Carlota de Torres went to church on the day of her wedding and in which she made love with Francesc for the first time.

In her mental journey round the inside of the convent, Malena could not shut her eyes to the paintings in the refectory. She wanted to remember only those that dated from the happy times, without crossing the threshold and entering the nightmare zone, but it wasn't possible; her memory kept on going, and dragged her through the whole traumatic chronicle of events. In the case of Romaguera's death, the pictures were fleshed out by her recollections of the desperate screams of his wife and daughters the night that he was taken away. It was the price paid for the murder of Arnau Terrer. Of the bloody deeds that were carried out in the area, the only deaths were Romaguera's and the priest's. The latter was given the chance to leave and even supplied with everyday clothes, but he returned and his presence and his unwise remarks proved intolerable for the squads who had come to the town calling for all the bourgeoisie to be shot. When a group went to the Germans' farm the day after the rebellion, von Müller, his monocle and his followers had vanished into thin air. The Left had an absolute majority and were in control of the situation from the outset, refusing to execute the gentry and the few right-wingers in the area, despite the demands of a handful of extremists, although this led to the town's isolation. Until Caspe finally fell into Republican hands, they were under threat from a possible incursion of rebel forces from the other side of the Ebro; and on the road to Lleida which ran alongside the Segre, from the Anarchists in Cinca. Long, confused days in Malena's memory, with the Caspe bank beyond the bridge and the Fraga road packed with dynamite which the miners had laid to protect the town. Shotguns at the ready, the men were on permanent alert. And then the war: young men leaving for the front, death, the brief excitement at the presence of soldiers resting in the town – the Red Shock Battalion, Aleix told her once, pointing at a line of military vehicles along the wall by the Ebro – and his increasingly despondent and sombre moods. After the collectivization of the coalfield, he had been employed at one of Senyora Salleres' mines, now controlled by the General Union of Workers, but the war went on and on, and devoured everything. Suddenly, at the end of March 1938, disaster struck. First, a flood of soldiers: a Fascist offensive had broken through the Aragon front, the Republican troops were withdrawing. The bridge over the Ebro was a continuous procession of men and vehicles and the town was in ferment. On the 26th they began to hear a kind of muffled thunderclap in the distance, which grew louder and louder.

"They're mining the bridge," muttered Aleix, looking at the river from the gallery of the convent. "The Fascists must be close."

Almost immediately, above the clamour of the streets, they heard the voices of the members of the municipal committee advising the inhabitants to evacuate the town. From that point on, Malena's memory was a confused muddle: feverishly stuffing clothes, jewels and money into a suitcase with Anna's help, the scrum of people pushing their goods and chattels along in carts, aggravated by the presence of retreating military vehicles. She remembered seeing the party leaders load filing cabinets full of documents into a lorry from the Segre mine outside the committee's headquarters, and long lines of people walking off down the Ebro. The quayside was thronged with crowds hoping to be taken on board the few available barges; the captains were attempting to establish order in the midst of chaos. There wasn't room for everyone; there weren't enough boats and so they could only take old people, invalids, women and children. One by one the ships sailed off down the Ebro, the water almost up to their gunwales, overloaded with terrified folk; those who didn't fit had to escape by the Lleida road or cross the Segre by the pontoon at the other end of the town.

Aleix pushed a way through the groups of militiamen down to the Town Square Wharf. Nelson made room for her and Anna on his boat, the last one to get out. Night was closing in over the valley, shells had started to explode and bullets were whistling past. On the bridge, the last stragglers among the soldiers were still silhouetted against the evening sky. She looked despairingly at Aleix, who stood on the wharf and watched her as the barge drew away.

"Go to Barcelona, to Aunt Assumpta's," he shouted. "I'll come for you there."

Someone next to her burst into tears but an almighty clatter like a drum-roll drowned them out: the groom at Senyora Salleres' mines had opened the stable doors when he left, and the teams of horses were galloping along the wall by the Ebro, scared out of their wits by the mayhem and the thunderous explosions which were coming nearer and nearer.

The sailing barge skimmed over the black waters and Aleix soon faded into the darkness. As they rounded the confluence of the Ebro and the Segre, a wall of flames lit up the blackness and turned the valley blood-red, like a brief false dawn. They were blowing up the bridge. A moment later, the wave caused by the explosion nearly swamped the barge. But Malena didn't hear the terrified cries of the fugitives packed on to the ship or Nelson's curse. In the midst of the chaos she had a dreadful presentiment: she would never see Aleix again.

The vibration became stronger and more sustained, the cables were pulled as tight as possible and the pillars gave way: a fissure cracked the wall of the foyer from top to bottom, the staircase came crashing down with a deafening noise, the carnival masks fell to pieces. In the cells and the refectory, goddesses, satyrs, nymphs, weeping women and dead men were all reduced to dust. Then down came the old chapel where, a few days before the town was evacuated, Aleix, his heart already heavy with dreadful forebodings, had begun to depict his premonition of the entrance of the rebels: skeletons in dress uniform, whose sashes and braid used up all the yellow paint he had left in his paintbox, were being fêted by the town's worthies, most notably Carlota de Torres, who looked slightly the worse for wear but was smartly dressed in the best outfit from her wardrobe and jewels fished out from their hiding-place. Once the dust caused by the demolition had settled, the workmen noticed that part of the wall over the high altar was still standing. Near the top they could see a skull wearing a soldier's cap. The serrated shovel of one of the machines attacked the base of the wall; the skull fell down on to a fragment from the partition-wall of the former cell of the saintly nun, where the artist had immortalized in shades of pink the full firm breasts of an Aphrodite.

132

PART THREE

Calendar Ash

I

The ferry, which had ceased to exist fifteen years earlier, pulled away from the right bank and started across the river. The water meanwhile changed colour and the mild autumnal air of October 1971 drifted away. By the time the boat's gunwale gently nudged the landing-stage on the town side – where Alfons Garrigues stood, guiding the rudder from memory – the landscape had been covered in the freezing fog of winter 1939. The ochre and green tints of the Ebro had been transformed into a dirty grey, and sheets of ice floated slowly downstream like scales detached from a gigantic fish.

They came looking for him when the noise of battle moved into Catalonia, after the battle of the Ebro and the departure of the Fascist soldiers who had been occupying the town since the collapse of the Aragon front in March 1938. When the Republicans had blown up the bridge, it had cut all links between the two sides, and the rebel troops had installed a pontoon at the old ferry crossing, abandoned fifteen years earlier. But the army were leaving, so a ferryman was needed to take their place. At that time he was a lad of eighteen, who had been unable to escape when the town was evacuated because of his mother and his sick grandmother, and was apparently the best person for the job. He was a Garrigues after all, wasn't he? A scion of the Garrigues family of the Carrer Major, town ferrymen since the dawn of time.

The first occasion was a winter's day when the stagnant water between the landing-stage and the military pontoon was frozen and blocks of ice kept hitting the boat, causing its metal floats to clink mournfully. He thought back sadly to his grandfather, who had lost his job as ferryman when the construction of the bridge during the dictatorship of Primo de Rivera ruined his life and forced him to go down the pit. He hated his job as a miner but pride forbade him from signing on as a deck-hand on the barges, and he swallowed coal-dust until the day he died, shortly before the Civil War. How could the old fellow ever have imagined, reflected Alfons, that one of his grandsons would see the destruction of the bridge he had always hated – while acknowledging the progress it signified – and that the boy would turn to the traditional calling of the Garrigues family? If it hadn't been for the hunger and poverty his family were suffering, and fear of the consequences were he to turn down the job – when it was all too easy to end up in prison or in front of a firing squad – Alfons would have flatly refused to work on the ferry; he would have preferred to avoid the trauma of the homecomings when most of those who had left in 1938 returned after the defeat of the Republic signalled the end of the war.

Some people came by the Lleida road; Alfons Garrigues couldn't remember them, but those who got off the train at Faió station and walked up the Ebro along the riverside path were engraved forever on his memory. News got out the moment a figure was spotted in the distance, and the few people left in the town – those who couldn't or wouldn't escape during the evacuation or who, in the confusion of the moment, had hidden in mines or farmhouses where they were cut off by the Fascist offensive – peered out of their balconies or windows, came down to the wall of the deserted wharves and anxiously studied the silhouettes, trying to see who they were, an impossible task given the distance. The people waiting (and who in that dead town wasn't waiting for somebody, wondered Garrigues) would eventually give up and make straight for Ferryboat Wharf. There they stood, the tips of their toes right next to the water's edge, or huddled on to the wooden jetty, and tried once more to make out the features of the still anonymous figures. This feverish, anxious scrutiny became unbearable as the ferry crossed the Ebro, picked up the new arrivals and started back again. As the distance gradually shortened, the patches of light and shade came to life and turned into faces nearly always emaciated by privation, fatigue and worry. Over the final metres of the crossing, the figures acquired names, and there were often cries and tears of joy alongside much silent and bitter disappointment. On foggy days they were unaware of their presence until the distant, muffled voices wafted over from the other side to ask Alfons to ferry them across. The waiting was even crueller then; in the fog's murky haze the secret was not revealed until the very edge of the landing-stage.

Women, old people and children were the first to come back.

Some time later, soldiers started returning from the concentration camps, workers' battalions and prisons. Alfons Garrigues had enduring memories of that grey tide, a mixture of faces and days, sun and fog, since there was no end to the people returning. The leaden eyes of his cousin Ramon, who came back ill from the concentration camp, stayed with him forever, full of the desire to die in the town, where he was to be buried four weeks later. As though time had stood still, Alfons could see Jordi Blanques, the old blacksmith from the Torres i Camps mines, who never came ashore; on the far bank he met a relative of his who told him during the crossing that his wife, whom he had dreamt of night and day during their long separation, had gone off with a Fascist soldier who had been garrisoned in the town. Jordi Blanques didn't set foot on the quay; he stayed inside the boatman's shelter until the pontoon made its next trip and then disappeared for ever down the riverside path.

Memories came flooding back non-stop. How could he ever forget Antoni Canals who, when he was in midstream, glimpsed his younger brother on the wharf and shouted to him, saying what the hell did he think he was doing, hanging round the town during the olive harvest. He could also have testified to taking a car across on the ferry, driven by Francesc Romaguera in his uniform as second lieutenant in Franco's army, accompanied by von Müller, dressed as a German commandant.

The mists of time parted to reveal the indelible image of Eduard Forques, builder of river boats by family tradition, and tenor saxophonist by irrepressible vocation, the son of Ramon Forques, the former conductor of the River Harmony Band. He spent the whole ferry trip practising a funeral march which he couldn't get quite right. He had got his hands on an excellent saxophone at the França railway station in Barcelona; a starving tramp had let him have it in return for some tins of sardines and a few bars of chocolate. From Faió station to the town, the faltering notes of the unfinished piece had followed the towpath, ringing out wistfully in the Ebro valley, which was still battle-weary, still in mourning for the dead. When he came ashore, he greeted everyone on the quayside, then started up his music again and walked off home, followed by a band of inquisitive children.

Neither would he forget the homecoming of Joanet del Pla, a

member of the *Neptune*'s crew and Nelson's right-hand man. When he jumped from the launch on to the landing-stage, they all assumed that it was to tie up the mooring ropes; in fact, he went and stood in front of Joaquim Mestre, who was lazing round as usual, waiting with the others for the ferry to get in, and said in his quiet gentle voice, "Give me back my boots, lad."

Everyone on the riverbank knew the calm tone of Joanet del Pla's voice. It was usually accompanied by an almost imperceptible flicker of his left eyelid, and when the sailor adopted this instead of his usually lively manner of speech, it was always the prelude to some memorable event such as the hair-raising fight on the quayside at Faió between the crew of the *Neptune* and some sailors from Ascó, which all began with a blow from Joanet's fist that smashed the captain's jaw, or the commotion at a brothel in Tortosa when the deck-hand, after exchanging a few well-chosen pleasantries with some fishermen from the Ebro Delta about a tart they fancied when he had already chosen her for himself, proceeded to knock them for six with Atanasi Resurreccció's enthusiastic and selfless assistance. Joaquim Mestre knew all about this, and realized moreover that neither defeat nor the hardships Joanet had endured in the workers' battalions had changed him: his voice was as polite as ever, his eyelid was flickering as clearly now as in the old days. Yet even so, Joaquim tried acting dumb.

"What do you mean, Joanet?" he managed to stammer out as the crowd gathered round them.

"Don't come the innocent with me. I mean the boots you're wearing. They're mine. I spotted them a mile off."

"He must have pinched them from your place, the thief," chimed in one of the women. "Some good-for-nothings have been up to all kinds of mischief while we've been away. When I got back, the whole house was topsy-turvy."

The woman had hit on the truth and Alfons Garrigues recalled Joaquim Mestre's terror as he tried in vain to wriggle his way out of the situation.

"Take your boots off."

"Hang on, Joanet!"

"Take them off, I said . . ."

Loudly protesting his innocence amid the taunts of the

bystanders, the burglar was forced to take off his boots and hand them over. Barefoot, his feet freezing in the wintry weather, he ran off as fast as his legs could carry him along Quay Hill while Joanet took the pair of magnificent boots – a present from Nelson, who had received them from Arquimedes Quintana, who had been given them by Mr Oliver Wilson – and carefully polished them on the sleeve of his frayed jacket.

Alfons Garrigues recalled the emotional return of Estanislau Corbera with his wife and little daughter; but he knew nothing of his bitter tears when he found that the café had been ransacked first, so he was told, by some straggling militiamen on the day of the evacuation, and then by Franco's soldiers. The building had been left wide open, exposed to the biting north winds and the sultry southwesterlies; the mirrors were coated in dust and a layer of grime covered the mess the soldiers had left behind them.

As his memories poured back, Garrigues didn't overlook Nelson, a good friend of his dead father's, or Berenguer de Serra. As keen as ever to get his hands on female flesh, he swept his wife up in his arms the moment he reached the quay. When they got home, he couldn't wait to go up to the bedroom, but began pulling her clothes off on the landing. Pasqual de Pons, the best card-player in town, flashed into his mind. He had got up a card school on the train home and cleaned out four Carlist militiamen from Navarre who were going home on leave. The arrival of the chemist's wife with her son, the future Honorat del Rom, stirred up memories in the young ferryman's mind of the stampede on the day the town was evacuated: the teams of horses from Senyora Salleres' stables had bolted down the river wall in terror at the uproar coming from the panic-stricken crowd and the explosions. They were on a level with the Widows' Wharf – from where Nelson's barge had just set sail – when the wall of flames and the noise from the charges of dynamite laid to blow up the bridge frightened them so much that they suddenly turned up Pebble Alley. The cry of horror from Honorat del Cafè as the animals rounded the corner and crushed him under their hooves put the fear of God into young Garrigues, who was watching the chaotic exodus from his balcony . . . Along with all these memories of people returning home, the ferryman was haunted by thoughts of those who had been taken away in black cars, which he was made to ferry across the river in the small hours or at dawn, after interrogations at the Town Hall or the Civil Guard barracks.

Alfons Garrigues, of the Garrigues family from the Carrer Major, town ferryman from 1938 to 1942 – the year he left the job to go and sail on Senyora Salleres' barges – turned his back on Ferryboat Wharf and started to climb up Quay Hill. As soon as his back was turned, the colours of autumn 1971 suffused the landscape once more and the ferry melted away in the gentle glow of September. But the retired ferryman couldn't help seeing one last time the look given him by Sebastià Noguera, Julia Quintana's husband: the prisoner's eyes were already inhabited by the shadow of the death that was waiting for him at the hands of the firing-squad in the city. The sadness of the workers' leader knew no bounds when his gaze fell for the last time on the famine-stricken town, where the unforgiving victors were making the starving, louse-ridden children play at war with wooden guns, to the beat of trumpets and drums.

Alfons Garrigues' reminiscences evoked no response among the townspeople. Estanislau Corbera scarcely noticed the fleeting vision of a far-off, vandalized Quayside Café which flashed on to the mirror facing the bar. While a blustery autumn north wind, still tempered by the warmth of late summer, rattled the windowpanes and imprinted the warm brown colour of the first fallen leaves on them, the café proprietor listened attentively to his customers' lively chatter.

If Eduard Forques had paid just a little attention to the notes that were trying to take shape in some corner of his memory, he would undoubtedly have found the solution to his funeral march. On his way back from the concentration camp in 1940, he had got stuck after the first few bars and had never been able to finish it. The notes fluttered for a moment on the edge of his consciousness and then sank into oblivion among all the other things the tenor saxophonist had forgotten.

Joanet del Pla didn't remember taking Mr Wilson's boots off Joaquim Mestre's feet. Nelson listened to his friends talking in the bar, unaware of the image of the town struggling to resurface on his retina, and Honorat del Rom heard the bang from Pebble Alley but didn't recognize it as the sound of the horses who had crushed his father to death, reawakened by the ex-ferryman's reminiscences as the quay was smashed to pieces.

A few weeks after the convent had been bulldozed (while Honorat del Rom scrabbled about among the debris and managed to retrieve a fragment of wall bearing a portrait of Estanislau Corbera crowned in a wreath of vine-leaves and a skull with a soldier's cap), the situation of the battered town took a turn for the better: the first houses in the new town were finished. The population's will to survive was starting to bear fruit after all the years of ceaseless struggle. Previously, when houses were knocked down, whole families had been compelled to move to the city because of circumstances such as the lack of jobs or prospects for the children – as happened with Julia Quintana. From now on, there would be no more goodbyes, each house demolished in the old town would mean another house finished in the new one, a state of affairs few people had actually believed in until then. The mutilated streets were alive once more with optimism and euphoria.

And it was this sense of anticipation that was dominating the conversations of most of the regulars at the Quayside Café, while Alfons Garrigues, the former Ebro ferryman, remembered them coming home from the war. But his recollections passed unnoticed. And most of the residents were to react in the same way to the event that would occur a few hours later, and which would erroneously be placed by the future anonymous chroniclers at the beginning of the demolition and regarded as one of the omens of the evil to come.

II

Something was missing, although she couldn't put her finger on what it was: the first member of the Torres household to become aware of it was Carmela, while getting out her mistress's mourning clothes. They had spent the last year stored in an oak chest in the General's Room – so called on account of the equestrian portrait of the beheaded hero of the battle of Tetouan, which had come to rest there after a lengthy pilgrimage: on the death of the general's widow, the soldier, his horse and the swarm of Moors that the unknown painter had squeezed in round his charger had been shifted from wall to wall through the entire mansion and were finally banished to the secluded room in the west wing where the maids went just once a year for the funeral garments. These garments were kept in an impeccable state; their severity, redolent of catafalques and obsequies, was offset by the silky light in the bedroom, full of the autumnal ochres that filtered in through the curtains. On this front, the maid wasn't too concerned, although her mistress was always capable of behaving unpredictably. What really annoyed her was the prospect of having to dress her. Each year that passed, this operation became more of a nuisance, and not just because of the strictly sartorial problems which came to light when her mistress stood in front of the dressing-room mirror and had to admit that her clothes were rather tight, when in fact they were bursting at the seams with the effort of holding in her considerable bulk. This gave her an excuse to vent her anger and shout loud enough to exorcize the legion of ghosts that always appeared at anniversary celebrations. The ageing maid guessed that the ceremony would be even worse than usual. The symptoms preceding the anniversary had been more worrying than on previous occasions: the demolition of the houses on Ferryboat Wharf had left the liquorice-extract factory surrounded by debris. This debris foreshadowed the fate of the whole building, which had been shut down many years previously, when the fall of France to the Germans in the Second World War spelt disaster for the French importers and the collapse of the business. Thirty years had elapsed since then and the immense factory now stood in isolation; its empty bays were silent and the huge yard, where rust was destroying the pergola covered in dead vines, was a barren waste. Yet even so, it was a symbol of the family's power and Carlota could not bear to see decay encroaching on its walls. Francesc Romaguera's presence in the town had deepened her irritability. She had been hoping in vain that he would visit her, although nothing would make her dream of letting on, particularly to the harpies who sat in her lounge of an afternoon and never stopped reminding her on every possible occasion that her former lover was back. As she nibbled her biscuits, Nàsia Palau claimed untruthfully to have seen him in Church Square. Teresa Solanes capped Nàsia's fib with another, stating bold as brass that Francesc Romaguera had greeted her in the Carrer Major. And even though Isadora Rubió went further than the rest, she was no competition for Estefania d'Albera, who topped the whole web of invention with an alleged conversation on Bakers Hill. Carmela was on a knife-edge. All this spiteful gossip was having a bad effect on her mistress. In spite of her apparent nonchalance and strong character, the remarks about Francesc were undermining her. So long as her former lover was in town, she would jump if there was any noise on the stairs or a knock at the door; when Sofia or Teresa went to open up, she would follow them impatiently and prick up her ears. Romaguera never once appeared on the landing bathed in the diffuse light that shone through the skylight and softened the green of the household plants. When Carmela finally decided to inform her that Francesc had left town after sorting out the details of the sale of his family home, empty since the end of the Civil War and soon to be demolished, all hell was let loose. The house became unbearable and the slightest little thing would trigger off a storm of anger and abuse.

The feeling that something was missing hit old Carmela again and drove all thoughts of Romaguera from her mind. She uneasily checked through the funeral clothes but everything was in order. She picked up the outfit to take it to her mistress's room, and it was as she was crossing the hall that the tick of the grandfather clock made her realize what was unsettling her. To confirm her suspicions, she went to one of the balconies on the north side of the house, overlooking Juniper Square, a square dominated by the church clocktower. She hadn't been mistaken: the hands on the clock – "the mileometer of death", as Horaci Planes called it – had stopped at half past eleven; that feeling of something missing had been caused by not hearing the siren, which was synchronized with the clock to sound at one p.m. Carmela didn't know then that it would never be repaired, that from then on, its immobile hands would preside over the period of the destructions. A premonition did however momentarily flicker within her as she looked at the weathercock on top of the belfry, which showed a north wind stirring up the dust from the recently demolished buildings near Ferryboat Wharf.

The siren had been installed at the outbreak of the war to warn of rebel aircraft. When the town fell into Fascist hands, it warned of Republican planes. After the war, someone had the idea of using it to sound at one o'clock, the time that the miners knocked off for lunch. Synchronized with the church clock, it had always been punctual since then and caused the neighbourhood dogs to howl mournfully: they would lift up their heads and join in the wailing. And thus it was – Honorat del Rom maintained many years later in the Quayside Café – that what started off as a harbinger of death and destruction, driving people to take cover inside the mines, was transformed over the years into a stimulant of the town's appetite; mouths started watering as people subconsciously associated the siren's wail with their midday meal.

Carlota was unaware of her maid's foreboding that the clock had stopped for good. In her mind, the siren was linked to the day that the Torres family returned to the town after the Civil War. That memory briefly displaced the recollections that had been evoked by the anniversary of her father's funeral.

The military car jolted over all the bumps in the road, which was scarcely more than a track of tamped-down earth covered in gravel. Both the driver, an Andalusian corporal with a tattoo on his right forearm (a heart and dagger with drops of blood and a woman's name), and the passengers, Senyor Jaume de Torres and his daughter, exhausted and soaked in perspiration, lurched forward whenever the wheels got stuck in a pothole or bumped over a rut and made the car's suspension judder. The truck which had also been placed at the family's disposal by an infantry colonel (a former classmate of Senyor Jaume de Torres and his companion on visits to the city's brothels) was following them, laden with trunks and suitcases. Carmela was sitting with the mistress's eldest daughter on her lap, next to the driver, a sallow, clean-shaven lad, somewhat intimidated by the surliness of the maid, who was even more unbending than her employers. The landscape became less bleak once they left the uplands and turned off the main road. They were within sight of Fraga, which could just be glimpsed beyond the fields dotted with fig-trees, nestling among the hills of clay. The harsh, dry light of the empty wastes of the Monegros plateau which they had been crossing since Saragossa gave way to the misty atmosphere of the Cinca valley. Everything was swathed in a fine blue-grey film. The vehicle drove away from the village of Torrent de Cinca, silent among its irrigated fields; a little beyond the confluence of the Cinca and the Segre, following the course of the latter – a gleaming thread that wound its way through burning white pebbles – they crossed the town boundary. The castle rose up in the distance; everything looked dead. There wasn't a soul to be seen in the Soler mine; the black lignite had almost vanished again under the flesh-coloured ochres and the warm brown of the earth. Senyor Jaume ordered the car to stop at the Lluïsa mine, which belonged to the family as did two more by the Ebro. Derailed trucks were lying on the overgrown ballast, the stables had been bombed and all that remained of the smithy was a scattering of scorched bricks and a piece of wall holding a windowframe that looked out on to a scene of desolation. They were burning brushwood on the other side of the embankment and a gust of wind enveloped the vehicles in a pall of acrid smoke. The passengers started to choke, so Senyor Jaume gave the order to drive on. The wind from the Ebro blew away the mist, revealing the midday sun and making the panorama look harsher. An eagle circled slowly high in the sky. On the next bend they saw the remains of an army lorry which had overturned: the heap of burnt, twisted iron looked like the skeleton of a strange animal left to rot instead of being laid to rest beneath the parched earth.

As they drove through olive- and almond-groves towards their journey's end, fury was replacing the sadness that Carlota de Torres had felt the previous day when they had dropped the two boys at the Jesuit boarding school in Saragossa, where the older one had been a pupil prior to 1936. Once the Francoist troops had taken the town, they had spent the rest of the war in Valladolid with the parents-in-law of her brother Ramon. The long year she spent there had been plagued by constant homesickness, which reached its peak on the death of her mother. She suffered from intense loneliness when her mother, who had been ill for some time, died shortly after reaching the capital of Castile. Senyora Adelina de Camps passed away full of concern for her sons, both of them second lieutenants serving at the front in the Fascist army, and for her son-in-law, who was stationed at a supply depot at the rear, thanks to the intervention of the colonel, a friend of Senyor Jaume's. Ignorant as she was of military matters, the poor lady imagined that this entailed the same amount of danger as the front line, an opinion reinforced by Hipòlit's heroic letters. How different her last days would have been in the town – her daughter often complained when she secretly unburdened herself to Carmela – with a houseful of friends and relations! And the tiny procession that accompanied her to the cemetery would have been unthinkable back home, where people were generous when it came to expressing their grief and everyone stopped work to attend funerals!

Near the town, the vehicles skimmed past the builder Bakunin de Planes and showered him in dust. He reacted with resignation and even tried not to cough too loudly. He hadn't recognized the passengers but the fact that they were in a car, and an army one at that, was enough for his common sense to warn him not to behave in a way that could be taken as a protest which, coming from someone with such a suspicious name, would automatically be considered subversive. The builder had problems enough that morning. If the proclamation of the Republic on 14 April 1931 brought any joy at all to Bakunin de Planes (who knew nothing whatever of politics and didn't want to, because it made his head reel), it was the task he was assigned by the new mayor who had taken over from Sadurní Romaguera: to knock down the wall that divided the graves in the town cemetery into two sections, segregating those whom the Church considered unfit for hallowed ground in a part that was reached through a side gate in the wall and was bitterly termed the "backyard" by the townsfolk. When Bakunin de Planes started work on it the very next day, he broke out in goose pimples. Under the gaze of Jeremies the gravedigger, who leant against the marble door of the Salleres family vault in the meagre shade of a cypress-tree and chatted as he smoked his sooty, foul-smelling pipe (whose yellowish stem Honorat del Cafè, when still alive, swore was made of a dead man's bone), the builder took a mallet and knocked down the wall surrounding the tombs of the damned. As he did so, he was ridding himself of a sense of anguish that had been weighing on him for a long time. This sense vanished once he saw the stone on his father's grave through the hole in the wall. As well as Bakunin, the old Anarchist had fathered a Germinal, a Felicitat and a Perfecte but he never married in church and when he died in 1928 the rector wouldn't allow him to be buried in holy ground. As a public sinner, his remains were interred in the "backyard" between Octavi Oliver, a romantic doctor who had blown a hole in his head with a pistol after an unhappy love affair, and Libori d'Escarp, a one-time captain on the Camps' boats and the founder of a new religion which, at the time of the visionary's death, had three followers – an innkeeper from Miravet, a cobbler from Ascó and a Tortosa prostitute who, without the spiritual guidance of their master, split up into rival sects which finally collapsed in confusion. Other stones without crosses on them marked the graves of unbaptized infants, a Protestant and a few suicides. In one corner, an epitaph in French composed by Madamfranswah and engraved on a small marble plaque on the wall (*Je m'en fous du Pape*) sat over the grave of a chorus girl from the Eden who had died of typhoid in 1917. Once he had finished demolishing the wall, the builder furtively wiped away a tear: his father and the other souls buried in that ignominious spot were finally the equals of the rest.

But that midday in 1939, Bakunin's heart was heavy once more with the sorrow that the proclamation of the Republic had lifted. After the vehicles transporting the Torres i Camps family back home had coated him in dust, he walked down the hill from the cemetery, which stood among the silent olive-groves on the outskirts of town. The priest – the first one they had had since the Civil War – had sent him there to rebuild the wall which he had knocked down a few years past. He could still hear the words of the gravedigger, who watched him from the shade of the same cypress as he placed the last brick.

"You've packed them off to hell again, Bakunin. But don't go fretting yourself about it; they're better off down there with the devil than we are with Franco."

When the vehicles entered the town through the Segre Gate and began the climb to the Town Hall Square, Carlota de Torres was overwhelmed by the sensation of being back home after so many months as an outsider in Castile: she was herself again, she felt confident, she had recovered her authority. But hand in hand with her relief, the hatred that distance had kept at bay re-emerged in all its fury. She relived the humiliation, the anguish, the constant fear, which had stalked them until the arrival of the Francoist troops, of ending up like Sadurní Romaguera. They drove along dead streets where most of the shops were shut, but when they reached the Plaça d'Armes, the group that was assembled in front of the mansion to welcome them home was proof that everything was back as it should be. As the car braked, Carlota de Torres glanced at the people who had been waiting for them since mid-morning, when Graells received the telegram from Senyor Jaume in Saragossa to say that they were on their way home. Standing alongside the old faithfuls, whom Graells had gathered together and now headed, the entire membership of the Casino de la Roda had turned out, but no representative of the Romaguera family. The vehicles stopped in front of the entrance to the mansion. Ramon Graells was overcome with emotion: he drew away from the group and, in a theatrical and solicitous move, went to open the car door first for Senyor Jaume and then for Carlota. From the arms of the administrator, who had never been treated so effusively by his employers before – nor would be again – the travellers passed to those of Doctor Beltran. The good doctor – the most effective killer of the town's inhabitants since the cholera epidemic of 1885, as Honorat del Rom was to say in later years – had proclaimed himself a staunch Republican and made passionate speeches against the rebellious soldiers, yet he was the first to greet them warmly at the gates of the town. The pompous, blustering doctor came out with the same empty phrases which

148

he had used to welcome home other members of the gentry, and he was just about to embrace the powerful body of Carlota de Torres, which he had always secretly lusted after, when the hands on the church clock reached one and the deafening wail of the siren burst forth.

Years later, the event was discussed in the Quayside Café and the most reliable and complete account of it came from Anselm de Rius, who had witnessed it all firsthand. According to the grocer, who had a good view of the square from the door of his establishment, the first person to start running with a scream of "The planes, the planes!" was Carmela, followed by Senyor Jaume shouting, "Help, help! The reds!" and Carlota de Torres crying, "To the shelter!" The rest of those present followed suit; although now used to the new function of the siren, its wail was still inextricably linked in their minds to bombs falling, and they too ran off in all directions like angry hens, infected by the travellers' fear. Among those who fled was the skinny, moustached Civil Guard sergeant, whose panic not only ruined the salute he had been intending to give the family, but forced him to seek refuge in Anselm de Rius' grocery. In his blind terror, the brave guardian of the law tripped over a crate of tomatoes and fell headlong into a pile of salt cod which was virtually the only item on display in the gastronomic wasteland of the shop.

As the grocer feared, this heroic action led to a barrage of insults, accusations of black-marketeering and threats hurled at him from the sergeant, in a vain attempt to shift the blame for this ridiculous situation, while he dusted the salt off his uniform and extracted his three-cornered hat from the drum of pickled sardines. And consequently, Anselm de Rius wasn't able to see the group reform in the square or witness the travellers' bad-tempered entrance into their family home.

Carlota's irritability marred the first tour of inspection although Carmela, who had got over the shock of the siren by now, dismissed every one of her mistress's complaints about the state of the house as clearly unfounded: during their masters' absence the Graells family had done their job well and everything was gleaming. The mistress's attitude was all the more surprising since she had never cared about these things before. Suddenly, halfway through an argument over the portrait of the general's widow, which the mistress said was dusty and the maid said wasn't, Carmela understood the underlying, maybe subconscious reason behind this inspection and took note of it: now that Senyora Adelina was dead and buried in a faraway grave, Carlota de Torres was taking possession of the house. Her intuition was amply confirmed over the next few days. Carlota's attitude didn't betoken a lust for power kept in check during the life of her mother, whom she treated with all the tenderness she was capable of; no, it was simply that Carlota de Torres was taking over from her. While Senyor Jaume began to put his affairs in order, to visit the mines that were now back in his hands after the wartime collectivization, and to try to get them producing coal again, Carlota received her visitors beneath her father's portrait in the Hall of the Martyred Virgins. The ladies would go there every afternoon: this was the time of triumph, the time of security regained and the suspicious post-war hot chocolate served by two new maids who were still rather clumsy. They had replaced Adelaida and Veronica, who left the house for good shortly after the rebellion (Adelaida in silence and Veronica shouting, "Long live Anarchism!" and calling for the heads of her employers as she walked down the great staircase). Carlota de Torres learnt what had been going on during her long time away: the pregnancy of Senyoreta Soler and her hasty marriage to the infantry lieutenant who had seduced her in a tower of the castle after the Francoist occupation; the absence of any news about Aleix de Segarra and Malena, whom nobody had heard anything of since the evacuation; the townspeople who had died, those who had crossed to France, those confined in concentration camps or locked up in prison waiting to be court-martialled. Most afternoons, the local headmistress – a moth-eaten, bossy old hag who attended Mass every day and harboured unmentionable feelings towards her pretty young charges – recalled how sad the town had been to hear the sorry news of the death of Senyora Adelina de Camps in Valladolid and repeated every single detail of the funeral mass said for the eternal salvation of the good lady by the army chaplain. An extremely elegant lieutenant colonel, a house guest of the Alberas, had conducted the ceremony, which was very moving, although, said the schoolmarm – unaware of the drop of hot chocolate that always got caught on the hairs on her chin, and matched the wart on her nose – the aroma of incense hadn't quite blotted out the smell of petrol which reminded them that the Republicans had turned the church into a garage after they had stripped it of its altars, images and ornaments, and burnt or thrown them into the Ebro when war broke out.

At night, the faint light cast by the street-lamps made little impression on the darkness, which served as a cover for all sorts of comings and goings. This was when her other visitors came to see her. While her father was with his friends at the Casino de la Roda, Carlota de Torres would take pleasure in exacting revenge on those women who swallowed their pride and went to ask her help in getting their husbands, brothers, fathers, sons or fiancés out of prison or the concentration camps. She didn't offer them a seat: if they wanted favours from her, they had to stand, and they never left without experiencing the bitter taste of mortification. But the people Carlota de Torres was waiting for most anxiously didn't appear, which made her tremble with fury. She often looked down from the balcony of the hall at the large deserted square and the café tables empty of customers and thought that that was where they should have shot Sebastià Noguera, the late Arquimedes Quintana's son-in-law, and the rest of the townspeople who had had the effrontery to try to make the revolution, to confiscate and collectivize the mines, lands and factories of the ruling class (particularly those of the Torres family) and subvert the immutable order of the world.

The war had hurt Carlota de Torres even more deeply than she let on in her blistering tirades against her evening visitors: it had robbed her forever of Francesc Romaguera. The Torres family were in Castile when he came back in the company of von Müller, but she knew what he had done: accuse the town's gentry of treachery and complicity with the Reds. They hadn't physically taken up arms to kill his father, but they had sold him, dangling him as a bait in front of the murderous hordes in order to save their own skins. Someone, maybe Carlota's father-in-law, Gelabert de Móra, had retorted that there had been nothing they could do and that they had been lucky enough to escape the mass executions. And when he raised the old question of whether the real motive for the crime was revenge for Arnau Terrer's death, Francesc's shouts put the fear of God into the timid members of the Casino de la Roda. What a bunch of cowards they were! If only they had behaved like real men at the proper time, things would never have gone that far. A bunch of cowards and hypocrites: for hadn't they benefited from the fear that Arnau Terrer's death had instilled among the miners? Carlota knew it all, starting with the insults that Francesc had flung against her father – "that chicken-hearted coward holed up in Valladolid" – and herself – "his slut of a daughter". Harsh, unkind words, but she was prepared to forget them in return for hearing Carmela's discreet tap at her bedroom door one more time and seeing Francesc's face behind the maid. However, her lover was never to walk down those long nocturnal corridors again and Carlota would never smell his semen on the rumpled sheets. She only saw him once, almost straight after her return from Valladolid, when the lawyer visited the town to collect his mother and elder brother and take them to live with him in Madrid. In spite of the begging messages she sent to the Romaguera home via Carmela, Francesc didn't come. She stood in despair and spied on him from her attic windows as the sailing barge they were leaving on drew away from the Town Square Wharf. She stared after the ship until it disappeared down the Ebro and faded into the distance as though entering the grave. When she went down again to the drawing-room, her eyes red from weeping, she saw her father listening anxiously to the radio: Hitler's army had just invaded Poland.

III

In the summer of 1939, the blast from the siren didn't merely send the Torres family and their entourage scurrying round the Plaça d'Armes; it also interrupted Senyora Salleres' new administrator in mid-speech.

This was the second hiccup in his carefully devised plan. The first had ruined the impression that the former clerk had been hoping to make when his visitor walked into the room. The doorbell would ring; the maid, who was against the whole farce but well rehearsed, would go and open the door, tell him to wait as if she didn't know him and then announce him. After a deliberately long time, he would be ushered in. The administrator would position himself in such a way that the sun shone into his visitor's eyes, thereby flustering him and robbing him of any remaining shred of self-confidence. At first it had all gone according to plan; but how could anyone have foreseen what Rem, the mistress's gun-dog would do? The maid opened the study door, he took up position, with his back to the balcony, ready to impress the new arrival, and then in ran the dog, barking rapturously, and jumped up and licked Nelson all over his face.

The furious administrator caught an ironic smile flickering across the maid's face as she managed to remove the dog. He was just striking a stern pose for the second time prior to launching into the speech he had rehearsed in front of the bathroom mirror when the blessed siren ruined his plans yet again.

The noise of the siren, on top of the yelps emerging from the room where the dog had been confined, forced the administrator to abandon his monologue, which had been intended as a preamble to a eulogy of the new era. Nelson looked at him from the other side of the table in disgust and contempt. He had spotted straight off the sort of welcome the cretin had in store for him. It came as no surprise. The five days he had been back had given him a good idea of how things stood; he had had a taste of it at the railway station at Faió when someone from the town had pretended not to see them getting off the train. It was the same story on the ferry: the only people to dare say hello were the Garrigues lad, who ferried them across, and a cousin of his wife's. The other passengers, in the main peasants on their way home from working in the fields, cut them dead; they were too scared to speak to someone who, for all they knew, might land them in an awkward situation. Their behaviour had been depressing enough, but the sight of the ruined bridge was the final straw. When they had fled on board the *Neptune* packed with fugitives in March 1938, the explosion had been a distant blast, a brief red gleam in the black waters. Now he could see the consequences next to the ferry crossing: mutilated supports jutting out amid debris and rusted iron struts from the water, intensely green on that summer's morning. It had taken just one day to put back the clock by many years. And now that the ferry which had lain idle for so long had replaced the bridge, it seemed to be transporting them to the darkness of the past. They came ashore in a town gripped by fear, a town full of evasive eyes that reflected the nervousness created by people such as Senyora Salleres' new administrator, a jumped-up office boy and self-styled anti-Fascist, who had just been outsmarted by a dog. The hound – the widow's constant companion on her visits to the mines, an inveterate sailor on board the *Neptune* and a friend of the crew – was one of the few to greet him unreservedly.

Thrown off his stride by the siren, the new incumbent of the widow's bed – "the carboniferous ponce" as Honorat del Rom would later refer to him in the Quayside Café – made a second attempt to look imposing and authoritarian with his ridiculous little Franco-style moustache, his hair smarmed down with lashings of brilliantine and his flabby features. All in vain: his imperial air was nothing but an absurd, pretentious grimace.

The outcome of the interview didn't become public knowledge until some time later, when one of the maids talked out of turn. Estanislau Corbera had been told all about it by Nelson in person and seeing that the captain himself said nothing, he felt that he must intervene in order to dispel the malicious rumours being circulated by the hot-chocolate brigade from the Hall of the Martyred Virgins. And so it was that the town learnt that neither the first punch, which lifted the administrator out of his chair and sent him crashing against his office bookshelf, nor the second one, which loosened a couple of his teeth, nor those that would have continued to rain down on him had the maids not been alerted by the hulla-baloo and his feeble screams and come rushing at the double, were the result of an altercation between Nelson and the pen-pusher over who should bed the widow. What made the captain's blood boil was the collaborator's scathing reference to the townspeople who had died in the war and in particular to the death sentence that a court martial had just passed on Sebastià Noguera.

"If they hadn't pulled me off him, I'd have killed the filthy bastard," he confessed the same day to Estanislau. And the café proprietor, who was still working hard to repair the damage before he could open his establishment, worriedly shook his head and poured the boatman a glass of rum from one of the bottles hidden away in the cellar which had escaped the keen attention of the pillagers.

"You and your friends lost, Nelson, and a loser can't afford to go round punching administrators' teeth out, especially one who was on the winning side," the widow told him the next day after sending a servant to fetch him. "He'll keep quiet this time. I've made it plain that if there's any trouble I'll give him his marching orders. For the moment, we can be pretty sure he'll keep his mouth shut, not least because it's blown up like a balloon. You really let him have it and no mistake! When I saw all that blood, I thought you'd finished him off . . . Relax, keep your wits about you. I don't want to lose my best captain just when I need him most. There's been enough disaster! I don't care about the past. You collectivized the coalfield, you staged your revolution, but you didn't do us any harm and I don't want to hurt anyone. I want to open up the mines as soon as possible and I couldn't care less if the men digging out the coal are reds or blacks, they've all got to eat. Now do what you were telling me about. And later on we'll talk about building the barges we need to start transporting lignite."

These words came back to him as he journeyed down the Ebro on the widow's own private launch. He had chosen his fellow sailors in direct consultation with her, so as to avoid problems with the snivelling administrator, who skulked all day in his office for fear of people seeing his black eye and puffed-up cheeks. The widow only balked at one name, that of Tomàs de Xerta, who used to work as a captain for Torres i Camps, and who always referred to her in the cafés as "the old floozie from Rudder Street". Nelson argued that Tomàs was a good captain and that later on he could be entrusted with commanding a barge, which she knew to be true, so she gave in without making a fuss. All she said was, "Tell him he can call me a floozie as often as he likes. But if he wants to sail on my ships, he'd better not call me old."

Tomàs de Xerta had been out of work since he left the concentration camp. Those who had been politically active during the Civil War were generally ostracized and Senyora Salleres' attitude was the exception. The firm of Torres i Camps was ruthless in its thirst for revenge, in most cases because of Carlota, who, hand in glove with Ramon Graells, hired and fired behind Senyor Jaume's back. Now that he was rid of his wife and had the excuse of setting the firm on its feet again, he redoubled his business trips to the city and eschewed matters such as these, which were in any case not nearly so urgent as the alluring blonde he kept in Lleida.

Crammed into the boat, far too small for the five of them and their tools, they sailed along a sluggish Ebro. The water flowed indifferently past the silent landscape of empty trenches, rusted wires, ruined houses, land ploughed up by bombs. All that obstinacy and death, thought Nelson, hadn't altered its course: it rose with the autumn and spring rains and receded with the summer heat, but the waters had no memory of the battle. Memory was a human affair; the river, the Ebro, was a force insensitive to the troubles of the folk who fished in it, cut through it with the keels of their boats or met their death in its cold, muddy depths.

They kept quiet as though they still had the eyes of the sergeant and his two men on them. The Civil Guards had arrived out of the blue as dawn was breaking over the deserted wharves: the boat had just been launched and they were loading ropes, pulleys and tools. They had no option but to give a detailed account of what they were doing, under the suspicious gaze of the police. Nelson could feel the sergeant's inquisitorial eyes trying to pierce his thoughts. He knew he was a dangerous brute who openly regretted the fact that the townsfolk hadn't committed atrocities against their employers and the right-wingers because then he could have enjoyed taking his revenge and executing the vermin who worked in the local pits – as dangerous, so he said, as the miners from Asturias. It was his obsession when he interrogated people returning from the work camps and prisons; it infuriated him to find nothing that would justify his blood-lust. He wasn't after murderers, simply the losers of a war they hadn't even started themselves and which had caused the deaths of so many of them. And then would come the shouts, the blows, the beatings, night after night when the patrols cleared the streets after curfew. Nelson had to prove where they were off to with the boat, and take him to the widow's house. The mistress was woken by her maids and saying, "What does the fool want?" she unceremoniously sent the Civil Guard packing.

The guards, furious at the gaffe they had made with the Senyora, who they knew had influence in the capital – a relative of hers occupied an important ministerial post – observed them as the boat, a blue shadow etched against the orange sun, drew away from the bank. Luckily they didn't catch, or maybe didn't understand, Tomàs de Xerta's muttered words as they started rowing: "Back in 1936 they weren't so fond of throwing their weight about . . ."

The boatman's words met with grunts of approval from the others. They alluded to the stance taken by the town's guards when the military rebellion broke out in Africa in July 1936. The garrison was cut off from the area headquarters and the guards remained inside the barracks with their families, not knowing which way to turn. The townspeople surrounded the barracks and, tired of waiting, informed them that they must either reach a decision straight away or else let the women and children out because they were going to blow the building up. "A spontaneous demonstration of their loyalty," was how Honorat del Cafè sarcastically described the Civil Guards' ardent support for the government which was manifested the moment they saw preparations being made to dynamite the building, and which inspired them to emerge from the barracks shouting, "Long live the Republic!" By now these cheers had turned to harsh reprisals: the evidence lay before Nelson in the bow of the boat where Joanet del Pla's left cheek was swollen from a blow he had been landed from a rifle-butt for not standing to attention in the café while the national anthem was being played on the radio.

The captain had something else on his mind. It was troubling him the entire journey down the glinting river, amid a silence broken only by the occasional remarks of his companions and the muffled sounds that wafted across from the bank. He started to feel that they would never arrive. The endless expanses of near stagnant water seemed to go on for ever. His anxiety came to a head at Horseshoe Island where in July 1936 they had found some of the religious statues flung into the water from the riverside villages, and which from then on was known as Thirteen Saints Island (the anonymous enumerator casually throwing in one devil and three angels). The statues had gone: at the outbreak of the war, the crew of the *Christopher Columbus* from the Vallcorna mine had amused themselves by standing them upright along the edge of the islet and there they stayed until a Fascist plane, attracted by the September sunlight reflecting off the polychrome of their uncannily stationary enemies, strafed them and smashed them to smithereens. The great flood of 1937 swept away their remains for good, but the name stuck forever.

Nelson didn't relax until they reached a poplar-shaded backwater; motionless in its green depths he saw the outline of the *Neptune*. Many hours later, after much hard work, the pulleys dragged the boat out of the opaque swirling waters, and when he saw it he nearly burst into tears. He and his crew had secretly scuttled the barge in March 1938 after landing the fugitives at the railway station at Móra. They had joined the exodus fleeing from the Fascists to the hinterland of Catalonia, but his thoughts had often turned to the barge. After numerous dramatic adventures, he, his wife and their youngest son had ended up in a tiny flat in the Barcelona suburb of Gràcia, where his spirits reached rock-bottom. The city was in chaos, his family had broken up – his eldest son was fighting at the front and his pregnant daughter-in-law had gone with one of the groups of refugees from the town to live with her parents in Figueres – and he was tormented by thoughts of the distant river and the *Neptune* hidden away in the depths of the side-stream. He spent long hours brooding at the bar run by Carlota de Torres' half-sister, the Cafè del Sol, where he would go when he clocked off from the munitions factory where the union had found him work. During the battle of the Ebro, he thought the boat must be lost; it seemed impossible for it to have survived the fighting unscathed: its hiding-place was safe but it was in the heart of the battle zone. That morning, as he watched it emerge safe and sound, Nelson recovered his reason for living, he was himself again in spite of the disaster.

Ever since its launch, the *Neptune* had been a part of Nelson, the ship's one and only captain: the coal-blackened vessel was an extension of the sailor's own muscles, brain and nerves. Through the creaking of its timbers, the vibrations of its hull and the way it slid through the water, he came to understand the Ebro, to forge a mysterious link with it which Honorat del Rom described graphically when he said that Nelson had a bow for a breast-bone and a tiller for a cock.

They cleaned off the mud and inspected the hull. The boat's stay underwater had helped keep it in good condition. The only thing to have suffered was the paint on the sides of its prow which had become loosened in the water and been partly chipped off during the rescue and clean-up. The top coat, applied at the outbreak of the war, was flaking off and revealed fragments of the letters of the vessel's original name painted by Aleix de Segarra and repainted each year during the summer inspection of the barges. Unless you'd known it was there, you could never have pieced together the puzzle and sorted out the patches of blue from the red and the dirty white surrounding them, to come up with the name of the god Neptune; after a Jupiter and a Mars this was the name Senyora Salleres had chosen to continue the mythological sequence which began at the time of the Great War with the short-lived *Polyphemus*. In the wake of the changes brought about by the Civil War and the collectivization of the mines, the *Jupiter* became the *Lenin*, the *Mars* was transformed into the *Liberty*, and the *Neptune* had had a skimpy coat of white paint daubed over its name and an enthusiastic though none too skilful shipwright had traced in red the name of Karl Marx.

This was the second time that the barge had been saved from destruction, as though fate had decreed that it should see the town through all its ups and downs. The first time was in 1937, a few months after the army had requisitioned most of the barges to construct a pontoon at Gelsa near Saragossa during the Republican offensive on the capital of Aragon. Apart from those that were needed to transport lignite from the collectivized mines, the remaining barges were taken to Faió; there the military pontoniers raised them out of the water and loaded them on to trains. One after the other, the convoys of boats left for the front amidst billows of thick, acrid smoke. Nelson went to hand over the *Karl Marx* and two other barges from the mines once owned by Senyora Salleres and now controlled by the General Union of Workers. On his return he became very morose. He was given another barge but was never happy sailing it: the tiller wasn't the sort he was used to, the mast didn't suit him, and the sails weren't to his liking . . . And he didn't have his old crew. Atanasi Resurrecció was at the front fighting as a volunteer with the Komsomol brigade; Joanet del Pla had been called up, as had the mule-driver . . . His thoughts often turned to the *Neptune–Karl Marx* chained up to the pontoon near Saragossa and this made him feel even worse. His black mood only lifted when his eldest son came home on leave. But when the lad went back, his spirits plummeted again as he took him down on the barge to the station at Faió. On the homeward journey, though, he was galvanized into action by the first hint of the disaster that was to come. The full force of the squall hit them in the Canota valley; all of a sudden a terrifying wind sprung up, the sky blackened and the heavens opened. It was all over in a quarter of an hour; the clouds scudded off downstream, leaving the sky intensely blue. The skipper was nonetheless filled with a deep feeling of unease and hurried the mule along the towpath. He sensed the menace of the river, a strange flutter in the ship's keel. The second squall caught them at the confluence of the Segre and the Ebro alongside the first houses; they tied up at the Widows' Wharf in a downpour. In the stables the animals were straining at their halters and braying with fear; the old stableman, as foul-mouthed as usual – "it's all the fault of those fucking Fascists" – was trying in vain to calm them down. The black gale blew this second squall away too. But as Nelson and his men were walking up from the wharf, darkness closed in on the town; it was the beginning of the disaster.

The rain came lashing down with an intensity never seen before in this dry land where, except for the lush vegetation that grew in the places where the Arabs had built irrigation channels, the arrival of spring could only be inferred from the tiny flowers that appeared on the aromatic herbs, the burst of almond-blossom, or the subtle shifts in tone of the intense ochres and dusty greens of the landscape. By day a blazing sun burnt in the sky; by night it poured non-stop. The two rivers both began to swell, the noise was deafening. The waters rose and rose, higher than the marks left behind by previous record floods, and the streets in the lower part of the town were awash. Houses had to be abandoned, animals were taken from their stables. The Ebro flooded the cellars of the Quayside Café and the two Honorats sailed round in a canoe inside the Venus Cinema, Theatre and Dance-hall, which was now a lake where only the dress-circle boxes stood out above the water. In Gelsa, many kilometres upstream, the flood broke through the military bridge, swept the boats away and destroyed most of them; the debris got caught up with dead animals and uprooted trees and floated down the ochre-stained waters past the horror-stricken town. When the rivers subsided several days later, somebody remarked that two boats had run aground by a poplar-grove near the Lliberola Gorge. Nelson was dispatched to see if they were worth salvaging. He went on foot up the right bank, skirting the fields that still lay underwater, shimmering like mirrors. As he neared the place where they had run aground, he suddenly knew what he would find; once there, there was no need for him to scramble down to the river full of driftwood and rotting objects to know that one of the mud-covered hulls, still joined by the chains of the pontoon, was the *Neptune*.

On that occasion the barge had sailed once more for a buoyant town that still believed in victory; in 1939 it emerged from the river into a world of losers. Of its crew only he and Joanet del Pla were left. The mule-driver had died at the front; Atanasi Resurrecció was never to return from exile in France.

In his whole life Nelson would never forget that journey on board the *Neptune*. With no animals to tow it upstream, the men had to drag it as in the olden days along an overgrown towpath which in some places had been obliterated by the fighting. They stumbled over barbed wire and trenches, had to watch out for unexploded bombs and shells, and twice had to show their papers and be subjected to interrogation by the Civil Guards from the villages en route, who were watching for people on the run or in hiding.

They didn't tie up at the wharf but took the boat straight to the shipyard on the right bank, next to the ferry landing-stage. Three weeks later it came out freshly caulked with a brand new mast, sails in mint condition and a different name; its brief existence as the *Karl Marx* had ended and the old *Neptune* was now the *Virgin of Carmel*, a name much more in tune with the winds blowing down the river since Franco's victory than its previous ones. This trend was best exemplified by the Bishop's new boat which its captain, who had made a timely move to the Fascist zone when war broke out, had christened with the pontifical name of *Pius XII*.

As Honorat del Rom remarked several years later, in the course of a lively discussion at the Quayside Café on the conversion of the barges to National Catholicism, the first meeting between the *Virgin of Carmel* and *Pius XII* was none too successful. To put it bluntly, it didn't come to blows simply because of the providential arrival of a train from Barcelona. The Bishop was standing in the prow of his boat, sporting more medals than ever on his chest – as he kept adding those of the legion of virgins and saints whose miraculous appearances all over the place had multiplied since the Fascist victory – and he had begun to preach to the workmen shovelling coal nearby. Joanet del Pla uttered a blasphemy on banging his foot, at which the Bishop, bursting with righteous indignation and with the scrap iron clanking on his chest, reprimanded them all and exhorted them to repent and seek forgiveness. Seeing their lack of interest, he decided to skip the bullshit about forgiveness: he flew off the handle and began insulting them, calling them Red bastards, filthy brutes . . .

Malena de Segarra never knew that her presence on the quay at Faió that day averted a disaster. Nelson had had just about enough of the Bishop's abuse and was making for the gangplank of the *Pius XII*; his coal-covered face was distorted with anger as he muttered, "you priest-loving traitor, you son of a whore, you Fascist shit". He was poised to give the preacher a bloody nose when the sight of her and her maid, weighed down with bags and cases, stopped him in his tracks. The men had laid down their tools to grab hold of him and stop him boarding the barge when they saw him halt at the bottom of the gangplank and suddenly walk over towards two women who had just appeared on the path from the station between the heaps of coal.

That night, the captain's wife cross-examined him: was it true that Malena de Segarra had lost her looks? Had she tried in vain to get into France after the war because she had heard that Aleix, whom she had waited for in vain in Barcelona, was in Paris? Had she burst into tears as they passed the convent on the way to her house with her luggage? But Nelson reacted noncommittally, giving monosyllabic answers to the barrage of questions. He had been profoundly shaken by the vision of Malena de Segarra on the quayside at Faió. It had stirred up many intimate memories and his wife's prattle irritated him. He was concerned about Aleix since nobody had had any news of him since the evacuation, but his great respect for Malena had stopped him from raising the subject with her. The sails had billowed out in the strong southwesterly wind on the journey up from Faió and the two women had sat in front of him on a seat that he had rigged up so that the coal-dust wouldn't dirty their clothes. Malena de Segarra was downcast and her despondency grew manifestly deeper the nearer they got to the town. Seeing the familiar landscape which he had painted so often must have made her memories of Aleix all the more poignant. After leaving Malena at the door of the Segarra home – with no sign of the tears she was rumoured to have shed, as invented as those at the convent, which she passed by quickly and with her eyes averted – Nelson was only to see her once or twice again in her life. Cooped up in the house with Anna, her faithful maid who had gone with her when she fled, she anxiously awaited news which never arrived.

That midday in 1971, old Nelson realized that the siren hadn't gone off and, like Carmela, he sensed that the church clock had stopped for good. He slowly ambled home, following the wall from the Ebro, alongside which the barges were rotting as they hadn't set sail since the beginning of the destruction of the town. After lunch, he went down to the Quayside Café with the image of Malena all those years ago still in his mind. In Stone Street, he was surprised to hear bells ringing. But they weren't marking the passage of time on the clock which had now run down forever: they were ringing for a funeral. That was odd; he hadn't heard of anyone dying. Estanislau Corbera put his mind at rest by informing him that, along with that of two personalities of universal importance, it was the twenty-first anniversary of the death of Senyor Jaume de Torres.

IV

After a suffocatingly hot siesta punctuated by the sound of the funeral knell, it was time to change for her father's memorial service and Carlota de Torres exploded with unbridled fury. She had a sacred, unshirkable duty to offer an annual Requiem Mass for the soul of her dead father but it entailed a high price: stirring up old memories of the shameful incident at the burial.

Carlota's irritation had been mounting for some time, ever since she realized that the big day was getting nearer, and it boiled over when she saw Carmela standing in the middle of the room with her mourning clothes draped over her arm. The maid knew this chain of events by heart and responded with extreme patience. There would be shouts, insults, complaints and threats and finally she would let herself be talked into getting dressed, still snorting with rage. Sure enough, after a period of time that had grown longer each year, Carlota de Torres decided to rise from her double bed. The bedstead emitted complaining creaks and the maid noticed, not for the first time, that Senyor Hipòlit had left no mark behind him. Carmela always had the impression that the mistress either slept alone or else with Francesc Romaguera – who Carmela cursed each and every day, particularly after his latest visit to the town. Hipòlit de Móra's presence between the sheets had gone almost as unnoticed as his absence, since he passed on two years earlier from a death as insignificant as himself. Nothing unusual about his death throes; he didn't go out with all guns blazing like the general's widow. Even less was his a sinful, romantic demise as Isadora Rubió described the death of the profligate Torres in the arms of Madam-franswah on the banks of the Seine. One day in September, Senyor Hipòlit de Móra simply dropped dead like a chicken caught in the wind. The chemist remarked that Dr Beltran didn't even get the chance to finish him off; the only thing the old quack could do when someone came running to inform him was to issue a certificate for the dreariest death of his long and lethal career as assistant to the Fates.

They held memorial services for Hipòlit too, but they were drab affairs and didn't rake up past grievances in the same way as Senyor Jaume's. Quite the reverse: to begin with, the Mass for her dead husband provided an excuse for bringing the children together at least once a year, even if it did mean her two daughters-in-law and her son-in-law coming too. Senyora Carlota de Torres held them responsible for her children leaving home; her elder son and her daughter had moved to Madrid with their uncles, the younger boy to Barcelona, and they rarely came back. They found the mines tedious, the river of no interest and life at the house extremely boring, unlike their mother who couldn't stand the noise and anonymity of the city. She also tried to get them to come home for their grandfather's memorial, but their numerous excuses compelled her to abandon the attempt. As on other occasions then, the bells that heralded the service for the eternal rest of Senyor Jaume de Torres echoed through a semi-deserted house where absences, both temporary and permanent, had sealed off entire corridors and rooms and reduced life to the area round the Hall of the Martyred Virgins. The hall itself was under threat from the increasingly opaque and dense silence that reigned behind the locked doors.

Nineteen seventy-one was the second year of the demolitions and the town was crumbling to pieces around Carlota. More than ever she felt oppressed by loneliness and nostalgia for her father. Standing in her dressing-room, while Carmela did her best to squeeze her into her widow's weeds, which reeked of camphor from the drawer in the general's room, she saw all the old shadows emerge from the mirror. Behind the reflection of his daughter, the whiteness of her well-fleshed shoulders contrasting with the black of her brassière which matched her dark dress, Senyor Jaume suddenly appeared as he had on that June day in 1940 when he opened the door without knocking to inform her with a mixture of excitement and fear that the Germans had just entered Paris.

As he said goodbye to the local worthies on his return to Germany, von Müller had warned them that Europe and the entire world would soon be engulfed in flames. ("Give our regards to the Führer and his good lady, the Führess," Isadora Rubió had exclaimed ecstatically, putting Dr Beltran off his stroke just as he was about to embark on a flowery piece of rhetoric). Months later, the members sat in the pro-German atmosphere of the Casino de la Roda, where the smoke from their contraband cigarettes and the aroma of black-market coffee wreathed the immense photo of General Franco – *caudillo* of Spain by the grace of God – which had pride of place on the lounge wall. They were cheerfully discussing the vagaries of a conflict which had given rise to a familiar phenomenon: the growth in demand for lignite, first experienced at the time of the Spanish-American War and repeated so spectacularly during the First World War. This turn of events was breathing fresh life into the moribund coalfield, where the only pits that had been operating at full capacity since the Civil War were the Salleres and the Torres i Camps mines. Most hadn't bothered to reopen or had been struggling to survive. Barcelona desperately wanted coal and the mines were in a position to provide it, in many cases due to the period of collectivization, when the unions not only employed a rational approach to working the already functioning mines but reopened some old ones, pre-viously abandoned by their owners who had been unwilling to carry out essential work on the infrastructure.

There was a need for coal; there was also a need for barges to transport it, but there were none left. The only one to have survived the disaster unscathed was Senyora Salleres' boat, captained by Nel-son; those that were used to evacuate the town had been destroyed afterwards, during the fighting on the Ebro. There was a burst of feverish activity. The sounds of the boatbuilders working on the other bank of the river drifted over to the Hall of the Martyred Virgins. The north wind blew wisps of smoke from the bonfires out over the water and brought the smell of hot pitch to the town's quays. The factory-owners were now squabbling over the boatmen and miners who had been condemned to starve because of their political activities during the Republic and the war. Fights broke out when recruiting captains and crew. "When there's money to be made, that lot will come cap in hand, even if you've strung up their own dads," philosophized Estanislau Corbera, on seeing the proprietors urgently summon foremen, bargemen, quarrymen, carters or drillers when only a few days earlier they had slammed the door in their faces. In Carlota's mind, that period was charac-terized by the bustle in the shipyards, the clanging from the forges on Bakers Hill where the blacksmiths were busy repairing and fitting trucks, rails and tools, the sight of harnesses being made in the saddleries and the hurly-burly of people constantly on the move. If you went up Pedret Street you heard Casimira Rius' sewing-machine stitching sails for the boats; if you went down Rudder Street to Widows' Wharf, you were hit by the sharp smell from Senyora Salleres' stables, occupied by mules once more. The gypsies came to town in their loose black shirts, with long, slim canes and glib, fulsome tongues and sold replacements for the animals killed in the war; outside the ancient Old Boar Inn administrators, veteran stablemen and sailors spent all day in wary haggling with the horse-dealers. This was how Nicanora, Nelson's favourite mule, came to the widow's stables. Many years later, Nicanora grew fond of Honorat del Rom after a trip he made on the *Virgin of Carmel* and she would wander into the chemist's whenever she was passing by. Ignoring the customers' shrieks of panic, she would stick her muzzle through the grille of the counter to be patted by the chemist and would refuse to leave until he fed her a handful of mint pastilles.

Carlota de Torres resumed her sessions on the balcony, a practice she had abandoned during the humiliating break forced upon her by the war. She often went out there, particularly in fine weather, and contemplated the vast square and the brand new barges being launched on to the green surface of the Ebro. And she could frequently be spotted there on cold days too, standing behind the wrought iron railing and imposing her presence and power on both people and objects. The balcony was her throne: from there she listened, proudly and defiantly, to the blood-curdling squeals of her pigs being slaughtered on the Town Square Wharf one clear, frosty morning in the first winter since the war. The Torres pigs were always killed on the family estate in the old Moorish farmlands down by the Ebro, but that December the lady of the house ordered the animals to have their throats cut and be butchered on the quayside in full view of everybody. She stood on her balcony and saw the maids and the people sent by Graells walking up and down with large wicker hampers full of pieces of meat and offal under the hungry gaze of the famished population. And it was also from her balcony, accompanied by her father and other gentlemen who often included top members of the regime who came from the capital, that she watched the processions: the paramilitary exercises of the schoolchildren in time to the music of trumpets and drums; and meetings where the silent townsfolk were subjected to floods of imperial invective with frequent references to Hitler and Mussolini. Once the pits were back in business, she watched the miners come home at nightfall from the other side of the Ebro; the line of yellow flames from their safety lamps wound its way down the Aubera Road like a garland of light and subsequently regrouped at the landing-stage where the workers awaited the arrival of the ferry. According to her father, who often stood by her side during these contemplative moments, it was a sign that things eternal were now permanently back to normal after the turmoil of 1936.

Senyor Jaume had taken on a new lease of life. The war had almost finished him off, what with the collectivization of the mines and fears that the calm in the town could be whipped up into a storm at any moment. He was nothing but skin and bone when they ventured out to welcome the Fascists on the day after the evacuation, which they had spent indoors, fearing a last-minute attack from the fugitives. It was hard to discern any trace of his former arrogance in that stumbling figure. His stay in Castile had started him off on the road to recovery despite the dramatic – and eminently forgettable – hiatus of his wife's death. Returning to the town for good had given him a fresh burst of energy, but the passing years had made their mark on him, as his daughter noted wistfully whenever she compared Senyor Jaume as he was then with Aleix de Segarra's portrait. The stack of work created by post-war developments and the new world conflict put the finishing touches to the miracle. However, Carlota and Graells, mainly through self-interest, particularly in the case of the latter, did all they could to spare him the bulk of the work and feigned ignorance of his mistress in Lleida, whom he unwittingly shared with a chief inspector of police, a bank manager and the proprietress of a candle shop. ("*O tempora! O mores!*" exclaimed a melancholy Latin teacher, the blonde's true love, caught up in that tangled web of passions played out to the accompaniment of the National Anthem, Koch's bacillus, ration books and black marketeering).

The launch of the *Carlota II*, the first in a succession of ships to leave the yards when the *Virgin of Carmel* had already been sailing

169

for a month, was the crucial moment in his recovery. He was jubilant as he stood surrounded by the group of ladies and gentlemen who had gathered on the docks for the ceremony on their way out of High Mass one crisp, bright Sunday in early winter. Although Carlota was pleased to see him so happy, she was alarmed at the attention he was lavishing on the new schoolmistress, which grew more and more overt, almost scandalous, as the banquet progressed: the simpering madam had an ample bosom (one of Senyor Jaume's weaknesses) and was egging him on non-stop despite a pretence of coolness. Her guile was so shameless that when Carlota was getting dressed after her bath the following day, her maid Carmela, who was helping her, informed her of what the other lady guests had had to say about Senyor Jaume's behaviour. None of them could help mentioning, with as much malice as possible, the fickleness – "Alas!" – of human emotions. Over dessert, someone referred to the death of Adelina de Camps in Valladolid: her ghost walked among the strawberry sorbets and her cries rang out as on her deathbed, imploring them to bury her barefoot as was the custom in the town, since she was terrified to think she might enter the other world with her shoes on. Estefania d'Albera (a long-standing and secret candidate for the vacant post, who, in an attempt to ensnare the widower, used cotton falsies to pad out her depressingly flat chest) even said that she would dedicate her bedtime mysteries of the rosary to the memory of the poor woman, buried in a distant cemetery, who would turn in her grave if she knew of her faithless husband's infatuations. As she slowly smoothed her mistress' dress over her solid hips, Carmela kept up the flow of information: Nàsia Palau, who had just let a telegraphist escape from her clutches, scared off by the threat of imminent marriage, spoke of Senyor Jaume's obsession with women. To hammer home her point (Carmela left out this section), Nàsia had gone back a long way and recalled certain gunshots, the departure of a girl from the town with her entire family, the birth in Barcelona of a baby who could have been Carlota de Torres' twin sister, and the latest scandal: the mistress in Lleida ("*Ad majorem Dei gloriam*", the melancholy Latin master had been mouthing ever since a canon from the cathedral had taken the place in the busty blonde's bed vacated by the bank manager, gaoled for embezzlement).

The coquettish and self-seeking schoolmarm rekindled a dormant fear: what if her father remarried? Carlota de Torres spent several sleepless nights plagued by this niggling worry. She was alarmed. Were it to happen, there would be such an upheaval that not only would her own position in the house be threatened, but it would also spell disaster for her children. She suddenly turned away from the mirror which now bore only the reflection of her maid, who was unsurprised by her mistress's furious reaction.

To the astonishment of everyone except Carmela, the teacher, having been summoned to the city by a schools inspector, a former classmate of Carlota de Torres' eldest brother, immediately decided to request a transfer, and she upped and left without a word. During their lengthy ceremonies in the dressing-room, the maid was pleased to see that her mistress was once more relaxed and even smiled at her own powerful image reflected in the cold glare of the mirror ("*Amor omnia vincit*", muttered the melancholy Latin master from Lleida when he saw Senyor Jaume back in the blonde's bed after a month's absence).

"Hurry up, or we'll be late!"

"I'm coming," grumbled Carmela, suddenly jolted back into the present by the church bells; her daydreaming as she dressed her mistress had made her forget all about them.

"Wretched bells! Why can't they stop their ringing?"

"If they did, no one would know that we're holding a service for your father, may he rest in peace. They'd think we'd forgotten him."

"But if they remember the anniversary, they'll also remember what happened when he died."

"It's donkey's years since then."

"You don't really think they will have forgotten about it, do you, Carmela?"

She didn't reply. She was all too familiar with the dilemma facing her mistress: she couldn't discontinue the memorial services for Senyor Jaume. What would people say? They would accuse her of being an ungrateful daughter, of breaking with tradition and depriving her late father of the consolation afforded him by the annual Masses and prayers. But if she went ahead . . .

171

The funeral knell rang out repeatedly over the half-destroyed town. Dressed in black from head to toe and followed by her three maids, Senyora Carlota de Torres swept down the marble staircase and reflected bitterly that each time the clapper struck the bell, it jogged the town's memory and no doubt reminded everyone of the most humiliating and painful episode in the entire history of the two families, the Torres and the Camps.

V

Honorat del Rom's comments on the nightmare of the demolitions
tended to diverge from the often pompous and vague official version.
He dismissed the idea that the dust responsible for whitening
Senyora Carlota de Torres and her three maids at the door of the
parish church came from the debris of Nicanor de Sansa's house.
There was wisdom in his argument, although Forques the shipwright — who would have given his saxophone not to hear him,
despite knowing in his heart of hearts that he was right — termed
it treachery. The pharmacist stated first that during the week prior
to the memorial service for Senyor Jaume de Torres the bulldozers
had demolished five buildings in Straw Square; he then examined
the undoubtedly slim possibility that the wind, a scorching northerly turned golden by the wheat from the high plains, had raised the
dust from only one of these so as to carry it through the labyrinthine
medieval streets to the rectory on the corner of Bakers Hill, where
it enveloped the four women. The likelihood of the house in question
being Nicanor de Sansa's was even more remote and was ruled out
by one indisputable fact: on the day of Senyor Jaume de Torres'
memorial service in September 1971, Nicanor's house had not yet
been demolished. There was ample evidence to back this up, including photographs taken by the chemist, who was recording the stages
in the destruction of the town with his late father's old Leica. The
theory that the cloud of dust that landed on Senyora Carlota and
her servants was Nicanor's posthumous and symbolic revenge on
the Torres family for their underhand behaviour was thus exploded.
The chemist regarded it as a poetic piece of nonsense born of help-
lessness (and if the shipwright had parted with his sax in order to
prove Honorat wrong — which no one thought he would — everyone
knew that the latter would gladly have forfeited his telescope from
the Napoleonic War, the most valuable of his apothecary's jars or
the two Goya engravings of bullfights which he had salvaged from the
scrap heap if it meant that he could side with Forques). In lending
money to Nicanor's widow, alone in the world with three children

since the death of her husband in France after the Civil War, and subsequently taking her house in lieu of the original amount and the
interest that had accrued over the years, Senyor Jaume de Torres had
merely employed a traditional and ancient method of getting rich.
How had most of the well-to-do families in the town amassed their
wealth? Years of poor harvests, disease, debt aggravated by poverty,
with the legal backing of craftily-worded documents initialled with a
cross by illiterate people, were the basis of the family fortunes of the
Torres, the Salleres, the Alberas, the Vallcornas . . . If the wind and
the dust – to which Honorat del Rom flatly refused to attribute a moral
conscience – were acting as righters of wrongs by sullying Senyora
Carlota de Torres' black dress, the chemist didn't see why they
shouldn't attack a wider sector of the community. They could start
with him, since he had doubtless done well out of the thefts committed by his unscrupulous ancestors, and end with the Graells clan, the
seconds-in-command of the Torres family, who had learnt by their
masters' example and followed the same course in a fashion both ruthless and profitable.

The various issues that the town's residents raised later were open
to debate but there was no question as to what actually happened:
a gust of wind bearing earth and chaff coated the women in white
dust outside the French windows of the Quayside Café. The black-
shawled ladies were thrown into panic, as witnessed by the customers seated on that side of the café, drowsy in the noonday heat,
and by a hound that was flat out in the shade of the sorting-office
doorway.

"She'll need a good soak to get all the dust out," said Joanet del
Pla as Carlota attempted unsuccessfully to brush herself down with
the help of her maids.

"It'll take a bathtub as big as the Ebro," added Nemesi Cordes
before swallowing a mouthful of coffee.

"If she climbs inside, we'll all be flooded out," prophesied Estanislau Corbera, looking up from his game of patience. He was stuck.
He needed the king of hearts but it was nowhere to be seen. Jacks,
queens, aces . . . Where in God's name was that bloody king
hiding?

"She's so white with dust that her own father won't recognize
her if he comes down from heaven for his memorial."

"From heaven?"

"Of course, you fool. Where do you think people with money go? When they reach the crossroads all they have to do is stick their hands in their pockets to get out their wallets and hey presto. Haven't you ever heard that money talks?"

"He won't come. He must still be embarrassed."

"No, you're right."

"Who would ever have thought it! What a cock-up! Things like that only happen to down and outs like us; not to toffs like Jaume de Torres."

"I don't need any reminding. It's as if it happened yesterday," exclaimed Joanet del Pla. "The whole affair gave us all a real scare on the *Virgin of Carmel*. Do you remember, Nelson?"

The sailing barge was on the point of leaving Tortosa. The Salleres agent, Ramon, arrived out of breath on the quayside to pass on to the captain the message he had just been given over the phone. When he learnt what it was, Nelson wrinkled up his nose and let out a string of the most blood-curdling oaths in his repertoire, which wasn't particularly large, but substantial enough to make the clerk's hair stand on end. Ramon couldn't help glancing round. Since Franco's government, in league with the Church, had put up posters everywhere banning blasphemy, accusations and fines had been rife. Barely a week had passed since the Bishop had reported a prostitute from the Colonel's Lady, his favourite brothel in Tortosa, for swearing when he pinched her bottom in a brutal fashion, inflamed by a fortnight's penitential abstinence.

"I don't like it one little bit," muttered Nelson, once he had finished cursing. "Isn't there a Torres barge that could do it? It's no concern of ours."

"They all seem to be up at the town today, worse luck! They couldn't get here in time. But you can do it. You can see the way things stand. You know the widow. She can't abide the Torres family, but in a situation like this . . ."

"I see. I don't have much choice in the matter, do I?"

He told the crew what was happening and dispatched them to help the clerk, with strict instructions not to waste time. It was nearly midday and he wanted to press on as far as possible before sunset. This assignment had really got him rattled and he jumped a mile when the mule, lying peacefully on the sacks of rice they had taken on board after delivering the lignite to a brickyard, brayed loudly, signalling the return of the crew. No, he didn't like it, but he had no choice: he must transport the coffin which was to hold the mortal remains of Senyor Jaume de Torres, who lay on his deathbed at that very moment. Ramon had been given the news over the phone along with the macabre errand: the previous day, Senyor Jaume had blacked out while drinking coffee at the Casino. The young Dr Puiggròs, Beltran's rival, had told Carlota that there was no hope. It would be pointless and cruel to attempt to take him to the city; he would die on the way. The end was imminent, just a couple of days at the most. It would be sensible to start making whatever arrangements seemed fit. One of his daughter's first moves – as the whole town learnt from Teresa – was to charge Graells with the responsibility of putting in an urgent order for a coffin from the undertakers in Tortosa who had always supplied the family. Needless to say, it must be vastly superior to the one the same firm had made for Praxedes Maials, the owner of the Venus Cinema, Theatre and Dance-Hall. From being a miner he had gone to staging the first film shows in the town in a garage on Ferryboat Street, shortly after the Lumière brothers' invention made its first appearance in Barcelona, and had made a fortune from this business. There must be no comparison between his coffin and the casket of Senyor Jaume de Torres. This point was rammed home in a telephone conversation between Graells and the director of the funeral parlour. The latter, striving to maintain his professional enthusiasm insofar as the painful circumstances allowed, had keenly assured the administrator of such an illustrious family – long-standing patrons of the firm on similar sad occasions – of the unsurpassed quality of the product.

The upper classes were never buried in coffins produced by local carpenters; they were too roughly-made to hold the bodies sent off to eternity by the top families. How could anyone expect a Torres or a Vallcorna to journey to the beyond in a coffin made on St Francis Alley or Fish Square? Whenever death cast its grim shadow over one of the town's noble houses, the luxury of the casket was the prime concern: to such an extent that the last wishes of Senyoreta

Dolors d'Albera, Estefania's sister, were flouted. This old spinster had requested – at least so Honorat del Rom said – to be encased in a coffin made by Dalmaci Pons, the carpenter from Partridge Alley, whom she was secretly in love with, but family pride had her crated – this was Estanislau Corbera's expression, not the chemist's – in a de luxe coffin from the Tortosa undertakers.

The post-war boom in mining had led to a wave of prosperity which had revived the fashion for lavish funerals among the gentry. When Nelson received the macabre order on the quay at Tortosa, people were still reeling from the luxury surrounding Senyor Praxedes' funeral in mid-spring that year, 1950, a dismal season of treacherous cold winds, freak heatwaves and icy squalls which had lain low many a delicate or aged soul. Now it was up to the Torres family to go one better than the splendidly carved wooden casket with bronze handles and an ivory crucifix on the lid in which Senyor Praxedes had lain in state inside the Venus. The day after the funeral was a Sunday and the young people had exorcized death by dancing boleros played by the band that the deceased had formed.

Nelson anxiously loaded the coffin on board as fast as possible and threw some sacking over it, more from a desire not to see it than for its protection. He gave the order to leave. The men cast off the moorings and hoisted the sails; the *Virgin of Carmel*, borne along by a southwesterly, started off up the Ebro. The clerk was left behind on the quayside, wishing them a safe journey and highly relieved to see them depart with their ill-omened cargo.

They sailed uninterruptedly all that morning and afternoon, except for a short break for lunch. The presence of the coffin on board had reduced them to silence. At night they slept on shore. They took palliasses and blankets and sought shelter in a farmhouse, leaving the coffin alone on the barge. The next day, there was a message for them at Ascó. A former captain of the widow's was waiting for them: they would have to hurry, Senyor Jaume was sinking fast. They must sail through the night . . .

"At night?" muttered Nelson.

"We'll be dicing with death!" exclaimed Joanet del Pla.

"He says don't worry. Graells has had a word with the Civil Guards. In the circumstances there's no problem."

"All right. But there's no telling what may happen . . ."

They sailed until dusk, halted for supper and then a sustained tail wind propelled the *Virgin of Carmel* into the misty night, cutting through the starlight painted on the surface of the Ebro. Not far from Faió, the wind suddenly dropped and they had to land the mule so that it could tow them the rest of the way. Thick clouds were hiding the stars by now and the ship was shrouded in darkness. The only sounds were the water gently splashing against the sides of the barge, the clip-clop of the mule's hooves on the towpath, the towline brushing against the branches of a shrub and from time to time a brief command to the mule. A couple of hours later, voices sounded on the riverbank, the mule's steps fell silent and the towrope slackened.

"What's up, Alexandre?" Nelson shouted to the mule-driver.

A confused mumble of voices came from the shore.

"Alexandre!"

"Draw the barge into the side, Nelson," he finally replied.

"What's the matter?"

"Do as I say."

"Come on, lads," he ordered anxiously as he turned the tiller to bring the vessel close in. The two deck-hands employed boat-hooks to make the manoeuvre easier. Nelson could vaguely distinguish the solid frame of the mule standing still in the dark. A couple of silhouettes came up to the barge but he didn't think he could see the much-feared shadows of three-cornered hats. If it wasn't the Civil Guards, then there was no doubt: it must be the maquis. Bands of exiles had been coming in from France, particularly since the defeat of Hitler, to fight against Franco's dictatorship. They were so common in the area that some years back, the army had been stationed in the town. Their numbers had declined steeply but from time to time there were bursts of activity. Nelson was relieved not to have met the Civil Guards even if the Torres family did seem to have gained permission for them to travel at night, according to the captain from Ascó. In an attempt to stop sailors from ferrying the guerrillas from one bank of the Ebro to the other, thereby avoiding the checkpoints on the bridges, the Civil Guards had forbidden sailing from dusk till dawn under severe penalties. Failure to respect this order met with fines and beatings and, despite the guarantees he had been given, Nelson breathed a sigh of relief not to see any around. He didn't object to the maquis; quite the contrary, although he felt that theirs was a lost cause. There were many folk prepared to help the guerrillas in and around the town; they were given shelter in farms and mines or even in people's homes. To avoid reprisals, those who had put them up would then go, as the guerrillas themselves told them to, and report them at the barracks, where they claimed to have been forced to feed them or provide refuge under threat of death. When their spies tipped them the wink, the Civil Guards and groups of right-wingers would make night-time raids, faint-hearted and shambolic sorties which seemed to be aimed at alerting the guerrillas rather than capturing them. Their attitude was ironically described by Honorat del Rom as "commendable for its generous helping of heroic prudence" to his cronies at the Quayside Café, and was even more blatant when they ventured out of the town. The sergeant commanding the post would then call upon the services of guides who were familiar with the maze of pathways in the area, men whom he suspected of conniving with the maquis since they unfailingly led the posse to the wrong spot. The heroic sergeant preferred the safe haven of the barracks: there he could thrash the detainees unmolested and invent daring, brilliant traps such as the one he set to catch a guerrilla who, he learnt to his fury, had the nerve to pop in whenever he felt like it to a certain house on Fish-Hook Street. The operation culminated in the arrest (oh dear!) of the town judge in his underpants (the confidential report modestly draped this item of underwear over the truth of the matter which was flagging somewhat due to the shock) as he was studying the civil code with the president of the Ladies of Saint Barbara.

Orestes de Campells, the sailor who Nelson had taken on to replace Atanasi Resurrecció, lowered the gangplank and the shadows came on board. One of them went towards to the stern. The captain noticed how sure-footedly he was moving along the gangway between the mast and the stern bench, a fact that rather surprised him and set him wondering.

"Good evening, Nelson."

"Good evening," he replied to the figure standing barely a metre away from him, next to the bulky coffin. His memory sought in vain to identify the vaguely familiar voice, which must belong to a man of the river.

"We knew you were sailing upstream, although we didn't expect you till later. You've sailed fast, but you needn't knock yourselves out to get there; as far as we know the bastard they're going to stash away in here," – he kicked the coffin where it lay under the sacking, – "hasn't given up the ghost yet. We shan't bother you for long, we just want to get over to the other bank. You can leave the mule here, it's not worth taking it on board."

The guerrilla went back to the rest. They held a rapid conversation but all he could hear was whispering.

"We're ready, Nelson," the one who'd talked to him said.

"You stay with the mule, Alexandre. And the rest of you, ready to row!"

Orestes de Campells and Joanet del Pla pulled up the gangplank and placed the oars in the rowlocks.

"Now!"

They started rowing. The barge slid through the slow-moving water, which couldn't be seen in the dark but could be heard lapping against the prow. Nelson didn't need any light; he knew the Ebro like the back of his hand. He knew exactly where they were and where they would land on the opposite bank. As he offered up a prayer that they wouldn't bump into the Civil Guards, a shadow came and stood in front of him in silence. There was something even more familiar about it than the voice of the other one. A metallic noise, probably a weapon, rang out above the muffled splashing of the oars. A beam of moonlight suddenly filtered through the clouds and enabled him to glimpse the guerrilla, who was fiddling round inside what looked like a shepherd's bag. He heard a rubbing and the flicker of a match illuminated the darkness. At first the red light dazzled him and made the figure even blacker. The flame rose up towards the end of a cigarette, the match was held on a level with the man's face for longer than necessary and Nelson's blood ran cold as he realized that out of the pattern of light and shade that constituted the man's features, the eyes of Salvador Riells were observing him.

He said nothing. Salvador threw down the match when it was almost burning his fingers; the flame traced a red arc then fizzled out in the blackness of the water. He fumbled round in his bag again, then took hold of Nelson's arm and placed a piece of paper in his hand. It felt like an envelope. Nelson hid it under his beret, still staring at the dark blur Salvador's face had become again.

Seven years had elapsed since December 1943, the night when the town silently filled up with secret police from the city. Before daybreak they began arresting members of the armed group of the CNT* which was being set up in the town and which had been uncovered, so it was said, by means of an inside agent. Salvador Riells was leaving to go and clock on at Senyora Salleres' mine where he worked as a blacksmith, when he came face to face with a policeman and two Civil Guards. His unflappability was legendary in the town: the policeman asked him if a certain Salvador Riells lived there and he replied that they had indeed got the right address; they would find the good-for-nothing asleep in his room on the second floor. As they all hurled themselves up the stairs, brandishing the weapons they would point at one of the municipal dustmen and his wife, Salvador Riells slipped away. How he got out of the town had always been a secret. None of the *Virgin of Carmel*'s crew ever let on that an hour later, Nelson, about to set sail, discovered the Anarchist hiding in the cabin of the barge and set him ashore at the Canota valley. A few months later, the town learnt from a guerrilla that Salvador had crossed the border into France.

Seven years had gone by. Salvador Riells had come back to risk his life again while the rest of his fellow fighters, except for the one who hanged himself before the police could catch up with him, were rotting in Franco's gaols. Nelson would have liked to talk with him for a few moments but it was too risky. The *Virgin of Carmel* reached the left bank. A deck-hand lowered the gangplank and the other two guerrillas started to disembark. Nelson felt Salvador squeeze his shoulder hard then follow them and disappear into the night.

The sight of the women in black outside the church where the Mass to commemorate the twenty-first anniversary of Senyor Jaume de Torres' death was to be held, reawakened these memories. Nelson remembered how they silently docked at the wharves of the

---

* CNT: the Confederación Nacional del Trabajo (National Confederation of Labour) – the Anarcho-Syndicalist Trades Union. (Translator's note)

still-sleeping town, where the street-lamps shone out over the riverside wall; and how they delivered the coffin to the house, where
crowds of people were at the bedside of the dying man. He sent
the crew home to sleep and when he himself got home he read
Salvador Riells' piece of paper. He slept fitfully as his brain was
overactive despite his physical exhaustion and by the time the funeral
bells awoke him it was nearly midday.

"Senyor Jaume has just died," his wife informed him from the
door of the bedroom.

He lay there, staring up at the ceiling, with no desire to get up.
The letter was a note from Atanasi Resurrecció, now living in exile
in Toulouse, which had affected him profoundly. It wasn't just
painful memories of Atanasi and all the other people scattered by
the disaster of the war that were tormenting him: he had to go and
see Malena de Segarra and dash any last glimmer of hope she might
still be cherishing by informing her that Atanasi, who had been
detained by the Germans in France and deported, had seen Aleix
die. He had come across him in the concentration camp at Mauthausen, very ill by then and with only a few days left to go. In
their brief conversation, the painter's obsession was Malena, a distant
Malena maybe dead, who hadn't answered his letters from Paris,
where he had ended up after a string of adventures and where he
had been arrested by the Nazis when they took the city. Unknown
to Atanasi, there was someone else in Mauthausen besides Aleix de
Segarra whose thoughts had gone back to the faraway town at the
last moment: the poison gas cut off the trembling threads of another
memory desperately weaving old reminiscences of happy days by
the Ebro. Although the sinister lists of the camp's victims were
consulted years later in the search for those townspeople who went
missing while in exile, nobody noticed that Jewish surname among
so many. They didn't know it. The person it had belonged to
in life had always been known to those who remembered her as
Madamfranswah.

The wind that had covered Carlota and her maids in white dust
swirled round Church Square, then headed off down Mill Lane
towards the river and blew itself out over the stationary barges.
Meanwhile, in the Quayside Café, the fragments of memory that
had been brought back by the sight of the women came together
like pieces of a jigsaw and re-created among the ruins the unforget-
table scenes at Senyor Jaume de Torres' interment.

An undulating black mass of people were lining the streets between
the mansion house in Plaça d'Armes and the church door. It was
the same inside, where every inch of the nave had been occupied
for some time by people anxious to miss nothing of the ceremony.
There was no proper procession until after the Mass, when the coffin
emerged amid billows of incense and the nauseous stink of sweat
and melting wax. According to Honorat del Rom, who made a
minute examination of the event, this funeral – in common with
all the funerals ever seen in the town except for the civil ones during
the Republic and those held for people whom the Church deemed
unworthy of burial in hallowed ground – was led by three altar-boys
dressed in white surplices and black cassocks. The middle one carried
a processional cross and the other two, bronze candlesticks with
candles that blew out at every crossroads. The sight of the cross
always irritated Orestes de Campells. His anger dated back to the
day when the town received its first post-war rector. On seeing the
church still bare after being used as a garage by the Republican
army, he decided that it needed decorating. He went to the town
council – a docile body, keen to emulate at municipal level the
passionate love that united the Church and Franco's regime – and
subjected them to a barrage of stale, scholastic syllogisms. The local
dignitaries burst into applause when he finally concluded that
the images and ornaments must be paid for by the atheistic Reds
who had burnt the originals or thrown them into the river when
the war broke out. The conservative assembly therefore gave its

whole-hearted, unanimous backing to the rector's proposal: to deduct from the workers' wages the amount that was needed to purchase new fittings or to restore those that had survived, such as the harmonium, which had turned up in a builder's yard (although the instrument never recovered from having the Internationale played on it in 1936 by Communist hands – sacred music, particularly Glorias, always sounded like revolutionary anthems, which disturbed the parishioners, who couldn't see why). The priest's suggestion brought polite, though unsuccessful, complaints from the handful of miners who had been doing their military service in the Fascist zone when the rebellion broke out, and who had been forced to fight for the rebels; and protests from some migrant workers who had just started working at the mines and who had obviously had nothing to do with the events. From that time forth, frequent ceremonies were held to welcome a growing number of religious statues to the town. The ever-zealous Civil Guards added to the splendour of such occasions by turfing recalcitrant customers out of the bars and cafés and forcing them to join in. This constant march-past caused a great deal of resentment and became the butt of Honorat del Rom's caustic wit, which reached its peak during the victorious welcome afforded Saint Barbara, the patron saint of the miners. In the billiard room at the Quayside Café, the chemist allocated the share in the new church statues and ornaments that, if the situation ever changed, should by rights belong to each of those present, in line with the amounts they had had deducted from their pay. Along with other beneficiaries (Estanislau Corbera, for instance, would be entitled to a red velvet prie-dieu, which he traded that same night with the pastry-cook for a confessional door), chance rewarded Orestes de Campells with one of the arms of the processional cross. Since then, whenever the sailor caught sight of it on public occasions such as the day of Senyor Jaume de Torres' funeral, he would start wondering whether, come the revolution, he could sell his few ounces of bronze to a scrap-metal merchant in return for all the money he had had docked from his wages.

Behind the altar-boys with the cross and candlesticks came eight men dressed in black, led by Ramon Graells and his sons, proud of the honour they had been accorded. They bore the magnificent coffin shipped up from Tortosa, which had commanded greater admiration than that of the late Praxedes Maials. Ramon Graells had scrupulously planned each and every detail of the solemn occasion and since he couldn't foresee the disaster menacing his handiwork, he looked relaxed. He had seemed a little put out early on, more from concern over the disastrous consequences the sorry event could have for him and his children than from any grief. His worries receded when the mistress gave him carte blanche to deal with all the arrangements during this sad time, and vanished completely when she asked if his wife and daughters-in-law could wrap the body in its shroud (the supreme accolade). Among tears and laments – the loudest of which came from Sofia, Carmela and Teresa, successors to Camilla, Adelaida and Veronica, and quite terrified the relatives who had been hastily mustered from Madrid and Barcelona – Ramon Graells stood in front of the mistress and received her instructions: he was reaping the harvest of his devotion to the family. From then on, apart from the odd headache caused him by Hipòlit, who was destined to survive his father-in-law barely two years, the family business was his to command. All the same, Ramon Graells tried to tone down his satisfaction during the ceremony until the deceased was actually laid to rest, since he didn't want his thoughts to penetrate the solid varnished timber of the casket that lay between him and the mortal remains of Senyor Jaume de Torres.

The master, the involuntary cause of so much mortuary splendour, was impervious to the thoughts of his right-hand man. But if he had been able to tune in to Graells' machinations, they would have been nothing new to him. Unlike the rest of his family, he had never believed in the administrator's selfless loyalty, since he knew all about the secret intrigues, the small-scale but continuous pilfering that went on in the production of lignite, the ruses he used to get a rake-off from suppliers, the racket with the petrol coupons for the two lorries they had bought for a song after the war, and, most importantly, his manoeuvres to outsmart rivals who could eclipse him in the estimation of the family. Senyor Jaume turned a blind eye to his peccadillos, mainly because the administrator knew too much about him and the business and because he was nervous of him. In return for his master's acquiescence and the chance to flatter his own vanity by presuming on the friendship of his employers – a fundamental weakness in Graells which Senyor Jaume knew well and had always played on – he was a trustworthy servant and useful as a procurer after the death of his mother-in-law and his wife: he had no scruples about arranging for one of the town's beauties to welcome him in her bed, or doing whatever was required to hush up any breath of scandal which might lead to a repetition of the 1914 shotgun story. The only person Graells didn't dare approach, in spite of his master's insistence that he should, believing that her precarious situation since the execution of her husband made her easy prey, was Julia Quintana. What dissuaded him was not so much her inevitable rebuff as Nelson's reaction. If he ever found out, he was capable of killing both him and Senyor Jaume.

But all that had just ended. Nothing remained of the master, not even the sensation on his hands of Sofia's firm breasts as he fondled them in the darkness of the corridor on his way to the Casino de la Roda a few moments before his illness struck him down. His brain was a black void cut off from the rest of his body, now stiff with rigor mortis and bundled into the coffin. From outside there came the muffled chanting of the priest.

"Dominus vobiscum!"

The town's rector, Father Ambròs, walked behind the coffin, weighed down by his purple silk and silver-embroidered ceremonial cope; he was flanked by another pair of altar-boys carrying the censer and the aspergillum required for the ritual at the graveside. He was as oblivious as the rest of them to the disaster that lay ahead. One of the after-effects would be to drive a considerable and painful wedge between the parish church and the Hall of the Martyred Virgins. Their excellent relationship had been built on a time-honoured tradition of taking hot chocolate and biscuits, blessing boats, celebrating Masses and dispensing alms in return for glory in the other world and impunity in this. There was ample evidence of this new coolness. Honorat del Rom learnt from Sofia of the reasons why Senyora Carlota de Torres felt so annoyed. They were encapsulated in two key questions. How could He (she obviously meant God, since no one other than the Eternal Father was allowed to interfere in her family's affairs) have allowed such a disgrace to occur? And what had the Torres i Camps family received in return for all the favours it had done the Church? Carlota de Torres' visible chilliness often turned to scathing criticism ("that parson's a thief," she remarked apropos of the collection to repair the bell-tower; "that parson's a filthy pig," she commented when the priest was rumoured to be carrying on with one of the pillars of the Church). It all started when the sabre of the hero of Tetouan was removed from the family altar where it had lain ever since Franco's victory, and came to a head a few weeks after Senyor Jaume's funeral, when his daughter flatly refused to give anything towards building a new altar in honour of the patron saint. The gentry were up in arms: the priest said that the project had been suggested from on high. One night, the electric lights on the old altar had come on of their own accord and the rector interpreted this phenomenon as a sign, preferring to turn a deaf ear to the electrician whose opinion it was that the problem lay in the switch, although he was careful not to say so in public for fear of being branded a Communist from the pulpit and packed off to gaol. The holy martyr had presumably had enough of the smell of Republican petrol given off by the old altar and was demanding a new one. Carlota's cynical reaction to the supernatural communication was to send fifteen 60-watt light bulbs, thereby turning the rift in relations with the clergy that had opened during Senyor Jaume's burial into an abyss. The regulars at the Quayside Café saw this as a turning-point in the town's spiritual history. It was the beginning of the so-called Age of Miracles and the end of the Decade of the Redeeming Flame, which had been characterized among other things by the remarriage in church of those couples who had had registry-office weddings during the Republic, the punishment of blasphemy and the imposition of modesty in the way people dressed, with the ever-faithful assistance of the Civil Guard. The force, led indefatigably by Father Ambròs, (Estanislau maintained that the biretta and the Civil Guard's tricorn were interchangeable), had already covered themselves with glory in daring, even risky, manoeuvres in the area. Provided there were no maquis around, they went out with the aim of catching and fining any sinners who were working on Sundays and other days the Holy Mother Church had declared days of rest. And so, after Senyor Jaume's burial, Father Ambròs was frequently to regret Senyora Carlota's hostile attitude. But to tell the truth – at least this was what Feliça Roderes told the Bishop of Lleida in an anonymous letter she wrote defending the rector – he couldn't have had an inkling of what was going to happen or of how it would affect the behaviour of Senyora Carlota, whose presence the priest sensed a few yards behind him as the funeral procession lumbered up Carrer Major.

The family group – a huge black blob spattered with the white of the men's shirt collars and their faces sallow after two nights spent in the company of the corpse, and the surprised-looking faces of the boys carrying the wreaths – walked slowly, almost treading on the priest's cape. It was led by Carlota de Torres' eldest brother, who had the same thought as his younger brother: to get back to the city as soon as the will was read. They had been cut off from the town for many years since settling in Madrid as government employees, and found the rituals surrounding their father's death both tedious and disturbing. It was worse, though, for their wives, cast out into the cold by the disparaging attitude of their sister-in-law, whose contemptuous gaze they could feel resting on them. Carlota's naturally imposing personality was accentuated by the funeral: the veil that she, in common with the other women of the group, wore over her face, conferred a certain mysterious charm on her as she stood a good span taller than the other mourners, even the men. Before the funeral, when the deceased still hadn't been cut off for ever from the light of day by the coffin lid, Carlota de Torres had left the mortuary chapel in the hall to climb up to the high attic windows. She had taken a peek at the crowd massed in the square. Glad to see so many of the townsfolk turning out, she went back to be by her father, and while Ramon Graells and his sons screwed down the lid, she gave herself over to her tears, followed by Carmela and the other women. This was one of the few if any chances to glimpse an approachable Carlota, stripped of her surnames, her mines, her boats, weeping in fear, all on her own in front of the luxurious coffin (which had survived the kick from the Anarchist guerrilla, thanks to the hessian thrown over it). This vulnerable woman, who would probably have been less hurt by what happened, was just a fleeting image. The events at the burial took their toll not on some poor grief-stricken person, but on Carlota de Torres i Camps, the lady who, just a second before the catastrophe occurred, sent one of the family to tell Father Ambròs that the procession was walking too fast for the solemnity of the occasion.

Although Carmela, Sofia and Teresa were sobbing and weeping uncontrollably behind the throng of dignitaries and civil servants that came after the family group in this lengthy procession, their expressions of grief were swamped by the booming music.

In his analysis, Honorat del Rom described the orchestra's performance as infuriating, and it has to be said that he was right, although his musical talents were slim: to quote Forques the boat-builder, he was hard put to spot the difference between a Strauss waltz and the screeching of the circular saw at the dockyard. The old and much-loved River Harmony Band, which dated back to the days at the Eden, had been badly hit during the 1918 slump in the coalfield and was virtually wiped out in the Civil War. No replacements were found for the casualties (a trumpeter who died at Teruel, the tuba-player at Carrascal, a clarinettist in the battle of the Ebro), or the helicon-player who was living in exile in Mexico. The ensemble, which in the olden days always played for boat launches, public ceremonies, funerals and lavish anniversaries, had ceased to exist. Three of its surviving members set up a small combo with the help of Praxedes Maials, and a couple of novice musicians joined later to inject a bit of life into the first dances held after the war. On special occasions, fiestas, gala football matches, high-class funerals or carnivals when the town ignored the official ban and let rip, the group could call on the services of a blacksmith from the Salleres mine, a virtuoso on the cymbals, and a foreman at La Carbonífera, who had taught himself to play the slide trombone. However, that afternoon Graells had felt that the cymbals were unsuited to the pomp and circumstance of the occasion, and it was out of the question to call on the trombonist from La Carbonífera, who until recently had been the talk of the town. Three weeks earlier, the nightwatchman had noticed during his evening round that the Ebro ferry wasn't tied up at the quay; feeling concerned, he had gone over to the landing-stage and anxiously scanned the river. The lamp on the street-corner was too faint to see anything much beyond the bank. He listened hard, but all he could hear was the gentle lapping of the water against the barges tied up at right angles to the quay. The ferry couldn't have drifted off downstream; there was no current to speak of, and it would have taken an unimaginable jerk to snap the steel cable that ran from side to side and along which the boat slid during its crossing. Someone had obviously just crossed the Ebro without permission and left the ferry on the right bank. The nightwatchman went and woke up the ferryman and they both hurried back down to the quayside. While the ferryman, still half-asleep, was vainly staring into the gloom and suggesting that they take a rowing-boat across to bring the ferry back from the other side, the first bars of the Internationale played on a trombone floated out of the black night. The nightwatchman and the ferryman were both thunder-struck. Windows and balconies overlooking the Ferryboat Wharf were opened halfway; incredulous townsfolk cautiously put their heads out. No, it wasn't a dream: someone was playing the forbidden anthem. The Civil Guards came running at the double, armed to the teeth, and took up position by the wharf. The instrument fell silent but after a long pause took up the subversive melody once more. And over and over again, for several hours. Excitement mounted as the townspeople waited to see how it would all end. In the early morning, as the river was set aglow by the red light of a lazy sun, they all saw the ferry stationary in midstream and the figure of the foreman from La Carbonífera seated next to the rail, cradling his trombone. He didn't appear to hear the sergeant-major shouting at him to surrender. From time to time he raised his trombone to his lips, as he had done during the night, played an excerpt from the Internationale, then fell silent. Several ideas were dismissed, such as the commandant's suggestion to request re-inforcements and artillery from the city, since it might well be a cunning trap set by the maquis. The mayor, who on the one hand couldn't quite see what purpose this alleged trap would serve, and on the other, had just had it mysteriously confirmed to him that there was no sign of any guerrillas on the ferry (the two who were in town were at that moment both sound asleep in the cellar of the Frog Café), decided to go with the nightwatchman and the ferryman to negotiate with the musician. After a lengthy conversation which the townspeople, by now unashamedly crowding on to the riverside wall and the moored barges, couldn't catch because they were too far away, the mayor and the ferryman returned, leaving the night-watchman with the foreman. The town was astonished to hear that the musician was at that very moment standing outside the Kremlin in Moscow, where he had just arrived after an all-night journey on the ferry, and was killing time until the private audience he had been granted with Stalin . . . Many years passed before he came home from the lunatic asylum and the absence of his trombone had a serious effect on the sonority of the orchestra at the solemn funeral of Senyor Jaume de Torres.

The crowd, divided into separate groups of men and women, were almost treading on the musicians' heels. The men's group contained representatives of all the town's various social strata, other than the gentry, who were with the family. The Quayside Café, the Oar Tavern and the Frog Café had in the main provided sailors, miners and craftsmen; most of the farmhands came from the Ploughman's Café, while those from the world of industry, commerce and administration were regulars at the Castle Bar, also known as the Phoenicians' Hideaway. The young people, regardless of their background, came from the Sportsmans Café and most of the pensioners had taken up position in the door of Benjamin's Bar to see the cortege pass by. Two slightly tipsy blacksmiths from the Pla mine brought up the rear of the men's section, and behind them, the women's group had just set off; the front of the extremely long procession was meanwhile entering the Town Square, where the council officers, headed by their secretary, were waiting to join in.

It must be said – and he readily admitted it himself – that Honorat del Rom's analysis of the situation lost a great deal of its rigour and objectivity when it came to the female mourners. Everyone was familiar with his taste in women and it was all too clear that he let himself be carried away by excessively personal preferences when, of the vast number of women who had congregated on this sombre day, he only remarked on Adelina Terrer's phenomenal legs, Rosa de Costa's ripe, full beauty, Elena Segarra's powerful hips, Eulàlia Rius' green eyes, Berta Montull's elegance and the youthful splendour of Irene Vallcorna.

Passing over the only questionable point in Honorat's account ("What about Maria Campells?" protested Estanislau; "And Fermina Berenguer?" asked the boatbuilder, followed by other less justifiable claims), it should be noted that he refuted the theory that the maquis had orchestrated the whole débâcle, which occurred just as the choirboys with the cross and candlesticks were in the middle of the Town Square. He said it was pure invention. The idea was scotched by one of the guerrillas – almost certainly one of the silent shadows who had crossed the Ebro on board the *Virgin of Carmel* – who confirmed that at the moment the funeral began, he was in one of the town's cafés. Not wishing to attract attention when it emptied, he had joined the cortege along with the rest of the customers and, like everyone else, had been caught up in a commotion he knew nothing of. The pharmacist disagreed with Estanislau Corbera's opinion that the crucial spot lay just in front of the tobacconists; his version placed it outside Manuel de Vidallet's bakery, where Palmira Sansa saw a famished-looking dog in a doorway, its eyes resting on the crush of people, and cried out: "What a skinny old mongrel! Look at its ribs sticking out! You'd think it'd got rabies . . ."

Carlota de Torres refused to accept the explanation she was given by Carmela, who, in common with most of the town, supported Honorat del Rom's theory. The maid pleaded with her, she tried to make her see reason, she swore on the Bible and her mother's grave that it was true, but her mistress angrily repudiated the chain of events that had led to the catastrophe: Palmira's words were overheard by the row of women in front of her and in Matilde Roca's mouth they were reduced to a more laconic version, stating for a fact that there was a dog with rabies in a doorway. Three rows further on, terror had crept into the phrase – since the town had chilling memories of this dreadful disease – and it was transformed into Filomena Planes' cry: her blood-curdling scream instantly sowed panic from one end of the long procession to the other.

On the afternoon of the twenty-first anniversary in 1971, the event was still fresh in people's minds, although many of the details were blurred. The changes in the setting even misled the wind: before it covered Carlota de Torres and her maids in dust, it had been led astray down previously unknown alleyways which the demolitions had opened up in the old heart of the town. The clock had stopped for good, but the rest of the church was still unaffected by the destruction. Estanislau Corbera's wife, leaning on the counter while the regulars reminisced, could clearly recall the noise and the pandemonium that broke out inside. Shouts rang out warning of a rabid dog on the loose in Carrer Major and a group of women who were still standing at the foot of the church steps, the tail-end of the cortege, ran back inside. The women were scared out of their wits and sought refuge anywhere and everywhere. She had climbed up the narrow steps into the pulpit, feeling the beast's feverish breath on her ankles and its fangs tearing at her flesh. On seeing that the dog wasn't behind her, she calmed down and was able to view the uproar inside the church from the pulpit. Those who had been shut out in the street battered desperately at the doors, locked after the first onslaught, while one group took cover in the sacristy and another climbed up the choir steps. The butcher's wife from Fish-Hook Street and some of her friends squeezed in through the belfry door. Later on, when the flood of people subsided, a feeble moan led to the discovery of sanctimonious old Isadora Rubió, pale with fear, inside a confessional in the east aisle.

Vidallet's bakery had gone by 1971. It was one of the first buildings on the Carrer Major to be knocked down at the beginning of the second year of the demolitions. The memories of those terrified folk who had gone in there twenty years earlier could no longer find the oven, the sacks of flour they had climbed on or the kneading-troughs they had huddled under, men and women thrown together indiscriminately, who didn't take long to turn what had until then been a funeral ceremony into an orgy. It was the same story at the dress shop, La Mode de Paris, where, because of the stampede, five crews – two of Senyora Salleres' and three from L'Ebre Coals – coincided with the ladies from Basket Alley. In the Town Square, the lightning dispersal of the crowd affected most of the porches beneath the colonnade and the entrance to the Town Hall, but with uneven results. The largest group, which Nelson remembered perfectly as he himself formed part of it, went into the Town Hall, climbed upstairs and entered the rooms on the first floor. By then, a highly organized, effective opposition to the dictatorship was functioning clandestinely in the coal-mines, run chiefly by the Communists, and it so happened that most of its leaders were among the group who took refuge in the municipal building. Leaving to one side the sarcastic remarks that Honorat del Rom inevitably slipped into his account, the unvarnished truth is that the priest, the family mourners, a large section of the gentry, four Communists, a Socialist and three Anarchists fortified themselves inside the town gaol after smashing down the door, to the horror of a tramp who had been locked up for stealing domestic rabbits: on seeing the sinister group dressed in black, with the priest at their head, the poor fellow thought that his last moment had come and that he was about to be marched off to the scaffold. As well as this unplanned gathering (regarded as the first assembly of the town's political forces during the Franco period, with the exception of the Trotskyists who were holed up in the telegraph office), it also came to light – although the authorities were never informed – who had painted a hammer and sickle on Franco's portrait in the council chamber, who had taken the mayor's fountain pen and who had maliciously tripped up the corporal, precipitating his nosedive on to the first-floor landing. But no one ever discovered the identity of the person who took advantage of the mêlée to punch the sergeant and knock his tooth out. And despite much bawdy speculation, mystery was always to surround the name of the owner of a very dainty pair of panties, embroidered with tiny red hearts, which were found by the bailiff in a store-room at the Town Hall among the giants and carnival figures brought out each year for the fiesta.

On that afternoon in 1971, the second year of the demolitions, the route taken by the funeral procession was a long gash in what had been the town's main artery for nearly one thousand years. The memories of the Quayside Café's patrons often got lost in the ruins. Joanet del Pla, who chronicled every detail of the stampede from the iron grille at his window, had difficulties pinpointing in his mind the exact spot where the bass drum from the orchestra, after rolling along the pavement for a while, had collided with Senyor Jaume de Torres' coffin, that gem of the undertakers' art, abandoned in the empty square.

PART FOUR

The Black Wind

I

By the autumn of 1971, Honorat del Rom had been arrested four
and a half times – not counting the never-ending years of the
dictatorship, when the entire country was under arrest, and the
collective incarcerations for rowdiness that often followed events
such as football matches, when the home side felt let down by the
referee. The pharmacist had little interest in sport but went along
out of a sense of fellow feeling and an inability to resist the lure of
a good fight.

Estanislau Corbera kept a careful note of the arrests in his memoirs
and according to his reckoning, the first one was in 1945. Honorat
had just obtained his degree in a sad, defeated, starving Barcelona:
he came back home, reopened the family business and started fre-
quenting the Quayside Café, contrary to the wishes of his mother's
brother, Uncle Ferran, who had strict ideas on social class and bad
companions. The old reactionary lectured him long and hard, urging
him to disown certain members of the family who were "not
altogether proper", as he timidly hinted, lacking the courage to go
any further in his veiled criticism of the late chemist in front of his
nephew. In fact, the uncle was firmly of the opinion that Honorat
del Café's death under the hooves of the stampeding horses on the
day the town was evacuated in 1938 had been a stroke of luck, and
he often said as much to his high-class friends. Heaven had thereby
spared the family the shame of imprisonment, which would
undoubtedly have been the fate of that odious, impertinent and
godless Republican, who was always rubbing shoulders with the
riffraff at the Quayside Café. His nephew should become a member
of the Casino de la Roda as befitted his family position and his
brand-new degree in pharmacy (or as Honorat himself put it, his
"official authorization to become Dr Beltran's accomplice in legal-
ized murder"). He always preached these homilies behind the back
of his sister, who missed her husband terribly; they ceased when he
finally despaired of his nephew ever listening to them. Honorat
del Rom never confirmed ("or denied," Estanislau Corbera added

maliciously) a rumour that the old fogy had abandoned his edifying, if tedious, speeches on account of a casual remark the young chemist had let drop about some mysterious poison that killed its victim without leaving a trace ("particularly maternal uncles", he was rumoured to have stated with a sinister smile).

At first he was intimidated by the Quayside Café; it also filled him with profound sadness. He would lean on the counter, imbibing nothing more than the indefinable liquid Estanislau called coffee – a word he accompanied with an impotent shrug, a cautious expression of the shortages bedevilling those grim and impoverished post-war years, never mind the dictator's pretentious claptrap about building a universal empire. The pharmacist observed his father's old friends, but couldn't bring himself to break into their world, a wary, enclosed world in those difficult times. The rest greeted him amicably enough but watched him out of the corner of their eye, fearing that the reactionary uncle might have influenced the young man, who they had hardly seen since he was a child. They gradually found out about his character and ideas. They laughed at his rumoured relationship with his uncle, recognized qualities he had inherited from his father and began to spread tales of his womanizing in the pharmacy store-room. The lady next door had spied on these activities through the skylight and she broadcast the names of the heroines of tender itinerant seductions which took place among the showcases of the family collection of old instruments and professional formularies; she repeated passionate declarations of love delivered under the pots of the Labiatae (nearly always the lemon balm) or else she disapprovingly recounted vigorous, noisy couplings with unusual variations, on the cushions of the divan that stood beneath the precious jars of the Aristolichiaceae . . .

Honorat meanwhile became a keen spectator of card-games. He sat near the card-players, watched, listened and avidly absorbed not just the secrets of the game – which was what mattered least to him – but something else more recondite, a hinterland as old as the rivers, present in those figures gathered round a table under pretext of playing cards. One Saturday, Eduard Forques had raging toothache and couldn't go to the café, so Nelson, deprived of his usual partner, invited the pharmacist to take his place. The agony of the boatbuilder and tenor saxophonist lasted a week and when

198

the patient, his face still swollen, came back to join his friends, Honorat had been tacitly awarded the seat left vacant by his father, even though he wasn't particularly good at *botifarra*, a game he never mastered. A few days later, maybe to put the seal of approval on his admission, Estanislau invited him to the small party he was giving for his closest friends to celebrate his daughter's wedding. Nobody suspected that the following day, the chemist would be arrested for the first time.

On this occasion he was arrested by the army, in the person of an officer from the Engineering Corps who turned up in the town with a lorryload of soldiers and several rolls of barbed wire. It was a crisp September morning and the autumn-gilded poplars by the river were starting to shed the first of their dead leaves which sailed off down the Segre and the Ebro in melancholy convoys and brought out the romantic side in the nightwatchman's nature, leading him to step up his nocturnal visits to a certain beauty who lived in Carp Square. The army lorry was a creaking old rattletrap on its last legs; it drew up with a squeal of brakes outside the chemist's, where Honorat was lounging about after selling a bottle of *Aigua del Carme* to the Alberas' maid. Her mistress supposedly took this elixir to recover from her frequent and spectacular fainting-fits, but it had turned her into an unwitting alcoholic, in common with several others ladies of the town. The chemist was pleasurably inhaling the fragrant airs of early autumn, now that the sweltering heat of summer was past. He was feeling cheerful anyway, irrespective of the boost to his spirits from the change in season. He shared the secret hopes expressed by the guests at the café proprietor's little get-together the night before: Franco's dictatorship had one foot in the grave. After the defeat of Nazi Germany and the surrender of Japan, the victorious democracies would never stand for a Fascist regime such as Franco's, which had blatantly supported the Axis powers. This was also the belief of the guerrillas, who had been intensifying their activities in the Peninsula ever since the liberation of France. Of course, not everybody cherished these dreams, which were, in any case, to be cruelly shattered. Amongst those not of the same mind as the pharmacist was the newly promoted officer from the Engineer Corps, with his freshly-polished stars and watered-down brain, who was just now driving into the town.

The soldier left his vehicle and, without deigning to say good morning, asked the way to the bridge over the Ebro. When the chemist replied in faltering Castilian that should he wish to cross the river he must take the ferry, since nothing was left of the Ebro bridge but its columns, the officer countered with barrack-room bluntness: he knew what those Red bastards had got up to in the war, but once it was over, the bridge had been rebuilt by the triumphant forces of General Franco. It was on the military plans.

When he recounted this tale, Honorat couldn't avoid a retrospective shudder at his own temerity. He excused it on the grounds of a keen desire to see what would happen if the lieutenant were exposed to the counter-irritant of truth ("much safer to play with dynamite than truth", was the opinion of Horaci Planes, who drilled coal in the Torres mines before taking over from his father as night-watchman). He should have sent the loud-mouthed bully straight off to the bridge without further ado, but he made a big mistake: he informed him that the townspeople were aware of this story. After all, no one could have missed the article about the inauguration of a new bridge on the site of the one destroyed by the Republicans. On reading the paper, the amazed townspeople had all leant over the wall by the Ebro, eager to view the miracle. For what other explanation could there be? How else could such a mammoth project be carried out overnight without disturbing a single soul? God (at least so His ministers preached from the pulpit) seemed to hold the Head of State in such high regard that the most extraordinary things proved possible. When all was said and done, building a bridge over the Ebro must be child's play for the powers of heaven.

"Any little angel", Forques the shipwright reasoned out loud, "could do it with a half-hearted flick of its wing. You'd just need to say, 'I want the bridge here,' and abracadabra! Or even simpler than that . . ."

They were to be sorely disappointed: there in front of them stood the same ruined supports they had left the night before. Being easy-going folk, the chemist insinuated to the soldier, understanding when the Press made mistakes and prepared to forgive angelic oversights, they resigned themselves to crossing the river by ferry as before. Best be grateful for small mercies. This, however, was stretching the officer's sense of humour too far: in a matter of seconds a look of such savage fury darkened his face that Honorat del Rom feared his end was nigh. It was plain to see, bawled the lieutenant with a malice that foreshadowed glorious back-room campaigns and petty manoeuvrings to reach high rank, that the chemist was a typical Red, only concerned with belittling the achievements of the glorious regime of General Franco, *Caudillo* of Spain. How dare he feed him such a pack of barefaced, downright lies? So the Press was telling stories, was it? The military plans which showed the reno-vated bridge were wrong; and so, needless to say, were the written orders, signed by the regimental colonel, to seal the bridge with barbed wire and stop the guerrillas from crossing . . . But the lieutenant didn't do things by halves, oh no! He knew how to deal with recalcitrant crypto-Communists, he was a past master at bringing them into line. For the time being, while he and his men went off to carry out their mission, the pharmacist could consider himself under arrest. He'd be back as soon as they'd laid the barbed wire at the bridge and then they would sort things out properly. The balconies, porches and windows round the chemist's had been slowly filling up with people. When the officer marched off, the soldier who had been left behind to guard the chemist, clearly a new recruit, had no idea what to do with his gun or his prisoner. And he had such an awful hacking cough that Honorat popped into the pharmacy to get him some syrup. As he was handing him the bottle – "one large spoonful every six hours" – the lorry screeched back down Bakers Hill. It stopped just long enough to pick up the sentry; the officer didn't even glance out of the cab window. After a while, Honorat del Rom decided that he was free to go, free in a relative, precarious way, of course, given that the whole country was one huge prison, and he ambled off to tell Estanislau Corbera all about it.

The second time, it was the bailiff who went to arrest him (albeit very unwillingly since Honorat let him have medicines for his sick wife on credit) and take him to see the mayor. The chemist had thrown into the wastepaper basket the four letters – the last one of which was handwritten and threatening in tone – which he had received, telling him to report to the mayor's office. He was to answer certain questions regarding an incident that occurred after a marble plaque was affixed to the façade of the parish church with the names of the dozen inhabitants of the town who had died in the Civil War while fighting for Franco: there had been a ceremony with imperial speeches, flags and patriotic music, and on the following day, a list of the eighty or more Republican casualties had appeared nailed to the door of the Town Hall. Doctor Beltran, who had just been appointed mayor and in the first council meeting which he had chaired had seen to it that the demand for General Franco's canonization was carried unanimously, wanted the matter investigated. An informer had accused the chemist of the dastardly deed. The streets were soon buzzing with the ins and outs of the interrogation; it was almost impossible to connect the normally calm and ironic appearance of the pharmacist with what the bailiff let slip about the meeting with the mayor. Even Honorat experienced one of his habitual retrospective shivers when he recalled how close he had been to instant imprisonment and sleepless nights, expecting to hear the Civil Guards bang on the door at any moment. It was whispered that youthful hot-bloodedness had been the key factor in the unexpected reversal of roles whereby Doctor Beltran switched from accuser to defendant. Paternal to start with and condescending as befitted an old friend of the family, he had suddenly found himself red and trembling like a partridge, forced into a corner of his office, having to withstand the furious broadside of the younger man. It only took a few minutes for the whole sickening truth to emerge: accusations, reprisals, gaolings, interrogations and beatings, not to mention the torn-up letters from people in exile and the situation of the wives and children of those rotting in prison . . . What convinced the outraged doctor to forget this scene was not Uncle Ferran's well-meaning attempt to calm his rage – "all childish nonsense, my dear Beltran, and the bad example he's been set by those scoundrels at the Quayside Café, all of them tarred with the same brush as my brother-in-law" – or the pleas of the chemist's mother. No, it was an idea of Estanislau Corbera's: an invented threat from the guerrillas, who were in the area, that if he took reprisals against the youngster, they would come and get him.

The third arrest occurred some years later, when demand for lignite had brought prosperity back to the town. Two Civil Guards, Romualdo López and Ciriaco Fernández, burst into a pharmacy overflowing with customers and dragged the chemist off before he even had time to remove his white coat. They pushed their way through the crowd which had gathered in the street and took him to the rectory, where Father Ambròs accused him with inquisitorial severity of such a wide assortment of crimes that in the opinion of Estanislau Corbera, rather than one charge it should by rights have been three. Putting to one side the fact that the chemist never came anywhere near the church except for the weddings and funerals he was obliged to attend – the traditional attitude of the vast majority of the townspeople – the rector wished to ascertain whether he had any inkling ("you know what I mean, my dear fellow: chance remarks, confidential information . . .") of who had composed a ballad which was being clandestinely circulated round cafés, shops, barbers' and other hotbeds of gossip and which cast doubt on, or to put it bluntly, openly poked fun at the miracles at the parish church. The dear fellow replied in shocked tones that he hadn't: after all, he had only been responsible for the introduction ("Come one and all, both young and old, the Ambrosian marvels to behold . . ."), as the real author, the nightwatchman, couldn't find an opening that was rousing enough. The priest had then enquired whether there was any truth in the "irreverent and arguably illegal and subversive" views the pharmacist was alleged to have aired on the value of holding processions to beg for rain from a heaven that had sent the scourge of drought to punish the entire nation and which was deaf to all entreaties. Father Ambròs was deeply vexed at the lack of rain, an obsession with the dictator. At the Casino he would sprawl in his favourite armchair, swathed in the bouquet of old brandy and the aroma of a fine Havana while the local worthies chewed the fat, and speculated in a loud, puzzled voice about what the reason could be for such celestial ill-will. It was beyond his comprehension. They had waged a war, a crusade indeed; they had given Republicans, Reds, masons and separatists a sound thrashing on God's behalf, proclaimed the good churchman in evangelical tones, reinforcing his words with vigorous movements of his authoritarian beak, a florid pimply proboscis which Hõnorat identified as the seat of his ambition to become one day a bishop and maybe a cardinal; they had buttressed up the old heretic-roasting Spain, but their only reward from Heaven was a persistent drought. All over the State, people were offering up prayers but the land was turning into a desert. Meanwhile in France (and these were the words of Honorat del Rom that made the priest grind his teeth), in Republican France, the cradle of Voltaire and Rousseau, home to numerous exiles, atheists and fallen women – ah! those tantalizing derrières, those thighs which Father Ambròs had ogled salaciously at the Folies-Bergère during a surreptitious journey to Paris, under cover of a pilgrimage to Lourdes! – in that frivolous and corrupt land of devil-worshippers, the rain fell in torrents without the need for a single miserable procession . . .

Experience had taught the chemist to deny any knowledge of these scurrilous remarks. He unhesitatingly ascribed them to evil tongues and reacted in the same way to the inevitable question about the affair of Manolet de Ribes, the baker from Fish-Hook Alley: "You know how it is, Father, another spiteful accusation." How could anyone think that he and the baker, supposedly aided and abetted by the nightwatchman, would spend an entire night secretly slaving away at the bakery so that in the morning the ladies would find their usual loaves of tough, rationed bread transformed into weird and wonderful shapes: funny faces, fish, rabbits, aubergines, carp, horses, boats, hens, dragons and pumpkins? The chemist's mock horror reached unprecedented heights when the priest opened his desk drawer and brought out an enormous bread phallus; its crust was covered in greenish mould which endowed it with the noble patina of old bronze. He informed him that this lewd, perverse object had been baked and sold along with the other shapes he had mentioned, in with the cottage loaves, rolls and baguettes. While feigning shocked surprise, the pharmacist wondered amusedly what adventures the phallus had had between the oven and the priest's hands. Of the twenty or more that had provoked hilarious laughter and ribald comments when the customers found them mixed in with the other artistic inventions at the bakery, this was the only one that had been heard of since it was sold. Eventually, realizing that it was no good trying to pull the wool over the wily priest's eyes and fearing more for the baker and Horaci Planes than for himself, Honorat hinted at a sizeable donation to the new altar in honour of the town's patron saint (a miracle in progress since the last sermon). The rector stopped speechifying and brandishing the phallus, dismissed the Civil Guards who were standing outside, rang for his housekeeper (who over the years bore comparison less and less favourably with the young ladies at the Folies) to bring them coffee, and began to make conversation about the fortunes of the local football team – "Dear me, dear me, what a sorry bunch!" – who were in a hopeless situation.

The fourth arrest, also known as the Aspirin Rebellion, came about when the chemist parted company for good with a mistress who left him for a Navy captain. Forsaking his usual abstemiousness, Honorat partook of too much rum and climbed up on to the parapet of the Ebro bridge – which had finally been rebuilt ten years after its official opening – to pronounce an impassioned defence of the virtues of aspirin in the treatment of rheumatism. The speech may have been couched in abstruse scientific terms but a Civil Guard informer spotted that it contained anti-Francoist references and coded messages urging the miners to strike. In spite of his accuser's blunder ("acetyl-salicylic acid is a medicine, you fool, not a Communist agent!" the sergeant informed the spy as he boxed his ears for his stupidity), the chemist was still detained and fined for delivering a speech without prior permission from the provincial civil governor.

What the café proprietor thought of as a half arrest took place when an outbreak of flu had confined the whole garrison to their beds, with the consequence that the station commandant sent the only person available, Corporal Bernardino, to bring the chemist and Joanet del Pla in for questioning on the events surrounding the funeral of Senyor Jaume de Torres. The corporal fainted from weakness in the pharmacy while informing him that he was under arrest. The chemist brought him round and slipped a pick-me-up into the pocket of his tunic; he then took him in person to arrest the deckhand on the quayside. The two of them helped the corporal back to the barracks.

By the autumn of 1971, many years had passed since the fainting fit of Corporal Bernardino, who fell victim to galloping consumption only a few months after Honorat's half arrest. Time had flown like a whirlwind even for Estanislau Corbera, who tried to pin it down with his reminiscences; the process leading up to the destruction of the town occupied the past so completely that it felt as if there had been nothing but emptiness before. There was hardly anyone left in the houses now, except for the last residents who couldn't wait to depart and hand them over to the bulldozers. The café proprietor leant on the counter and looked bitterly round his establishment, which would soon be part of the advancing debris. Nelson's voice broke into his thoughts.

"You'll have to get someone else today," the boatman was saying, "I can't stay to play cards. I've got a job to do."

He shot him a rueful glance. He knew perfectly well where he was going, although the captain never said. Lost in his thoughts, he watched him through the window until a cloud of dust blotted out his image as he was about to round a corner. Two Civil Guards appeared on the other side of Church Square.

"Pounding the beat as usual. It would never do if we started the revolution without letting them know," he muttered as he saw them walk up to the café door. He could never have dreamt that he was about to witness the fifth and a half arrest of the pharmacist.

II

The dust forced him to screw his eyes up, so he didn't notice the Civil Guards walk across the square, clutching their patent-leather hats, their green capes billowing out in the wind. He had felt mortified by the gently ironic look on the café proprietor's face when he took for the rum. Estanislau had been right to suggest some time back that the best thing was to forget it all, to let it drop; nothing could be done, so the sooner he put it out of his mind the better. But Nelson couldn't just turn his back. Immersed in his thoughts, he reached the top of Carters Hill and suddenly found desolation staring him in the face.

Since the demolitions began, he had almost unwittingly reduced his movements inside the perimeter of the town. He avoided those places where the ruin was furthest advanced; if he strayed from his usual route, what he saw made him sick at heart. Unfortunately, the stretch between the Quayside Café and the saddler's was one of the areas most affected by the unstoppable march of destruction.

He reached the shop, took what he needed, exchanged a few words with the saddler on the eternal subject that had been haunting them all for more than ten years by now, and then left. Seeing the devastation on the way down, he was finally overcome by despair. Not a single soul crossed his path and the oppressive silence weighed heavily on him. Memory inevitably took up residence in the ruins; it restored demolished houses, traced streets, rebuilt squares, brought people back to life. But Nelson realized that his mind was playing tricks on him. He became confused by so much dilapidation. The town he re-created in his imagination wasn't the old town. He brought families together in the wrong place and was misled by piles of bricks, shattered beams, broken door- and window-frames and wrought-iron bars from balconies and galleries. He would muddle up house numbers and shop signs, turning a grocer's into a tailor's, or a wine-shop into a barber's; he would transform a basket-maker's workshop into a bank, or relocate the presses from the old oil mill on Rudder Street in the dress-shop on Castle Hill.

Placing the buildings was bad enough, but it was even worse when he tried to recall and piece together the sounds (cocks crowing, blacksmiths hammering, bells ringing, carts trundling past, the clatter of horses, the chug of tractor engines and coal lorries, the clamour of the sailors on the quayside, the hustle and bustle in the market and the drills in the mines) which in the past had provided the accompaniment to everyday life, split down the middle by the noonday siren which had itself lain silent for many months now. He would never hear them again. Their absence was a measure of the disaster, which had initially caught the town unawares and surprised it by its magnitude.

The first rumours did create a minor stir, the old man recalled as he rested on top of the ruins of Rampart Street, but no one took them very seriously. It would be a nine days' wonder, a topic of conversation for a few months, as on previous occasions in the past; some heat would be generated and then it would all blow over until the next scare. But this time the predictions got it wrong. Rumours intensified, the story appeared in the papers, concern mounted and, to everyone's amazement, on a carnival day in 1957, when the whole town was given over to dancing and processions, the invasion was launched.

Lorries laden with gangs of strangers came in via the Lleida Road, their powerful engines drowning out the festivities and causing many faces to turn pale behind the carnival masks. The vehicles didn't stop in the town; they carried on upstream along the track by the Ebro for a couple of kilometres, but they left a trail of anxiety in their wake. The revellers dispersed and a clammy darkness fell on what had been a day of dense fog when the boats' melancholy sirens had never stopped wailing in midstream, interspersed with the screeching of seagulls. It was the first of many nights of anguish which were to mark out the future of the town.

The trucks kept coming day after day; the wall by the Ebro vibrated as they drove past. The time for rumours was over: they were going to block the course of the Ebro with two enormous dams. One of them, upstream, not far from the town; the other downstream, at Riba-roja. Faió and the town would disappear beneath its waters.

*　　*　　*

He remembered the disaster: men and bulldozers trespassing on farmlands, surveyors at every turn with their equipment, taking measurements and drawing up plans, workmen erecting prefabricated wooden huts by the river so they could hide away while the townspeople sought to fight off this brutal onslaught, calculated to sow despair and block any attempts at resistance.

"They want to make electricity," exclaimed Joanet del Pla at the Quayside Café, echoing the remarks that could be heard night and day all over the town.

"Yes, at our expense . . ."

"Two reservoirs."

"And us in the middle."

"They've got a bloody cheek!"

It was all illegal – or so Forques the boatbuilder muttered furiously, repeating the argument that had been employed time and time again in futile protests aimed at averting the disaster: the plans still hadn't received government approval. And Estanislau Corbera mentally agreed with him as he lay awake, afflicted by the insomnia that he was to suffer from then on. But they would be beaten, there was no hope for them. The firm who were constructing the dams belonged to the State, to the people in charge. And no one needed reminding that the people in charge were the same bunch who had rebelled against the Republic in 1936 and who were responsible for the savagery of the Civil War . . . What point was there in talking about legality? The counter in the café was the reef on which their anxieties crashed: the land, the houses, the mines would be expropriated, the town would be flooded . . . And this led on to the next question: what future was there for them? Where would they go? What would they do? But why did they care, why did they worry? Weren't the exact words of His Excellency, the governor of the province, that he was sick to the balls of that shower of whining Reds, and that if they didn't stop pestering him, he'd personally load them all into a lorry at gunpoint and send them up north to work in the mines in Asturias? The solution according to Horaci Planes – whose job as nightwatchman meant that he suffered from insomnia in the daytime – was to push the esteemed gentleman just a little bit further until they burst his honourable balls (billiard balls? footballs? punch-balls? wondered the customers), and the threat became a reality. At least it would set things straight and they wouldn't have to live – if it could be called living – in the atmosphere of uncertainty that existed now . . . At the same time, the town was swarming with people. The first wave of the invasion had been merely a taste of things to come, of the huge tide which exceeded the district's capacity to absorb it. Even people who remembered the hordes who had overrun the coalfield in the Great War had never seen anything quite like this massive influx. In the main they were a sorry-looking bunch of poor folk who had come from far and wide to scrape together a few pence to send home to their families; the counters at the Quayside Café and the other hostelries in the town were filled with faces and accents from all four corners of the State. Every doorway became a shop, a tavern or a bar. The streets were paved with gold but even though his clientele had rocketed – mumbled Estanislau Corbera as he lay tossing and turning – it was easy money, short-term prosperity, its warm recesses a breeding-ground for maggots.

They never suspected that most of them would grow old, indeed many would die, still prey to that sense of anguish; they never suspected that thirteen years of uncertain struggle lay ahead of them, caught like rats in a trap. Estanislau didn't realize that he would have thousands of sleepless nights to reflect and commit to memory each bitter setback in the agony of the town's stubborn defence. In the course of this process it managed to irritate not just the governor's testicles but those of the entire machinery of government: the moth-eaten testicles of the pallid, dusty clerks; the testicles of the wily, devout technocrats, softened in holy water; the testicles of the bloodthirsty sabre-rattlers, steeped in alcohol; the mummified testicles, embroidered with a swastika, of God's chosen one, whose face appeared on the coins . . . A long path leading to desolation, which old Nelson was treading that afternoon in 1971 as he walked down Soul Alley.

III

"The chemist's been arrested!" exclaimed Teresa, seeing Honorat del Rom flanked by two Civil Guards in the Plaça d'Armes.

Carmela didn't hear her. While Teresa had been polishing the windows in the Hall of the Martyred Virgins, she had been dusting the chairs. The tiresome, sterile battle against the dust kept her busy. Since debris from the first house to be demolished had settled in the room in 1970, it had been impossible to restore objects to their former brilliance; in time the dirt had become permanently encrusted, the furniture was coated with a stone-like veneer that started off fragile but gradually built up until it became indestructible and as durable as the particles of lignite that had clothed the town in mourning for a century. Not being able to get things clean usually made Carmela bad-tempered, but that afternoon she didn't grumble. She was distracted, her mind was elsewhere; it was as though she could foresee events to come.

Whenever in later years the old servant was to recall the misfortune that befell the house on the same afternoon that the chemist was arrested for the fifth and a half time, she always went back a long way in her search for the underlying roots of the tragedy, back to that accursed day in 1957 when the lorryloads of strangers came to spoil the fun of the fair. Besides implying a threat for the future, the invasion was the first blow to her mistress's pride to come from the new arrivals, by whom she clearly didn't mean the gangs of workmen – "squalid and repulsive" in Senyoreta d'Albera's words – who had descended on the banks of the Ebro like a plague of locusts. When Carlota spoke of them, she meant the top brass, particularly the engineers, behind whom she placed somewhat condescendingly and at a distance the rest of the team from the hydroelectric company (surveyors, lawyers and technicians). Didn't common courtesy, if nothing else, demand that they call on the leading citizens (at least the most important ones, and it went without saying that that honour belonged unquestionably to the

Torres i Camps family) and inform them, the town's dignitaries, of their plans? The noble families couldn't be treated in the same way as the hoi polloi . . . The townsfolk's fierce struggle, which her pride had led her to boycott, should be transcended by a meeting of minds, a consensus between people of refinement. But they never bothered with anything like that and over the years, as the problem of the future became more and more pressing, they went down in her estimation from being "uncouth" to being "disreputable" and finally "the dregs of society", the whole lot of them, from the engineers to the humblest worker.

"They're savages," Estefania d'Albera, hypocritical to the last, would inevitably remark if the subject came up during their afternoon get-togethers.

"Barbarians," added Teresa Solanes.

"Beasts," agreed Nàsia Palau.

"They're, they're . . ." stammered Isadora Rubió as she searched for a forceful, emphatic word before she plumped for her usual one, which she delivered with a sudden flash of inspiration. "They're Soviets!"

When the first conflicts arose with the hydroelectric company over the illegal occupation of some olive-groves belonging to the Torres company, Carlota was most upset. No one attempted to apologize for the upheaval or take the opportunity to go and pay their respects at the house. They just compensated her for the damage and left the matter there. She shouted, hurled insults, protested and cursed them, but when she complained about their high-handed behaviour to her brothers, cloistered away in their ministry in Madrid, their advice was clear: she would do better to give up any ideas of a confrontation. She couldn't win, so she might as well back down. This was the second in a long chain of unforgivable slights she was to suffer over the years to come: Carmela was often made to listen to them when her mistress arose from her siesta, the lowest point in her day. If there was no reply to her first knock at the bedroom door and she had to go in and wake her up, Carmela knew that she would be forced to hear a diatribe against the hydroelectric company, the State – what good had come from winning the war? – and the town in general, particularly the upper classes. Because, although the members of the Casino de la Roda often talked of the offence to their dignity ("in other words their pockets have been hit," rectified Estanislau Corbera) and arrogantly proclaimed their intentions to repel the invaders, the defections had started up at once. And the long-suffering Carmela would have to listen for the umpteenth time to the tale of some important person from the firm who was invited to dinner at the Móra's (whose relations with Carlota had cooled considerably, sinking to arctic temperatures after Hipòlit passed on); or another one who went to lunch at the Serras'; or a niece on the Torres side who brazenly consorted with a surveyor from the site. In the course of the obsessive years that saw the construction of the dams, Carmela followed each and every stage in her mistress's decline through her tirades: it hit rock bottom with the crisis at the mines.

She always prefaced any mention of this subject with a reference to her late father. Day after day, in one tribute after another, while Carmela sympathetically said nothing, Senyor Jaume de Torres became more and more perfect in the mouth of his daughter. She gradually absolved him of all his faults and by the end of this canonization, not even the evidence of Aleix de Segarra's huge portrait in the hall and the framed photographs in the office would make her hesitate before describing the deceased as an Adonis. Nothing could make her doubt the moral rectitude of her departed father; not his swindles, not his underhand dealings or his lechery (the last episode to reach her ears had been the pregnancy of the blonde from Lleida whom he had finally accused of public immorality along with the canon).

"He was a gentleman through and through," declared Estefania d'Albera, following in the same line of thought between a sip of hot chocolate and a nostalgic sigh, while concealing her old disappointment at failing to hook him for her husband.

"A most charming man," Teresa Solanes asserted daringly.

"A service-corps general," breathed Nàsia Palau, who during the war had had an affair with a captain from that corps and since then had felt an almost sacrilegious devotion for the provisions service of the army.

"A . . . a . . ." stammered Isadora Rubió in her usual fashion before making up her mind and saying in enraptured tones, "a Rudolph Valentino."

However, even if he had come back to life in full possession of the faculties the loquacious ladies ascribed to him, this paragon of virtue could have done nothing to halt the decline of the coalfield. The threat posed by the reservoirs came on top of another crisis, which had started to cripple the mines when he had already had ten years enjoying eternal rest – as he was fully entitled to after the pandemonium at his funeral – in a niche of the family vault between his mother-in-law and the general's wife in the shade of the cemetery's melancholy cypresses. The villain of the piece was oil, that obnoxious black liquid, as Graells called it in a broken voice, which was causing the world to change out of all recognition. Industries were forsaking coal for the advantages and lower price of this new fuel, orders were falling off, and alarm was widespread among the mine-owners. As on previous occasions, heaps of unsold coal began piling up outside the pits. The hydroelectric company seized the opportunity to step up pressure to expropriate them.

"I shall hold out till the bitter end," had been the heroic response of Il.luminat de Móra, brother of the ill-fated Hipòlit, in the Casino de la Roda two hours before signing his mine over and going to live in Barcelona with a freckled chorus girl from the Parallel, who would end up deceiving him with a bird-seller from the Ramblas.

From then on, Graells' insistence on the matter became more and more stubborn. The administrator was an elderly man by now and in failing health, although still clear-headed. However, he would call round nearly every day after the ladies' tea party and Carmela would overhear his monologues, which her mistress listened to with mounting impatience and resentment, ensconced in her favourite armchair.

There was no hope for it, he always began, before adding – in the knowledge that the dig amused Carlota – that even one of Father Ambròs' miracles couldn't save them now; the coalfield was on its deathbed. It was a pipe-dream to think, as some poor fools did, that wars between Arabs and Jews could affect oil supplies and revive the fortunes of coal. And even if the dream came true, there was another hurdle which couldn't be overcome: the Torres i Camps mines, in common with most of those in the area, were below the planned level of the reservoirs. Sooner or later, they would be compulsorily purchased. To hang on and resist along with all the simpletons who were defending the town to the death would merely prolong the agony and, to make matters worse, lose them a considerable amount of money. What was the point of standing up to an invincible enemy? And anyway, her brothers were at the centre of things, and what did they say? Giving in to pressure from the State-run company would save them from a slow, ruinous death. And then, with deliberate circumspection, he would recite the ever-growing list of those who had decided to sell, the mine-owners who were shutting up shop – not always as heroically as Il.luminat de Móra – pocketing the compensation and leaving for the big city to get away from the disease-ridden town.

Apart from Carlota's mines and those of Senyora Salleres, scarcely more than two or three were still in business when she eventually gave way, swayed by Graells' pessimistic litanies. The pleas of her eldest son, her favourite, who was hand in glove with the administrator and who helped by visiting her occasionally and writing and telephoning her non-stop in an attempt to convince her, finally won her over.

Carlota suffered a harsh blow on the day that the mines were sold. In Carmela's opinion, it was this that sparked off something inside her which was to explode in the future, coinciding with the pharmacist's final arrest. When she came home, Carlota de Torres i Camps had changed: she was no longer the same woman whose maid had dressed her in the most elegant outfit in her wardrobe, who had demanded a complete make-up and summoned the hairdresser from Cross Street, the best in town. Afterwards, there was complete silence for a week: even Graells kept away from the house and the telephone never rang; her eldest son also vanished without trace once he had achieved his goal. The silence was broken by a blistering tirade far worse than all the rest and the maid understood with horror the bitter pill her mistress had had to swallow that morning.

Against Graells' advice, she had insisted on taking a last look at the mines before they went to the hydroelectric company's offices to sign the contract, and although she never admitted that the administrator had been right, the tone with which she recounted her visit to the first mine and her refusal to go round the rest made

Carmela realize that she regretted not having listened to the crafty old fox.

When she got out of the car, flanked by Graells and the family solicitor, Senyor Nicomedes Taverner, the ever-present image of her father, which was by now verging on an obsession, flashed into her mind. What would her poor father have said when faced with the awful spectacle of the mine now shut down for good? In spite of her expression of disdain as she walked from the mouth of the main gallery – where the coal trucks stood idle on the rails – to the river, the sight of the *Carlota II* came as a shock to her. When the workers had been told of the shut-down a few days earlier, they had downed tools instantly and the boat was left half-laden beneath the Ebro rubbish-tip.

"Take it to the town quay immediately," barked Graells. "I don't want it to stay here."

Memories came flooding back and engulfed her. Suddenly she felt three pairs of eyes fixed on her, belonging to the remaining workmen left after the rest had been dismissed, who were busy stripping down a motor under the supervision of the foreman. She shivered. They were the same stares that had upset her in 1925 when she drove past the groups of strikers on the Faió road. Only now she didn't have Francesc Romaguera at her side. She was drawn into the whirlpool of time: she relived their meeting at the railway station at Faió, the journey, their wild nights together while out in the streets the strikers squared up to the Civil Guards . . .

"Excuse me, madam . . ."

Graells' voice cut across her thoughts, telling her to be careful stepping over the rails. Her past had been resurrected among the heaps of lignite – black tumuli in the graveyard of the mine – and its abrupt extinction left her with an emptiness she couldn't bear.

"Let's go!"

They returned to the car as fast as the administrator's arthritis would allow and she told the chauffeur, Graells' eldest son, to drive back into town. However, the morning wasn't over yet. Visiting the mine had depressed her, but going to the offices of the hydroelectric company and signing all the papers for the sale of the mines had meant a humiliation almost past enduring. Firstly, because she wasn't seen straight away. She had to sit in a waiting-room, next to one of Senyora Salleres' sailors, who was there to put in a claim against the firm for trespassing on some small piece of land. The miserable fellow went in first and when they were eventually shown into the office, there was no engineer to meet her, just a lawyer who didn't even have the decency to realize that the lady in front of him was Senyora Carlota de Torres i Camps. He confined himself to a well-mannered "Good morning" (which was doubly annoying since it deprived her of the pleasure of sending him to hell), handed the papers to her solicitor for him to check them, and indicated where she should sign. He had shown them to the door with the same cool politeness. As they were leaving, he reminded them – the third nail in the coffin – that although she no longer owned the mines, she could dismantle the fittings and do with them as she pleased; the hydroelectric company had no use for them. She was in high dudgeon when she had the solicitor and Graells dropped off outside the bank where they were to deal with the finances; she herself went home. From the Hall of the Martyred Virgins she watched the *Carlota II* plough through the waters of the Ebro, still murky and stained red from a flood. In compliance with her orders, the vessel was taken to the Town Square Wharf and there, where it had been launched in 1939 – and Carlota thought back wistfully to the music and the celebrations – it was moored to await its death.

From that time on, the rift between the house in Plaça d'Armes and the rest of the town grew wider and wider. Although Carmela made every effort to cover up the tell-tale signs such as the steep decline in the gifts of produce and game and the number of courtesy visits, one relentless measure of this change remained impervious to all her attempts to conceal the truth: the memorial services for Senyor Jaume de Torres. The congregation got smaller by the year. In the old days the church had been chock-a-block with dignitaries and Father Ambròs doing his utmost to curry favour with the Torres family by lashing out on candles and incense and singing the funeral hymns till he was blue in the face. But things had gone downhill since then. Only some dozen people had attended the last service, apart from the Senyora and her maids, who had been covered in white dust by a wind that evoked memories and comments among the customers at the Quayside Café. They had been such a small group as to be nearly invisible inside the vast temple, made even larger by the harmonium – still damaged from playing the Internationale – whose chords echoed round side aisles where the chance reflection of the candles from the catafalque made the silver candelabra gleam or restored the faded altar cloth to its former whiteness. Carmela had found no arguments to allay her mistress's anger; after accepting the condolences at the church door, while the wretched north wind returned once more from the quayside and buffeted the meagre cortege, she shut herself up indoors where she succumbed more and more frequently to fits of depression and complained of severe migraines. Every day she went up to the attic and spent hours staring at the *Carlota II*, its cargo of lignite turned white by the dust, or at the town crumbling away around her home. Nearly all the buildings still standing among the rubble belonged to her. This time Graells' ploys and the letters and phone calls from her children would be of no avail. As the population moved out and went to live in the new town which was springing up on the other side of the Castle mountains, she stayed put in the ruins and deferred any suggestion of selling the houses as she had the mines.

"They're not coming . . ." she often muttered bitterly. "They're not coming . . ."

These words intrigued Carmela; ever since the anniversary she had had a feeling of doom and it would soon be confirmed, that same afternoon, the afternoon when the pharmacist was arrested for the fifth and a half time.

IV

When his fury subsided, Nelson would regret insulting the rivers with a curse of "may you run dry!" and take back his words with a mixture of tenderness and fear. He sometimes lost his temper and blamed the rivers for the disaster, for not resisting or defending the population. Early on, when the workmen started damming the Ebro upstream from the town, the captain had cherished the secret hope that the river would refuse to be tamed or turned into a stagnant pond. How could anyone possibly conquer or humiliate it? At any moment a flood would come to sweep the whole site away, to hurl fittings, machines and workers into the sea. This had been Nelson's dream for years, although he felt some guilt about all those innocent folk who earned their living as workmen on the vast site. And so he restricted the disaster to a moment when it would be deserted, but work never ceased in this immense hive of activity. There were flash-floods, the Ebro caused damage, some of it severe; the dam wall, a massive slab of cement and iron built into the mountains on either side of the valley, emerged unscathed. Nelson saw it grow almost by the day when he sailed past on the *Virgin of Carmel* to load lignite from the widow's mine.

On the afternoon of Honorat del Rom's final arrest, Nelson's anger was beyond calming. He stood among the ghostly, mismatched buildings that his memory had erected and cursed all those years of anguish. After the failure of their first savage onslaught, the invaders had purposely employed delaying tactics, seeking to undermine the town, to divide it and suppress any individuals set on defending their own interests and the survival of the community. Thirteen years of constant doubt and uncertainty, thirteen years of advancing decay . . . No one who hadn't lived through it themselves could begin to imagine the inhuman pressure that had been brought to bear, made worse by the dictatorship's attempts to gag them. Maybe Honorat del Rom was right to say that the regime was using the situation to make them pay for their loyalty to the Republic during the Civil War. And what a price! The years inflicted deep wounds; feuds were underhandedly stirred up among the town's inhabitants to break down their resistance. And at the same time, several families had opted to leave, given the bleak prospects for the future after the closure of the mines – and here Julia came back into the captain's mind.

"You can't ask everyone to be a hero, particularly when the cupboard's bare. The other side aren't in a hurry; first they shut the mines, next they'll finish building the dam and there'll be no work left . . . That's what they want: to wear us down so that we'll end up handing them everything on a plate," Estanislau Corbera snapped when someone passed an unfavourable remark on the first people to leave the town after the closure of the Móra mine. "Why don't you feed the poor buggers and give them a job, and then they won't need to pack up?"

In the same way that he had nursed a hope that the Ebro might react, Nelson fantasized about an unexpected event, some unforeseeable turn of fate's tiller that would save the mines from being abandoned and the barges from death. If nothing else, he pretended to himself with deliberate naïveté that Senyora Salleres' mines would never disappear.

"I shan't close, Nelson, you needn't worry," she confided in him on their way down to Amposta on the *Virgin of Carmel* to see the former merchant-navy captain, now retired and in poor health. "You can tell them in the café that the floozie from Oar Street is no Il.luminat de Móra; she'll hold out till the last moment against those bullies. So long as she's got a few pence left, she won't turn her miners out on the streets. It's a disgrace."

But the erstwhile smuggler, now nothing but a pathetic shell of what she once was, was to die a few months later in hospital in Barcelona. Her nephew, a sanctimonious milksop, was ashamed of his aunt – "an immoral Messalina who will burn in hell", the confessor whispered in the ear of the prim, effeminate heir – and couldn't wait to get his hands on the compensation money. He put up no resistance before selling off the mines. The townspeople were deprived of their wish to attend her funeral, since they didn't even say prayers for her at the parish church. The hearse came from Barcelona and drove straight to the cemetery. By the time anyone heard of it, Senyora Salleres was already safe inside her niche. Her demise cast a shadow over the assembly at the Quayside Café, and as he went round his customers, pouring out glasses of rum in memory of the deceased, Estanislau Corbera pronounced a brief, heartfelt epitaph: "She was a good woman, ardent and strong-willed. The grim reaper has cut her down in the prime of life."

The reference to her youthfulness was an act of posthumous gallantry. In recent years when there were no longer any powders or creams that could mask the ravages that time had wrought on her features, she had had all the mirrors removed from her house so that she wouldn't see herself as a sickly old woman.

Her death coincided with the completion of the first dam. The labourers were then either dismissed or transferred to Riba-roja, where work had begun on the retaining wall of the second reservoir, which would flood Faió and the town. After years of hearing lorries and bulldozers roar past and people on the move, the streets never rang again to the old sounds. Only silence and anguish remained. Time was running out, but the population clung on to the old black carcass and refused to give in until they were granted the one request they were standing out for, seeing there was no chance of continuing the fight for their homes. The death of the town had been a *fait accompli* for some time: the waters would engulf the most important part, leaving just a few lifeless streets like limbs from a butchered body. The residents condemned to stay there would be as badly affected as those who were made homeless, but would have no claim to compensation. They couldn't be forgotten. Everyone must be compensated, not just those who lost their houses or their livelihood. If they could obtain this, they could set up their new town without any assistance from a government that turned its back on them and only sprang into action in order to harass and crush their leaders, silence their suffering or send in reinforcements of police and Civil Guards when the tension boiled over into demonstrations that threatened the sacrosanct law and order of the dictatorship.

Construction of the Riba-roja dam was nearly at an end when the hydroelectric firm decided to give way to the unyielding pressure from the townsfolk and meet their demands. Old Nelson swore. He shared the universal relief, but not the euphoria that some felt: a cruel and lengthy nightmare was drawing to its close, a back-breaking fight to obtain the minimum any human being in that situation had had a right from the first moment to expect.

"Thirteen years of war, to get money for our own coffins," grumbled Forques the boatbuilder.

"That's fine for the lyrics," suggested Estanislau Corbera. "Now why don't you write a tango melody to accompany it?"

The town stumbled broken and defeated from this battle to face a more uncertain future than ever, but it was irrevocably committed to going on as a community. They would sign their houses over to the hydroelectric company but would only vacate them as those in the new town – which they were going to build themselves – became available. However, many hardships still lay ahead of them: while living in the old town they had to suffer the whole cruel, unnecessary process of the demolitions, which began one spring morning with the flattening of Llorenç de Veriu's house on Horseshoe Hill.

Nelson's house, Honorat's pharmacy and the Quayside Café were in the last sector of the old town to be moved out. In consequence, the skipper was forced to endure things too painful for words. He became more and more upset over the prospect of having to empty his home and relinquish it to the bulldozers. He felt it was steeped in his own life. Its rooms held memories and ancient voices: it was there that he had experienced the happiness of the early part of his marriage, so quickly dispelled; there that his children were born; there that his parents died, and his little daughter whom he still missed. His children . . . After the death of the little girl, they had three more: two boys and a girl. Neither of the boys had been drawn to the river or the mines. They had set about learning other trades: the elder one was a mechanic, the other an electrician and both of them were keen to go to Barcelona, dazzled by the bright lights of the big city, where most of those who left ended up. His daughter was the only one who would be staying in the new town.

He was getting near Plaça d'Armes, crossed a short while earlier by the Civil Guards and Honorat del Rom. The Torres mansion was all that remained in the big square, which at one time had been at the hub of the town's life. Try as he might, there was something old Nelson couldn't understand. All over the town, in areas which had been abandoned and where nearly all the buildings had been demolished, the only houses left standing were those belonging to Carlota de Torres. What was she after? Was she holding out till the very end to get a higher price for her property and rake in more money? She hadn't run away like other members of the bourgeoisie who vanished the instant they pocketed the compensation money for their mines, land and houses and then washed their hands of the town's fate; and neither had she applied for a house in the new town, unlike that leech Graells who had been one of the first in line to join the co-operative in charge of the construction. Well, that was her look-out. If everyone had had her money, those years of struggle and despair would have been a different story. The old boatman was concerned for the people on the breadline, not for the likes of the Torres family.

A maid – it looked like Teresa to him – stepped on to the balcony and shook her duster against the balustrade as the captain cut across a pile of rubble and walked down to the wharf through what had once been the Salleres stables.

The boats' graveyard: barges tied up at the quayside of a moribund town, a harsh mistress who refused to let them sail away and who demanded, like some ancient war-lord of his faithful followers, that they should perish with her to ferry her down the rivers of the afterlife. As the mines closed, the boats were stripped of their fittings and stood idle, rusting away. The dried-out hulls started to crack and green water lay stagnant among the ribs and inside the cabins. At the beginning, some of the sailors would occasionally take the trouble to go and wash down the decks and inspect the moorings. As time progressed, they stopped bothering with such a nonsensical task since, in all honesty, the sooner the river carried them away, the better. "Out of sight, out of mind," said Joanet del Pla. Old Nelson was the only one to persevere in caring for his barge, even if it did mean putting up with Estanislau Corbera's gentle irony. He couldn't caulk it or cover it with pitch but at least he could clean it, bail it out and do minor repairs. That morning, an old sailor who had once worked for the Móras had told him that one of the vessel's hawsers had snapped, which was why he had forgone his game of cards at the Quayside Café: to go and buy rope at the saddlery. He repaired the damage, checked the ship, sat down in the stern and let himself be swept away in a flood of memories. The barges were fitted out again, the old crews were back on the landing-stages. Pulleys creaked, mules brayed, deck-hands placed oars in rowlocks and the boats slipped away from a town still asleep, gliding across a drowsy dawn Ebro; Arquimedes Quintana was leaving for Amposta, Sebastià Peris and Roca for Faió, Uncle Cristòfol and his squint-eyed shipmates were hoping to reach Tortosa by nightfall and were drooling at the seductive thought of the girls at the Colonel's Lady . . . But none of it existed any more, ashes were all that remained: dilapidated houses, remembrances of dead people and rotting boats . . . What a filthy trick life had played on him, sparing him neither the death of the town nor of his own trade.

"They've sold off the river, lads," Estanislau Corbera informed his astonished customers one day, then launched into a detailed account of the whole operation: the names of the citizens who had signed away their navigation rights on the Ebro, and the millions each of them had collected in a move that had released the firm from any obligation to keep open a shipping lane across the Riba-roja dam.

A further instance of high-handedness, the old fellow mused; one more link in the chain that was dragging them all down. Not only their fathers, their grandfathers and their great-grandfathers but many other folk too had sailed on the Segre and the Ebro since a time too distant for people to recall, so they had to read about it in books, as Honorat del Rom sometimes explained. How could this be ended forever? By what right? Who were those people to sell off the river?

He remembered his last journey. He had had a sense of foreboding at the quayside in Faió – a village which was to meet a sudden tragic end beneath the waters, so different from the slow decline of the town – where the *Virgin of Carmel* had moored on its way upstream from Tortosa to allow the crew to rest and where he learnt of Senyora Salleres' death. He locked himself inside his cabin and curled up on his mattress, trying to take it all in. His cramped quarters, made stuffy by the hot August sun beating down on the boat, were visited by ghosts. The noise on the docks came from a far-off world. Time spun round like a top inside his brain, throwing off momentary images: his first interview with the widow, the smuggling trips, the explosion of the *Polyphemus*, coming home after the war . . .

Before leaving the boats' graveyard, he checked the moorings again. As he made his way to Bakers Hill, where he learnt of Honorat del Rom's arrest, he remembered how that grim journey from Faió five years earlier had ended. By the time they reached the town quay and tied up alongside the other boats that had lain rotting for years, he knew that neither he nor the *Virgin of Carmel* would ever sail again.

V

"They aren't coming . . . What time is it, Carmela?"

She often thought back to her mistress's obsessive question on the afternoon of Honorat del Rom's last arrest; these anxious words had signalled the passing hours from the moment she had stepped back into the drawing-room after a shorter afternoon nap than usual. She paid scant attention to Teresa, who was standing on a chair with the window-cleaning rag in her hand, keeping her informed in her sparrow-like twitter of what the chemist was doing. She made a thorough inspection of the preparations for the party, complained of a headache and sat down in her favourite armchair beneath the portrait of her father, as still as a stone sphinx, staring blankly out of the windows. Her fingers gripping the red damask of the arm were the only clue to her inner turmoil.

"What time is it, Carmela?"

"Half past three, madam."

During the spell of foggy weather that descended on the town after that afternoon, Carmela was often racked by feelings of guilt. Could she have foreseen or prevented what happened? Although she nearly always decided that the answer was no, she still felt a gnawing doubt; maybe if she had known the identity of the guests whom her mistress was expecting . . .

Since receiving instructions the day before to make the hall ready for her mistress's birthday party, she had been trying to puzzle it out. What was the point of the celebration? Bringing out the silver, the best crystalware, the finest table linen . . . It was madness, nonsense. Who would come? The Graells family would turn up halfway through the morning to pay their respects as they had other years and Carlota would accept their bouquet of flowers and then talk for a short while with the sons and daughters, the sons-in-law and daughters-in-law, the grandsons and granddaughters, the whole well-scrubbed, embarrassed and servile brood. Apart from Graells senior, none of them was invited to the afternoon party, which was solely for people of the same standing as the hosts. They never made any special preparations for the morning visitors: they were offered pastries, liqueurs or soft drinks and nothing else. The proper party was held in the afternoon, which was when the gentry put in an appearance, brimming over with congratulations and hypocritical wishes for her health, wealth and a long life. But who was left in the town of those ladies and gentlemen of the past? Almost no one. After the closure of the mines and the departure of most of the owners, the festivities had gone rapidly downhill and now, since the start of the demolitions, they had dwindled to Graells' morning visit and a couple of extra guests at the usual afternoon get-togethers in the hall. On top of this, the angel of death had recently accounted for several of the few members of the leading families who hadn't yet left for the city.

A few months after the convent was knocked down, Malena de Segarra gave up the ghost. Since returning to the town at the end of the Civil War, she had scarcely set foot outside her home except for the occasional family funeral. Nelson's sad visit to pass on Atanasi Resurreccio's news of Aleix's death in Mauthausen – which he had heard of from the guerrilla – had merely confirmed her fears. She cut herself off completely; the noise of the outside world fell silent at her threshold. Even the controversy about the reservoirs had done nothing to disturb the hush in the Segarra family home, the dead time that lurked therein. The disappearance of the convent finally broke her delicate health. The end was swift: she died a few months before the move to the new town, one October day when the breeze muted the autumnal emerald tint of the rivers and cast a grey film over the still-golden fields. By the time the maid told Nelson, her mistress was already in her shroud. Beneath the dress they had clothed her in were the Venetian masks behind which she and Aleix had hidden one far-distant carnival day. A long line of mourners followed the coffin which was carried, as Malena had requested, by Nelson, Estanislau Corbera, Honorat del Rom, Joanet del Pla, the boatbuilder and other regulars at the Quayside Café. This show of grief was derided contemptuously during one of the last sessions in the Hall of the Martyred Virgins, where the malicious gossip about the affair between Malena and Aleix was also dragged up again. Carmela couldn't help showing by her brusque manner that these

venomous remarks had offended her. Her mistress was so angry at
the rebuke that she went an entire week without saying a word to
her, although all that was water under the bridge by the afternoon
of the birthday party.

"What time is it, Carmela?"

"Four o'clock precisely, madam."

Not long afterwards, Carmela recalled as she sadly leafed through
the obituary, the Baron's last descendant was struck down by a heart
attack during his annual pilgrimage to Lleida. It happened in a
brothel where, drunk on rum and naked as the day he was born,
he was dancing a sensuous, plaintive tango with a cross-eyed strum-
pet clad in nothing but a single black stocking, on her right leg.
Several days after the funeral, the authorities at the town hall
received the deceased's straw boater, which had been left behind in
the hall of the bordello by the undertakers' lads. In an accompanying
letter, the poor harlot in whose arms the aristocratic waiter had
expired, profoundly shaken by the tragedy, told the mayor of the
deep spiritual crisis she had been through and announced that she
was turning her back once and for all on the sins of the flesh and
the delights of the tango. She wanted to shut herself off from the
world. She had asked to be admitted into the calm of the cloister
and hoped to be accepted thanks to a Carmelite Mother Superior –
"a saintly woman, Sir" – who was cousin to the widow of a cavalry
colonel – "another saintly woman" – who ran the house of ill repute
in Tortosa where she had embarked on her career at the age of
nineteen.

The uplifting story of the Lleida whore was the prelude to a
spiritual revival among the guild of godfearing ladies still left in
the town, who had been rather concerned at the downturn in
miracles since the start of the demolitions; Honorat blamed it on
the supernatural beings getting lost among so much dereliction.
The ground was thus prepared for the passing of Senyoreta
d'Albera.

This ancient spinster, older than Carlota de Torres, was exceed-
ingly frail. Neither medicines nor tonics could restore her health.
She had stopped going to the gatherings at the Hall of the Martyred
Virgins and her spiteful tongue, which had once lashed the whole

town, had now ceased to wag. By the end she was fit for little more than babbling away incomprehensibly. One autumn morning when there was thunder in the air, her niece discovered her stone-cold in her little room overlooking the Widows' Wharf, seated in her rocking-chair as though she were asleep. Clasped to her bosom was the nun's habit that she had once worn to stimulate the libido of the unfortunate clerk of the court during the Great War. Mothballs fell to the ground as these robes, whose real purpose remained a mystery, were prised from the dead woman's stiff fingers. Her gesture was taken as a desire to be buried in them; they were covered in slashes which her niece devoutly attributed to penitential scourgings, but which were really the result of the late secretary's impatience to reach the flesh hidden beneath them, so fresh and provocative at the time. And thus, surrounded by rumours of her saintliness, Senyoreta d'Albera passed on to the other life dressed as a nun, but she never achieved her dream of being compensated for the compulsory purchase of her houses and land and ending her days in the city.

None of the ladies was left who used to go to the Hall of the Martyred Virgins, none of the old guests at the Torres family celebrations, practically no one at all.

"Ah, sweet friends! Time marches on apace and the sad hour of our tearful farewells is come," Teresa Solanes stated dramatically the day before she left for Tarragona, where she was to die four months later of a heart attack.

"The unfathomable ways of destiny are taking me to a second-floor flat in the Carrer de Cavallers," announced Nàsia Palau one week later, as she left for Lleida with her youngest son.

"Ah, Carlota my dear," said Isadora Rubió, the last to forsake the salon. "To think that by this time tomorrow I shall be in Barcelona fills my heart with springtime joy. It's such a . . . such a renowned city!"

And meanwhile, the general exodus to the new houses was leaving the town deserted. As she furtively peered out of the window and witnessed yet another family leaving, Carmela wondered what her mistress, who was becoming more morose and bizarre by the day, would eventually decide to do. Soon phantoms would be the only ones left in the old houses and tumbledown streets. As she put the final touches to the table, she wondered whether these were to be the guests, phantoms and ghosts.

"What time is it, Carmela?"

"Almost a quarter to five, Madam."

The doorbell rang at nearly half past five. Carmela rushed anxiously from the kitchen where she was getting on with her chores, but when Teresa opened the door, it was only the hesitant figure of Graells accompanied by his eldest son. A few minutes later, the mistress's voice rang out in the hall, low at first but then angrily, until it became a torrent of abuse that ricocheted from one ancestor to another down the line of paintings that hung in the immense corridor. The corseted ladies and the stern, worthy gentlemen pretended not to hear their descendant's stream of invective; but all of them, from Senyor Jaume de Torres to the most obscure relative, were forcibly acquainted with the list of grievances vented that afternoon in the Hall of the Martyred Virgins. Her opening remarks disturbed the founder of the dynasty on the Camps side, who was confined to a corner of the so-called Old Hall, where, almost unseen in the murk of the blackened pigments, he slept alongside an ebony cornucopia and a mechanical bird. The good fellow – a shoemaker who made his fortune by impregnating the filthy rich widow of a francophile, in need of protection after the Napoleonic wars – was called upon as a glorious witness to the family's origins and the unforgivable slight the town had just inflicted on the dynasty. Carlota proceeded to cite many other family members including Pau Camps, an illustrious moneylender who had acquired most of the houses and properties the family owned, and Nicanor Camps, the first to venture into mining in the early days of prospecting for lignite in the area. Filomena Sants (whose contribution to the family had been her holding in the liquorice-extract factory), the heroic general's widow, her grandmother, her mother and Senyor Jaume were the last in chronological order in the roll-call of family members (which even included the dissolute uncle and other unworthy specimens) who were subjected to their descendant's bile.

The Senyora's voice thundered for a long time among the preparations for the party before Carmela, Sofia and Teresa discovered, along with the ancestors, why she was so angry. When the demolitions had started eating into the old town, she had said nothing, she had waited in her mansion for the residents to allocate her a place in the new town; not just any place, a house like all the rest, but one worthy of Carlota de Torres i Camps. How could anyone even imagine the community without her family! She didn't intend leaving like certain others, she wouldn't drag out her days in a city where no one knew her name, cut off from her possessions and the people who had always been connected to the family. But naturally enough, they would have to come and beg her. She couldn't enrol in the co-operative they had set up . . . How could the names of Torres and Camps appear alongside those of shopkeepers, farm-hands, butchers, bakers, tailors, dressmakers, or – even more demeaning – former sailors or workers in her mines? The same list and the same rights! She wasn't just another resident: they would have to plead with her to do them the honour of going to live in the new town, they would have to earmark the best spot for her and build a new house even bigger and better than the one that dominated the Plaça d'Armes.

However, the architects had designed the houses and planned the streets, the building sites were sprouting pillars and walls, by now nearly everybody was living in the other town and still no one had come knocking at her door. Carmela learnt later from Graells' eldest son that his father had guessed what she wanted and suggested that she have a house built just outside the new town where the family owned sufficient land: a house worthy of her, seeing that those designed already weren't to her liking and neither was the demo-cratic way they were being allotted. The old buffer was given a furious dressing down. If the Torres i Camps house had to be any-where it wasn't outside the town but slap in the middle, where it belonged . . . What was it to her if building land was scarce and the townsfolk had already refused to sacrifice a single inch of it to erect a church? The priest could go and say Mass in a field if he wanted and the archbishop could condemn the whole godless lot of them to burn in hell. She really couldn't care less. But what was the town without the Torres family? She had to have a place of her own, as much space as she needed, and it must be in the main square. The rest would have to fit in as best they could. How had the wretches survived, if not thanks to her family's factory, lands and mines? The scoundrels fancied themselves home-owners now, but who had rented them houses in the past? They would have to come to her on bended knees to ask her to choose the place she wanted.

But none of this had happened and her patience had eventually worn so thin that she made the mistake of trying to appeal to the residents' representatives and win them over by flattering their vanity with an invitation to her birthday. In the past she only invited the top people; half the town would have given an arm and a leg to be there in those days. Fool! How could she have stooped so low? Hurtful as it was when they turned down her invitation, it wasn't as humiliating as the letter they sent back via Graells – whom she had dispatched with the message – which informed her that if she wanted a house, it would have to be the same as the rest and that, like everyone else, she would have to go where she was sent. These were the rules and they couldn't be bent for anyone. Rules? It was a conspiracy, and she could see the old enemy lurking behind it: the enemy who had shot her father when she was a little girl, who had brought the miners out on strike, who had collectivized the mines during the Civil War, who was set on doing away with the ruling classes . . . They had been soft, far too soft with the rabble back in 1939 . . . !

The shouts were getting louder. Carmela crossed the corridor and tiptoed up to the door of the hall, where Sofia and Teresa stood aghast at the increasingly raucous cries of their mistress. It would never happen, she was bellowing, she would stay in the old town, inside her own home surrounded by her own houses which would never be knocked down. She would reopen the mines, get the barges sailing again! Tell Graells to summon the foremen and give them their instructions, to get the builders in to repair the house . . . ! She wasn't like the rest of them: she was Senyora Carlota de Torres, she belonged to the Torres i Camps family.

"I shan't let them, father; I shan't let them," she exclaimed, addressing the portrait.

She frenziedly repeated these last words over and over again until her voice suddenly gave way and the fearful maids and the long line of motionless ancestors caught Graells' horror-stricken cry of "Madam, what's the matter, madam?"

VI

The generally accepted version of Honorat del Rom's last arrest was that the prisoner was taken straight from the Quayside Café to the Civil Guard barracks. But it was an erroneous conclusion, an automatic assumption based on the number of times they had witnessed this same horrific spectacle during the interminable Franco years, for that afternoon the barracks no longer existed. Some months had passed since the garrison moved out of the building near the old fort by the Segre Gate and into makeshift wooden huts near the new houses. Scarcely had the last three-cornered hat left the barracks – clamped on to the shiny bald pate of Officer Trinitat, who was staggering under the weight of a cabinet full of files on citizens suspected of subversive activities – when other occupants moved in: the stray dogs from the ruins. The simple-minded waiter from the Central Café, feeling sorry for the poor creatures, had hit upon the idea of letting them take shelter there. The inquisitive dogs roamed all over, from the guard-room, the cells and the post commander's office to the living-quarters of the men's families. They sniffed all the corners, marked out territory with their urine and under the armoury window a cinnamon-coloured hound mated with a bitch on heat after fiercely seeing off a rival hunting dog. The following day, although the waiter brought them buckets of water and crusts of bread, they were anxious to leave; the rubble-encircled edifice was transformed into a deafening chorus of yelps. The demented animals spent three days locked up inside, staring out of the windows and balconies and desperately pawing at the doors until a passer-by set them free. Workmen came and sealed the door straight away and the barracks were knocked down a month before the chemist was arrested. In fact, he was taken to a court office in the Town Hall, where the clerks were already packing up council documents, and his interrogation took place on a pile of legal documents topped by the Register of Deaths.

The moustached sergeant, a dull-witted stickler for the rules, first went to great pains to establish his identity, to make sure that he really was the proprietor of the pharmacy where he himself went regularly to buy *Aigua del Carme* tonic wine, aspirins and, in strictest secrecy, imported condoms, since he blamed those made in Spain for the brace of ginger-haired twins his better half had brought into the world three years earlier (an incorrect supposition since you only had to look at the youngest member of the garrison, a smart fellow with bright ginger hair, to realize that the much maligned home industries bore no responsibility for this double fault). Once the chemist's personal details had been verified beyond any shadow of a doubt, the questioning began. His answers were direct and to the point. He had been racking his brains since the arrest but couldn't work out what it was all about. He hadn't understood what was going on until he entered the office and caught sight of the cardboard box out of the corner of his eye, and the corporal guarding it. The first of the sergeant's questions elicited a yes: the night before he had gone out quite late. Exactly how late? He couldn't remember, it must have been about half past twelve. Where had he gone? Well, he'd gone down Fish-Hook Alley as far as the river wall, then headed for the ruins of the Venus Cinema, Theatre and Dance-Hall. But he took the utmost care to avoid telling the sergeant, who was looking at him from the other side of the table with a Machiavellian glint in his eyes, how it had felt to be back inside all that remained of one of the town's most popular night-spots. As he stood on top of the tottering piles of fresh debris in the faint yellow glow of the street-lamp, he could scarcely believe that such a tiny space had once held an institution like the Venus, which had seemed so vast to him as a teenager on the day when his father had taken him to hear Aleix de Segarra's piano recital celebrating the proclamation of the Republic; or that, at the height of the Civil War, it had been turned into an enormous muddy lake by the great flood of 1937. He and his father had paddled their canoe in through a window; they had journeyed up the shadowy corridor behind the boxes and ended up backstage among old pieces of waterlogged scenery. His father had pushed the sodden curtains aside with an oar and the canoe had sailed out on stage. It had felt as though they were interrupting a ghostly play performed to an underwater audience, the seats all taken by sailors who had gone down with their ships long since. Last night as he stood there, happening to spot a fragment of the painted plaster of Paris cornucopia that always had pride of place at the front of the stage thanks to an odd whim of Senyor Praxedes, the site hadn't even seemed big enough to contain the boxes, where the darkness during the film-shows was conducive to what the rector termed "sins of the flesh" during the wave of hypocrisy and moralizing that followed the Fascist victory in the Civil War. The couples in the back row couldn't care less about the wishy-washy films the censors passed for screening and they devoted themselves instead to far more stirring activities – with such rash and embarrassing enthusiasm that Senyor Praxedes decided to save appearances if nothing else. He had a bell fitted that rang a few minutes before each interval or break in the film to give the audience time to regain the demure, genteel appearance that the regime's iconography held up as a model of propriety. In spite of this invention, there were several sticky moments. Now and then, people would reminisce about Casilda Quintana's legendary orgasm, and each time it was mentioned it grew louder, more violent, syncopated and full-throated and less bothered by lights and bells; Estanislau Corbera was infatuated with her, never guessing that such frenzied passions lay beneath the fragile exterior of a girl always involved in Masses, viaticums, rosaries and novenas. Mentioning Casilda inevitably led on to the guardsman who was landed in a similar situation by the manual dexterity of his fiancée: he didn't heard the interval bell and, taken by surprise when presenting arms, he exclaimed "Franco, Franco, Franco!" in a rich baritone, an opportune and patriotic thought that saved him from being disciplined. As the sergeant said to the rector and the mayor when they held an extraordinary meeting to investigate the case, could anyone really find it in their heart to condemn someone who at such a juncture had shown such spontaneous and deep-seated devotion to the Head of State?

The chemist steered clear of any dangerous ironies. He merely went along with the sergeant in reconstructing the events of the previous night. Was he alone? Yes. Was he carrying anything? Yes, he was carrying that very cardboard box which the other Civil Guard was meanwhile positioning on top of the table. Without waiting for further questions, he corroborated what the sergeant obviously knew already: the night before, he had secretly gone and buried it in the remains of the Venus.

After a few seconds' silence cleverly calculated to heighten the suspect's tension, the sergeant undid the box, put his hand inside and pulled out part of what it held. Somebody burst in at that moment and Honorat heard the familiar voice of Susanna Castells behind him saying, "Might I ask, Sergeant, what you're doing with the skull of poor Ildefons in your hands?"

The grotesque sight of a pot-bellied Hamlet in uniform and three-cornered hat, holding the dusty skull in his right hand, became a favourite talking-point during the final days of the Quayside Café. Honorat del Rom regaled them with all the details of the affair, beginning with the astonishment of the sergeant, who had been poised to confute the detainee with the indisputable evidence. Susanna's voice broke in on the Shakespearian scene, transplanted from the northern mists of Elsinore to the banks of the Ebro. The Civil Guard let go of the skull, which fell into the box with a mournful thud, landing on the rest of the skeleton. The sergeant's bid to unmask a criminal who had tried to destroy the evidence of a misdemeanour undoubtedly committed many years ago had come to naught.

The Civil Guards had been alerted to the pharmacist's suspicious behaviour by one of their informers (the baker thought it was La Lloca, the boatbuilder plumped for Joanet d'Escarp, and Joanet del Pla resolved the dilemma by giving the pair of them a bloody nose). On the previous night, the individual in question – a dangerous revolutionary according to their files, like the rest of his drinking companions – had buried a cardboard box in the remains of the cinema. Weapons? Explosives? Subversive literature? Banned books? The sergeant secretly disinterred it a couple of hours later and found proof of a crime: a dusty skeleton, unquestionably the victim of a murder.

The remains of Ildefons Albaida, the hapless Republican soldier who had once been the owner of the bones in the box, turned up in 1938 among some juniper shrubs near an olive-grove belonging to Susanna Castells' parents. His wasn't the first corpse to be discovered in the district, which had been badly scarred by the folly of war. The circumstances of the macabre find seemed to indicate that Ildefons, on being wounded (there were machine-gun bullets on the ground beneath his smashed rib-cage), had hidden in the bushes where he died in solitude. When Susanna's father had found the skeleton half-covered in a few shreds of rotting clothes next to a rusty helmet and a leather bag, his intention had been to bury it, but inside the bag he found letters and documents bearing the deceased's name and address. Ramon Castells was moved by the ever-present memory of his own eldest son, who had died at Brunete and probably lay in some godforsaken foxhole; if he could prevent this poor fellow from spending the rest of eternity far from home – the cruel fate of what remained of his son – he would do so. He gathered up the bones, furtively carried them home and hid them in his attic waiting for a reply to the letter he had sent to the address on the document. "I wrote it myself, your honour, because Father couldn't write. We sent four letters over two years." But they never heard anything back. They wondered whether Ildefons' family were dead too or whether the war had forced them to flee. They would surely have said something otherwise. But they couldn't bring themselves to get rid of Ildefons; they thought that maybe their respect for this stranger was being echoed somewhere else with their son who died in the Battle of Brunete. "Because you see, Sergeant, we never got over my brother's death." The remains were always kept in a basket hidden in the loft at home. The children would sometimes go and take a peek or show them to their friends – "innocent pranks". When the old folk died, nobody thought of evicting poor Ildefons until she, Susanna, who had been in service for many years with Honorat's grandparents and was on her own now that her parents were dead and her married brother had left for the city, had to leave the house to go and live with cousins in the new town.

"I can't turn up on their doorstep with Ildefons," she said to Honorat when asking for his advice on what to do. He said not to worry, that he would take charge of the bones. He would bury them under one of the demolished buildings. It was for the best; like that there would be no complications or gossip.

* * *

237

Little came of this event, which ended with the pharmacist and Susanna Castells being fined for contravening public health regulations. The townspeople didn't care that the sergeant had made a fool of himself. They had no interest in the tale told by Susanna, who had guessed what was going on the moment she had heard that Honorat was under arrest. They were indifferent to the news that a distressed Carmela had come to the court looking for the chemist because Senyora Carlota de Torres had had a severe attack and the doctor urgently needed some medicines. By now they had nearly all settled in the new town and were totally caught up in their own future. The soldier's dusty skeleton and his skull – still echoing with the noise of battle – belonged to the land on the other side of the frontier and they wanted nothing to filter across from there. They would leave the past behind among the ruins in the hope that the north wind would scatter it along with the dust of the flattened town.

EPILOGUE

One-way Exile

Her puffy, smarting eyelids painfully opened a fraction like part-healed wounds; her pupils were suffused with the crimson light of dawn that set the warm stale air in the bedroom aflame. Carlota de Torres looked in the mirror and saw the bedside table stacked with medicine bottles and Carmela wrapped up in an eiderdown, asleep in an armchair by the bed. She forced her rheumy eyes wide open and sought to clear her thoughts. Since experiencing that red-hot twinge of pain in her head on the day of her birthday when the room, the maids, Graells, the party preparations and her father's portrait had all suddenly begun to spin round in a fearful whirlwind that became darker and darker until everything went black, she had been incapable of distinguishing night from day. A black spot was always bobbing around inside her head. She noticed it when she came to after her first attack; it had stayed with her ever since, like some horrible strange seed bursting with the darkness that swamped her whenever she fainted. She could feel it pulsate slowly and rhythmically until for no apparent reason the beating suddenly grew faster. The seed expanded rapidly, she felt the pain shoot through her brain and then came the terrifying whirlwind, the agony, and the darkness. She heard herself groaning and was vaguely aware of voices and movement around her bed, the strong smell of surgical spirits and the pricking of needles. When she came round, the hideous seed was always slightly larger, as though the fatal embryo were building up stores of darkness inside its shell ready for the next sinister germination. She glimpsed people on the other side of a stretch of stagnant water untouched by barges, sailors, fish or waves; they often drifted over to her as though floating on the water. At times she had seemed to see the faces of her children . . . Or had she dreamt them along with her daughters-in-law in their Sunday best, her snub-nosed son-in-law and the family solicitor, Senyor Nicomedes, always so punctilious and with that annoying little cough?

The light turned from red to pink in the big mirror. She could blink her eyes more easily now. The eerie waters and the bizarre figures had gone from her head and although the black seed was still throbbing, it was superimposed on the familiar sight of her room, the dressing-table and Carmela sleeping like a baby in the armchair . . . It was like waking from a nightmare. Then the afternoon of her birthday surfaced in her mind and she began to panic. She must get up and see if the builders had started repairing the façade of the house and her other properties, as she had instructed, if Graells had arranged a meeting with the boatbuilders and taken the barges to be overhauled at the yards, if work had started at the Veriu valley mine, an abandoned working owned by the family. Were the captains and their men ready to sail? Were the stables full of animals? . . . The new town . . . ! She wasn't moving from the old one, they wouldn't humiliate her, they would never turn her out of her ancestral home.

She pulled herself up with great difficulty. Her body ached and her knees sagged when she put her feet on the rug. Carmela was so exhausted after nursing her for weeks that she slept through it all. She stood up. A shiver ran through her as she looked for a dressing-gown to throw over her naked body. She couldn't find one. And so she lurched towards the door unclothed, using the wall and the chairs to steady herself. All was silent except for the maid's regular breathing. She must stop. She was panting. She was in constant fear that her legs would give way and she would fall. Beads of sweat were running down her back. Once she had recovered a little, she opened the door. The darkness in the corridor made her stop. She groped for the light switch and the glare of the bulbs forced her to shut her inflamed eyes. When she opened them again, she didn't see Bernabé Camps, the ancestor whose stern features always met her when she came out of her bedroom door; in his place there was the mark left by the picture frame on the pale blue flowery wallpaper. Her uncle had gone missing, but he wasn't the only one; her grandparents weren't there either, nor her aunts. Not a single picture remained. In total amazement she made her way to the entrance hall. And there she discovered several wooden crates full of pictures. Propped against the wall next to an empty crate were the portraits of the general's wife and her uncle who died in Paris, apparently waiting to be packed. What did it all mean? Who had given the order to take down the paintings and store them? Who? The black seed began vibrating rapidly in the middle of the colourful group of Moorish tribesmen depicted in the equestrian portrait of the General, which somebody had brought down from the room where the mourning clothes were kept. Where was the cornucopia and the writing-desk? Where was the statue of Saint Barbara, the patron saint of the miners? And her wicked uncle's collection of porcelain? What had happened to the display of sabres and pistols belonging to the hero of Africa? She leant back against the wall. Her legs could barely hold her, her breathing was very laboured and she had broken out in a cold sweat. She rested for a few minutes before entering the dining-room where she bumped into another pile of half-packed crates. Silver, crockery and the general's weapons lay heaped on the table; she saw that the painting of the false martyrs had been brought down from the attic. She staggered out and into the study which had been kept as it was when her father died. The room was empty. On the verge of collapse, she entered the drawing-room which was nearly as bare as the study; all that remained was Aleix's enormous painting which had been taken down and was standing by the balcony. She stumbled across the room. How had this disaster occurred? Who was emptying the house? What was happening?

Feeling faint, she grabbed hold of the picture frame. She was terrified and tried to call out but the words stuck in her throat. Why didn't Carmela, Sofia or Teresa come? Where were they? The black seed was beating faster now. She felt dizzy; the seed burst, darkness blotted out the window, the acacias in the square and the quayside now home to nothing but rusted ships. She was slipping, sinking down into the night. Once more she tried to call out but no one came to rescue her from that well of dark oil slurry.

Senyora Carlota de Torres i Camps had never looked ahead to her own death, unlike Carmela who had even planned her last words and written down the arrangements for her passing and burial on a sheet of paper: from the memorial cards, the coffin and the type of tombstone to the number of priests officiating at the ceremony, the music and the epitaph (in Latin because it looked more distinguished). Had her mistress ever pictured her own end, she would probably never have guessed that she would have the dubious honour of being the last person to die in the old town. And she couldn't have envisaged the circumstances, so different from the grandiose deathbed scenes of her forebears. It would never have occurred to her that her lifeless body would be found next to the French windows in the Hall of the Martyred Virgins beneath her father's portrait. Oblivious to his dying daughter's naked body stretched out on the tiled floor, he smugly and contentedly surveyed a distant family scene – young Carlota gazing in rapture as Aleix de Segarra mixed his paints and immortalized her father on the large white canvas.

The merciful darkness descended on her before she could hear Carmela's harsh words. Aghast with horror, the maid flew into a rage and heaped abuse on Carlota's sons and daughters-in-law, who had rushed to the hall on hearing her cries, the ladies in their nightdresses, the men in their pyjamas. Her mind was distraught, she couldn't forgive herself for her negligence or put out of her head her mistress's final moments on seeing the state of the house. She blamed the children for their greed: why were they in so much of a rush when they would be inheriting it all anyway? The mistress hadn't got long to live, there was no need for such haste. The poor woman could have been allowed to die without undergoing this ordeal, she didn't need to see the house ransacked and guess that the legal documents which they had made her sign without realizing what she was doing had enabled her sons – who had come the moment she was taken ill – to sell off properties and buildings and even her own home, which would be razed to the ground as soon as their mother's coffin crossed the threshold. Teresa and Sofia dragged her from the room. Carmela ignored the insults of the sons and daughters-in-law and kept on shouting; her laments echoed endlessly through the deserted chambers.

Carmela survived her mistress by three melancholy years which she spent living in the new town with distant relatives who had decided that she was not long for this world and had designs on her savings. She frequently voiced her disapproval of the shabby funeral – not one of the usual showy affairs the gentry went in for – which she had attended separately from the family group. The day before, the eldest son had shamefully ordered her out of the house for berating the heirs and, despite her fervent pleas, even refused to let her dress and sit with his mother's corpse.

There was no ornament other than two miserable wreaths carried behind a hastily-bought vulgar coffin, unworthy of the remains of Senyora Carlota de Torres. The funeral prayers were interrupted by the roar of the bulldozers knocking down the houses on Bakers Hill and there was nobody to play the harmonium in the deserted choir-stalls.

The news had spread straight away. The sordid details of the wake, held as the workmen noisily finished dismantling the house, went round and round inside Nelson's mind. Being one of the few inhabitants left in the town, he had joined the small procession as it threaded its way through the ruins en route to the cemetery, trailed by the poignant figure of Carmela. Hardly anything was left standing. The only witnesses to the hearse's journey were walled-up houses, nameless streets and piles of rubble. There were no shops to close while the funeral cortege passed by or cafés to clear of customers. The only remaining one, the Quayside Café, had been evacuated a few days after Honorat del Rom's last arrest and the onset of Carlota de Torres' illness; by now it was just a heap of stones, and Nelson averted his gaze when he walked past. Grass was growing everywhere. Nature was fast reclaiming the land it had lost many centuries past, sowing seeds and populating it with wildlife. Long armies of ants explored paths between broken tiles, crumbling eaves, shattered beams or stretches of wall where the elements had effaced all sign of human warmth. Lizards and geckos scaled the walls; spiders spun webs between the branches of the thyme and rosemary bushes, and snakes shed their skins among the fallen masonry from the arcade round the Moorish square. Former houses and streets were alive with the rustle of animals, birds flapping and chirping. Foxes were getting bolder and at night would venture inside the town to hunt stray cats. Sometimes as he lay in bed, Nelson could hear their desperate yowls and all that remained the next day were a few drops of dry blood to mark the spot where they met their end.

Carlota's funeral procession left by the Segre Gate near the old fort – an ineffective bastion in this lost war – and took the main road. Halfway to the new houses, at the junction with the path down from the cemetery, a group was waiting for them. Nelson saw Honorat del Rom, Estanislau Corbera, the boatbuilder and other old regulars from the Quayside Café. On their faces he could discern the indefinable imprint that they all bore. Although the same name stood at the entrance to the new town as to the old ruined one, at a certain point on the path between the ancient olive-groves that lay between the two towns there was a vacuum, a kind of no-man's-land where people underwent a subtle change. They themselves were probably unaware of the phenomenon, which made it seem pointless and pathetic, for instance, when Estanislau Corbera tried as hard as he could to recreate in his new establishment the atmosphere of the old one: the mirrors reflected a different light, the rear windows didn't look out on to the quayside, the Moorish fez had got lost in the upheaval of the move and the crack on the marble counter no longer brought back memories of General Prim's sabre. The north winds were broader than before and came direct from the Monegros plateau; the straight streets with their rows of identical houses got more of a battering as there were no cul-de-sacs where the winds could swirl around, no maze of alleys where they could blow themselves out. The complex networks of age-old neigh-bourhood relations would have to be re-invented and now that the rivers were no longer the town's main arteries, their lives would be conditioned by other factors. But only the youngest inhabitants, the babies, would forget completely; a part of the memories of the rest would hang on like a root beneath the waters of the Segre and the Ebro. They would often hear old words in the new rooms where the furniture still smelt of varnish and in the mists of winter they would catch the raised voices of old crews and the screams of other seagulls.

Carlota de Torres' cortege began its climb up to the cemetery. Her remains were to lie in the family vault – a replica in death of the house in the Plaça d'Armes. They would preside over the city of silence where generations of invariably drunk gravediggers put the dead, segregated by the other town, into rows of graves and niches, ready for their journey into the void. Above the cemetery walls, the cypresses began to cast the first shadows of evening against a purple sky. Old Nelson paused and turned to look right, at the new settlement where he would be moving the next day. They had won for themselves a place where their descendants would carry on the name of the town but he was aware that he could never feel that that red and white geometry was his own. A sailor deprived of his boat, an exile with no hope of ever going home, he now belonged to that endless night where his father, his daughter, Arquimedes Quintana, Malena, Aleix de Segarra, Senyora Salleres, Joanet del Pla, Atanasi Resurrecció, Madamfranswah and so many other beloved ghosts were sailing silently towards oblivion.

Shortly before the sluice-gates of the Riba-roja reservoir were shut, heavy rain began lashing the empty, demolished town. Floodwater from the Castle mountains burst furiously on to the quayside, the frayed moorings in the boats' graveyard snapped and the aged barges were scattered. They drifted off down a seething Ebro – which had forgotten the furrows that their keels made and the cadences of their oars – and came to grief in gorges and rapids. The *Virgin of Carmel* was smashed to pieces near Thirteen Saints Island, her prow ran aground among the riverside poplars. When the river subsided, no one recognized the debris; the raging storm had obliterated all traces of its third name. The old *Neptune*, which had been launched from the Widows' Wharf with speeches, flag-waving and music on one of the splendid days of the Eden was for ever more an anonymous carcass of dead wood.